About the author

Martin Morton lives mostly in the Adriatic on a boat.

Visit Martin Morton at www.martinmorton.co.uk

Careless Hours

Martin Morton

Careless Hours

Chimera

CHIMERA PAPERBACK

© Copyright 2020
Martin Morton

The right of Martin Morton to be identified as author of
this work has been asserted by him in accordance with the
Copyright, Designs and Patents Act 1988.

All Rights Reserved

No reproduction, copy or transmission of this publication
may be made without written permission.
No paragraph of this publication may be reproduced,
copied or transmitted save with the written permission or in
accordance with the provisions
of the Copyright Act 1956 (as amended).

Any person who commits any unauthorised act in relation to
this publication may be liable to criminal
prosecution and civil claims for damages.

A CIP catalogue record for this title is
available from the British Library.

ISBN 978 1 903136 69 0

Chimera is an imprint of
Pegasus Elliot MacKenzie Publishers Ltd.
www.pegasuspublishers.com

First Published in 2020

Chimera
**Sheraton House Castle Park
Cambridge England**

Printed & Bound in Great Britain

1

"That went really well!"

"Thank you, Andy." She hesitated. "Are you taking the piss?"

"No. I'm serious!"

She looked hard at him, trying to find irony in his expression, but that wasn't normally Andy's way. "I wasn't sure when Peter asked me if he genuinely wanted me to lead the session, or whether he just thought I'd been too quiet in my first two Gatherings." She'd known about the half-yearly Gatherings before joining the Group, just Peter and the twenty-seven business heads. Two had joined since her start-up, both Chinese who made a real attempt to integrate themselves and attracted a lot of attention from the established members. A lot had also spoken to her, but she would admit to using Andy and Sandy Nicholls as her chosen society and had perhaps done too little active networking herself.

"Come on! You know he thinks what you do is important to them all, he's got you five clients already."

"Six," she corrected him.

"Whatever," he said, smiling. "I know he thinks more of the guys here should be working with you."

"And they want to. I think I'm the bottleneck. Two more of them have spoken to me in these two days and asked for some time. They'd be new clients, but it's hard to get round them all."

"You couldn't send your other guys?"

"I suppose I'll stay small time if I don't start doing that here. I do it in Europe; I let Alan look at new business opportunities now. I don't think you know him, he was the first guy I took on. But in the Gathering here, the guys are all Dickinson Group and I don't think Peter would be impressed if I didn't look at each one personally. But how are you doing? How's Tania working out?"

"Everybody loves her, especially Eddie. Well, a couple of the VPs maybe not so much. She's inclined to tell them directly when she thinks they're not being supportive enough," he said with a laugh. "She's very refreshing. How long do you have her for?"

"Her father asked if she could do three years with me, then he'll want her back at Giddings, but he might have a problem with that. I think she enjoys living in New York — and the businesses she works with all adore her."

"Hey, did you know she'd studied in Japan?"

"Now you say it, I think I did. It was a year of her degree, wasn't it? Why?"

"It came up the other day. We're getting more problems with a Japanese competitor and we had some of their products and literature lying around. She poked her nose in, like she does." He was smiling, he plainly approved. "She read a bit of the text. I was blown away. She gave us a little impromptu talk on Japan."

"Serious competition?"

"It's a niggle, at least." He mulled that over a moment. "Well, it's more than that, if I'm honest. They got a foothold here when we weren't doing so well. You'll remember that those were the problems you identified."

"Well, Eddie was on the same page already."

"Yes, but you gave us the way of getting everyone together and focused on the right things but the Japs, well their US distributors anyway, had already spotted the weakness. Now they compete on service and on price and some of our customers are saying that the quality is as good. That's crap, of course, but it is telling us what's important to them."

"What are you going to do?

"Good question. I was going to talk to you about that."

"Me? I don't know anything about Japan."

"I'd guessed that. Tania's the only person I know who does. Can I get some more of her time?"

"Andy! She's stretched with our new business — and she was only in Japan as a student. Surely Peter has some connections."

"I'm talking to him later. I'll need to try a few angles, but I just want someone to talk to who I can trust, it would be a big help."

Claudia was torn. She'd been delighted when Arthur had called her the previous year with his proposition. The programme had started really well at Giddings and Tania, with Marybeth, had been instrumental in that, but longer term he hoped that Tania would run the place, so he wanted her to see more of other businesses to broaden her outlook. He thought Brodie Associates would be ideal. Claudia agreed instantly. She rated Tania very highly and needed more people for the US, where they were picking up more business.

"I don't like saying no — and you certainly never like hearing it — but I should do on this." She was getting Andy's puppy dog look. "Listen, I don't mind if you talk to her, but let me talk to her first. I can see why she might be interested, she's trying to get the broadest possible business education, but she gets so committed to things that she's a danger to herself. She's working over sixty hours every week as it is, not including a big travel load. I'm trying to look after her but if I say no, I'm probably not being fair to her or Arthur."

"Or me!"

"Oh, you can go fuck yourself!" They laughed loudly.

"You two having fun?" Peter was walking past. "Oh, Claudia, that was splendid earlier on, by the way, thank you very much. It was important, but I think you thought I was doing it just to give you a higher profile, didn't you?" Andy and Claudia looked at each other, smiling. "But what's funny?"

"Being told to go fuck myself is funny, especially when I'm a client." They all smiled. "But now I've got you for a moment, I might need some help with Japan, that's what we were talking about."

"Is this Nakamura?" Andy nodded. "I wondered when you were going to ask."

2

Jack always felt relieved to be flying back. There was a lot to enjoy in Brazil but a lot to be nervous about. The security guys advertised themselves as discreet, but he was almost glad they weren't. He felt more comfortable with Jorge's massive, shaven-headed bulk beside him and was fairly sure that would be a sufficient disincentive to any would-be kidnappers. Jorge wouldn't be indestructible, but there were surely softer targets around.

Eight years before, the wife of the then general manager had been kidnapped. Jack had heard nothing about it until the Old Man and Saunders had talked to him when offering him the job two years ago ('It'd be wrong not to acquaint you with the dangers and the security coverage you'll have to endure, Jack, but, the simple fact is, we don't want to have to replace you or find some money to get you out of a situation'). They'd also made the point very forcibly that they wanted a total information lockdown if anything similar happened again. And they hadn't told him what they'd paid to get her released. They had changed the security company.

He was frequently made aware of the distractions and temptations Brazil could offer and the secondary benefit to the high level of security became apparent to him. Jorge was able to provide safe and discreet addresses for an occasional but rare diversion. It was too uncomfortable returning to the car an hour later to repeat the adventures very often, but the mild embarrassment was not a great price to pay for the necessary security provided, and the girls were invariably beautiful and imaginative. Jorge had also made it plain that there were other options for 'special tastes' should Jack so desire, but past experience in the Far East and his DC arrangement made him decline.

And while he was usually flying back, from anywhere, with a weekend of activities planned, it was always to an empty apartment that should, at least sometimes, have had Claudia in it.

The occasional visits from Lavinia, usually coinciding with his return from a longer trip, had brought, initially, a bizarre excitement but now, in addition, brought their strange frustrations. When he checked his phone on landing, one of her usual texts was there:

You should receive my submission at 5pm, I hope that will be convenient. L
It will be dealt with appropriately. J

It was a ritual they had developed over more than a year of these appointments. They were apparently necessary for her; they were enjoyable, in their way, for him, but the attendant frustrations were best dealt with by subsequent date nights, so five p.m. Friday had become a regular slot. She would leave after their session, to do at home what he could only guess at, while he got ready for whoever he was taking to dinner. Before they'd established their routine, Lavinia had left him with time and frustration and his thoughts could only focus on memories of Claudia. That made the experiences more poignant and more painful.

But tonight, he would be having dinner later with Jessica. He liked her — fortyish, funny, smart, not quite divorced (ideal), lovely, just a little bit vanilla. He doubted she would understand Lavinia's needs. But that was fine, the evening as a whole would suit him, and he pushed to the back of his mind that it was all a little hollow.

He worked from home during the day; there were plenty of phone calls and emails to deal with and reports to read and, dammit, after a heavy week and an overnight flight, a nap in the afternoon was necessary (and healthy but impossible to manage in the office). He was freshly showered and changed when Lavinia arrived, five minutes late. That was part of the established ritual: punctuality meant one treatment, tardiness another (always exactly five minutes though). It gave him five minutes to adjust himself, move the armchair in front of the window, adjust the drapes to allow for the slight possibility of being observed (in reality, almost zero, even by desperate, distant telescope peepers but that frisson was, for her, important) and retrieve the cane. (Claudia's cane! Would she mind? Did she ever think about it? He did, whenever he used it!) The ritual had been refined in phone calls: texts, because insecure, were always terse and deliberately ambiguous; meetings were pared to the experience itself, nothing should disturb the way the roles were played.

"Come in, Lavinia!" (She had knocked on the drawing room door, the front door had been latched to allow her access and then shut behind her). "I need hardly say how disappointed I am."

"No, sir." A tall, elegantly dressed woman stood before him, head bowed, hands clasped in front of her. (Her bags and any other paraphernalia would have been left by the hall table.)

"I think I am entitled to expect punctuality, don't you?" (Claudia had never valued the role-play elements, she focused on the experience itself, but he liked it — and it was vital for Lavinia, as was him taking his time.)

"Yes, sir, you most certainly are. I am very sorry, sir."

He managed a theatrical sigh. "I'm afraid, if you recall, that is exactly what you said last time, isn't it?"

She nodded, seeming to shrink slightly. "I'm afraid you know what this means, don't you?"

She nodded again. "What does it mean, Lavinia?"

"It means thirty this time, sir."

"Exactly, thirty with each." And she nodded once more.

He'd had, in the two years he'd had dealings with her, only one official meeting. He'd been aware of Henderson's covert operations through a telephone conversation relating to unfortunate circumstances of his own in Singapore. When a problem arose in his US organisation in the early days, he'd had to have direct contact with the Networks business and had visited Henderson's office downtown. The PA was a formidable, statuesque woman, dark-haired, somewhat formally dressed and too fierce-looking, he thought, to be called truly attractive — the famous Lavinia that Claudia had referred to — the source of her mysterious invitations. He had been surprised to be rung by her a month later. ("I wonder if you and I, Mr Stephens, might talk confidentially about a very delicate personal matter?" She had handled it cleverly, making him feel awkward and defensive about his Far Eastern misdemeanours, letting him imagine the call was somehow about his strange tastes and behaviours. In a way it was, but she came slowly, very tangentially, to her own frustrated interest in such activities.)

Now this striking, self-possessed woman stood before him, passably imitating the body language of a naughty schoolgirl.

"Now, Lavinia, you will, of course, receive these punishments on the bare bottom. Is that clear?" She nodded again, this part of the ritual was unvarying. "Then I must ask you to remove your panties and hand them to me." ('Bottom' not 'ass' was agreed early on; 'panties' had taken four phone calls to fix: 'knickers' — his favourite — 'pants', 'undergarments' and 'underwear' having been tried without finding a consensus.)

She hooked her thumbs up under the skirt of her dress and slid the panties down, retrieving them with an elegant stoop from the floor and handing them demurely to him — never once, at any time, revealing her delta. He found that strange, slightly sweet even, that he had no idea if she waxed or how she shaved. It was an incongruous modesty, considering how obviously open she would be shortly across his lap and then, subsequently, over the armchair, how she would be almost gynaecologically available.

"Now I must ask you to place yourself across my lap, and I warn you, this will be painful!"

She was a tall woman, well-shaped, rather than slender. By reaching across him she could lower herself gently on to his lap. When she finally relaxed there, he always found her somewhat heavy. After the first few visits, he began to enjoy that, her size helping him feel free to slap harder. They had a code for too hard, but he'd forgotten it — probably because she'd never used it.

He lifted her skirt up to her waist — who should lift had also been a telephone topic. The agreement reached was that he would lift when she was on his lap — which would be awkward for her; and she would lift on the armchair — allowing him to stand back and admire the reveal — this element of humiliation being important to her — her shapely bottom wonderfully framed by the suspender belt and stockings. It was a splendid view and a certain amount of stroking was permitted — 'but not too much!' this was from an early, difficult phone call, when he'd let his fingers slide between her legs to find her very wet, but unwilling, 'I just need this to be about spanking and punishment, are you OK with that?' and he'd agreed he was. It made the experience frustrating at the time but, as he looked again at her magnificent, beautifully rounded white buttocks, still very thrilling.

He brought his hand down very hard on her right cheek. She twitched and gasped — never very loud but always audible — and he loved the feel of the blow on the flesh, the movement of the cheek and the slow appearance of the red hand print. Its partner soon followed on the left and then he could take time to admire the handiwork and gently stroke her again. After a dozen slaps in these longer sessions both her cheeks would be a full bright red and his hand would be stinging but attempts to go softer or introduce a paddle had met a firm refusal in the follow-up call. But, stinging or not, he loved the feel of her flesh as his hand made contact.

Her hip bone would also be making contact with his very firm bulge but that was never referred to. It would stay very stiff though the entire hand spanking. They never counted aloud but he was always aware by the way she slumped that the end of the first thirty had been reached. She allowed him time to study, and it did look wonderful to him, but if he began to stroke now, she would rise and move to the chair, standing beside it and awaiting his next instructions. Today he just looked, and she stayed unmoving. If she even squeezes her hip against me, he thought, that could be embarrassing.

"Now, Lavinia, we must address the issue of your tardiness, please go and stand by the armchair." She rose, quite elegantly, her dress falling easily to her knees again. Her clothing was always well-chosen for these occasions, slightly loose but never compromising on style. It made access easy and recovery simple and the suspender buttons were never discernible.

"You will lean over the chair with your bottom in the air — and bend right down, please." She moved slowly down into position. These were the moments he probably enjoyed the most. "Now, raise your skirt to your waist, please, I must have your bottom completely clear."

He stood behind her to watch the slow reveal, she never expected him to move until she was positioned how he wanted her (and how she wanted to be, they had agreed).

"Now I shall fetch the cane." He left the room; he'd left the cane on his bed but he moved slowly and waited a while before returning. He closed doors (bedroom, drawing room) quite audibly for her. He could always tell from the small movements of her thighs that her excitement was mounting — her lips were glistening.

"Now, I am growing tired of having to deal with these offences. I must make today's punishment especially severe in order that you finally learn a lesson. Is that clear?"

There was no reply. He brought the cane down quite viciously across the middle of her buttocks. It brought a loud gasp from her.

"I am still waiting for a reply. Is that clear?"

"Yes, sir, very clear."

"Very well. Now I may begin with the thirty." But he never rushed. He always moved to stand behind her after each fresh stroke. He loved admiring the build-up of lines, always across the fleshiest area, almost never down on to the thighs or near her back.

After ten it already looked savage and there were few spaces between the parallel stripes. At this point she usually spread her legs slightly as if to show him how wet she was, how excited, encouraging him to continue. So he kept the speed slow and the intensity high. Just occasionally a gasp would be particularly loud, but he was not to ease off ('sometimes one falls exactly on top of another, that's all') then, when confronted with two rectangles of the deepest crimson, he would see her slump again. He always knew when it was roughly thirty and, on the few occasions he'd counted, he'd always found her exactly correct.

"Very good, Lavinia, stoically borne, now you may rise." The dialogue and the choreography had become exact. He returned to the sofa and watched her stand erect. "Now, you must come and thank me and promise to do better."

She walked slowly, stiffly to him, the only evidence of any discomfort.

"I am truly sorry, Mr Stephens. Thank you for correcting me. I shall do better next time."

"Very well, Lavinia. Here are your panties. You may dress in the bathroom." She took them from him, her face showing no emotion, and left the drawing room.

There were always several minutes before the front door closed. She probably repaired her face, but he never saw any evidence of distress when she rose from the chair, and she would certainly be applying creams to the red patches — by the time she came again the evidence would be long gone. He never saw her once she'd left his room. Each visit would be followed by a text two or three days later. She wrote once:

Thank you for dealing with the matter appropriately. L

And that was typical. He was always grateful to be under time pressure to go out after the visits. But even when the frustration seemed excessive, he was honest enough with himself to admit that his addiction almost matched hers, and he was aware that falling on her and trying to enter her would ruin what had become an intensely erotic experience.

3

Andy was never comfortable in New York. The bank had done their best, as they always did, to make him feel important and well supported, but he was always conscious that three bankers in a room was going, ultimately, to cost lots of money, so he visited rarely.

Peter had set the meeting up, it was true, but their fees would be paid by Andy's business. So, he'd had a lot of high-level attention, but that was attention appropriate to Peter Dickinson Enterprises and would attract appropriate costs, but Dickinson as a whole was about fifty times larger than Molloy!

But there was no way round it, competition was eating into his sales and his margins, so he needed to get Nakamura looked at, and the bank was the best place to start — and that would involve their Far East operations doing some analysis. More expense! He cursed himself again for not acting sooner on Hank. Peter had seen the problem straightaway, his old buddy just hadn't been growing with the business. The closest Peter had been to an 'I told you so' though was a 'loyalty's not a bad fault, Andrew, but it is a fault'.

And now to Skinner Peabody to meet Ozawa, another contact of Peter's, or rather of the mysterious

Mr Henderson who seemed to work somewhere in the shadows of Peter's empire. He'd had one phone call with Mr Ozawa. He had never talked with anyone who spoke so slowly. "Ah, Mr Molloy," pause, "I am delighted to hear from you," another pause, "Mr Dickinson has told me something about you," pause, "but I should need to understand a great deal more about your operations and, of course," pause, of course, "about these irritating competitors of yours," pause, "Nakamura, I believe it is, but I'm afraid I know so little about them, however," pause, "I'm sure a great deal can be gleaned or made available," pause, "indeed I should need this in order to assess how I may best help."

By the time he'd reached the end of his excruciating sentence, Andy was wondering where the billings clock had got to. He tried hard to finish the phone conversation in less than fifteen minutes to prevent a second quarter hour being booked but, when he put the phone down, (seventeen minutes, fuck it!) he recognised he was in the presence of a master. A master who had, nevertheless, already made some startling observations on how to do business in Japan and forced Andy to conclude, grudgingly, that his support would be essential.

After the call he took a few moments to laugh at himself; there was no value in the petty irritation he felt. Ozawa's time would have a cost, and a very high one, but Peter's time was more valuable and that, on the face of it, came free, or was a sunk cost anyway. The conversation, the morning before he called Ozawa, had been unusually lengthy and he'd been unprepared for it:

"I'd just like you to open your mind, Andrew." If he was using Andrew, it meant that Peter was at his most fatherly and at his most irritatingly didactic. "You don't know what you might find."

That probably meant that Peter had already found something himself. "What are you thinking? You think we should try to buy them or something? Seriously?"

"It may be one option just as, may I remind you, allowing ourselves to be bought is also an option. They may have greater ambitions than you."

Andy found that thought a little chilling. "You'd never sell a business."

"I've sold two, if you remember, or at least my parts of them."

"Yes, but I'm not a cokehead; and my dozing wife, when I placed her tea by the bed this morning, omitted to tell me she was divorcing me."

"I'm not saying it's a preferred option. I have bought a lot more than I have sold, obviously, but I would prefer an approach that avoided the continuing, and apparently inevitable, margin and share erosion. Think radically."

"I thought it was very difficult to buy a company in Japan."

"It is, you can't just go and buy the shares, that's not how Japan works. Well, it isn't how we work either, but you'll find that Nakamura san's fifteen per cent holding is augmented by his effective control of at least another sixty per cent of the business, which will be held by tame institutions. And his directors will probably do as he tells them, that's another ten per cent. So, if he doesn't want to sell, it won't be sold."

"How do you know this?"

"Andrew, if you paid closer attention to your own accounts, you would see that you pay a one per cent fee to Dickinson every year. This enables me, amongst other things, to keep a small finance team that can look into opportunities like this."

"So, do they know what it would cost us?"

"Nakamura trades at around a thousand yen per share, so the market cap is around four hundred million dollars. We'd have to find six hundred million, give or take."

Andy was stunned. "OK, I can understand that may be what it's worth, but that's a lot of money, even for you."

"I won't deny that, but it could be done if we thought there was a good case. But you would have to build that good case. At the moment all I'm hearing is your lingering death scenario."

"That's not fair, we've done a lot of good things on quality and service levels. It's starting to have an impact. We can beat them back like that, it just takes a little time."

"Ah, the 'fair fight' mentality, Andy, very noble, very noble. Personally, I'd rather watch a boxing match where one guy suddenly pulls a knife from his shorts. Change the rules of the game."

"Is that what your finance team's proposing?"

"They've outlined a few options but they're numbers people, it's up to us to decide which of those make any sense. Nakamura is a public company, remember, we already have quite a lot of information on them, so it's quite easy for finance guys to play around with a few scenarios. But you and I know that business is about ideas, emotions and people. Numbers are merely signposts, so this initiative has to come from you. I'm just encouraging you to think more radically. I'll be behind you if you come up with a good plan."

"Can you show me what these options are?"

"No, I won't do that, because you won't like some of the ideas they've come up with and that will distract you. I will send you a dossier on Nakamura that they're putting together. You'll get that this week — it will be pretty comprehensive. I will also send a copy to Ozawa before you meet him, provided you tell me that you want to work with him. I think you'll find him a little unorthodox, but that's why he can charge a lot of money."

***

"Mr Molloy," said this unorthodox man, beaming at him and bowing as Andy went through the office door held open by the PA, herself clearly Japanese — ah, thought

Andy, Asian certainly, only probably Japanese—. Ozawa was holding a business card to him, held in both hands. Andy put his bag down and began to fumble for his wallet. "Please, just take a seat, we can catch up on the formalities later. My country makes too much of these funny little ceremonies, perhaps. Yoshiko san, could you provide some refreshment for us, please? A coffee, Mr Molloy, or a green tea, perhaps?"

"I'll stick with coffee, please. My wife drinks green tea but I've not acquired the taste."

Ozawa merely smiled and nodded slowly. He was a short man, but maybe average for his people, thought Andy. He was immaculately dressed in a black jacket with a crisp and brilliant white shirt and a perfectly knotted tie. Andy never felt comfortable in his city suit and would have struggled to locate a tie that morning even if he'd been motivated to look.

He'd made it to the hairdressers the previous day but would never have matched the shiny black sleekness of Ozawa's perfectly cut hair. It looked a very healthy growth too, all brushed straight back. It gave nothing away about his age. It was the hair of a much younger man. Ozawa, Andy thought, for all the absence of wrinkles, must be sixty plus. "Should we sit here, Mr Molloy?" He gestured to one of the leather sofas that opposed each other across a low coffee table in the corner of the rather large office: large for tenth floor, Sixth Avenue, thought Andy.

"I will make an observation to you Mr Molloy," said Ozawa, once they were seated, "and it is an observation that few of my countrymen would make directly to you. We tend to like to remain, and it is a word often used about us here in the West, inscrutable." Andy smiled slightly and nodded. "And we would also greatly fear giving offence. This means that many important points can be lost in circumlocutions unless we develop an extraordinary sensitivity to subtler signals." Andy was still nodding, becoming mildly irritated by the preamble. "But that is not the western way and, from what I observe about you, it is manifestly not your way. You are allowing, I believe, a meter to run in your head and it is telling you that every interminable minute you are forced to listen to me speak is costing you upwards of thirty dollars," Ozawa continued, smiling gently, but raised his eyebrows slightly. Andy guffawed but then checked himself quickly, realising that Ozawa's smile would probably be there at all times, whatever was being said — maybe a samurai smiled as his sword sliced though a neck. "I find that quite a common trait here, although one should never generalise. Your Mr Dickinson, for example, is a very attentive and sensitive listener, but he is, in my experience, a rarity. My only point to you at this stage is that there are few things more expensive than deafness."

Somehow, Andy felt as though he'd just been told off, but Ozawa was smiling, more broadly now, and still appeared to be very friendly — *why not, at thirty-odd dollars a minute?* — and appeared to be offering Andy the chance to respond.

"You got me. I confess, I'm sorry."

"No need to apologise, I assure you, our time is very valuable. It is important for me to assess whether I am reading you correctly. Am I reading the signs?"

"Well, I guess I made that pretty easy for you. I'm often told I look impatient. Well, fuck it, I am impatient I suppose." Andy was reading Ozawa too. If he'd shown sensitivity or distaste for customary working profanity that would have irritated and made a partnership more difficult. He hadn't reacted.

"You will find I am happy to work at a high tempo, but I do strive, at all times, to avoid impatience and, if you will permit me in any ongoing relationship we may enjoy, I will indicate to you when I see you succumbing to that failing."

"When?"

"In my observations already, I believe 'when' to be a more appropriate word than 'if'. Now, would you care to describe your thoughts to me? Mr Dickinson has encouraged you to be radical, I think." Andy nodded. "I should add that, if you are not prepared to think radically, then you are very much wasting your time and money by sitting with me, and I should prefer to fully justify my reassuringly expensive fees," he said, with a sly smile.

"I'll admit that my first thoughts were that we should simply out-compete. We created the opportunity for them by letting standards slip in some areas, but we've been working on that for two years now and we've made some big improvements. I'd say we beat them now on everything except price, but they've got some momentum and a customer base, so it would take time and money to beat them back. That's made Peter ask the question of whether we should buy them." Ozawa nodded. "He also asked, to be entirely frank with you, whether we should consider selling to them." Now Ozawa smiled. "Is that realistic?"

"Yes, but not very. It would have been, maybe, but before your time. We Japanese went on a big buying boom in the US in the 1980s, that's partly why I established a base here. Japanese businesses acquired some major American companies and they wanted lawyers they could trust, or at least speak to without an interpreter. There are still many bad memories from that time and a reluctance to engage again. I also doubt whether you would make your company available at a low enough price to interest them, and they are unlikely to see the value of a global picture. You could find other buyers elsewhere who might be attracted before Nakamura. Would you like to look at that?"

"I wouldn't, but Peter may want to dispose of his forty per cent before its value declines."

"But he's looking for you to make some proposals, is that not right?" Andy nodded. "And I'm not hearing anything radical other than assessing whether you could purchase, correct?"

"I guess so," said Andy, glumly.

Ozawa was smiling. "That has the great merit of keeping us focused."

Yoshiko san knocked quietly and came in with the drinks, placing the cups carefully on the table in front of them.

When she had left, Ozawa began again. "It seems to me that the issue of whether they will be open to being purchased depends entirely on the attitude and motivation of Nakamura san. I know almost nothing about him. He is sixty-eight, no great age in Japan. He owns, or at least controls, an attractive company, that gives him status as well as money; that may be important to him. It's profitable, it's growing, although not rapidly any more, and he could presumably have sold to a larger company in Japan at any time he chose in the last ten years or more. Might that be right?"

"He has good technology with some unique features so it might have been attractive but I don't have the impression that the big guys over there are too ambitious these days. We've been less worried about their innovation in the past five years. They seem to be trying to consolidate and cut costs, even using Chinese manufacturing."

"Yes, that would have been a real blow to Japanese pride. But Nakamura san has not done that."

"No, it seems he's kept everything in Japan."

"So, our task is clear. We must understand Nakamura san."

"Will he talk to us?"

"Oh, I am sure he would. I am equally sure we should get nothing useful out of that conversation and we might give a great deal away."

"Mr Ozawa, you're looking a little, if I might use the word, inscrutable." Andy was relieved to see him smiling in response.

"Now, Mr Molloy, I must tell you some things about how we acquire information in Japan."

4

"I may need a favour in a month or so."

"Of course, Peter, anything," said Claudia.

"You don't know what it is yet."

"I'm looking out over open fields. Pat's in the outer office next to me and the kids have friends in the main house. I really don't think Alphonse was challenged to persuade me this was my perfect spec for a property, and this is all funded by your purchase of a part share in my business, so I'm hardly going to refuse you anything. Besides, to make a point you're fond of making, you know what my daily fee is now. This isn't going to be altruism. What's on your mind?"

"My dearest thing, for the first time in my life I'm mixing love and commerce. I do adore you."

"OK, now I'm starting to worry."

"No, no, I'm serious but not serious. I'm calling about Andy's project."

"The one he wants Tania to help on?"

"Yes. She may be an impressive young lady, but I'm not sure she will be of much help in this case, I seriously doubt whether she has enough relevant experience — and I would have other concerns anyway."

"I share those, too. I mean to talk to her before I let her get involved. I want to do it face-to-face, though."

"I trust your judgement, of course, but being timely is better than being personal, so please don't wait too long. My major concern, however, if he makes any progress, is trying to assess how two halves of the combined business could actually work together. I wouldn't expect them to integrate but I do think it will be important that they work in similar ways to Molloy and have similar goals and philosophies. This would be, effectively, bringing a new business into the fold. If he does get as far as talking about an acquisition, you're the best person I know to have a look at how they work."

"Well, I feel flattered but a little out of my depth. No, that's rubbish. I actually feel completely out of my depth. Do you not have other connections?"

"I do, but none I am used to dealing with directly. Henderson has some people but none I know personally. Ozawa, the lawyer, seems very sharp and pleasantly unscrupulous but I have had only one telephone conversation with him. The bank will help but not with anyone I know. It will come under Martha Weddle, but she'll use her Tokyo people."

"Martha Weddle?"

"Yes, she's the bank's head of all Asian business and a very impressive lady. She's Singapore based, so she helps me a lot with my interests in the region, including the two Chinese companies whose heads you met recently. I believe they're also Collins's bank globally. She may well have known your Jack."

"I think that was a name he'd mentioned." The name was a stab that hurt deeply for no logical reason, it was a very painful memory and she needed to move on quickly.

"I'm sorry to mention that connection, my dear, and I won't pry. I suspect you'd rather move the conversation on than have my sympathetic ear."

"You're right," she snapped, but then made herself calm down, "but unwelcome knowledge, as Alphonse said at the time, is better than unwelcome ignorance. So, moving on, who else?"

"One of my finance team thinks of himself as a Japan specialist but his knowledge is all from computers and news reports, none is gleaned from personal contact — and I suspect it still wouldn't be if I left him there for a month, although he's done quite well for me in China. So, he will have a role to play, but a subordinate one. So that's it; I have you, whom I trust completely, and I may have Ozawa whose loyalties will always remain obscure and, I suspect, biddable."

"You have Andy."

"Ah, my dearest, an acquisition is a hunt, the goal becomes all-consuming. It will be hard for him to remain objective. I will also worry if he spends too much time out there without Jen near him."

"I did hear you. I will work on that. And thank you for trusting me to remain immune if you're asking me to be out there with him. I hope I can help, though. I've only been there once and, in business terms, I was completely focused on the Collins unit there. I loved the place, though. I thought it was fascinating."

"Good. It may well come to nothing but, knowing you, you'd rather know weeks ahead so you can prepare a little."

"That's true, so you're maximising your use of my non-billable background study hours."

"Of course, but now you can return to gazing idly out on your pastoral idyll."

"No, I think I'll call Tania. Thanks for the heads-up. Will I hear from you or Andy?"

"You should hear from Andy. I'll talk to him now. If he hasn't contacted you within a week, would you please let me know?"

"Of course. See you soon. Well, that's a sentiment, not a plan."

"I know, my dear. I love working with you, we tune in so well, but sadly we've had to bid adieu to our careless hours."

"Ah, Peter, no one phrases bullshit quite like you do. Bye, my love."

"Bye, my love."

***

"If I've woken you, it's your own silly fault, girl."

"Good morning, boss. And it's set to mute unless it's you who's calling."

"Seriously? Can you do that?"

"Ha, gotcha. Actually, I've no idea but it sounds like a useful facility. It would be like having a permamute for David. I suppose I could block his number but that seems too crude and obvious."

"My goodness, is he still pestering?"

"I think he's getting the message, very slowly though. That was a fringe benefit of coming to New York. Oh, please don't get me wrong. This has been such a brilliant move for me."

"I think your father's sorry he bought you the apartment. He worries he won't get you back."

"Well, he bought it for Debs too and I love sharing with her, but she has such an odd taste in men. Maybe it's to do with being in medicine."

"And your taste in men?"

"Ha, that's a very good question from my slave driver boss who utterly prevents me from having any opportunity to ever meet them. One of the reasons my father loves you is that he regards you as the chastity belt on my life. At home he even calls you CB. Mum thinks he's just taken to using your initials, but he winks at me when he says it. He's never called you that to your face, has he?"

Claudia chuckled. "No, no one's ever made that joke before, not to my knowledge anyway. And it certainly wasn't my intention to fill that function. I thought you might have more fun in New York."

"Ha, chance would be a fine thing. I mean, what's this call about? How are you going to ruin my Saturday now? Shall I tell Ryan Gosling our Fifth Avenue shopping trip is off this afternoon? Oh, please don't make me cancel dinner at Le Bernardin, he's been so looking forward to that."

Claudia could almost see the smile on the other end of the phone. All of their conversations were topped and tailed with the irreverent or the absurd. "Now, I'm going to talk to you about Japan and you're going to get embarrassed and try to pretend that Andy hasn't spoken to you."

"You're right!"

Claudia had learned to live with this; just when Tania threatened to become tiresome, she found the right moment to become serious. They were almost there — but not quite. "I'm right about what: he's spoken to you already; you're pretending; or you're embarrassed?"

"You would have been so much fun as an older sister but now I can hear the boss in your voice. You know I don't embarrass easily." This was true. "So, either I'm pretending, or he hasn't actually spoken to me — and since my newly won cynicism about males stems solely from your training and you're never wrong, he's obviously spoken to me, so you know I'm just pretending. OK boss, the clock ticks on to eight ay em

Eastern time on this glorious New York Saturday morning and Tania Gunter has her game face on. Andy Molloy needs help with his Japanese problems, and he needs Superwoman Junior's help — why wasn't there a Batwoman, then I could have been Robyn with a 'y'? He does have Japanese problems though, doesn't he, bigtime?"

"Yes, he does."

"The Nakamura stuff's quite good. I can almost tell the difference in sound quality, although I'm probably kidding myself, but everything I saw when I was there for that year tells me that out of box and service performance is going to be much better than Molloy's. We're getting better but it was still embarrassing when I got there, and they'd been working at it for a while. I know it's not what I'm supposed to be doing but he does need help."

"Do you think you're the help he needs? And I am also conscious that we have a new client coming on stream that you were instrumental in winning and also that you're already working very hard, I'm very aware of that. And I don't like being your chastity belt. There were a couple of compliments in there. I hope you noticed."

"All I heard was you don't think I can help Andy with Japan."

"I want you to tell me more. So far as I'm aware, you had a year living in Japan as a student. I don't know what you did there so I've no idea if it's at all relevant to helping Andy evaluate a Japanese business. You've obviously impressed him with what you've said already, but you might merely be the one-eyed man in the kingdom of the blind."

"That's all true, boss. I am painfully aware of that and I won't let you down here, but it was my third year in a business studies degree, and I was focusing on Japanese tech industries, so my experience is at least a little bit relevant. And I loved the place. Well, it's also a bit of a giant chastity belt for a girl who won't date shorter men, but it fascinated me. I think Andy's just a bit overawed by it though and wants his hand held until he's got someone working with him that he can trust. That will have to be a Japanese person."

"So, you're happy if I rule you out?"

"He was making a very strong case for a little help up front, and I'll have to admit I told him I'd like to help. I also told him, when he asked me not to say he'd spoken to me, that you and I don't have any secrets and I was going to talk to you the next time I got a chance. So, I would like to give him a week but on the strict understanding that he's got to have a team in Japan after that that doesn't include me."

"Is that what you told him?"

"Nope. I just said I'd like to help but I wouldn't do anything without asking you first."

"Thank you."

"So, can I go?"

"I'm very reluctant."

"I'm hearing yes."

"Do you have boyfriends like that? Reluctance means yes?"

"Not these days. As previously discussed, I'm a holy fucking virgin. So I can't even offer to do this in boyfriend time, 'cos there isn't any. But I'll discuss schedules with you before I commit. I won't drop any balls here. Brodie is definitely priority one."

"OK, I'll keep an open mind but please let me know about any conversations you have about this and I like the way you've set conditions. It's a max of one week and he has to have a non-Tania project team at the end of it."

"Thank you, boss. I am a little bit thrilled about it, I admit."

"OK, but just one more point very briefly — I'm sorry to keep Ryan G waiting — oh, fuck him, he's not until this afternoon anyway — this could develop into an acquisition project. It's absolutely essential that you say nothing, repeat absolutely nothing, to anyone other than Andy and me about that possibility, understood?"

"What, not even Ryan?"

"You'll find other stuff to talk about."

"Sure, we shall, and Claudia?"

"Yes?"

"Thank you. Wish I could hug you."

"Hugs to you too, my love." For all her goofiness, Tania always seemed to have an old head on her shoulders. Claudia felt she could trust her to limit her efforts and, if she had to get involved herself later, it would be very helpful to have Tania's perspective.

5

It wasn't unusual for the Old Man to call him in for a chat, but Jack was conscious that he seemed to be taking particular trouble that the office was relatively empty. Saunders was on holiday, Davis was traveling, and Adams, who he felt should run the US from one of his factory sites and not camp out in HQ, was actually on a rare road trip. It could have been coincidence, thought Jack, but nothing with the Old Man ever seemed mere coincidence.

Oscar Maguire was certainly over sixty-five, but it seemed impolite to try and fix an exact age, and if he'd been only sixty you would still have said he looked good: hair nearly white, but enough of it; no discernible flab, he looked fit; and a slim, tanned and handsome face. He'd had nearly twenty years at the head of the corporation. Jack could barely remember the time when he hadn't been there; certainly, he could remember no other name as the corporation's senior executive. The announcement that he would add chairman to the CEO role ten years ago had made no impact on Jack since the preceding chairman had no profile within the business whatsoever.

"How are you getting on, Jack?" The open question was his usual gambit, even when he had something specific on his mind. Jack had not fallen into too many traps, but he suspected that the Old Man's encyclopaedic knowledge of the corporation came, to a large extent, from people answering questions that they hadn't, in fact, been asked.

"I'm good, Oscar, thank you. We have our hands full in Argentina because of the economy again, but I'm happy with Brazil. Finding a Brazilian to run it has given the team real momentum. I could imagine him being headhunted soon, our success down there is pretty obvious, but we have a good number two in place and if anything happened with Oliveira, I'd promote within — unless you've got someone who needs a development move?"

"I like getting more native talent moving up. I like your Robert in Singapore. We're too fucking Anglo-American — and white — and male. It seems to take for ever to change that picture. I tell you, it's gonna be a crusade when I can hand on the CEO job. I know I'm a hypocrite, I watch the bottom line every quarter like the next man and don't force the people moves I should, but you just wait to observe the Olympian majesty of me being able to ignore the urgent and focus on the important."

"Davis has data that show we're in the top decile for diversity."

"I think you know how much you would disappoint me if I thought for a minute that you took that shit seriously. You pushed for Robert to succeed you and you have a Brazilian lined up for Oliveira's job? What's his name?"

"Hanna!"

Oscar guffawed loudly. "You did me there, you asshole! Which one is she?"

"Well, I could tell you she's dark and beautiful but that's sexist and it won't help you one bit, they're all like that as you know — but she had more to say than the others when you were down there, and she gave the sales presentation."

"Got it! Excellent. Well, I don't want you losing Oliveira but if you want to give her some encouragement, I'm happy for you to say we've talked succession planning. And you should think about what we could do with Oliveira."

"Thank you, I'll do that."

"Will do? Or have done?"

Jack smiled. "The former. It's hard enough to fulfil promises when you have authorisation. And I don't like taking risks on people's career steps, having something taken away if it doesn't happen can be shattering."

"Now what about the US?"

Was this the question? "I'm OK, we're just about on plan, well, for profit anyway, we might duck under on sales by a per cent or two."

"Why does that prick use here as his base? He's a fucking unit head, he's not on staff."

"He says here's good for flight connections. He managed to get his family settled here and it would be hard to budge them now. Harris let him do it when he back-filled his job and I think he thought he'd be getting the region when Harris moved up."

"Exactly illustrating the point you made a moment ago."

"I think so."

"You could tell him to move. Hell, we move people round the world, going from DC to Chicago ain't no big deal."

"He's got Saunders and Davis on his side."

"Well, he'll soon be a blocker where he is unless his attitude changes." He paused, stroked his chin — ah, was it coming now? — "And what about you? How are you doing? I thought you were going to settle down a little domestically."

"That didn't work out, unfortunately."

"Well done, son, lost us a damn good manager for no personal benefit. Programme still seems to be running OK, though."

"Well, she's still running that, but from outside."

"Ha, genius, I'm willing to bet we pay her more now for one day a week than her whole salary back then." Jack felt slightly stupid, but nevertheless more than a little proud. "But how settled are you then? Do you think of America as home?"

"I suppose I do. I hadn't really thought about it."

"But you haven't put down any roots."

"But I'm not thinking of going anywhere."

"Good, 'cos there ain't any jobs you can do for us that aren't based here."

Did the Old Man want reassuring? "Oscar, I like what I'm doing. The teams need developing more in South America. I'd like to refresh our product ranges faster, but I do have some input into that, including into who we might buy."

"Yeah, I like your ideas on that, but I was really asking if you feel settled in DC as a place."

"It's at least as good as anywhere else. I don't have any family pulls now the boys are grown up," he said, with a smile. "And the dating scene isn't bad."

Oscar looked thoughtful. "But no one special?"

"No, no one special, but I can always find a plus one for any occasion. Do you want to tell me what's on your mind?"

Now Oscar smiled. "Now that wouldn't be my way, would it?" They both laughed.

"Well, I always think of you as the master of decisiveness and clarity, but that's only after a pretty lengthy Knätphase, as the Germans say."

"I'm in a Knätphase now, Jack, that's kneading the dough, isn't it?" Jack nodded. "I think we've got a bit stale and complacent so I want to shake things up so the place is ready for me to give up the CEO job. I like how you develop your teams and I like your ideas on how we should expand, so you're quite an important player in running the place. It gets noticed, Henderson tells me there are one or two big corporations who'll need new CEOs in the next couple of years." He stopped there and looked hard at Jack.

"I've had a couple of enquiries, but I don't follow them up." Oscar raised his eyebrows, Jack laughed lightly. "I don't tell them to fuck off, I just say the time's wrong. Besides, I wouldn't put it past you to set something up to see what your senior guys are planning."

Oscar smiled. "You give me too much credit, I'm not that Machiavellian."

"Which is exactly what Signor Machiavelli would have said."

"True." He smiled again. "But I didn't. I am keen on keeping you though, Jack. The big question for me, though, is in what role. Ken Saunders is very good on operations, but you offer more on people and products and, not that I like the word, but on vision. You seem to be thinking further ahead than the others. So, yes I'm in a Knätphase and I'm not clear yet how this place looks in two years' time, but I want you in the picture in a bigger role than you have now and you and I will be having a few talks like this to help me get my thinking straight. OK?"

"Yes, very OK. Thank you."

"But they're strictly between us."

"Of course."

6

Leaving home Sunday morning to get to the hotel on Monday evening had struck him as pretty stupid when he looked at the bookings.

"It is a direct flight, Andy. It's the only one. And on Friday at least you land back in Boston before you leave Tokyo, if you see what I mean," his girl said, not looking convinced her ploy would mollify him.

"I get that, Karla, logically I get it, but it does feel weird and like a fucking waste of time."

And once again he cursed himself for not dealing with Hank sooner, for letting these Japanese problems arise. But maybe, maybe this was an opportunity. He could double the size of the business and make Molloy almost invulnerable. Ozawa seemed to think that there might be a realistic possibility; he'd hinted darkly about the content of his confidential conversations, the Tuesday meeting would tell them more.

He'd had little curiosity about Japan, apart from being an avid watcher of sumo contests on one of the more obscure cable channels. He'd got hooked in his time as a college line-backer and was intrigued by how the big guys made such rapid hits. In truth, there wasn't much learning to bring into football techniques but, by then, he'd already become an addicted viewer and, even now, he could name the current yokozunas and the ozekis at the top of their sport.

His body felt out of sorts; he wasn't a good plane sleeper and he had no idea how this time difference would affect him. A five p.m. landing and already getting dark. He told himself not to even think about his body clock. He'd set his watch to Tokyo time on take-off and would deal with the US by email. At least he had no plans for the evening apart from meeting up with Tania. He wanted to meet a face he knew, but he wondered how he'd deal with her apparently perpetually energetic enthusiasm.

There was a smooth serenity about the Okura. It was Ozawa's recommendation. He was shepherded in by attentive staff. Reception personnel looked uniformly quiet, neat and friendly. "We are very happy to welcome you to Hotel Okura, Molloy san. This is your first visit, I believe?"

Disoriented and mildly grumpy as he felt, the smile switched on his better side. "Yes, it is. I've been looking forward to it very much." And when he thought about that, he realised that he had been.

"We have one message for you." She handed him a small envelope. "Fujimori san will show you to your room." She handed the key folder to the young bellboy hovering behind him, holding his bags.

The room was simple but pleasant. Bland maybe, with just a few hints of Japan, and understated certainly.

It would do for four nights. Then he couldn't think of the last time he'd spent four nights in the same, strange place, not without Jen.

Call me in 907. Can we meet for a drink?

Tania was waiting in the Highlander Bar when he got there.

"How are you feeling?"

"A bit shitty but I figured it's best to try and stay up until a proper bedtime. When did you get in?"

"Yesterday. No point in coming all this way and not making the most of it. I'm staying until Saturday. I've promised myself a night in a posh *onsen*. I've always wanted to do that and I couldn't afford it when I was a student here."

"Now you have to tell me what an *onsen* is."

"It's a hot spring. There are thousands of them but the one I want has the hot tub on the balcony with a view of the mountains. Then you sleep on a mat on the floor. I thought taking twenty-four hours to relax properly might be a good idea." Only Tania would bring her fierce enthusiasm to the pursuit of relaxing. She probably would get a big benefit out of it. "You should think about it."

Andy harrumphed mildly. Four nights was already too many and the schedule had been left irritatingly open at Ozawa's insistence: 'We must be ready for follow-up meetings, Molloy san.' He wasn't sure when the switch from mister to san had been made but it was fine with him, it made the experience feel a little more authentic.

Thursday was fixed. Ozawa had arranged for Tania and him to be given a guided tour of the Nakamura facility. They would be posing as potential distributors for Nakamura products in the US. Andy was uncomfortable, this was borderline unethical — *nah, Andy, scrub borderline* — 'But this is Japan, Molloy san, and my contact is aware of your true purpose, but you will need a good cover story. Please give that your full attention'. This had surprised Andy, no doubt he would find out more tomorrow.

Apart from that, only the Wednesday afternoon meeting at the bank was in the diary. Three more expensive bankers for two hours, he thought; Peter's bankers, Andy's bills.

"Are you hungry?"

"I don't know what I am but maybe eating isn't a bad idea. I suppose the last meal on the plane was a sort of breakfast but that's a long time ago now. But I'm not feeling ever so adventurous foodwise at the moment."

"That's fine. There's a good teppanyaki on the twelfth floor. That will seem relatively normal. OK?"

"Is that the hot plate one?"

"Exactly, you can see them cooking everything in front of you."

"Well, that'll be mildly reassuring."

His attention drifted a little as small waves of tiredness washed over him, but Tania conducted a lively seminar on Japanese history and culture as the courses were served. He even had the impression that she was following a script prepared for him, bless her. She was going to make her presence felt, not just provide him with the comfort of friendly support. And she hadn't been shy of bullying him when he'd tried to leave some of the sashimi. But the Kobe beef had been unlike anything else he'd ever eaten, so rich in flavour and meltingly tender. He'd been unable to restrain a loud 'Wow' on the first mouthful. The chef had smiled quietly. Tania beamed at him. "That was unbelievable. I'd heard about it, but nothing compares, does it?"

"Nope. I only had it twice in my year here but nothing's like the real thing. You have to beware of cheap imitations. They try and sell you Wagyu as something similar in the West."

"Oh, nowhere near, nowhere near. Well, that settles our dining programme for the week."

"Aren't we moving to the dictates of Ozawa san?"

"Aren't we expecting Molloy san to pick up all the tabs?" She smiled. "But you're right, of course, and we should know more about his dictates after tomorrow morning's meeting. He doesn't want you in that, by the way, at least not until his contact has gone."

"No, I was pretty sure he wouldn't. I am a mere woman." And she fluttered her eyelids at him coquettishly. Tired and mildly wretched as he felt, it registered for the first time with him that he was with a woman as well as a consultant in his business. "I do want to meet your Ozawa san, though, he sounds a bit dark."

"I guess we'll be doing lunch, unless he persuades his contact to stay. I suppose that might be a good sign. We'll see tomorrow. I'm going to have to crash now."

"Yup, you look like shit. But I thought I should try to keep you awake as long as possible."

"I appreciate that, thank you. Can you do the check, please? I feel like you said I look." But they managed to smile at each other.

As arranged, he was in Ozawa's suite at eight for breakfast. "Not the cheapest, this suite, I know, Molloy san, but we do need privacy and we must impress. Endo san is from an old family and he will have standards. Will you be wearing a tie when you return later?"

"You think that's necessary?"

"I think it advisable, and a suit would be appropriate, one should not show disrespect."

Andy smiled. "I thought you might insist, I'll be ready, assuming he wants to meet me. Are you going to tell me a little more about him and why you've got your hopes up?"

"I am not yet hopeful, Molloy san. I have been a little guarded in my conversation about our exact purpose, but I have said enough to let him deduce."

"So, one guarded telephone conversation with a man whose role you've yet to explain to me and I've flown seven thousand miles, right?"

Ozawa smiled. "I believe I told you, Molloy san, that I would let you know if I felt you were beginning to succumb to the demon impatience." He looked straight at Andy and raised his eyebrows. "Things move slowly but quite surely here. We take small steps though a fog of ambiguities, but the wise man can discern a path."

"Is that supposed to be some piece of ancient Japanese wisdom?"

"It is assuredly wisdom, Molloy san, but I do not yet qualify as ancient."

"OK, funny." It had made Andy smile. "But who is he?" But then there was a ring at the door, a gentle, tasteful noise, and breakfast was brought in and elaborately arranged on the dining table.

Ozawa had gestured for silence from Andy until the lengthy preparations were at an end and he had signed the tab.

"I have been doing research. Nakamura san is the younger of the two brothers who founded the company forty years ago. His brother died seven years ago. Endo san is one of only two directors appointed before that date. He will have been appointed by the older brother, Nakamura Taro, whether the younger brother fully supports him I do not yet know. He would have been compelled to keep him because he manages the older brother's shares in trust on behalf of his widow and I imagine that both she and the institutions who own shares will have wanted Endo san as continuity, but that is my assessment, not my knowledge."

"What do you know? What have you told him?"

"I have merely asked him if he would be prepared to meet with another old gentleman from another old Japanese family in order to discuss issues relating to two companies of mutual interest. He will have understood what I meant, although I have not yet identified either you or your business by name. I suggested a subterfuge for your Thursday visit, and he was comfortable with that, but it will only go ahead if today goes well."

"And what will going well mean?"

"Endo san, I think, will want to guarantee a stable and prosperous future for all the employees of the company and a generous settlement for the widow he advises. I have, from other sources, a picture of the younger brother as the wilder of the two in his youth and this reputation has pursued him into old age. Not that sixty-eight is old here." Andy smiled, now he knew roughly how old Ozawa was. "What that does mean is that there are some quarters where he is still seen as prone to recklessness. Your task, if we do all have lunch together, is to present a picture of growing prosperity through a global enterprise. I hope, in fact, that that is your vision. The more limited objective of merely wishing to keep the fucking Nips out of America will not engage him." Ozawa smiled while Andy burst out laughing, the profanity had sounded so absurdly incongruous in his cultured, lightly accented tones.

Ozawa's meeting was scheduled to begin at ten. At eleven Andy received a call asking him to join them. Tania had insisted that he have double-sided, dual language business cards produced and had trained him in bowing and the two-handed exchange. It had felt foolish in his office. He felt relieved now, however, as Endo san and he exchanged their *meishi*. Endo was taller and slimmer than Ozawa, grey-haired and probably even older, slightly gaunt and disconcertingly unsmiling.

Ozawa invited Endo and Andy to sit on the opposing sofas by the coffee table, he moved a dining chair to the end of the table and sat looking down on his two guests. He first addressed Endo san and then turned to Andy. "I have told him that I will first explain to you what he and I have discussed and then I will ask you to talk about how you see the industry evolving, and particularly how you would like to see the relationship between Nakamura and Molloy develop.

He then spoke briefly to Endo — *this is rapidly going to get fucking tedious*. Turning again to Andy, he said, "Endo san was with the brothers from the start. He was at university with Nakamura Taro, the older brother, and was his close friend, even before Nakamura Taro met Keiko san, Endo san's sister, who became Taro san's wife. Taro san was an engineer, Endo san had trained in finance and Jiro san, Taro's younger brother, who did not attend university, was a salesman. They all had a passion for music and wanted to make better sound systems. They bought a small specialist company with money from Nakamura's father and became very successful. They had several offers from the largest Japanese electronics companies to buy them out, but Nakamura Taro believed in his products with a passion, enjoyed the engineering development of them, and wanted to remain independent. Nakamura Jiro remains a very energetic salesman and has continued to expand the business in new regions of the world." Andy, while listening to Ozawa, studied Endo who may have understood Ozawa's account of their conversation but betrayed no comprehension. OK, thought Andy, Ozawa's our man but I wonder what games he's playing with the translation. "So, Molloy san, you should speak freely about why you are here, I will translate." In that moment Andy wondered where Ozawa's loyalties truly lay. He had positioned himself exactly between his guests and, sitting higher, seemed to be judging them.

"I started Molloy corporation twenty years ago when I left MIT and we make the best audio systems in the world." Endo showed no reaction but there was a pause before Ozawa responded with his translation. Andy hoped he had startled him slightly. "I know the Nakamura products well and I have been impressed over the years by the innovation I have seen. They are the only products in the world that produce accuracy, fidelity and richness that is close to Molloy products."

He let Ozawa translate again. "What I hear from your customers and distributors in America is that your quality and reliability are more consistent than ours and that, when issues arise, your Tokyo team is very quick to respond." This time Andy looked at Ozawa, who was now smiling and relaxed as he began to speak. Then Andy began to build a case for a collaborative partnership that would share innovation and quality techniques and could dominate the market sector globally. Both businesses were small in China but could grow rapidly there and they could penetrate that market more quickly together without a damaging price war. Business in other developing market economies could be grown much quicker together than separately. As he spoke, Ozawa seemed to be becoming more animated in his translations. Endo remained impassive.

When Andy had finished his prepared remarks, he received what he thought was an appreciative nod from Ozawa who then seemed to invite Endo to speak. Endo began a series of questions about product development, information sharing, manufacturing collaboration, most of which Andy was prepared for. He saw the two organisations remaining independent but collaborating closely. He could see, over time, more products being manufactured in Japan, since performance was better and it was closer to the new markets, but he could see more development being carried out in Boston but would definitely retain a development function in Tokyo. The conversation moved on to more general issues about doing business in each country. Endo had visited America only twice. Andy had to confess his ignorance about Japan but was able to demonstrate his relatively wide knowledge of the sumo scene. For the first time in nearly two hours, Endo showed some emotion, nodding when Andy expressed his admiration for Kisenosato san, the only pure Japanese wrestler in the top two ranks, which had come to be dominated by Mongolians and Pacific Islanders.

"Endo san would like to have stayed for lunch, but he has meetings he must attend this afternoon." Ozawa was plainly concluding the session. "He will discuss our conversation with Nakamura Jiro and with Nakamura Keiko and he has arranged for someone to welcome you at the factory on Thursday. He is happy that you will pose as a distributor. He does not expect to share your proposals with anyone else before then. It is possible that Nakamura Jiro might wish to meet you on Thursday evening." Endo was nodding as Ozawa was speaking but his face had returned to its impassive mask. Andy just managed to restrain himself from offering a handshake and returned Endo's bow.

Lunch was arriving as Endo left the room. "Good," said Andy, as the waiter began to lay three places. "This will please Tania." He called her. "Eleven zero two, Tania, it's lunchtime." He turned to Ozawa. "I don't mind her hearing everything."

Ozawa shrugged slightly but raised no objections. Andy had explained her role.

"These are interesting times for the Nakamura family," began Ozawa when they had settled at the table — Tania plainly thrilled to be picking pieces of sushi and sashimi with her chopsticks, Andy waiting uncomfortably for the waiter to return with knife and fork.

"You'll have to try Andy." She turned to Ozawa. "Can you tell him, please, Ozawa sensei, we can't go out to dinner anywhere Japanese with him expecting a knife and fork."

"Tania san is quite right, Molloy san. If we are to meet Nakamura Jiro on Thursday you will be expected to show willingness, if not dexterity."

"OK." Andy shrugged. "You win." Tania placed the sticks in his hand and moved his fingers to the best position.

"That's it. Just try bringing the points together. Come on, sushi's easy." She turned to Ozawa again. "I am sorry for interrupting you, Ozawa sensei, I just felt he must learn." Ozawa nodded and smiled.

"Why are you calling him sensei? I thought everything was san."

"Because he's a lawyer and a very senior person. I am right, aren't I?"

Ozawa beamed and nodded. "Quite correct, Tania san, I hope, by the way, it is not inappropriate for me to address you that way. Would you prefer Gunter san?"

"Oh no, that would just be confusing, and we might make mistakes on Thursday when we visit the factory.

I've had cards produced for us. I've used the name and address of Andy's best distributor, it's a married couple called Edwards. I'm sure they won't mind. I'll be your wife for the afternoon. Would that be OK?"

"Good idea," said Ozawa. Andy nodded. "So, back to the meeting. I was saying these are interesting times. Keiko san has one daughter. she is a doctor and has no interest in the business. Jiro san has two children, one male, one female. The man worked in the business years ago but showed no aptitude or interest. Nowadays he does very little; my information is that he is an embarrassment to his father and has created difficulties for him. The woman is married with three children and does not wish to return to work, so the family is at a crossroads. They have not agreed what they will do with the company. From other sources I know that Jiro and Keiko seldom agree on anything on the rare occasions they meet. I also know that Jiro's health is declining. I will find out more about that in the coming days."

"How will you do that?" asked Andy, genuinely puzzled.

"This is Japan, Molloy san, many things are possible. You may prefer not to enquire more deeply." Andy wasn't sure but felt that was a point better raised with Peter. "What that all means is that this is an unusually good time to begin these discussions, but we may, ultimately, have to deal with two partners separately."

"Will we have to meet the lady?"

"That is unlikely, I think. I believe she is happy to have Endo san representing her. His position is, shall we say, uncomfortable. Powerful, but uncomfortable."

"It sounds like you picked the best place to start," said Andy, with some admiration but not a little suspicion.

"Yes, sometimes there are happy accidents." Ozawa paused. "And sometimes there is good intelligence."

7

"Do you think we could actually meet normally some time? Dinner or something?" asked Jack.

There was a long pause. It was Lavinia's way. "I don't think that's a very good idea, Mr Stephens."

"Are you worried about us being seen? I know your work is all a little twilight

"Oh, it's not that. Well, it is that as well, of course, but that's not my prime reason."

"Can you help me on that?"

"If you have to ask then I'm not sure I can."

"Let me try. We have an arrangement, I won't call it a relationship, but it seems to suit us quite well. I suppose meeting in different circumstances might change the nature of that. Is that it?"

"Well, I'm pleased you understand that. As you know, I'm always prepared to discuss minor changes in the arrangement — and I think you've chosen a good word for what we have. It took me a long time to find something that suited me, however, and now I enjoy having this as a compartment in my life. My impression has always been that it also suited you. I found it fortuitous when I read the details of your case in the Far East. I thought you might be amenable to something like this, but it took a great deal of courage for me to broach the topic with you."

"You managed it with a lot of tact and sensitivity, I must tell you that. I never guessed what you were hinting at until after I'd exposed my willingness, eagerness even, to consider this — and that wasn't a risk-free step for me to take. It might have been a trick by someone to see whether I'd really left the past behind. But I just didn't feel that you were operating that way."

There was another long pause and when she responded her voice was softer. "Thank you for saying that. I should warn you though that I can operate that way. In fact, I have to sometimes, but you gauged it correctly on this occasion. As you can imagine, I have to be extraordinarily discreet in what I do, maintaining integrity in what you quite rightly call 'twilight areas' is not straight forward but I have a reputation for sustaining it. If you'd exposed me, I should have been in very serious trouble. I took a big risk in trusting you, but I felt fairly secure that what I was offering would appeal to you and that you would keep everything very confidential."

"Well, it certainly appeals very much and it's very much just between us."

"And what we do also appeals to me very much, obviously, I admit it, but I do want to keep it inside our agreed boundaries. It's special for me but I would like to keep it separate from the rest of my life. I had tried, on more than one occasion, to integrate the sort of activities our arrangement covers into my normal relationships, but it has never worked."

"I know what you mean. I thought I was finally succeeding, and I still think I could have, but I rather cocked that up."

"So, you can understand that it's problematical if we let it spill over into the rest of our lives."

"OK, I do accept that. But I do find you a very attractive and captivating woman, Lavinia, that's not putting it too strongly. I would like to know more about you."

"Mr Stephens."

"Jack, please."

"No, not Jack, definitely Mr Stephens. You are a very good dom and the formality of our meetings appeals to me very much. It excites me, I'll even admit that, although that must be very clear to you."

"No comment." Her wetness, particularly when her thighs were open, always became obvious to him.

"Thank you for your tact." He could picture her smiling but then he had to admit to himself that he'd never actually seen her do that. "I'll go a little further and say something else that I'm almost certain is clear to you. You are an attractive man and also a little fascinating so, in a different world, I should very much have liked to have met up. But I am not looking for a relationship like that. I am looking to sustain this rather special arrangement that we have contrived. If you feel that needs to change at all I am, as you know, quite prepared to discuss some adjustments. It has evolved somewhat during this year or so and I am happy for it to continue to do so as long as its core and its boundaries remain intact. Are you happy with it?"

"I'm happy with it. Although it does leave me feeling somewhat frustrated, as you know. We've discussed that before, but that's a small price to pay for a very rich experience." He wasn't sure what to say next. He'd rung her, very unusual for them, and been, effectively, rebuffed but she wasn't ringing off. "But while I've got you, is there anything you would change? Is the setting still good? Are you still enjoying the instruments?" He paused, it seemed fair to think she was thinking, or had something on her mind.

"Um, well, I'll touch on something delicate if I may?"

"Of course."

"I'm inevitably aware of your frustration, as you put it. When I am over your lap the bulge against my hip becomes very obvious." He laughed quietly. "May I ask what you do with him?"

Now he laughed loudly. "Of course you may. In the early days, before we got the Friday routine established, I would simply lie on my bed as soon as you left and masturbate. Nowadays, I try to hold on, take a shower and attempt to ensure I have an engaging companion for the evening. But that does raise a question for me." He paused.

"Go on." She must have been expecting something like this.

"May I ask what you do?"

"I go home and masturbate."

"Invariably?"

"Invariably."

"Are you happy with that?"

"Not entirely, I admit, but I do have another relationship that satisfies me in different ways but, of necessity, I need my body to recover before I can pursue that."

"I get that. I think if I had a Friday date who suddenly revealed a well-spanked bottom, I would at least have some questions. Well, as you can imagine, I would personally be very intrigued, excited even."

"I'm fortunate in that Friday dates are, for me, unusual but I must admit that having to make it home before I deal with myself is not the best way of closing our experience."

"Do you have an alternative proposal?"

"I was hoping you might have one." She waited. "I'm happy to have an open discussion on this. I'm flattered to think of you masturbating but maybe I shouldn't be, maybe you have entirely different thoughts and different situations in mind when you retreat to your bedroom."

"No, no." But he had hesitated.

"Don't worry, I don't think exclusively of you when I get home. Sometimes though." There was another long pause, then finally "I'm happy…" and "Would you…" came all at once.

"Go on," he said.

"No, you go on, Mr Stephens. You're the dom. I'm happy to hear proposals via the phone like this, as long as you respect the choices we make and, I have to say, you've invariably done that so far. So, do you have a suggestion?"

"I should like to touch you to make you come, no penetration, not even with fingers, but I suspect that gently touching where you're wet might be enough, then I would feel that all my build-up had been what you wanted and you're not faced with an unsettling journey home."

"I should like that very much. I've been hoping you would suggest it at some point. I realise I must have put you off when it happened before, but you surprised me, and I wasn't ready. I'm grateful you've come back to the topic, and you should feel free to touch me any way you wish, after all, it's the result that counts. But wouldn't that leave you, so to speak, a little up in the air?"

He laughed again. "It would. I doubt whether I'd make it to the shower without having to pay him the appropriate attention."

"I shouldn't like you to have to wait that long."

"You want to help me?"

"Not actively, no, that would be going too far for me, but I do like to think I excite you, I like to think of you having to masturbate. So, I should like to stay in position on the arm chair while you hold yourself and then squirt your blobs all over my bottom. Could you do that? Would you like to?"

"I should like that very much."

"Fine, I think we have something new to try, don't we?"

"We do, Lavinia, I shall very much look forward to that."

"*Bon, à bientôt.*"

"*À bientôt.*" Well, that will change Friday date nights, he thought.

8

Andy felt pleased initially that his delegation outnumbered the banks by three to two, then wondered, perversely, if he wasn't being short changed. Yamamoto san, with whom he'd exchanged emails — in perfect English, to Andy's relief, as were the greeting and introductions — had met them at reception and taken them to the twentieth floor, where the American woman was waiting.

American, but the *meishi* formalities were conducted in the perfect Japanese manner, Andy observed, although his own efforts remained clumsy and he felt self-conscious about the shiny, new *meishi* wallet that Tania had bought for him that morning. It felt like a first day at a new school. But he studied the cards, as instructed. "Ah, Martha, do I call you Martha?" She nodded. "I see you're not based here."

"No, but this is an unusual case, very few companies ever get bought here, so I wanted to be here to see how you plan to go about it. Yamamoto san will be your principal contact in Tokyo and, if it starts to fly, he'll get more support locally. I also wanted to be here for Peter. You're probably aware of how much we've been doing together in China, so he's quite important to the bank. Now, if you can forgive me for being forward, can I ask what role each of you plays in this process? Yours is clear, Andy, but I'd like to hear you tell us what kicked this off, but, Ozawa sensei, how involved will you be? And how come you got landed with this, Tania, in misogyny central?" Ozawa and Yamamoto managed to laugh but looked a little embarrassed. "Oh, don't worry boys, it's no worse than many of the other places I visit. So, can I understand your perspectives first, guys? Then we'll come on to the analysis Yamamoto san has prepared. I should add that he's done that with help from Peter's team."

She may have been working in misogyny central, thought Andy, but he couldn't imagine this woman ever being intimidated by anything, least of all by a mere male. She was shortish, dark-haired, slightly heavily built, impeccably dressed in a well-tailored dark grey suit and white blouse, good-looking, olive-skinned and green-eyed, perhaps a little hard, and she would pass for forty, but she was probably older.

Andy spoke as succinctly as he could about his products, trying to rein in the pride and the passion, and about the competitive pressures and how that had prompted him to think of a global scenario where he could combine the strengths of the two businesses. Ozawa was cagey and unforthcoming, 'I am merely offering legal advice' — Martha had looked unconvinced but hadn't pressed him — banks must be aware of these darker processes, thought Andy. Then

Tania spoke briefly but very clearly about her Japanese experience and interests, and about the necessary improvements the programme was bringing belatedly to Molloy performance. Martha looked impressed.

"I'd like to come back to you, Ozawa sensei. May I ask what contact you've had with the Nakamura people?"

"A very brief contact with a director, just trying to set up an exploratory meeting. I am very interested now to hear what Yamamoto san has to say about this company."

Andy couldn't read anything into Martha's expression. He would ask Ozawa later about the lack of frankness, which had bordered on dishonesty. The Endo meeting had been much more than setting up, it had been already exploratory. Tania had looked to Andy but remained impassive, Ozawa's words must also have surprised her, but, fortunately, she hadn't reacted.

Yamamoto gave a polished presentation, which covered rather more than the information in the dossier Andy had received on Nakamura from Peter's team and added a lucid and succinct description of how the stock market functioned in Japan, in particular in relation to buying and selling companies.

"Now, one interesting feature you may not have picked up on." Martha turned to Yamamoto. "Could you go back to the balance sheet?"

"Can I just say thank you very much," Andy interjected. "That was a superb summary, Yamamoto san, extremely helpful. Sorry to interrupt, Martha."

"Not at all." She smiled. "That's very welcome." She turned to Yamamoto, who was smiling. "Back a bit?" He went back three slides. "You'll see that twenty-two thousand number there, two two one seven three to be exact." Yamamoto pointed. "This is not uncommon in Japanese companies like this. They hold large amounts of cash. They don't draw attention to them, although it's one of the first things a banker will look for. They're there as a fund to keep up the dividend payments in any bad years. It would be a huge dishonour to have to miss out on those. But it's a very conservative philosophy, that's two hundred million dollars just sitting there, not doing very much. So, when you come to work out what it's worth to you if you can get them to think about selling, that money goes straight into your bank."

"Jesus!" said Andy.

Martha smiled again. "Yes, makes it a much more attractive target than you thought, doesn't it?"

"Sure does."

"Now what happens next is up to you. Of course, there's a lot we can do to help but the project would go nowhere unless they're interested. I imagine that's what you're trying to assess, Ozawa sensei."

"Yes, but that is very early."

"Do you have any conversations planned this week? It's a long way for Andy and Tania to come to do some sightseeing."

"I am still hoping to organise a conversation. I will speak to my contact this evening." This was either news to Andy or bullshit. He had no idea what Ozawa's game was.

"We'll be getting a tour of the factory tomorrow." Andy felt Ozawa touch his elbow, but he already guessed that Ozawa, for whatever reason, would not want that mentioned.

"Just as a tourist? They won't know who you are?"

"No, they won't know who we are." Andy didn't want to reveal the arrangement, but he sensed that Martha was concerned. She looked from him to Ozawa and back.

"Well, two things: first, I hope you don't meet anyone important who might recognise you later if a bid emerges; and second, please make absolutely sure that all discussions about a possible purchase are held within a very tight team of absolute must-knows. Any leaks or gossip will blow any deal and if it doesn't blow the deal it will make it much more expensive."

"Yeah, we're keeping it pretty tight."

Martha smiled but she was plainly making a very serious point. "I'm not letting you get away with 'pretty tight', Andy. Please look me straight in the eye and tell me that no one gets to hear a word of this unless they are a: essential and b: sworn to absolute secrecy."

"I get it Martha, I promise you I do."

She looked hard at him for several more seconds. "OK, I believe you. Now, there's a lot we can do for you once the process is underway, but we need you and Nakamura san to agree to trigger that. After that we would work with their bank and their finance people. Ozawa sensei would work with their lawyers, I assume." She looked to Ozawa and he nodded. "But there are some big steps before then. But what we can say." She paused. "Well, I think I'll hand back to Yamamoto san for his last slides."

"Thank you, Weddle san."

"It's OK, Yoshi, in this group we can be first names." She smiled at Ozawa. "Unless Ozawa sensei wants to pull his samurai sword out to punish you for showing disrespect." Ozawa didn't respond but Andy could feel the tension.

"Thank you, Martha. We have looked at some possible valuations for you. As you know from the current share price, the market cap is forty-five billion, around four hundred million dollars for you. You would need to offer around fifty per cent above that, but you would have the benefit of their cash hoard to offset the price. We've looked at profitability and cash flows and we think Nakamura is worth at least eight hundred million dollars to you as a stand-alone concern. If you add in synergies and enhanced market penetration benefits of acting together in the newer markets, and you'll see on the next slide what assumptions we've made, our view is that it's worth nearer a billion."

Andy's eyebrows were raised.

"It certainly makes it worth pursuing for you, doesn't it?" said Martha. Andy nodded. "OK, ball's in your court. Well, it's probably more correct to say it's in Ozawa sensei's court. I wish you the best of luck with your conversations, sir." He nodded and smiled perfunctorily. "Now I have another meeting for an hour, but do you guys have plans for the evening? I love eating here. I'd like to take you out."

"That would be great, Martha, thank you. Ozawa sensei?"

"I must make some phone calls, alas. I will catch up with you at breakfast."

Tania was smiling and nodding when he turned to her.

"Fine, I'll get somewhere booked. Be prepared to be adventurous, Andy. I'll pick you up at seven from the Okura, is that right?" He nodded. She stood up. "Nice work Yoshi, good presentation, thank you." She bowed to Ozawa, shook Andy's and Tania's hands and left, leaving Andy feeling mildly exhausted but exhilarated from having been in her company.

***

She was waiting at reception, talking to Tania, when Andy got there.

"Not late, am I?"

"No, but we don't drop our punctuality habits in foreign countries. Come on, car's outside."

The Mercedes pulled up immediately they emerged. The bellboy held two doors open and skipped to the far side of the car. "Will you take the front, Andy? We're not going far."

She was right. They emerged from the car less than ten minutes later at the end of what seemed like an alleyway. A tiny Toyota delivery van made its way slowly along it but, encountering its like twenty yards in, had to negotiate its way past with extreme caution and some help from pedestrians who moved bicycles leaning against shop windows. On either side there were small shops selling incomprehensible paraphernalia and restaurants with plastic food models to show their menus. There were bright signs above the alley but very few with any English text. After fifty yards Martha turned left at a small discreet sign down a long, narrow, dark alley at the end of which was a bright doorway with a sign similar to the one they'd turned at. It was the graphic design that had impressed Andy, its starkly stylish simplicity standing out among its garish neighbours, and it had offered English text, Minamino, below the indecipherable Kanji.

They pushed through the flimsy curtains and were greeted by a small, smiling grey-haired lady in the most ornate kimono Andy had ever imagined seeing.

"*Konban wah, watashi* Weddle san, Anglo-Asia bank, we have a booking at seven fifteen."

"*Konban wah*, Weddle san, very happy to see you again. Please." She gestured to a rack half full of shoes. The purpose was obvious, but Andy found himself slower than the ladies, who had anticipated the expectation.

The small lady led them through a labyrinth of rush-matted corridors between walls of wood-framed rice paper. Peering down one side turn, Andy saw a younger kimono-clad woman slide a door open to shuffle into what was obviously a dining room, but she was entering on her knees. Eventually, at the end of a blind corridor, the old lady slid open a partition on the right and showed them into a small space where a table for six had been laid for three diners around one end, the table surface approximately one foot above the floor of the room.

"Whisky Tango…"

"You're lucky. There's a hole in the floor so you don't have to sit cross-legged, and your cushion has a seat-back, most don't. You'll get comfortable, get over it." And when he'd squeezed himself in, he found he was. "We use this place for a few reasons. The food is wonderful, it's reasonably authentic — although the kaiseki cuisine here is a pretty modern development, truth be told — and it's private. That's a real wall at the opposite end to you, Andy, and there's no one in the room on the other side of the corridor at the moment. If we hear anyone going in there, we'll have to be more careful. With that in mind, we'll do business first. I'm going to order a set menu for us all, some sake and water. If you eat it all I'll be impressed, OK? Should I order a beer for you?"

"He's not drinking beer," said Tania, firmly.

Andy smiled and nodded. He opened the lapels of his jacket and looked at Martha. "Of course," she said. He took his jacket off and placed it carefully on the floor. He began to loosen his tie. "Don't push it, buddy!" He stopped, slightly shocked, but she and Tania burst out laughing immediately. "Take it off. Just get comfortable, we've got some important ground to cover and I'd like to do it quickly because I don't know if anyone will come next door. Also, I love sake and that will help me talk more freely about this country later, but we should get business out of the way first."

The old lady came in with the menus, Martha taking them before she could hand one to Andy.

"*Sumimasen*," said Tania and continued in Japanese. The old lady smiled and nodded and replied briefly. "They have a booking next door at eight."

"I'm impressed, young lady, I hope you don't mind me telling you."

"Compliments always welcome, ma'am."

Martha turned to the old lady and pointed to the menu. "And sake *onegaishimas*, *Junmai Daiginjo*." The old lady smiled, nodded and shuffled back out of the room on her knees, sliding the door shut silently behind her.

"OK, now tell me about Ozawa." She was leaning towards him and eying him intensely.

Andy, unusually, felt a little flustered. "I could sense some tension between the two of you this afternoon."

She seemed to relax slightly. "You're not wrong there. He may be what you need in this situation, but you do realise he's dangerous, don't you?" Andy felt reluctant to speak. "Have you worked with him before?"

"No, we got him from a contact of Peter's."

"But he's new to Peter?"

"Yes, so far as I know, Peter's only had one conversation with him."

"Right. Now, you need to understand that things get done differently here. They have their ways of doing things that we would think of as unethical and we couldn't, frankly, get away with. A case in point is your visit tomorrow. Who are you, if anyone asks?"

"We've had *meishi* prepared," said Tania.

"False identities?" Tania nodded. "Do all you can to avoid using them. You're just dumb Americans who've forgotten them, or don't have Japanese ones, no, don't say that, they'll want your US ones. Look, you won't get through this without bending some rules, and since your man works in both countries, he probably knows enough not to get caught. I mean, he's pushing seventy and he's not in jail, but you need to be sure you can be comfortable with how things are done. What's this conversation thing? Where is he on that? That was bullshit today."

"We met one of the directors yesterday. He's the one who's set up the tour tomorrow."

"How did Ozawa get hold of him?"

"He said he'd worked out from the directors list who would be most likely to talk to him."

"That may or may not be true. I don't want to seem too critical; he seems to have got you to the front door, at least. We might have been able to do that bank to bank, but we can't control where information goes at their end as well as maybe he can. Yoshi, Yamamoto san, is a good man, you'll be able to discuss any worries with him, just don't leave any paper or email trails. Does your contact think there's any possibility of them selling?"

"Well, it's run by a younger brother, but the widow of the founder still has lots of shares, our man, Endo, is her brother. Younger Nakamura brother is old and there are no children on either side who will be capable of taking over the running of the place. Our man seemed to think it might be a good time to have further conversations. Ozawa wants to set up a dinner tomorrow night."

Martha nodded. "OK, sounds like it might be promising. Ah, here comes your chance to practise your chopsticks." The door slid open and two kimono-clad ladies slid trays in and then placed them in front of the diners. Each tray had four different dishes, all small and exquisitely prepared, none of which contained anything that Andy could remotely recognise. He looked perplexed. Tania laughed at him.

"If it's any consolation, I don't know what half of this stuff is. I couldn't afford to eat like this when I was living here, but I always loved the food and you did well with the Teppanyaki yesterday."

"You'll have to be prepared not to be invited tomorrow, you know that?" Martha said to Tania.

"I realise that. I'm just going to make the most of being here. I'm staying an extra day to give myself a treat at an *onsen* up near the mountains."

"That's a wonderful idea. Are you going Andy?" Andy was struggling with the chopsticks while the ladies were finishing their courses.

"No, I'm heading back Friday evening."

"It's worth an extra day. You don't know if you'll be coming again."

"Go on, Andy, you should think about it."

"Nah, I should get back." But the thought had taken root.

"Well, tomorrow might be an interesting experience for you. Some of the entertainment offered can be quite old-fashioned." She looked hard at Andy. He looked quizzically back. "Just be prepared for anything — and my advice would be to avoid most of it." She looked to Tania. "I'm not taking a moral position on men's entertainment, especially not here in

Asia." Turning back to Andy, she said, "I'd just recommend keeping business and pleasure separate. It keeps the business side simpler."

"*Kampai*," said Andy, raising his sake tumbler and smiling. "Don't worry, ma'am, I'm a good boy."

They moved on to more general talk about Tania's time in Japan and Martha's business in China. Andy found the food mostly wonderful but with the odd dish of unappealing flavours or unmanageable textures, although the ladies managed all courses easily with chopsticks. He counted eleven different dishes, but they were all small and he barely felt full when green tea was offered — which he attempted to decline but was not permitted to. The ladies seemed to enjoy it, but he screwed his face up. "Come on, practice for tomorrow night," said Tania.

"I don't even know if we're meeting."

"If you are, I'd guess you have a good chance of talking about a deal some time, but not tomorrow. They'll want to meet you and decide if they like you, but it will tell you they're prepared to think about a deal. Good luck. OK, I've texted the car, he'll be where he dropped us off in ten minutes."

9

"I'd never thought of myself as cheeky but asking you on a date and then letting you buy me dinner, I think that qualifies," said Claudia.

Alphonse smiled. "I wish you'd do it more often. Anyway, *salut*!" He raised the champagne glass to clink with hers.

"I would seriously like to pay next time. Or rather Brodie Associates would."

"Would Brodie Associates also book the room? That would make me feel very unchivalrous." He was smiling more broadly.

"Well, you're the one who sleeps there."

"I wish you'd stay."

She placed her hand on his. "I would love to, I really would, you know that, but I already spend enough nights away and Pat needs to know what I'm doing and where I am. I'd love to have you back at my place but I'm keen to keep life simple for the kids. Anyway, I think we've proved once again this afternoon that I'm far too noisy for that." He laughed lightly. "But you should come for lunch one weekend, if you could. I'm thrilled with the place and I'd love to show you what I've made out of it now we're in. I'm so grateful you saw the potential in it. I hope you'll approve of what I've done. Well, lots of the ideas were yours. Anyway, it would be a kind of thank you."

"That's what you said about this afternoon."

"I know I said that, but that was an excuse. It must have been obvious I was desperate for you."

"For me?"

"Don't make me blush. OK, one bit of you in particular. And you certainly shouldn't make me admit that you're my only outlet at the moment. It's just that a girl has to meet her needs, you know." She raised her glass again. "But I would like you a little more often — this is almost the perfect relationship for me. But how are you doing?"

"Is that what we're going to talk about?" It was a friendly question. "I thought there were some business issues."

"You're teasing me. I thought I made it perfectly plain that I had one objective today."

"And that's been fulfilled?"

She smiled, and said, "Can we say it's been half-fulfilled? I didn't tell them I'd be home early. Or am I being too demanding?"

"By no means. I prefer the late nights, however wonderful the late afternoon was. And I especially love the combination."

"But I had asked you a question. You may have been evading that. Did you mind me asking?"

"About what?

"You know very well about what. I'm not really asking for details about any other ongoing relationships, but I do like to check that you're happy, well, maybe contented is a better word."

"Yes, I'm contented. I don't chase around like I used to, but I see a few different people. I'm…" he paused.

"Yes? What is it? Are you getting deep with someone?"

He had looked a little tense but now he seemed to relax. "I want to be careful how I say this, but this, you and I, this is my most important relationship. It has been for a while." He squeezed her hand. "It's a little strange, I know, because I think we both expect to be with different people if we do settle down, but this really works for me like nothing else has. Is that OK with you?"

Claudia was touched. "It's lovely for me, and you don't have to worry that I'm bringing any expectations about us. I think we both like to pretend that this could continue if either of us falls into a more permanent relationship somewhere else but, deep down, I doubt whether it could, at least not the whole afternoon and evening at Coworth, and I like to think I love you in a way that I would want you to be happy with someone else. And if that's what happens, I would try to help. I suppose it would hurt, though, but I am promising I will try."

The starters were served with the waiter giving each dish its charming but slightly tedious explanation, and Alphonse had to taste the wine. He sipped and nodded.

"It would be much easier for you. You have other distractions." She leaned towards him and whispered, "You my good sir, are my only outlet, that's why you find me so voracious when we meet."

"I wouldn't find it as easy as you think, but I would, of course, should you fall for someone, be noble and silent. But I would never speak to you again and I would send you twelve blue roses every Friday."

She laughed. "Why Friday?"

"Because we met on a Friday and I would want you to feel some of the pain I would undoubtedly be feeling." But he smiled and held her hand. "Don't worry, I would try to make sure you were happy. But there is no one? No one since Jack?"

"No." She shook her head. "I would have told you if there had been. I don't have your powers of discretion. I would have blurted things out to you. And you fill all my needs like this. Besides, there's no time for anything more. Well, a little more maybe, dinner dates a little more often, please."

He smiled, and said, "But do you miss him? We never talk about him."

"No, we don't. It would have been too painful before but I'm getting there now. Yes, I miss him still. I spent years waiting for a relationship with him without really knowing it, and then it happened suddenly but in the two years I had it, I hardly ever saw him. We weren't together more than ten times."

"But who actually finished it? I know I had to tell you what had been happening, but Peter only wanted you to know. I was never really clear about what happened between you afterwards. I don't need to know, my love, but I do want to be here for you if you'd like to talk about it."

"I suppose I do, and you're the only one I can talk to. I can't even talk to Peter about it because he was, as I see it, instrumental in it ending. That's not really fair, of course. He was just letting me have the unwelcome knowledge, as you called it. You had to tell me, but it was his information."

"Should we have said nothing?"

"Oh, heavens no. It was just something I should have dealt with better. I kept on insisting on openness and I'd already found it harder than I expected to, but when I found out there was another level I needed to descend to and that he'd failed, once again, to be open, I just felt lost. I didn't know how dark he was, I still don't, he'd taken me to places I'd never expected to go. I loved opening up, but I'd certainly gone as far as I ever wanted." She thought a moment. "Probably further actually — we had a night with two guys in Charleston that I don't think I would want to repeat, but he may have wanted even more than that. I just have no idea —

in his defence, I was utterly into it that night, but I haven't done anything unusual or outrageous since then.

"The boat was somehow different, we were friends, but these guys were just strangers. I don't know, I'm not sure I would do the boat again, but that's it with Peter, you just feel free to let go but it's all somehow safe. Maybe I'd just let myself surprise myself. I really don't know.

"But now, you're all I've got. Not that I think we're vanilla, you still make very good use of your triple A pass, I'm glad to say, so I am sitting here a little awkwardly." They both laughed quietly. "I should be more honest there. I still want all of that from you, let's face it, I asked you here today. I'm surprised I feel almost addicted to it all, especially the thing, I'm ashamed to say, that you do so well and that makes me feel very pleasantly uncomfortable. But I don't miss going further. Like I said, I might enjoy some of the party stuff I suppose, but I certainly wouldn't seek it out. All of my real needs you deal with beautifully." She put her hand on his, "Don't worry, I realise I can't be the same for you and I'd be disturbed if you told me I could be."

He squeezed her hand. "Thank you," he said, quietly.

"But with him, I'd gone so far but still ended up feeling that I didn't really know him and that it probably wasn't enough. That's what hurt, still does."

"Regrets?"

"Yes, hundreds, but at the time I was so hurt, and the business start-up just gave me something to completely focus on. It seemed like a massive help then. But maybe I should have given more thought to a life plan." She touched his hand again. "I'm sorry, I must sound ungrateful and insensitive. Your big break-up must have been similar, I assume."

He looked out of the dark window. "A bit, yes, but being told lies is a step nearer hell than not being open, isn't it? Especially when I found out how long the lies had been going on for."

She felt perplexed. "Well, I suppose it's worse, yes. Is that what happened?" He would talk if he wanted to, she knew that, and he normally didn't.

"Yes, ultimately yes, but I found myself wondering for a long time whether I had brought the situation about, whether I had imposed too many expectations, not been sensitive enough to what he actually wanted. But you can go on forever blaming yourself for other people's failings."

"Is that how you see it now?"

"Only partly. But I think I blamed myself too much. After all, he was a bit of a cunt. A very charming and beautiful cunt, but a cunt, nonetheless." He was speaking with a little venom but had lowered his voice. "But these things are never quite that simple, are they?"

"No, this is the nearest to simple I do. I love what we have, the yesterdays we already have in our memories, the tomorrows we should still have and the hope that, if anything happens for either of us, we will welcome that too for each other."

10

Andy arrived punctually for his Ozawa meeting. He'd asked Tania to join them half an hour later and asked Ozawa to have breakfast served then.

Andy took his position on the sofa. "What did you think of our banker?"

"I was impressed. He is young but I thought his presentation was good and that is an important point about the cash. You must have found his valuations very appealing, I would think."

Andy couldn't help smiling at the deliberate misunderstanding. "I did, unquestionably. And Weddle san, what did you think?"

"She is based in Singapore. She is American. She is very *gaijin*. She understands little of Japan." — *and 'she's only a woman' is one you missed!*

"She understands that Japan is different, I think."

"Yes, but I believe your young lady knows more about Japan. Things are dealt with differently here."

"I'm still an American company."

"But you wish to be a global company. It will be important to convince our hosts that you can be flexible."

"We have hosts?"

"Yes, we are invited to dinner this evening back here in Tokyo, after the factory tour."

"That's excellent news, isn't it?"

"Yes, it's very good news, especially since Abego san will join us. He is their lawyer. It would, of course, be inappropriate to invite Miss Tania."

"Miss Tania is not expecting to be invited. As you said, she does understand Japan a little, she knows there are still men's evenings."

Ozawa smiled. "We may be misogyny central, but the country is beginning to accept that women can play important roles. And let us not forget that Keiko san will have something to say about this, although we shall probably never hear her words directly."

"So, what has Endo san said exactly?"

Ozawa smiled again. "I think you already know that what he said exactly will not help you to know what he really meant. We talk of *tatemae* and *honne*, the face we show to the world and the innermost thoughts and feelings that we conceal. It is sufficient that we have been invited to meet them. That means there is interest. We shall have to see whether they like you and whether they think you will be a responsible steward for their people."

"Is that really their main concern?"

Ozawa smiled again. "That is a perceptive question. I can only say it will be a major concern, and it is a concern that Jiro san and Keiko san will be able to agree on, even if they agree on little else."

Andy knew he would find this tiresome at some point but, for now, he was intrigued by how these little games played out and he knew he had no choice but to be patient. "What are you not telling me?"

"There is nothing I am not telling you." He paused. "Well, eventually there will be nothing. What do you think will be their major concern?"

"I think if I were ever to consider selling Molloy, I would want to know that my people were going to be secure, but I sure as hell would want the best price I could get."

"You see, but that is with a decision you can make on your own. The Nakamura family owns only fifteen per cent between them. You need to get a very high percentage to be private, or at least have total control. I assume that is your wish?"

"Yes, I can't see me managing a company that is traded on the Nikkei. I don't need all that crap. I'm an engineer, not a politician. Peter could do that, of course, but even he would like to get on with more new stuff rather than get dragged into meetings with know-nothing busybodies. Does this mean I'm going to have to win over the institutions and the directors as well? They're not just going to be happy with a fifty per cent uplift?"

"If you make Jiro san and Keiko san happy, the institutions will be happy, fifty per cent uplift is a good price for them. That will almost guarantee you seventy-five per cent of the company. As Yamamoto san told you yesterday, when you get ninety per cent you can effectively take if off the market, no more stock exchange reporting. To get near that you need the directors. If the directors are unhappy, they will be able to make problems for you. Some may want to retire, but some you will need to run the company for you. It will be important to make a good impression when you come back. If you come back."

"I must admit, yesterday's presentation has made me more enthusiastic."

"Very well, we must do what we can. One question I must ask, when are you flying back?"

"Tomorrow afternoon."

"Ah, so if further conversations were advisable, you would not be able to meet people on Friday or Saturday?"

"Is that likely?"

"We are courting them, Molloy san. It is not a bad idea for the suitor to seem enthusiastic."

"Well, there was an idea to stay an extra night and visit an *onsen*."

Ozawa smiled. "That would be an excellent idea. If they see that is your plan, they will know you are interested in Japan."

Tania arrived at the same time as the breakfast things. Once again, Ozawa blocked any discussion while the waiter was in the room. When he'd left, Andy asked, "Do you really think a waiter is going to listen in?"

"He will do if someone has paid him to. And some of the cleverer ones know where to go with interesting information even when they haven't been asked. You must be very careful with your conversations. Your language protects you somewhat but not completely. You must be careful what you say to each other this afternoon. But Tania san, you should try to speak a little Japanese with them. Do not give away who you really work for, I think your cover story is good, the American lady worries too much, but the little birds will whisper to Endo san and Jiro san that their suitors have taken the trouble to bring along some Japanese language capability."

"I'm afraid my Japanese is very poor."

"Nonsense, you will impress everybody."

"OK, thank you, I'll try."

The car got them to the factory complex somewhere away from the city. Andy had no idea where they'd travelled to and the cloudy day meant the sun gave him no orientation.

"Excuse me?" he had said to the driver, as they set off. The driver turned, looking puzzled, and shook his head. Andy added, "No English?" Now he smiled and nodded and shook his head again — "*Hai, hai!* No English!"

Andy turned to Tania. "I'm just going to assume we can talk." But, as they spoke, the conversation moved away from Nakamura anyway and on to Tania's other projects and her father's business — and her ambitions to run it.

"I guess I'm a little ambivalent. It means a lot to me. It means much more to him, and I'm his son, really, is how he views it — and my sisters are well into other things, so it's me or no one. But I like what I'm doing with Claudia — and I'm loving New York, although that's a bit crazy. I'm working all the time. I've got a couple more years on this contract and there's no fixed commitment on a date for getting back to Giddings. But what will you do if this happens?"

"I guess I'd be spending a lot of time here until whoever becomes chief executive makes me feel comfortable. Wow, the idea of setting things up so that we can communicate between the two halves is a bit mind-boggling but, if I can put the panic to one side, it's exciting. But even finding that sort of money to start with is something that Peter will have to help with."

"What's he like? I've heard a bit about him from Claudia. She thinks he's wonderful."

Andy smiled. "Well, he worships her, I think, so it's a mutual admiration society, but I think he's one of the most remarkable men I've ever met. He'll try to convince you that he knows little about anything but he's a superb reader of people. Like Ozawa said, after one phone call, he just listens better than anyone else. He's also brilliant on numbers but he tries to hide that, and he's just prepared to be bold. You make decisions when you're with him. This is a case in point. He wants the programme you're running in Molloy to achieve dramatic changes in the way business operates but, being hurt as we were, he didn't want to wait when a more dramatic opportunity presented itself, if indeed it has. If it is there, I'm sure he'll find the half billion. Shit!"

"What's up?"

"I'm fifty-five per cent of the business."

"I thought you were fifty-one."

"No, we bought Hank out. That was a bit sad but we're still speaking — and he's a rich man now. Anyway, somehow I'm going to have to stand for fifty-five per cent of what we pay."

"You could IPO."

He screwed his face up. "Shareholders and directors controlling you? That wouldn't work for Peter or me."

"Yeah, my dad's not always happy about that."

The trip took over one hour but it surprised Andy that they seemed to arrive so soon. They walked to the reception desk. "Edwards san, we're here for a tour."

The girl looked a little shocked but quickly regained her composure. "Ah, ah, Edwards san, ah, please to come," she said, and she came around her desk in the rapid shuffle that most of them seemed to move with. Andy was only slowly getting used to it.

Tania said something and the girl relaxed immediately, smiled and replied.

"We're to wait in here, someone will be along shortly."

"You seem to be doing very well."

"Oh, I'm truly awful, they're just so happy they don't have to try to speak English." They sat down in one of the two reception rooms to the side of the entrance area, a small room with four chairs around a table.

After a few moments, Endo san came in. Andy was surprised. "Endo san, hello." Endo closed the door, nodded and addressed Tania. She replied to him, he nodded and smiled faintly. She turned to Andy and said, "Endo san had heard that I speak some Japanese. He wanted to make a few points before the tour."

Endo spoke in short sentences, making it easy for Tania to translate. "He thinks the Edwards distributor story is good and we should stick to it… I asked if we should use the cards and he said no… Only Nakamura Jiro and he know about our real purpose, plus Inui san, the oldest director, who will join you this evening… Our guide will speak English but not very well… He would be surprised if I spoke Japanese, so I should avoid it… but now I've used it at reception, I may use a few words, but I must pretend I know almost nothing… He will ask the guide to call him when our tour is completed… Any outstanding questions he will attempt to answer later."

For Andy, in particular, the tour was a slightly bizarre experience. There were so many similarities to his own business in many areas. Assembly layouts were similar, not really surprising since Eddie had adopted the best of Japanese manufacturing techniques years ago. The labs seemed smaller and less advanced than his own, but they looked to be a hive of industrious experimentation. There was more paper in all departments here than he had expected to find, almost everything at home was typed or went automatically straight into a terminal. And there were prominent graphs and pictures on the walls, and he was fairly sure they were carrying messages similar to those at Molloy. There was a quiet hum about the place, with grey-clothed people moving around purposefully and silently, talking, when they needed to, in low voices. Few looked up to pay them any attention. The guide's poor English discouraged too many questions, but Andy had told himself to remain restrained anyway. He knew the business well enough to absorb a lot by observation. He was impressed.

After an hour they were back in reception. "I call Endo san now. You like tea?"

"Could I have water please?" The man nodded — no more green stuff, thought Andy. "And thank you very much for a very interesting tour. I was very impressed."

The man smiled and bowed vigorously and left the room backwards, still bowing. Endo joined them moments later. "Thank you very much for allowing us to view your facility, Endo san, I was very impressed." Tania translated.

Andy wanted to know how they saw Molloy and what their own hopes were for expansion, in America, in China, and in the rest of Asia. Endo seemed to deal with those issues relatively openly, admitting that they saw Molloy technology as superior but also that they were aware of the opportunities created by Molloy's weaknesses in other areas. Tania's response seemed to go on longer than he expected, and Endo was nodding a little more vigorously.

"I've been telling him about the programme and how we are trying to get everyone focused on the important things. I think he was impressed."

Andy smiled at her. "Would you tell him now that we're very grateful for his time and I very much look forward to seeing him later."

She addressed Endo and this time it was his response that was a little longer and he was smiling. "He is very glad we have come, and he looks forward to seeing us later. He hopes very much that I will be joining you." Now she was smiling a little triumphantly.

"I am sure Tania san will be delighted to join us."

"I've already told him that."

"Then I have no further comment that I would wish you to translate." He turned to Endo. "I will see you later, Endo san."

"See you later," was said so parrot-like that Andy had no doubts that Endo had not been able to understand much, if any, of their English.

"You don't mind me coming?" was her first question in the car after they'd waved their smiling goodbyes.

"No, not at all. I'm quite looking forward to sticking that one to Ozawa but, of course, it makes it harder for them to host me around the fleshpots of Tokyo later. Martha will be proud of you, though, when she hears. Why do you think they've asked you?"

She looked suddenly thoughtful, almost crestfallen. "Oh, I just thought it was the language thing, although I'm sure they'll have an official interpreter there."

"I'm sure they will, Ozawa will have made sure of that, he can't fulfil such a humble function himself. Look, I didn't mean to upset you with the question, I'm really pleased they've asked you."

"Really?"

"Yes, really, for fuck's sake, don't go all girlie on me now, you've been doing so well. I just want to be very careful with these people. They probably realise you understand a great deal about the business, and they'll be trying to see if they can get information out of you that conflicts with anything Ozawa or I have said."

"Oh, OK," she said. She nodded thoughtfully.

"Don't worry, I trust you on that anyway, but you may need to be careful. Of course, it may just be that they're a bunch of dirty old men who will try to feel you up at dinner. You know more about this place than I do."

She smiled. "Yes, and that can happen too."

"OK, but no chaperone needed."

"No, I can look after myself."

***

"She must be careful," Ozawa said. "They will try to find out things from her to check them against what you and I have said."

"I've told her that. That was my first impression. But I also think they were impressed we had someone who could speak the language. How good is she?"

"Oh, she is terrible, but they can understand her, and we are always very grateful in Japan when any *gaijin* makes the effort. Besides, Molloy san, she is an attractive young woman, don't you think?"

Andy thought. "Yeah, that crossed my mind. You think they're just dirty old men?"

"Oh, they are assuredly that." He laughed. "But I think our first concern is the major one. We shall repeat your message to her in the car. I shall see you downstairs in half an hour?"

"Yeah, six thirty, see you then."

"Yoshiwara san is the old 'Floating World' district of Tokyo. It is more respectable now, but some ladies of evening commerce still work there." Ozawa was turning from the front seat to talk to them in the back. "The modern establishments like to hint at the old times but any ladies we meet in tonight's location will be very respectable. I am not sure how they will treat you, Tania san. It will be a little unusual for a lady to be entertained. I believe Molloy san has told you of our concerns."

"Yes, I have to be careful what I say. I've been thinking though, unless there's stuff you haven't told me, I'm pretty comfortable I'll be able to stick with our message."

"Well, you should be flattered you have been invited. They clearly think of you as knowledgeable and influential. But, of course, they will also see you as a beautiful young woman." He smiled and turned to face forward.

Tania looked at Andy, her eyes narrowed. She shook her head, poked her tongue towards Ozawa and then made to put two fingers down her throat. Andy struggled not to laugh.

The Yoshiwara district was surprisingly quiet. The traffic was light. The ornate, poorly lit buildings were not obviously advertising their purposes, unusual in a country apparently addicted to garish neon displays. The car pulled up outside the dark doorway of a four-storey building. Andy could see four or five small panels on the side wall of the entrance, lit only by the street lamps, all with different scripts, presumably the addresses of the different tenants or businesses occupying the premises.

Ozawa led them up the dim, stone stairway to a double door on the first floor, one half being held open by an elegant lady in a kimono with an elaborate cloud of shiny black hair, held in place by a variety of coloured combs and pins. Ozawa exchanged effusive greetings with her as they were bowing to each other. She gestured Andy and Tania to enter. Andy tried to let Tania go ahead, but she stepped aside, touched his arm and hissed, "Men always first here." They stepped into a long, wide hallway with a double door halfway along on the right, opening on to a brightly lit room.

The room was far too large for the low, u-shaped dining table positioned nearer one end. Between the table and the ornate lacquer screens, which traversed the room and foreshortened it, was a small group of men talking and being served with drinks by younger ladies in kimonos. The group broke up as they entered. Andy recognised Endo. It was he and Ozawa who initiated the bowing. Andy found himself reflexively twitching in small bows to no one in particular. Endo introduced Ozawa to the youngest man in the group. After a brief conversation, Ozawa brought him to Andy.

"Molloy san, this is Kitagawa san, he is our interpreter for the evening. He will help us make the introductions."

Kitagawa san bowed deeply to Andy. "I am very honoured to meet you, Molloy san."

Andy bowed back. "I am very happy to meet you, Kitagawa san. Molloy is my business, I am its founder, and this is Gunter san, who works with me there."

"Oh." Kitagawa looked confused. "I was expecting Tania san, who would help with translations."

Tania smiled and bowed to him and, to his evident relief, spoke to him in Japanese. The two strangers in the group nodded to Endo, as if in appreciation of their female guest, then turned to Tania and smiled. Kitagawa addressed them and Andy picked up Molloy san, Ozawa sensei and Tania san in his introduction. So much for his attempt to accord Tania an appropriate status, now he had no doubt she would be treated like a girl, a girl who might yield some insights for them but who would be principally regarded as décor. She would cope! And she had obviously dealt with the first challenge well.

Inui san was introduced, the oldest and shabbiest of the group, the director of development at Nakamura. His grey hair was thinning, and his broad smile revealed a mouth of teeth in serious need of attention.

Abego sensei, the lawyer, was a slightly extraordinary creature. He was short and slim, and very well dressed and groomed, the full, shiny, grey-flecked head of hair almost bouffant in how it had been sculpted up and back. The lizard smile brought no lines to his face, which may well, thought Andy — no expert in these matters — have had treatments to induce that sheen.

"Nakamura san," continued Kitagawa, "will be with us when his massage is finished." Andy smiled and nodded and hoped that his *what the fuck* reaction had remained inscrutably concealed. "May the ladies bring you some drinks? Molloy san?"

"I'll start with a beer, Asahi please if it's there?" If beer was the wrong drink, at least he would be drinking Japanese beer. Tania asked for the same, which surprised him slightly, but the men all nodded and smiled again. OK, he thought, if you have to be seen as a girl, at least be seen as a game one.

Andy was asked about his tour and he responded as he had done earlier with Endo, being as positive as he could without becoming too effusive. Ozawa and Abego peeled off together to begin a conversation in conspiratorial whispers. That's going to be an important axis, thought Andy but he could hardly think of two men who seemed less trustworthy.

The slightly stilted conversation continued as the drinks were brought by the three pretty young ladies. Inui san spoke about Molloy products and how he had admired them, then asked Andy how he had started his business. The mention of MIT brought nods from Inui and Endo before Kitagawa had begun to translate. Inui had been twice to the States, he said, each time to meet the distributors. He had taken Kitagawa with him.

There was a sudden noise at the door, and they all turned to see the madame, that was how Andy saw her, however respectable the establishment, accompanying a slightly taller, slender man in a grey silk suit and white open-necked shirt. He was smiling, looking slightly flushed, and well-groomed, his silvery hair lustrous and unusually long, swept back in a more modest version of the Abego style. He walked straight towards Andy, extending a hand and bowing slightly at the same time. "Please to meet you, please to meet you, sorry for late." It was an effusively warm welcome and Andy found it easy to respond with a smile. Nakamura then switched to Japanese and Kitagawa translated his apology. The room had become more animated. The madame despatched one of the young girls to fetch a drink, and she returned swiftly with a beer while Nakamura and Andy were still engaging in pleasantries. Ozawa and Abego moved towards them but Nakamura had plainly asked Kitagawa if he could first be introduced to Tania. Tania, hearing him speak, had moved closer and bowed low.

"You are the beautiful young lady who speaks Japanese," translated Kitagawa belatedly, forgetting that her guardian would want to be informed of any advances being made. Tania had been bowing and attempting to look bashful, obviously understanding Nakamura's compliment but remaining fortunately unwilling to repeat the gestures she had made to Ozawa in the car. She had dressed impressively, and Andy only realised now why she had worn such unfashionably low heels with such an elegant dress — she was a little taller than Nakamura; heels would have had her towering over him, even though he was the tallest native in the room. Eventually, Nakamura turned away to be introduced to Ozawa but, having done so, seemed to treat him with a great deal of respect as if, somehow, his reputation had preceded him.

The madame came and whispered to Kitagawa. "It is time to sit down," he said to Andy. Everyone else seemed to have got the message. Andy was invited to share the head of the table with Nakamura, Kitagawa positioning himself self-consciously between them. To Andy's right on the long side there was first an empty space, then Inui, Tania and Abego were seated. To Nakamura's left, Ozawa and Endo filled two of the four seats. Andy struggled to fit himself in; the chair was very low but there was no hole under the table this time to make it easier for his legs.

The reasons for the spaces became quickly clear as the young ladies brought trays with sake flasks, water and small dishes, which they placed in front of the diners before they joined them.

"I am Sachiko san," said his smiling, pretty neighbour as she introduced herself. "Speak a little English, I pour you sake, yes?"

"Thank you, Sachiko san, I should like that very much. I am Molloy san."

There was movement in front of the screen. Two ladies in robes, rather than kimonos, although the materials looked just as sumptuous and elaborate, brought seats for themselves and seemed to be preparing to play instruments, one, a simple drum and the other a primitive post, about the height of a cello, with three thick strings.

"We shall provide you with traditional Japanese entertainment, Molloy san."

Andy's eyebrows were raised. This was not what he'd expected as traditional entertainment.

"Do you know much about Japan, Molloy san?" Kitagawa had translated Nakamura's question.

"Much less than I should," began Andy, "but I am a huge fan of sumo. I have followed it for years, right from the Waka Taka time." It was a slightly desperate gambit, but it came off splendidly. Nakamura was plainly impressed, but Inui was an aficionado and established quite quickly that Andy was a serious student and historian of the sport. For the next half-hour they were engrossed, stretching Kitagawa's capabilities to translate the signature moves of the great exponents. Nakamura seemed to engage deeply with Ozawa and could be safely left but the paternal part of Andy's brain was partly occupied by the observations of Abego being plainly entranced by his beautiful dinner companion. And the body language of the peacock was plainly universal.

The music had started. It was a quiet diversion, nothing more, and didn't seem to demand that they tune in. Sachiko would occasionally move away to bring more food or sake, returning to compliment him on his talent for using chopsticks. He tried, with an indulgent smile, to persuade her that this comment was as unnecessary as it was inaccurate but getting her to abandon her attentive politeness was a hopeless task.

A third lady joined the musicians and began to sing with them accompanying her. That was more distracting than the music alone had been, and they were all compelled to give it some attention, although Nakamura continued to whisper with Ozawa across their young companion, who kept their sake tumblers full without appearing to become bored. Abego continued to give a no doubt informative commentary on the performance to Tania. Kitagawa explained to Andy that this was a classical Japanese tradition and it would be followed by some equally traditional Japanese dancing. Sure enough, after four mildly boring but not unpleasant songs, the drummer put down her instrument and joined the singer and the two danced courtly steps to the accompaniment of the cellist. They continued for what seemed an unexpectedly long time, but Andy had to admit to himself that tedium was an enemy of brevity, maybe it hadn't been that long. He tried to look interested but was relieved when the singer left, and the drummer returned to her instrument.

When asked by Nakamura about his plans for the rest of his stay, Andy mentioned the possibility of his *onsen* visit and managed to imply a curiosity about Japan somewhat in excess of what he truly felt. But Nakamura was plainly a fan and began to describe his favourite spa locations. That at least prompted a debate among them about which was the best in all Japan, and it was evident that the sake was beginning to have an effect as they became mildly, but always respectfully, contentious.

Andy attempted to be cautious with the sake, drinking only when a neighbouring '*kampai*' compelled him to. He could be surer of the effects of the beer that Sachiko continued to pour into his glass whenever it became half empty. The food had moved through its pickled vegetable, fish and meat courses, all small and all exquisite, if not quite as fine as in Martha's restaurant. He was glad he'd had that experience as preparation. He knew when the bowl of rice came with the miso soup that only the sweet stuff was yet to come. The musicians departed to polite applause but joined madame in sliding one of the large lacquer screens to one side and wheeling out a console, a microphone on a stand, two speakers, and two quite large monitors, also on stands, all with their attendant cabling. It was clearly a practised manoeuvre, soon completed. Andy felt stunned to see what was obviously karaoke equipment; it looked utterly incongruous in the setting. "You know we love karaoke, Molloy san," observed Kitagawa. "You like to sing?"

"Ah, yeah, a little," said Andy, an enthusiastic bathtime baritone, reluctant to appear reluctant.

Madame had the microphone. She addressed Inui san, who scrambled to his feet. "Inui san is our best singer," said Kitagawa. Andy had already observed that he had immediately shown that he was the most enthusiastic. He said something to madame who scrolled through some options for him on the screen, quickly finding something that he nodded to and the intro began. It was tuneful and Inui had a very good voice but the song, being Japanese, was unknown and incomprehensible, but dramatic and moving to all of the audience except one. Andy nevertheless applauded enthusiastically with them all as Inui took his bow.

Kitagawa leaned towards Andy as Inui selected his next song. "We have all English songs for you, Molloy san." This was what Andy feared and he noticed Tania giving him a wicked smile as Kitagawa was speaking. He was fatalistic, if it had to be, they would get Springsteen, that must be universal surely.

After Inui's two-song spot, Nakamura took the microphone. He also sang well and very much enjoyed the limelight, theatrical gestures underpinning the emotion in the songs, and accepting the generous applause with a big smile and a sweeping bow but then finishing his second song with a gesture to Andy to join him — *don't hesitate, big boy, show no fear* — He scrambled up, elegance was impossible, and moved quickly to madame. "Springsteen?" he asked hopefully.

"No Springsteen, sorry, Elvis?"

Elvis is probably easier. "Elvis is good, please." Nakamura handed him the mike and he was soon scrolling through the entire catalogue, his mind going blank, he seized on 'Suspicious Minds', then hoped no one would read anything Freudian into his choice, but the intro was playing, he was committed and, once he'd started, he began to enjoy singing again, twenty years since his student band days.

The applause was loud, and the smiles were large. "Next song?" Madame was asking him and he jumped on 'Love me Tender', trusting himself now with a slow ballad, and that went really well. Part of him was reluctant to give up, a decision taken out of his hands by Sachiko appearing at his side with a second microphone. "We sing Titanic," she said, and madame was already bringing the music up.

The girl, fortunately, had a lovely voice. This was plainly a favourite song of hers and she was well practiced. His duetting efforts were okay, but he was going to be glad to hand the mike on.

He didn't feel quite so gallant when madame was gesticulating to Tania to come forward, but she responded like a trouper and came up with a smile, asking for Adele. That madame could do.

Andy squeezed himself back into his chair and felt immensely relieved as he listened to a very passable version of 'Hello'. The applause was the loudest so far and madame frustrated Tania's efforts to hand the mike back.

Andy suspected that the 'Someone Like You' intro came up unprompted by Tania but, having succeeded so well with the first, was not going to be beaten by this and, truly, she was getting committed to it and the applause this time was, if anything, louder, but the two-song precedent had been set and she was able to hand the microphone back.

Ozawa was next invited and, to Andy's surprise, he responded eagerly and performed very creditably. When madame invited the peacock, however, there was a show of mock reluctance, a 'surely not me' with grand gestures, an affected modesty undermined by his waving Sachiko to join him and madame starting 'I Have But One Heart' before she arrived to hold his hand. He did sing well, though, Andy had to admit, even though he found the closing 'My Way' mildly stomach churning, but the all-round bonhomie induced by the sake and the music was, if fleetingly, genuine. After the closing number, they all stood up and formed two small groups, Endo joining Nakamura and Andy with Kitagawa to help them.

"You sing well, Elvis," said Nakamura.

"But you were spectacular, Nakamura san," said Andy. "You have a very fine voice." And that was not wholly untrue.

Nakamura looked coyly modest. "Perhaps next time we shall have the chance to sing more, or perhaps Inui san will invite you to a *basho*."

Andy, slightly startled and very pleased, nodded. "I think a *basho* would be fantastic. I have wanted to see the real thing live for many years." He risked a smile, and said, "I am not so enthusiastic about singing again." Kitagawa must have managed the unsubtle nuance, the hosts laughed very loudly.

Ozawa joined them. "Our car is here," he said to Andy and then gave an elaborate address to Nakamura, which appeared to be very well received. They began a conversation. Kitagawa looked concerned, presumably about whether he should be translating but Andy shook his head gently to reassure him it was unnecessary. "I must thank you, Kitagawa san, you've done a wonderful job, it can't be easy with all these voices around you and the music playing."

"Thank you, Molloy san. It has been an honour and a pleasure. I hope I may join you on your next visit."

"I hope you do."

And now goodbyes were being said. Ozawa was speaking earnestly to Endo. Tania's hand was inevitably being kissed by the lizard. Inui was being told, Andy assumed, that he would be host at a *basho* on the next visit. Warm feelings seemed to abound and the hosts accompanied them down the stairs and waved their car goodbye.

Ozawa waited until the car had turned the corner before speaking. "They like you, Molloy san. They want to have further conversations with me next week. I hope I may speak for you."

"Of course, but I won't speculate on what they might be thinking until you hear from them."

"No, you are wise to be patient. I think it was a very successful evening. You enjoyed it Tania san?"

"Oh, I thought it was wonderful, Ozawa sensei, but I think I'm going to have bruises where that slimy old goat was squeezing my leg." She was smiling, and the men laughed loudly. Andy felt relieved that she'd handled the situation so well.

11

There was no summons from Ozawa to further conversations the following morning, but he seemed to have been quite right about Andy's interest in the *onsen* experience, which, combined with his detailed knowledge of sumo, added to his obvious enthusiasm for karaoke, did seem to have pleased and impressed his hosts. The car picked them up from the hotel after a light lunch of sushi. It was a drive Andy could never have retraced. They'd got on to a high-level expressway and soon left the towers of the city centre behind, but it seemed to take ages to pass the miles and miles of little, huddled houses before they got into open country where the roads were small and surprisingly quiet. They began to climb hills and drive through small patches of woodland and any signs in English lay well behind them until, just emerging from a small town, the car turned into the entrance of a large modern-looking hotel.

He had to leave the check-in procedures to Tania; no English was spoken.

"I've said we'll eat at seven, is that OK? It gives us plenty of time to try the *onsen* first. Don't forget to shower before you get in. Your room will be completely bare. Don't worry, they'll lay your bed out while we're eating dinner. Here's your key, I'm in five zero two if there's anything you don't understand. You probably won't get much joy ringing reception."

"No, I got that impression. I hope this is worth it." His initial reaction was not particularly positive. The furniture looked sparse and austere and there were just a few plants dotted around the foyer but no other décor.

His room, when he'd been taken there, was as she had said, almost completely bare. The floor was covered in the same tatami matting he'd seen in the restaurant. A small credenza of dark red lacquer work stood against a side wall with only a drinks tray and a phone on it. Two small and tasteful pictures were on the wall above, and there was no television, which would have been useless to him anyway out here, he imagined. One end wall was of sliding louvred doors, forming wardrobes into which the porter placed his bags, the other end wall completely composed of sliding windows, which led out on to a stone balcony with a rectangular bath being fed with running water, and beyond it a view of... a wooded hillside.

He rang her and said, "I was promised distant mountains; I've got nearby trees."

"Oh, I guess I booked for myself earlier than you. I have a wonderful room, you must have the cheap seats. Come and see, my view's magnificent."

"I'll unpack. See you in a minute."

She answered the door already in her robe, wet from showering, he assumed. "Come in." The room was identical to his except that the balcony was larger, the stone tub was circular and beyond it there were snow-capped mountains.

"Wow, that does look spectacular. Now I can see why you're making a fuss."

"It'll be even better when you're in the tub looking out at it. I'm sorry you haven't got a view, you'll just have to share with me." She walked out to the balcony, took off her robe and stepped carefully into the tub. "It's hot when you first get in. Come on!" Her smile encouraged him and distracted him momentarily from her nakedness. He hadn't realised what a beautiful body she had. She was tall, slim and pale, with a perfect peach of an ass and smallish, wonderfully shaped breasts. That all soon disappeared as she immersed herself.

He showered, struggled to fit the spare robe around him, then joined her on the balcony.

"Jesus, Andy," she gasped, as he threw his robe to one side and stepped into the tub, then she looked away. The water was very hot, so he had to take his time lowering himself in. He finally settled on the seating ledge, the tub was big enough to be able to avoid touching her. Slowly, she looked round at him. Her face was flushed, but that may have been just the water's temperature. "I'm sorry, that really wasn't very cool of me. I assume everyone reacts like that."

"It doesn't make that many public appearances. I assume we're talking about the same thing. And in his defence, I'm climbing into a tub with a beautiful naked young lady and I'm finding it hard not to stare at a pair of perfect breasts, so, yes, he is reacting, I can't really avoid that in the circumstances." She slid down a little to let the water cover her nipples. "Thanks for trying but the water is perfectly clear, I can still see your tits, and I'm not spending the next half an hour looking only at the mountains, however magnificent the view."

She was hesitating. "Would you stand up for me, please? I'm going to have to admit I'm fascinated." He stood up slowly, exposing himself, feeling it rising slightly. She was staring intensely. "How do people manage?"

"I'm always slow and careful."

She reached towards him. "May I?"

"Please."

And she cupped him with one hand, which made it firm up and move to the horizontal. She moved closer to him and slid her hand round, helping him point upwards but, by now, with her grip firming and her hand moving slowly up and down, it was standing on its own. She suddenly let go and moved away, staring out at the view. He sat down and placed his forearm across it to make the head submerge. She sat silent for a few moments and then turned slowly to look at him. He released his arm and it popped up like a periscope. She laughed.

"I am sorry, I feel such a girl, so uncool, but I haven't seen anything like it. Does everyone say that, or are some of them more sophisticated? I mean, even in the movies I watch…"

"Many?"

"No, of course not, but a girl gets curious and maybe there have been a few monsters. I've wondered how the ladies cope…"

Andy was looking into her eyes. Her gaze was moving between his eyes and his cock. "I'm not actually going to forgive myself if I don't ask this question, but would you?"

"Would I what?"

"Please don't make me say it more directly than that, but this is an opportunity that won't come again."

He looked seriously at her. "He's standing up for a reason." He smiled. "He obviously likes you and I'll confess, it's not the first time I've had a request, but you have to promise to be a big girl about it."

"Andy, don't be such a fuddy duddy. I'm not going to fall in love with you or anything." She paused. "But I would seriously like you to fuck me."

He smiled. "It will be my pleasure."

She laid the soft bedding out quickly in the centre of the floor, it was no more than a thick duvet. They had barely dried themselves. "I assume you lie down, don't you? I'll have to be on top."

"That's usually the way it works." And he lay back on the bed.

"Do you mind if I sit on your face first? I'm feeling as horny as anything but towelling down after the tub's dried me out." She looked down at his cock, stiffening as he looked at her, and said, "I'm going to need to be very wet, but I also want to play with him first, is that OK?"

"As long as you don't make him come. I would love to have your pussy on my face but that will turn me on, I warn you, and you don't want to waste him. Remember your prime objective."

She knelt down beside him and held him. "Boss, this is going to be only one night for me." She looked greedily at him. "But I don't think it's going to be a one-time only night." She straddled his face. He held her hips and guided her slowly down on to his mouth; his tongue quickly found her clit, hot tub and dry towel or not, she was already wet again. She had one hand supporting her, the other was rubbing him gently. "I want to suck him, you won't push or anything, will you? I don't know how much I can take."

Did she expect a conversation? He assumed not; he was busy licking this soft and shaven pussy. It was very sweet and pink. He slid his hands from her hips to her ass cheeks and stretched them open. "Not there, Andy, please."

Now he did push her off his mouth. "You have a very sweet little asshole."

"Even if I were so inclined, this is absolutely not the night I am going to lose my virginity there."

He pulled her down nevertheless on to his outstretched tongue.

"No, please!"

"Don't worry, that's it. Sweet though," he said, and he moved his mouth back to enjoy her pussy and, after that moment of tension, she relaxed back on to him, moving her hips around, her excitement rising. He felt her leaning forward, she had him in both hands now, wanking him gently, then he felt her mouth envelop its head and she was pushing her clit down more firmly on his face. She straightened up suddenly, leaving only one hand on his cock. "I've got to come, Andy, sorry, I've got to come." He gripped her hips tightly to manage her movements, freeing his tongue to vary the pressure on her clit, licking her more softly, sensually, lengthening her orgasm. She was squeezing his cock hard now, but he was in control. She would want to turn round soon, he was sure, they always did. In a while she slumped on him, laying her face on his cock. "Hello, big cock, am I going to have to take all of you now?" She kissed it gently and sat up, lifted one leg and swung herself around to lie beside him without her hand leaving him. She was up on one elbow, her face on her other hand with a beaming smile. "Sorry, I wasn't planning it that way but now I think it was a good idea. I can take my time as long as you can go slowly, I'm feeling very ready now. Oh, I don't have any condoms — but I have been a good girl for months."

"I haven't played away for a long time, but I can't speak for Jen."

"That's your wife?"

"Yes, but most of her affairs are gay anyway. I'm happy risking it if you are."

"I'm afraid I wanted that way anyway. Is that naughty?"

"Maybe not as naughty as fitting your cunt down on to your boss's cock. Actually, I'm not your boss, I'm your client. So you really should be fucking me anyway as part of the service. Take your time, sweetheart. Go easy and you should manage everything. Most people do."

"That's not exactly romantic!" But she was still smiling.

"I find it's the best way to ward off the evil demons of love and romance."

"No chance of that anyway, mister, you're over forty." They both laughed as she straddled him. She sat down on him and rubbed herself along its length. "Mmm, feels nice and I'm going to make him wet."

Andy lay back with his hands behind his head. "I'd like to play with your gorgeous breasts but then I might come too quickly."

"No, don't do that, not before I've tried to take all of this monster. I don't want to worry you, but I am so ready to play again, I don't normally do multiples. Can you recover quickly?"

He smiled as she rubbed her clit on the underside of his cock head. "We'll find out sooner than I want to if you keep that up. Let's see how you get on the first time."

She lifted her hips, reached through her legs, grabbed his shaft near the base and held its head at her entrance. "Ooh, wow." She pushed down a little way. "Gosh, that's not bad, let me try a little more." She inched further. "It feels absolutely wonderful, Andy, I'm stretching but I'm OK. Christ, I'm such a slut!"

"You're doing beautifully, just take it easy."

"Oh, I can feel him somewhere in my tummy now. I've never had anything this deep. You're not all in though, are you?"

"Don't worry. Just move up and down a bit, enjoy it."

"I'm certainly doing that. I feel so dirty, it's wonderful. I've never had anything anywhere near this thick. I have a big vibrator I like to play with at home but you're bigger than that. Oh, this is lovely." He moved his hands to her hips. "Don't touch my clit, I'd come again already."

"I'm not touching your clit yet. I'm going to squeeze that gorgeous ass." His hands slid round to her ass cheeks. He reached down to touch his cock, which she had now thoroughly drenched. He slid his finger past her lips and up to her anus and began stroking her.

"I'm not ever so keen on that, actually."

He moved his hand away and smiled at her. "Then how do you entertain two guys at once."

"Obviously I suck one of them of course." She narrowed her eyes. "You jerk, I've never done that, ever. Don't tell me you have!" He nodded. "With that thing and somebody else? At the same time?" She began moving more vigorously, the thought had plainly excited her. "Well, it wouldn't be for me. Now stay still, I want to see if I can take all of him." She began inching down again. "I'm going to get a stomach ache, I think, but I'm nearly there. If my clit gets to your pubic bone I am going to be screaming. Oh, Andy, can you come? Can you come now? I'm ready again, I can't stop, I can't stop."

"Go on, don't worry, I'll be right there with you, but you need to pull up a bit first. I will push hard when I start to come and that won't be brilliant for either of us. You really do have to ease yourself up."

She was still thrusting wildly up and down. He put his hands on her ass and lifted her a little. Her insides were gripping the head of his cock tightly and he couldn't hold back any longer. He thrust back and forth as she was slowly subsiding on to his chest, trying hard not to bump her cervix but not able to avoid it completely. He pulled her on to him tightly and felt his cum pulsing into her until he was sure he was empty. As she rolled off, however, he still felt the dribbles falling on his stomach.

"Wow, to think I came here to relax. I've never felt so relaxed. My God, that was amazing." Suddenly, she was up on one elbow again, smiling at him. "Thank you, my good sir, and I'd just like to reassure you that I haven't fallen even the tiniest bit in love with you."

"I'm very relieved to hear that."

"Good, and I'm going to promise not to do it either when you fuck me again after dinner. Can you manage that?"

"What, and me over forty?"

"I suppose it is asking a bit much."

"You'll find out, but you'll certainly have your sweet ass slapped for your cheek."

"Well, that's new too, but I think that's a price worth paying. Shall we try the tub again? We have a little time."

"Of course, but there's a definite need for a shower."

"Come on then let's do it together. I get my one night with the big boy, I want to make the most of him. Let me wash him thoroughly."

"He'll enjoy that, and he'll enjoy you again later. Separate rooms for the night, though, phone calls can be awkward."

"I know, even I might get one from my mother. She's not very good on working out time differences. And although we're pretty open with each other, it won't go as far as 'Hi mom, I've just fucked a bigger cock than you've ever seen!' OK, separate rooms later. Let's go shower."

12

In spite of the agreement in the phone call, the visit had surprised him in a number of ways. Lavinia was ten minutes late, which had never happened before, and her 'I must be dealt with particularly severely' was unscripted, although her intention was unambiguous. Likewise, the purpose of the tissues she'd taken from a pocket to hand to him with her panties. He had placed a pack on the nearby table anyway, hoping to be asked to wipe her later. The phone, however, handed over in the same movement, had been a surprise but she had needed no more than a nod from him to reassure her that he understood its purpose. He had caned her severely, forty strokes and some of the lines even had little red flecks on them and some of her gasps had been unusually loud. He had knelt beside her after the caning, placing one hand on the small of her back, she'd seemed comfortable with that. When he touched her, and she had kept her thighs well parted, he found her astonishingly wet and very responsive. She began to move to create more pressure for herself, but he eased away when she did this. She was delightful to touch and he wanted to prolong the sensation but when he heard the breathy whisper 'please, please' he pushed two fingers further inside her and let the third press very firmly on her clit, by then he was needing to come soon himself, but first there was an explosion of noise as her orgasm hit and her hips moved violently, trying to take his fingers deeper, and the movements and the moans continued for an extraordinary length of time until he found himself saying 'you must let me, you must let me' and he stood and freed himself and found the first blobs flying randomly in the air before he had full control, but then managed to point himself to get most to drop on to the mounds of her bottom cheeks. Finally, he had slumped to his knees beside her but remembered to reach for her phone as she was whispering 'camera, camera' to him. He took several shots, regaining some self-possession at the same time as being fascinated by the sight of her gorgeous, brutally striped bottom and the flow of his semen as the little rivers dribbled down her thighs and hips. Reluctantly, carefully, tenderly he dried her. She rose without looking at him, retrieved her panties from the sofa and retreated from the room.

He used some tissues on himself and dressed. He would dispose of them after she had gone. He did not want to disturb her ritual in hall and cloakroom. She might be some time; he'd left a guest towel prominently on the seat in there in case she wanted to shower. He pulled back the drapes, leaned back on the sofa and watched the city's lights begin to win their battle with the twilight. He felt very relaxed and contented, wishing he'd taken his own photo but certain the memory would always stay vividly with him.

He listened for doors but heard nothing. He began to think she'd slipped away completely silently and had all but convinced himself when the drawing room opened and she took one step in, one hand remaining on the handle. Her eyes were red-rimmed, and she made to speak but then, just as suddenly, she turned, closed the door and left.

For a week there was no text. He struggled to think how he should communicate. The usual protocol was that she would text or call but he found himself worrying and, yes, he thought, caring.

It was on the Sunday, nine days later, when she finally rang. Mercifully, his Saturday date had left for a day with her children — thank goodness, the relationship was nearing its end — when 'Good' flashed on his phone, his code for Lavinia Goodman.

"I've been worried, but I've been unsure about whether caring fitted into our arrangement."

"I'm not sure about that either, which is why it's taken me so long to call you."

"But did our last meeting disturb or distress you?"

"Oh, no, far from it." She laughed lightly — a first in his experience. "And your shaky-handed efforts as a cameraman did finally produce a couple of shots I'm proud of — and you should be proud of how copious you were. No, I will look forward to the next time, although I will probably restrict myself to being only five minutes late."

"Was I too severe?"

"Not at all, that was exactly the treatment I wanted." She paused. "It was exactly what I deserved." Then a silence.

"I'm sensing there's a story here I should hear more about."

"There is," she said, slowly. "But, Jack, I'm going to have to breach our protocol and ask you to meet me. Are you around this week?"

The 'Jack' was already a breach of protocol. "I'm back from Chicago on Wednesday."

"Can I book a room at the Ritz in your name for Wednesday evening? I'm sorry to be mysterious but we need some privacy."

"OK, go ahead, do you want my details, card etc?"

"Jack, my dear, I have all that, remember the business I'm in. I'll see you on Wednesday." She rang off before he could ask a question.

My dear? What was that about?

13

"Where are you calling from?" Claudia was surprised by the call.

"Atlanta, Giddings is still a client, remember — and I do like getting a daily fee that tops what I used to earn here every week," said Tania.

"And you save me hotel bills. How are your mum and dad?"

"They complain things are too quiet at home, but they seem good now, planning more holidays together. They had a bad patch a few years ago. I was still at college. Mom didn't say much about it, but she wasn't happy. Still, neither was Dad."

"Isn't this early for you? It's not six in the morning."

"I could have called you two hours ago but then you would have said I was crazy."

"Are you recovering from Japan?"

"That's why I'm ringing now. I can't sleep and also I figured anything I do on Japan before eight in the morning, you can't count against me."

"That's fair but you were giving me twelve hours a day on Brodie stuff before."

"You're billing Andy for last week, though."

"Too right I am. How was it?"

"It was fantastic. Heads up, it looks like they might want to do business, so he might want you out there soon."

"Fuck!"

"What's up? You'd love it."

"You're probably right but I have a time management problem that's bigger than yours."

"Does Andy know that?"

"I'm not worried about Andy. It's Peter I'm under pressure from. Anyway, you'd better tell me about it." Tania went through the week's events and described the people they'd met. She was suspicious of Ozawa, and repulsed by his Nakamura counterpart, but impressed by the head banker she'd met. Claudia, this time, was prepared and asked for more on Martha; everything seemed to confirm the picture Jack had given her. She found herself momentarily distracted by the thoughts of a powerful, dynamic woman having the needs she obviously had but she focused again on Tania. It seemed that Nakamura really might be prepared to sell. Wow, she would have to go there and help. She was fascinated by the thought of a trip but there was so much else to be done in her own business.

"So, what was it like socially, I mean evenings et cetera. Obviously, you weren't socialising in the friends and party sense."

"Oh, I love the food there, so that was marvellous for me, and we had the most bizarre evening with the

Nakamura people in kind of a traditional Japanese setting with little ladies in kimonos bringing food and drink and making small talk, and then after the meal, they wheeled out all the high-tech karaoke kit from behind an ornate screen and everyone had to sing."

"You sang?"

"Oh, move over Adele, I was brilliant. Truth to tell I was glad to get up from the table to get the lizard's hand off my thigh."

"Oh, it's universal, is it?"

"Did you doubt that?"

"No, I don't think I did, anything else?"

"We went to a hot spring. It was an ambition of mine. It was wonderful, you sit in a hot tub on a balcony with hot spring water running through and stare at snow-covered mountains. Ozawa told Andy he had to stay on an extra day in case there were any more meetings needed, so he had time to come too."

"And were there extra meetings?"

"No, but it looks pretty certain there will be soon."

"Did you fuck him?"

"Claudia!" There was a long silence.

"Sorry to do that to you, but the shock question works best, I think."

"No, I didn't."

"My sweet girl, that took you just a little too long. I don't mind, I just want to be clear what his motives are when he begs me to let you go again."

"It won't have consequences like that. It was just…"

"Tania, my dear, I know all about 'it was just'." She paused. "Impressive, though, isn't he?"

"Claudia!" But this time she laughed.

"And Tania."

"Yes, boss."

"Don't ever call me CB again!" They both laughed.

Two days later Andy had texted to schedule a call.

"It sounds like it went very well for you."

"You've talked to Tania."

"Yes, she was her usual effusive self but, even allowing for all that enthusiasm, it sounds like you might have a chance."

"Yeah, I've been talking more to our man Ozawa, he's still out there now, having further conversations, and it sounds like we'll be needing to have more meetings. We're looking at two weeks next Monday for the week. Can you manage that?"

She looked at her diary. "I can't miss the Friday here, that's a big new client, but the rest I can shuffle. I'm only putting my own people out of joint, but Alan can handle that. But help me a bit, Andy, what am I really needed for? I know His Master's Voice has spoken but isn't that just him wanting some warm feelings?"

"Let me tell you what scares me and why I'd value you being there. Well, the money scares me first of all, it'll be half a billion and change. Our Master is used to that but for me it's scary. But after that I have to get two completely alien organisations working together and you just have an amazing sense of how organisations operate. I got a good feeling going around the place but that was one hour in an alien country with a guide whose English was poor. I'm not going to kid you, it's very hard to feel you're getting below the surface. In addition to that, we're trying to keep this deadly secret. Only two of them know, apart from the boss man, Nakamura himself, and they don't plan on telling the other directors until we've agreed an outline deal."

"Why would they not tell them?"

"If they're comfortable where they are and don't want the place taken over by dirty, hairy *gaijin*, they just leak the news, the share price goes up and the deal becomes uneconomic."

"*Gaijin*?"

"It's what they call foreigners and they don't use it kindly."

"But the ones in the know seem keen."

"I think so, but Ozawa is talking to me about special arrangements for them. That sounds a bit suspicious to me and I've been warned by the bankers to watch out for things like that."

"That would be the famous Martha?"

"Yes, how did you hear… Ah, Tania's been talking. Yes, those two seemed to hit it off really well. Well, being fair, Tania was brilliant with everyone. Ozawa says her Japanese is crap, but everyone understood her and wanted her around. She wasn't supposed to come to the men-only evening event, but the Nakamura people insisted. They'll expect to see her next time."

"I won't."

"But she's made herself important, why are you so against it?"

"Andy, you can't fuck her and then tell me she's vital for business. You're not a credible witness." There was a long pause. "Well, thanks for not trying to deny it, then you and I would have had a real problem."

"Sorry, Claudie, but she really was very valuable. They would find it odd if she didn't come."

"Or they might just think you'd brought along your pet vagina for the week again."

"That's unfair to her, she did an amazing job. Is there any way to get you to reconsider?"

She thought for a while. "If Peter insists, I suppose I'd have to. But do bear in mind that when he asks me, he'll get the full story, so you'd better tell him before I do."

"Is that really necessary?"

"I think it is, but anyway, it's my condition, along with her two thousand dollars a day and expenses. Think about it. Now, I've put the Monday to Wednesday in my diary, please work around that if you want me and, if that works, please send me all the information you've got."

"Ball breaker!"

"I've never really understood that expression, but I assume it's a compliment."

"It is if you see it that way. But anyway, I have to say thank you for releasing her for last week, she did make a huge difference."

"OK, and I'm really glad, but you guys, you do go where he points you, don't you?"

"Are you sure you want to put all the blame on my gender?"

"That's a bit unchivalrous of you but I suppose I have to accept it's not always your fault. But apart from the distraction factor, I would worry about her."

"I'm leaving it with you now, but you do have a star there."

"I know, but she needs to be, she'll be running a bigger company than either of us one day."

"You sure she wants that?"

"Hell, I don't know. Two years ago, I couldn't have imagined doing what I'm doing now. I'm pretty sure she'll make up her own mind, though, when the time comes."

"That's why I think you're worrying unnecessarily."

"I might be persuaded if your argument weren't so obviously self-serving. Anyway, I'll see you in two weeks or so probably."

"I hope so. Bye."

14

Jack let her into the room. It felt so odd to be greeting this woman, with whom he'd shared so many deeply intimate moments, as an almost perfect stranger. He felt he should at least embrace her, but Lavinia moved awkwardly past him, removed her coat and threw it on the bed, then took a seat by the table in the window. She glanced at him twice but, clearly agitated, satisfied herself by staring at the dull picture on the wall in front of her.

He'd never seen her dressed like this: black pants, smart and well fitted around the hips and tapering to the ankles, low black pumps, a cowl-necked burgundy sweater that matched her coat, and a large silver broach. Her dark hair and make-up were as immaculate as ever, but her face was even more tense than usual. He stood near her, holding out his hands, offering to hold hers but she wrapped her arms more tightly around herself.

He sat down opposite her. "I have no idea what this is about. It's obviously very important, to both of us I assume, but I have a very strong urge to put my arms around you. I want to tell you everything will be fine." Her gaze did not leave the picture. "Even though I have not the faintest, remotest idea about whether it could be fine or not." He paused. "Looking at you now, I have a growing suspicion that it might not be." Finally, she looked directly at him but her blank expression didn't change. He sat down opposite her. "I know that you and I have contrived a strange arrangement with each other over the past two years, but I have actually come to care a lot about you. I knew that anyway, but it's become especially obvious after these past two weeks. So, I'm unhappy that something's causing you so much grief." He leaned forward and offered his hand again, she looked at it but didn't move. "Now, please take your time, I'm going to order sandwiches and some wine. I'm happy to wait for you to say what you want to say but, as far as I'm concerned, and however reluctant you may be to admit it, we have a real relationship, it's not just an arrangement, and I'd rather we confronted this thing together, whatever it is."

He moved to the side of the bed and dialled room service. At the twentieth ring, still unanswered, he found her standing beside him. He put the phone down and wrapped his arms around her. He felt her sobbing into his shoulder. Slowly her sobs subsided, and she put her arms around him. Eventually she lifted her face, he kissed her tenderly, then she nestled into his shoulder again.

"I've probably ruined your shirt," were her first words.

"Well, that settles it, I'm wearing one dirty shirt and have three more dirty shirts in my bag, that's all. It has to be room service. I'll make the bastards answer the phone this time." He felt her relax a little. "Kiss me again."

"Can't leave the dom behind for a moment, can you?" She looked up at him, finally smiling and raising her lips to kiss him, more deeply this time.

He dialled again, keeping one arm around her shoulder. She kept both her arms around his waist. After another twenty rings he had a response and ordered a club sandwich and a bottle of Pouilly Fumé.

"I have not the faintest idea what you're about to say but I have a powerful conviction that it's a conversation better conducted horizontally. Fully clothed, of course, after all, room service will be here in forty minutes — why can't they commit to thirty? It's just a fucking sandwich — and any state of undress would not be appropriate to the topic of the moment anyway, I suspect."

"No, it wouldn't," she said, sounding dejected, "but I like the lying down idea." He kicked off his shoes and lay back, while she settled by his side with his arm around her shoulder and lay her head on his chest. "Too late to worry about the shirt now, but the tie can come off." They manoeuvred to remove the tie and get the top two shirt buttons undone. They settled again.

"Are you comfortable yet?" They both chuckled lightly.

"I'm comfortable now." She snuggled in a little tighter and draped one leg over his. "I sometimes used to imagine this when I got home after our little assignments."

"Is that what you call them?"

She laughed a little. "I didn't really have a word for them, I've just invented that now, but when I got home and touched myself, it would sometimes be you I was holding." He pulled her closer to him. "I never gave any thought to who you might have been thinking of — but I guessed you must have been thinking of someone, something."

"Well, we've both admitted it, our little assignments got us very excited. Do I have to use past tense now? How bad is this? While I'm lying here, holding you like this, it feels like we'll be facing something together and that can't be so bad, can it?"

"I'd like very much to think we could do that, but you'd better hear me out first." She paused. "You have been set up, Jack, in quite a serious way. I hadn't realised it until recently, but it happened once against you directly and I think it disrupted your life quite badly. Now someone's trying to make something similar happen again, not directly against you this time, but it would also impact you in a big way."

He tensed a little and felt her react. "Hey, steady, I am a little shocked, I admit, but you must have expected that. But I'm not hearing anything yet that says we can't do something about it together."

"I don't know what we can do together, but I knew I wasn't going to be able to do anything about it on my own."

"Come on then, cuddle in and tell me more. You've probably said the worst, haven't you?"

"As far as you're concerned, yes. The thing is, well," she said, pausing, "I need to go back a long way, OK?"

"While I'm holding you, I'm fine, take your time."

"I joined Networks ten years ago, freshly divorced and rebuilding my life. I'd married thinking I'd finally found someone who shared my unusual tastes but his were much more extreme and he moved on through bdsm, which I could just about tolerate because I did love him in strange way, and into what I finally realised was abuse, and that was made worse by his drug and alcohol problems. Then I had a miscarriage and got violence from him instead of support. Long story short, I finished with him and I was rebuilding. I got in with Rod, the work was mysterious, it had a funny kind of glamour, I enjoyed it and I was good." She paused, as if considering what to say next. "I had my obligatory three-year affair with Rod before that settled in to something more perfunctory. He still occasionally attends to some of my needs but never on a Friday." They both laughed quietly. "All his affairs seem to last about three years, the lady of colour in Atlanta must be coming to an end soon. He keeps some going in parallel. He was very keen on your friend, wasn't he?"

"I got that impression, yes."

"Well, she wanted nothing to do with him. I admired her, she was smart. But some ladies fall for it and then still keep something going, like me. But some think it's real love and get very upset when it ends. I was too wise by then, and I never fell that hard, anyway. So, I carried on, the work was intriguing, and we were, I thought, sorting out real problems for businesses. We highlighted vulnerable people or vulnerable situations. I think we genuinely helped the businesses and the people themselves. But things have happened recently, and this is where we come to you, where I've had to doubt what has truly happened, events maybe being distorted or even just invented. It could be that we're being misused, that's what I want to believe, or it might be that Rod has, somehow, gone over to the dark side. Are you still with me?"

"I'm still with you. I could jump in with questions but it's probably best if I just let you speak."

"Thank you, it's better for me that way. I had obviously taken a special interest in your case for selfish reasons of my own. That has been wonderful, by the way."

"Oh, it's been absolutely wonderful for me, especially now we've discovered how to finish our meetings, sorry, our assignments, properly." He stroked her arm. "I understand why you wouldn't risk giving me that photo but it's the most stunning visual memory I have of almost anything."

She slapped him lightly. "That isn't helping. Anyway, having seen the file, it seemed like a standard sort of problem; potential trouble for an executive in a far-off country that could be made to be embarrassing for him and his business. I didn't think any more about it, other than, selfishly, the opportunity it gave me. Then something else came up that involved you, and I will come on to exactly what in a minute, I promise, but it made me look back at the details of your original case and it was built on very flimsy foundations. I won't say Rod had invented the dangers, but he had certainly exaggerated them. I wasn't aware of us ever having done anything like that before. We use very, I want to say 'leading edge' methods. We have quite a powerful IT team to access lots of information, and I don't think our investigations are as clean as Rod likes to portray them. I suspect there may be more than a little hacking going on. But, so far as I was aware, we had always applied our findings fairly and ethically, even if we'd acquired them by dubious means. I was kind of proud of it in a way. But your name came up again recently in relation to something going on at Collins. Are there big changes happening? Changes affecting you?"

"Oh, Mata Hari, is this where I find out that this piece of subterfuge is part of the plot?" She tensed — he pulled her in again. "Hey, come on, I'm already aware of what you've risked for yourself by setting this up. In a perverse way, because of our 'arrangement' — it seems funny to call it that now — I think I trust you more than anyone else on the planet." She moved in closer again, undid another shirt button and let her fingertips lightly caress his chest. "I have had a conversation with Oscar and, yes, he does have plans for the place that could work out well for me when he gives up the CEO role and becomes just chairman."

"Ah, now it fits! That's why we're looking at Oscar."

"Oscar?" He was shocked. "I thought Networks was a chairman-only thing. It was Oscar who put me on to our little US problem when I came to your office and first met you. I remember that very well. I was a little in awe of you, you can seem quite forbidding, you know. When you called a few weeks later my brain was a bit scrambled, but I was very keen to see you again. I'd even been tempted to call you anyway, you'd intrigued me, but the area you worked in was scary and it would have made the business relationship really complicated as well. Funny, I did absolutely nothing, but look what then fell into my lap, so to speak."

She laughed, undid another button to let her whole hand stroke him.

"It should have been Oscar, he should be the only one we deal with, that's what alerted me when that began to change, and when I looked back."

There was a ring at the door. "Christ, they're quick."

"Make sure it is room service."

"My God." He turned to look at her as he stood up. "You do live the job, don't you?"

She shrugged. "I have to. You'd be amazed at how we pick some things up, hotel staff are good sources."

It was room service, he dealt with it as quickly as he could. She'd stayed sitting on the bed. "We'll wait before we eat, if you don't mind, this is getting serious." She nodded. He lay back down beside her.

"I still want these open again?" She undid the buttons he'd done up to answer the door and then continued until she'd freed his shirt. "I like this hair," she said, as she ruffled her fingers through it.

"Can I admit to one of my favourite post-assignment fantasies?"

"Go on!"

"This isn't getting your story told."

"Are we in a hurry? No, we're not!" She answered her own question. "I want to hear this."

"Well, it's a particular favourite of mine. I leave you on the chair, I tell you to stay there in my best dom voice. And I take off my shirt."

"I'm staying there, obeying you."

"And I kneel down between your knees and rub my chest all over your bottom and it feels so wonderful, caressing you with the chest hair."

"Lovely, but is that it?"

"No, I kneel a little lower, tell you to get your bottom a little higher."

"I do that, I do that!"

"Then I eat you, I run my tongue all around you and you start to scream. That's why it was so wonderful the other night when I finally got to realise how loud you are."

"Stop it!"

"No, it was wonderful, truly."

"And in your little chest fantasy," she said, as she stroked him again, "do you come over my bottom?"

"Er, no."

"No, you don't in mine either."

"What do I do in yours?"

"You pull him out of your pants and stick him into me as hard as you can, of course. By then I used to be back at home, lying on my bed with my naked ass in the air, playing with myself to make me come while thinking of you giving me a real good fucking."

"Ass?"

"Yes, I just need the word bottom for the perfect script in our arrangement. But yes, Mr Jack, you have actually come all over my ass, not just my bottom. But we'd better get back to the main story before you tell me what you get up to with all those Brazilian ladies of yours."

"Brazilian ladies?"

"Yes, I'm afraid that's all part of the plot, something else that made me suspicious." They settled back with her still stroking his chest. She looked up and kissed him, pulled his shirt open completely and lay her face on his chest.

"Why, what happened next?"

"This is long-winded, I know, but we have to jump back two or three years again, and some of this is what I've been piecing together. You'll have to tell me whether it seems to make sense. But Oscar, I've only ever called him Maguire, but he's Oscar now, was making changes at Collins and he was getting more and more unhappy with Rod and his methods. I think he was trying to push Rod out. But Rod latched on to Saunders, not a man I like, by the way, but I've only met him twice, and started using him as a channel of influence. What's clear to me now is that Oscar really favoured you and thought of you as a more likely number two longer term, above Saunders. I think Saunders concocted this plan to trap you in the Far East and somehow discredit you. Oscar dismissed it but somehow Rod made it stick with you, at least. You must have been doing something a little naughty, but I'm not the one to complain about that side of your life, am I?"

"No, I guess you've been enjoying that."

"Well, I got wind recently of Rod looking for something on Oscar, not to finish him maybe, but enough to keep Saunders in line for the number two job and then the chairmanship later. It's a live project for them. I worked it out, but I hadn't told you and I felt truly terrible, but I had a weird loyalty to what we do at Networks. While I was agonising over what to do, I came to you and asked for some special treatment. I thought it might help me straighten my head and, in a funny way, it did. My God, it did sting, though. I don't know that I'll be asking for that again in a hurry, even if the arrangement survives." He laughed lightly and she ruffled his chest hair more vigorously. "So here we are, I've finally told you. I don't know what they're trying to dig up. Rod can usually find something, either pervy sex or dodgy finances — it's always amazing how greedy rich people can become. So Oscar might be in danger, and your career with him. If it hadn't been for him, I think you might have been finished before now. Well, at Collins anyway."

"Wow, phew, I don't know what to say — apart from a huge thank you. That took some courage." He turned on his side and pulled her to him and kissed her. "I have no idea what we do about it, but I can't thank you enough. Oscar did talk to me a month ago and he did hint at the changes you described. I got the impression he was going to shuffle the pack soon. Maybe he won't now."

"I don't know what they've got on him, if anything. And I don't know what made Rod go dark. He used to seem so straight to me, so fundamentally decent. Maybe it was the threat of being pushed out, maybe Oscar's not the only one who finds those activities distasteful and Rod's worried about who he might tell."

"Do you? Find them distasteful, I mean."

"I didn't, I thought we were doing something useful. I also thought we were staying more or less ethical, but I suppose ethical doesn't really belong with more or less."

"I'm afraid it does. It would probably be a different world if we couldn't combine them and work in the twilight. I mean, I was surprised to get called in Singapore. I knew I'd been in some odd places and met some strange characters. Rod seemed to me to be exaggerating the dangers when he called me, but I accepted it and my job was changing anyway. Well, I guess now I know he was exaggerating. But I've had many occasions with you since to be glad that my little kink was on your file and it matched your needs. But where does the Brazilian angle come in?"

"You have a principal security man down there?"

"Yes, Jorge, huge chap, shaven-headed monster. I do feel relatively safe with him."

"You shouldn't."

"Really?"

"He's on Saunders' payroll. Does he organise little diversions for you?"

Jack felt himself blushing. "I suppose there's no point in trying to conceal anything from you, my worst excesses are either on file with you or in the pictures in your phone."

"Yes, Jack." She was smiling and nodding; they were still lying on their sides, facing each other. "So you can tell me quite honestly what you actually do get up to in a minute but I'm going to guess that Jorge has been suggesting more, how can I put this, more extravagant entertainment, yes? Something for special tastes, perhaps?"

Jack breathed in deeply. "Yes, on more than one occasion. And I'll admit that the girls he takes me to seem to be getting more and more adventurous."

"Are there many? I don't really need to know that, I'm just curious. But I do need to know what they're offering."

He shrugged. "I'm there once a month, Jorge will take me somewhere once on a trip, sometimes not at all."

"Well, it doesn't sound like they're catching you that way, but I think most of their efforts are focused on Oscar."

"Are we going to try and do something about it? I would want to, but that puts you in real danger."

"If we're not going to do good with what we do, I don't want to carry on, so I want to stop it. Are you OK?"

"Oh, I'm fine. I'm shocked but relieved, a lot of things make sense. But how are you feeling? This is tough for you."

"Oh, I'm much better now you know. Although I did take my punishment in advance."

"Was that too much? I was worried."

"I can admit it now, but everything came together perfectly for me that night. I was incredibly emotional, as you saw. I was very worried about you and starting to realise how much I cared. I was keeping important secrets from you, so I had an ideal discipline scenario for myself. I wanted the punishment to be as heavy as you could make it, I felt I'd deserved it, and it really worked for me, I came like I'd never come before." She was smiling broadly.

"Well, I was worried about how heavy I was being, but I got to fulfil a lifelong fantasy on a very beautiful bottom. I didn't think I was going to stop." He pulled her to him and kissed her gently. "Do we have to form a plan now?"

"I've been so nervous I haven't eaten all day. So, I'm having half of your club sandwich, that's my plan now. Come on, pour me some wine please, and tell me what you do with your adventurous Brazilian girls." They slid off the bed and moved to the chairs by the table. She began eating while he unscrewed the wine and poured two glasses. "Jack," she said, while she was still chewing, "I can't tell you how relieved I am to have got that off my chest. You're not angry?"

"Christ, no! I'm very grateful. I've no idea what we're going to do about it though. A part of me is thinking revenge but that would be silly and almost certainly counter-productive."

"Yes, please let's not aim for that. I know we're going to have to start to think clearly about what we do next but, cheers." She raised her glass, smiled and drank. "I'm just so relieved to have got that out — and not to have lost you in the process. I've no idea what we do now but what we had was very important to me."

"It was for me too, cheers," he said, and he raised his glass to her. "Maybe you saved me going off the rails in Sao Paulo."

"It sounds like you went a little off the rails anyway. You're not going to go all coy on me, are you? Come on, we've done the first half of the difficult stuff, give me some naughty stories while we're having a break."

"Seriously?"

She raised her glass again. "Of course, seriously. You think, after what we get up to, I'm not broad-minded? And I've told you, I've had a little bdsm forced on me."

"Well, when you put it like that, I've nothing to compare. Actually, it's all been pretty orthodox stuff."

"What's the wildest then?"

"Sometimes a second girl joins us. I never ask for that and I don't think I pay any more for it. Have you ever done threesomes?"

"There were times when he used to bring other people in, but I never liked that, so I didn't really participate. I've had to watch it though. I'd rather just focus on the person I was with."

"Well, the Brazilian girls do that very well, and they make sure they welcome you in every way."

"I think I understand you. You like your little friend to go everywhere, is that it?"

He raised his glass again. "I think you've understood." He drank, then poured them more wine.

"It's not everyone's taste, I know, but I've always enjoyed it. But only with willing ladies, I have to add. I've never tried to push anyone into having me in a way they don't want to."

She sighed and drank some more. "I didn't have someone who was as considerate as you are. I wasn't very keen on the alternatives, but he rather forced them on to me and I've never wanted to since."

"True confession?"

She looked puzzled. "Yes, what's coming now?"

"Sometimes, when you'd gone and I'd retreated to my bedroom to play with him, it was one of my favourite fantasies. You have such a beautiful bottom." He chuckled, saying, "it's going to take me a while to call it an ass, I'm afraid. But I would still be picturing you on the chair and I would make myself come by thinking about having you like that. I'd always thought it would be wonderful."

"Having my ass?"

"Yes, Lavinia, having your ass. Sticking him up your bum. My God, how blunt do you want me to be?" They laughed. "I'm afraid, in here," he said, tapping his forehead, "I've had you lots of times like that."

"And, how was I?" She looked curious.

"You were wonderful, of course, but you used to love it and beg for more, and I used to come like mad. But now I know what you really feel, I'm afraid that rather blocks that off."

"Do most people like it?"

"Steady on. I'm not claiming a statistically valid survey, but plenty do when they try it and then they get very enthusiastic. I suspect in Brazil that Jorge only takes me where he knows all services are available. The last few have even offered me canes and paddles as well. I suppose that was part of their attempts at entrapment."

"Well, did you check the ages of the second little girls when they came in?"

"Shit, I never thought about that, I was usually too busy, but they could have got me that way, I suppose. I was just thinking about the canes but, by then, I'd got into a pattern of always hoping for a text from you when I was on my way back and nothing would compare with that. I love all that role play stuff we've created. Just caning a beautiful Brazilian bottom wouldn't do it for me now. It's funny, isn't it?"

"What?"

"Well, I think we've developed a very special arrangement and it worked very well for us. We'd even finally found a perfect way of dealing with our frustrations at the end."

Now she chuckled. "Yes, apart from taking nearly a week for the marks to clear, that was almost perfect."

"Only almost?"

"Yes, Jack, only almost." She emptied her glass again. "You've just been describing what I now really want. But how are we going to be with each other after you've fucked me?"

He smiled, drained his glass, and nodded. "We have a very big challenge ahead of us, my dear, but that's not it. I'll just trust us to solve that little one ourselves."

"And, Jack." She stood up, quickly pulled her sweater over her head and threw it on the floor, unhooked her bra without yet removing it and waited, looking at him.

He wondered what was coming but he removed his shirt and threw it away. "Yes?"

"You're still my dom. Can you fuck me every way? Make me do everything you want, just like your fantasies."

"Of course."

15

It was hard to find the right moment. Asking to meet Oscar alone was not a common thing to do if Saunders were in the office. It would have been unusual not to talk to both, and Saunders would have felt free to walk in anyway. Now he was feeling almost paranoid about him and was anxious not to arouse any suspicions. And Oscar usually left the office first. He would say, 'Stay late and you're showing me you can't cope.'

He was, nevertheless, always in early but catching him then ran the risk of Saunders just wandering in and that would make the conversation very awkward.

It was a week later, mid-afternoon, when Oscar had just sat down in front of his desk. Jack quickly finished the call he was on. "Jack, my boy, you've looked edgy for days, maybe you should come and talk to me."

Jack quickly glanced to Saunders' corner. "I have got something on my mind, Oscar, yes."

"Well, now Ken's not around, perhaps you'd like to talk. Come on." He stood up and walked towards the meeting room near his corner. "No interruptions Barbara," he said to his PA, not at all quietly. "Not even Ken if he comes back." *How the fuck much of this does he know already?*

They settled in their usual chairs.

"So, what's on your mind?" *Always an open question, I wish I were better at that.*

"I do have a worry, Oscar, and I don't know if it just affects me or if it's bigger." Oscar looked impassive, not in the slightest bit curious. "When you brought me back from Singapore, it coincided with a phone call I'd had around that time from Henderson. Did you know anything about that?"

"Go on." *That wasn't an answer, of course.*

"I'd been amusing myself in odd ways in my spare time, generally with the same one or two people. Then I tried out a particular club. I have to be direct here, it was a bit sophisticated, well, kinky is what I mean, and I found that fun." He paused. Oscar shrugged. "I'd been invited by a friend, I was curious, it happened in a fairly classy situation and I didn't give too much thought to what was behind it, how it got organised. It wasn't cheap entertainment, so I assumed it was self-funding." He was leaving pauses between each sentence, hoping Oscar would interject at some point but, of course, he never did. "I thought most people were there on the same basis, interest in the same things, same kinks et cetera, but I didn't exclude the thought that some of the ladies might have been, well, let's call them professionals." Still impassivity. "Out of the blue, Henderson rang me one day and said he knew about some events I was visiting and that they were run by gangsters and would open me up to blackmail. It sounded far-fetched, I hadn't picked up on any of that. I didn't ask the contact who'd introduced me. I thought the best thing to do was just stop. I like that stuff but it's not an addiction and I had other outlets anyhow." Another pause, longer this time. "Then I got called back here to do the Americas job anyway, so the problem went away, I thought. I'm telling you all this now. At the time Henderson called me, he told me the way he operated was to head off vulnerabilities, that's what he called them, and if the impacted executive agreed to deal with the situation, then it would go no further. I told him I would sort it. I did stop going and I thought that finished it all — so when you offered me this job, that seemed to confirm that he hadn't raised any suspicions about me."

"So, why are you here now?"

Jack waited a long time. "I think I might be being set up again."

"Are you up to your naughty tricks again?"

"No, but I think my security guy is trying to put me in compromising situations."

"So, change him."

"He comes under Ken; all that stuff does."

"Tell Ken you want him changed."

"I don't think it's that simple."

"It looks simple to me." Finally, Oscar sounded a little tetchy.

"Oscar, I may be completely out of order here, I know it's your responsibility, but I'm a little worried about Henderson's operations." *Can I manage this without implicating Lavinia?*

"So am I, it's in the nature of the beast." He returned to impassivity.

"Do you want to tell me why?"

"Not particularly."

Can I play his game on this one? Just sit him out? I will not be next to speak — although this silence is lasting a long time — a very long time.

"Is that it? You sorted yourself out, learned not to be a naughty boy, eliminated the vulnerability and got promoted. End of story."

"I'm not sure it is end of story."

"Just because you think your security is trying to get you to do naughty things with Brazilian ladies?"

"But you admitted you were a little worried about Henderson."

"Why do you think that might be?"

"I can think of a couple of reasons. How he comes by his information may not be entirely clean. Is it all legal, or does he use methods that cross boundaries that could embarrass us sometime?" Jack hesitated.

"And?"

"Well, I have no grounds for suggesting this, but it's a channel that could be misused, there could be manipulation going on."

"What's making you say that?"

"I'm just highlighting vulnerabilities."

"Jack, most of the time I value your imagination. I think it makes you better at thinking about different futures for this place, that's why I'd prefer to think of you running it all." He took a deep breath. "But here you're sounding a bit paranoid."

"OK, let me try and put it a different way. What if someone were to use the channel to somehow have a go at you?"

"You think they are?" *Still unmoving, but not an outright dismissal.*

"I don't know, I'm just saying they could."

"And you want me to turn over our entire background intelligence organisation just because of your worries about a hypothetical possibility?"

"If you don't have any concerns, then I'm wasting your time, I'm sorry."

"I've told you I have concerns, Like I said, it's in the nature of an operation like that, but you're not giving me anything to go on."

"Oscar, OK, I do have a source, and I'm being told that you and I are under threat. Now I don't matter much really but, for us all, it's much more dangerous if it might be targeting you. I think the source is reliable or I wouldn't have been hopping around for a week trying to find a good moment to speak to you."

Silence, and then a slow nod from Oscar. "It was about time you came to the fucking point."

***

"I prefer this sort of Friday afternoon," said Lavinia, cuddling into him, "but are we still going to be able to do the old way now and again?"

"Oh, I definitely hope so. We just have to work out how we play the role play. Do we do it like the old days and then you come to bed here instead of getting dressed to go home and masturbate? Or do I have you over the armchair?"

"I know we fantasised about that, but I suspect, if you're doing your job properly, I might be feeling too tender to be had like that. I think I'd be coming in here and sitting on you." And she sat up and straddled his softening cock and put her hands beside his head, allowing the nipples of her heavy breasts to brush his face tantalisingly. "Anyway, either way, even with lots of this stuff," she said, picking up the tube of lube and waving it at him, "I still end up with a sore ass."

"Was it too bad?"

"It was better than last week in the hotel when we didn't have any."

"I warned you, but you were so insistent."

"I know but I wanted us to do everything."

"You nearly made that impossible at stage one. That was a wonderful blowjob."

"Was it? I'd had to do it before, a long time ago, but I never liked it, never studied it, but somehow I was curious with you, I was trying to make it wonderful for you."

"It was almost too wonderful, I nearly came."

"I found you having my ass just now was too wonderful. I did come."

"Well, I certainly did."

"I know that, I thought you weren't going to stop, and you were pushing so hard."

"Too hard?"

"Oh, no, not at all, it was you being so rough that made me come. And I think I'm going to be reminded all day tomorrow." She climbed off him and lay beside him, putting her hand on his cock. "But we're here to work, aren't we? I'll just warn you that I'll be having him again later," she said, and she shook the thing gently and unceremoniously. "This time you will be coming at stage one."

"You want that?"

"Oh, I definitely want that, especially as I'll be sitting on your face and coming like crazy as soon as I've swallowed you."

He laughed. "That thought is not going to make work easy."

She looked a little thoughtful. "Well, it is serious though, isn't it?"

"'Fraid so. I tried not to tell him who my source was. Well, I didn't tell him, but I think he may have guessed, and it was only then that he began to talk. He's a really cool character, totally unflappable, but it did make him go thoughtful and you were right, he had been trying to push Rod out. He'd got wind somehow that his methods were crossing boundaries, just like you said, and they might be actually causing us more danger than they were removing."

"But what about him personally?"

"Well, he wasn't very forthcoming there. He just said that everyone he knew probably had something to hide."

"Sex or money?"

"He only talked about money. I didn't get the impression he disapproved of my antics particularly, but he was definitely talking money and how it gets hidden."

"So how did you leave it, what does he want you to do?"

"He just said, 'why don't you go fuck the ass off Lavinia and then sit down and see what you can come up with'."

"What I'm going to come up with first is a mushroom risotto. I've brought everything. I still don't want to risk dining out, certainly not with what we've got to talk about."

"I agree with you. Although I'd like to do something a bit romantic some time. New York weekend, maybe?"

"I think that's a risk we could take. I'm glad you've said something like that."

"Why?"

"Well, when I said I'd brought everything, I meant an overnight bag as well."

"Well, you'd look shitty in the morning if you hadn't."

He let her shower first, she wanted to get on and cook. And then she would stay overnight. His feelings for her had been transformed since the last visit here and the hotel conversation. And one night was not a commitment. She'd gone home, very late, from the hotel. Tomorrow's breakfast would be a first. A few people had stayed for breakfast, some more than once, but this was the first time that a relationship had threatened to get deeper. Was that what he wanted? He missed Claudia very much, but they had never had to confront the issue of whether they should truly live together. Almost as soon as they discussed it, the chance was taken from them. He'd been surprised by how she'd broken it off. She'd always challenged him on openness, but they had recovered from problems before and he thought she'd begun to appreciate how hard it was to be truly open. Even she hadn't been open, as it turned out. They had both been leading lives with distractions and she'd been trying to impose standards on him that she couldn't meet herself. Now he began to wonder if there was some connection between her last calls, where she'd demanded to know more about Martha and what else he'd been doing, and whether that had any relation to what was going on now, or what had been going on then. Had Henderson somehow been getting through to her? It seemed so implausible. Anyway, he'd gone soon after to the obsessive demands of a new job and a new-found freedom from having to explain and excuse himself. In his own mind the switch from answering to his wife, then to answering to Claudia was seamless, but that was a distorted conscience talking. It had been ages since he'd had to bother explaining his movements to his wife. But now he'd had two years of not having to explain anything to anyone, then Lavinia emerged from the bathroom, wearing only a towel.

"There is a robe for you."

"I know." She untied the towel and let it drop. "But this just lets you appreciate me more quickly." He was genuinely more moved by the big smile, so much more than he had ever expected, than by the very slightly voluptuous body that stood naked before him.

"Hmm, I am going to want you again later."

"I could actually want you again now, but I suppose this other thing will nag us until we have a plan."

"It will," he said, and he slid off the bed and wrapped her in his arms, slid his hands down to her ass and let his reawakening bulge brush her belly. "But I like that you're giving us until morning to solve it."

"Do you think it's solvable?"

"I never abandon optimism. But it's time to get cooking!" And he slapped her ass gently.

"I'm going, I'm going, but I'll have more of that later too."

He went to the shower, the thought about Claudia began to trouble him again. How had that happened? What had made her push to know more? Was there some connection he hadn't understood? He'd put her reaction, which seemed to him extreme, down to all the pressures of getting her business set up. Their last few times together had been wonderful, extraordinary: the bench in Singapore; the guys in Charleston; the day out with the kids; the plans for the seaside house — but he did have a sense at the time that it was all just a bit too much, that maybe he'd taken her further than she wanted to go.

But he had loved her, he'd had too many lonely nights before he'd truly managed to patch over his feelings and for all the dating, the strange arrangement with Lavinia was the only really firm emotional connection he'd established. And now that was threatening to get richer. Oh well, he would see.

But there was something about Singapore that nagged him. Would Claudia be able to help?

16

May I call you? J

On my way to the airport. Not convenient. C

When can I get you? J

Awkward. I land in Tokyo at 4pm local time tomorrow. Don't know what happens then but I know I have to meet people. C

Tokyo? I really would appreciate a chance to talk. I have a big problem and you might be able to help. Please. J

I'll text you when I have some time. C

She wasn't looking to be unhelpful, but she really didn't know what would be happening when she arrived. Peter would be there, and Andy, and, much against her better judgement, Tania. Andy had tried to persuade Peter, who had initially supported Claudia, but then the Japanese lawyer had intervened — 'He says these relationship things are important, Claudie, and the girl had made a connection with them', so Peter had wavered.

More than eighteen months with no contact and then 'I have a problem'. Fuck him!

I'm meeting people at 7. I have a little time now. C

Six p.m. She had an hour to unpack and shower. If he checked his phone at five a.m. on a Sunday she would be surprised but at least she'd made an effort. She would rather take her time and absorb the atmosphere in this place. She'd already regretted that it was going to be so hectic and intense. The drive from Haneda though the city had astonished her, the ultra-modern buildings, the multi-tiered expressways — and then the delightful, simple serenity of the hotel. On her only previous trip she'd flown to Narita and had stayed at a hotel near the office and not gone into the centre; that was a stupid way of living. She was uber awake now and restless but keen to focus on the week ahead. Peter would be waiting later with the others. And now she might have to deal with Jack. But what were the chances of him calling at five a.m.?

But when she got out of the shower, there it was: one missed call — 'Jack'.

"You have a problem, I gather."

"Thank you for calling back. I'd like to talk a bit, but it doesn't sound like you have much time."

"No, I don't have. I'm meeting people in half an hour."

"I'd like to know what you're doing there. I'm intrigued."

"Get to the point, Jack, please."

"It's not an easy point, Claudie."

"Twenty-nine minutes and I'm not dressed yet."

"I'll ignore that."

"You'd better. What's this about?"

"I'm not going to plead innocence about my Singapore time, but I do need to know what alerted you. What made it so serious for you?"

"Jack, I can't really say you'd been lying but you had been concealing so many things that it was, at the very least, deeply deceitful. I just gave up on being able to trust you."

"I understand that, but who had been talking to you? What made you push so hard for details?"

"That doesn't matter. We'd been talking about dreams and futures and seaside houses and then, suddenly, it became obvious that everything was lies and deceit. Why are you calling?"

"Because whatever you heard then was a distortion…"

"So, you hadn't been to perverts' clubs and risked being blackmailed?"

"I'm not denying that bad things had happened…"

"Well, a worse thing could have happened, Jack, I could have found out too late. Just let's be glad I found out when I did." She was shaking; this wasn't right.

"I'm not trying to turn a clock back but there were things happening then and we were victims…"

"I was a victim, Jack. Why are we going over this now?"

"Because I was a victim too and someone else will be soon if I don't get to the bottom of what happened back then."

"Who?"

"Oscar."

"Oscar Maguire?"

"Yes."

"Bollocks! Oscar, a victim? Come on!"

"It's not bollocks. I think that something happens in the way Henderson does things and what may have been helpful and ethical once is now being distorted and perverted to suit Henderson and not the people he's supposed to be working for."

"You always were the most plausible bastard, Jack. But you've made me too cynical, I can't believe anything."

"Well, don't believe, but please do have a think. If I'm wrong and Henderson had no involvement, then I'm sorry I rang. It's still lovely to hear your voice but you won't appreciate me saying that. But if he was involved in any way, then anybody you know who works with him needs to be very careful. I'd appreciate knowing more because it may affect Oscar, it may affect Collins and, yes, it may affect me too but that really isn't so terribly important. But if I'm right, it already has affected me. I know I'd done wrong, Claudie, and I've had plenty time to bitterly regret that, but I've always felt we could have and should have got over it."

"Oh, fuck you, Jack, just fuck you." She turned her phone off. She was still shaking, but then the shakes turned to sobs.

She was late meeting them in the bar. She saw from Peter's reaction that her repair job was inadequate. "Here she is." But she'd already caught his concerned glance. "Claudia, my love, let me introduce everyone, well, not Tania and Andy, of course, but Ozawa sensei is our lawyer, working between Tokyo and New York, Yamamoto san is with Anglo-Asia, our bank and Will Uprichard is with my team based in Brussels. The boy is my Japan expert, but this is his first-ever visit." The young man looked bashful when he shook hands and then sat down again between Tania and Yamamoto. Peter placed Claudia between himself and Ozawa. He spoke to her in a low voice. "I have a private room for us upstairs, Ozawa will tell you that all conversations in open rooms are dangerous." Ozawa nodded slowly. "He will also tell you that conversations in closed rooms can be dangerous, but the hotel understands our needs for confidentiality, although we shan't work ourselves too hard this evening and we shan't be too late. You and I need to talk later."

"About what?"

He leaned back and smiled his big smile. "I don't know, that's what you're going to tell me. Now, drink?"

They soon moved to an upper floor and had a private dining room. The cityscape was unusual because of the vast number of red lights on all the tall buildings, just how much danger was there for helicopters and aeroplanes? But any adventurous architecture like she'd seen earlier was lost in the darkness outside behind the glaring lights. Ozawa, for all he spoke so slowly, was a very helpful companion for the evening. He had enough male vanity still to make him want to inform and amuse. All the food was new to her but years of Chinese meals with the kids had given her adequate chopstick skills, although Ozawa's compliments were certainly overdone. He explained every dish and wove its origins into Japanese history and culture. She'd managed to get through one book to lift herself above total ignorance, and it meant that he could feign pleasant surprise that she already knew so much. He asked a little about her role for the week and she could see Peter, on his own at the head of the table to Ozawa's other side, tuning in to her reply. Peter would have briefed him already; this was a lawyerly cross-check and the question was being posed after four courses and a few sakes. She allowed herself a quiet smile and made a mental note not to trust Ozawa at all, but then she talked about how the best companies worked, in her experience, and how Peter and Andy would want to feel that there were compatibilities in the two businesses.

"I understand you, Claudia san, but I think you might be pleasantly surprised when you get to see Nakamura. That is Tuesday, I believe."

"Yes, I'm very much looking forward to that." *I wonder why it's Claudia san and Tania san and the men get to keep their surnames.* Claudia didn't normally look out for sexist slights, but this seemed to confirm everything she had read.

Andy, to her left, spoke little to her, staying engrossed with the three younger ones. At least he'd not sat next to Tania, who was opposite her, apparently enjoying the attentions of Will and Yamamoto on either side of her. She would meet her at breakfast; she could catch up then.

The service had been unobtrusively efficient, it almost felt like fast food, and Peter was not going to allow the dinner to drift on. "It's been lovely meeting up with you, ladies and gentlemen. There's plenty to do tomorrow, I think we're all together at Anglo-Asia at two." He looked to Yamamoto, who nodded. "I suggest you all get some sleep."

The younger ones resumed chatting while Peter, standing now, mouthed 'come with me' to Claudia and turned and bowed very low to Ozawa who had also stood to reciprocate with an even more exaggerated movement. He then turned to Claudia. "Very honoured to meet you Claudia san, I look forward to meeting again tomorrow."

He bowed to her, not as deeply as to Peter and, unsure, she simply bowed slightly and hoped that no offence would be taken if a different response had been needed. Maybe she should check on all that before she met any Nakamura people.

"I look forward to tomorrow, Ozawa sensei." He smiled, at least she'd got that right.

Peter let him leave, then looked to her. She turned to the table, and said, "We'll see you tomorrow guys." The rest of the party stayed seated, and she fixed a hard stare on Tania, who managed to counter with a teenager's look of wronged innocence. "Eight o'clock breakfast?" Tania nodded.

"I'm meeting with Will," said Andy to no one in particular.

Peter's arm moved round her shoulder and he ushered her from the room. It was a silent walk through the long corridors and down one floor in the lift to his suite. As soon as the door shut, they moved towards each other into an embrace. She could feel her eyes prickling. "Just let yourself go, my dear. You've done so well this evening. You were obviously very upset when you arrived. Tell me when you're ready, not before. Come on, come and sit down." He moved her to a sofa. Now she was looking out in a different direction. There was more neon, which she'd expected, and a brightly lit Ferris wheel somewhere in the middle distance, and hundreds of those glaring red lights. She was dabbing her nose and eyes while Peter busied himself with drinks. "Tea, my love, or something stronger?"

"I think a cup of tea is our nation's cure-all, isn't it? Is it going to be green, though?"

"It doesn't have to be."

"That's OK, I'll go with green." And she composed herself while he went through a process of selecting bags and choosing cups that he must have been making more complicated than it needed to be. She kicked off her shoes and got more comfortable. Finally, he put down the cups and sat in the armchair next to her.

"I love this place, the courtliness with which everything happens, and everything is as it should be. I would come more often but it isn't really where the action is now, its peak time was thirty years ago. I was just getting started then and only just getting to America. This is the first real opportunity here that I've looked at, so my wise words of caution to Andy that he mustn't let the chase consume him, always a danger with acquisitions, will probably apply just as much to me. I shall need you to keep an eye on me too." She wasn't sure what she could offer but having an additional role in the process made her feel more comfortable about being there. "Can you do that for me?"

"I'll try, of course, but I'm not sure what value I truly have."

"Oh, you have a better feel for a business than almost anyone I've ever met. You understand how those complex organisms function. Very few people really do, in my experience. But between you and Martha, I should be very well protected from overoptimistic assessments. I just don't know about Ozawa yet. He seems really cunning, but I've learnt enough to be a little cautious here, it's hard to determine where the deeper loyalties lie. Money's always there, of course, but you don't know what other connections exist. There's family and class, there's still a loyalty to Japan at large and," he said, laughing to himself, "odd though it sounds, a strange sort of 'honour among thieves' loyalty in the legal profession. You know, the qualified criminals!"

"You mentioned Martha."

He went silent, closed his eyes, then spoke slowly. "Oh, Lord. This is not my finest moment, my dear. I am truly sorry for springing this on you, I should have warned you sooner. Does that somehow relate to what was upsetting you earlier?"

"There is a connection, I think, but only that, just a connection. And you shouldn't blame yourself, I'd guessed she might be involved with this when you mentioned the bank meeting. No, I heard from Jack earlier on, that's what upset me."

He moved over to the sofa beside her. "Are you going to tell Uncle Peter about it?"

"I am." She put her cup down, swung round and leaned against him.

"Jack and I haven't spoken in nearly two years. I was very upset, you know that, and our last conversations were, well, I was almost hysterical. I felt I'd been deceived and let down and humiliated and I still wasn't getting honesty, I didn't think, and it all felt so hopeless. At the same time, I was so excited about moving on with the business, you must remember, it all blew up when we were about to sign."

"I remember it very well."

"Anyway, I'm not going to pretend I was at my calm and wisest best. But I'd also been getting so excited about moving on with him, but I'd always felt a little like I was standing on sand, and then it began to feel like quicksand. Part of me felt, for a long time afterwards, that maybe he'd call and be sorry and try to build a bridge again, but he never did. I had a lot of bad nights when I wanted to call him, but I knew, or I thought I knew, that I'd never be able to trust him."

"So, what's happened now? Has he finally said sorry?"

"No, not really. Well, not at all in fact. Typical! All he was saying really was that things were distorted and out of proportion then."

"He rang you to tell you that?"

"No, he rang me because he has a problem in DC."

"How does he think that's connected? Has he been up to his old tricks?"

"I don't know about that. I expect he's enjoying an adventurous life. But, no, he was looking for a connection to Henderson, sort of accusing him of plotting, and asking whether Henderson was involved in Singapore." There was a long pause. "He was, wasn't he? But I didn't say anything to Jack. I knew I'd be seeing you." Now a longer pause. "You're not saying anything."

"I'm thinking." He was taking his time. "I've known Rod Henderson for about fifteen years, and he's saved me two or three fortunes. In more recent times I've become aware that his methods may not be quite so clean and ethical as I'd always thought. I'm afraid I'd just parked that. I know I have to face into it, but I'd assumed we'd just moved into a twilight area and there's no point in being squeaky-squeamish, there's always a dark hinterland in that sort of work. My agreement with him was that I didn't want any of our work to breach any of my guidelines, but I didn't kid myself that he might not have to work in other ways to keep other clients happy. But I'd never thought to question his motives before and that's what your Jack seems to be suggesting."

"He's not my Jack, Peter."

"Well, maybe we can throw more light on that tomorrow."

"Why tomorrow?"

"We'll be having dinner with Martha. She'll be in the afternoon presentation, just to warn you, but obviously we'll be staying very focused on the bank's ideas of Nakamura's value then. Then she and Andy and I will have a conversation about funding, I'm afraid half a billion is not small change for me, so I need her help. But in the evening, it's just the four of us, including Andy. Will you want to have a private conversation after dinner?"

"Christ, I'm not sure I could get into that."

"No need, if you don't want to. I'm not yet doubting Henderson, he's done too many good things for me. But Martha may see things differently in relation to what went on then, if she's prepared to talk about it at all. If you don't mind, I will explain who you are, it wouldn't seem fair to spring you on her. She's a fearsomely capable woman but we all have our tender spots and we may find that Jack was one of hers."

"Yes, you should mention it, please. But if she's happy to talk, it would be the weirdest conversation I could ever imagine having." She thought for a moment. "But I think I would like to, if she doesn't mind. Did you know about her interests?"

"I'd guessed."

"But you never?"

"No."

"What makes you?" She paused. "No, forget it. I'd love to have a long evening to talk to you about everything in the world but, as you once said to me, we have lost our careless hours."

He kissed her forehead. "We have, and I do regret it, my dear."

17

Tania was waiting. She had a seat at a table by the glass wall that looked out on to the formal garden. She stood and waved when she saw Claudia, a gesture remarkable among the minimal hushed movements of the other diners. They embraced and then sat down.

"How did you sleep?"

"Shitty — and I'm normally good. How about you?"

"I'm good, I usually am. Is anything wrong? You looked upset when you came down last night but, my goodness, at least you have that gorgeous old man to look after you."

"Ha, that does illustrate the difference in our perspectives. I don't think of Peter as old. But I agree he's gorgeous."

"He's the one who got you set up, isn't he?"

"That's right. He got to hear of what I was doing and thought it would help some of his businesses. The first was Andy's, and at the same time I'd been asked to look at your dad's, so there seemed to be enough opportunities for the idea, so he put some funding and guarantees in place — and here we are."

"But how did you meet him?"

That was the question Claudia had tried to avoid. "Just a mutual acquaintance. Anyway, how did you all get on last night?"

"Only one drink at the bar after you'd gone. Will's a poppet. That's what you'd call him, isn't it?"

Claudia smiled. "It's a word we use, I suppose. How about Yamamoto? Was that his name?"

"Yes, I'd met him before. He's nice but very serious. His English is superb, fortunately."

"I thought you spoke Japanese." Claudia gave a sly smile.

"Come on, I never pretended it was better than crap. I'm not kidding myself about why they want me here again. They will try and find out more about us by asking sneaky questions. Honestly, if I hadn't come, they would have just got suspicious. Anyway, I think you'll need me tomorrow at the factory."

"It's just the two of us, is that right?"

"Yes, they thought too many questions would be asked if Andy went again — but I don't matter, of course, a mere woman. But if we're all at dinner in the evening afterwards, you can have Abego sensei."

"That's your fondler?"

"Fondle might not have been so bad. It was serious groping, really."

Claudia thought about her next question just as the waiter came to take orders. "What about your other fondler?" she asked, when he'd gone.

"Look, we're cool, honestly. Nothing to worry about. I'm more worried about you and Peter. That looks like the same age gap as Andy and me but the two of you are all doe-eyed with each other. Seriously though, Andy's OK and I'm OK. It's like it didn't happen." She reached across and touched Claudia's hand. "I know you're just looking out for me. But you won't mind if I make a play for Will, will you?" They both laughed, and then almost laughed again when they saw the disapproval on the faces of the ladies on the neighbouring table.

"We're meeting them at ten, aren't we? I shall be chaperoning you. But what about this afternoon at the bank? I've met Yamamoto now, but Peter says the head honcho is an American woman."

"Oh, Martha, wow, one seriously impressive lady! I'd like to be her when I grow up."

"Long way to go, child." They laughed again but a little more quietly this time, although the efforts at restraint made them snort and giggle. "But seriously. Peter seems to value her highly."

"I'm not surprised. She seemed to have a clear grasp of everything and a command of all that needs to be done to make this work, although she did emphasise that these deals…" Then Tania seemed to remember that open discussion should be limited — she looked around. "Well, it would be a rare thing, apparently. But anyway, I liked her and, without being aggressive or anything, she kind of dominated Andy. She doesn't trust

Ozawa sensei, though. There was lots of tension there. How did you get on with him? He seemed to take a shine to you."

Claudia managed an exaggerated eyelid flutter. "It's easy, my dear, isn't it?" Tania laughed again. It was like having a younger sister; she was wonderful to have around. Claudia knew that, somewhere in the background of her reaction to Tania coming again, was her own awareness that she wanted to share her company — and that felt too much like self-indulgence. Still, Andy was paying — but there was an expanding business in the US that needed attention. She already had her next trip planned, she badly needed to recruit more people.

Claudia had been very unadventurous in her breakfast choices, but so was Tania, she noted. And there were knives, forks and spoons on the table. But the view out of the window was an idyll from the pictures in the books she'd been looking at. There were buildings all around the large garden but on two of the sides they rose only to two or three storeys. The high rises were a few blocks away, so the space was not oppressively imprisoned. The foliage was exquisitely tended. Water ran down large boulders in the taller trees in the far corner into a small lily pond quite near them. The acers were turning from their dazzling late summer crimson to their drooping autumn duns, but there were trees and shrubs in many vibrant shades from a palette of darker blues, moving though vivid greens and yellows to elegant silver providing colour. The plants, with all varieties of leaves, were pruned into pleasing shapes that seemed to complement each other perfectly harmoniously. There were two benches, discreetly hidden. "It's lovely," said Tania, appearing to read her mind, "but if you want to meditate outdoors, we should go to the Imperial Palace gardens. It's hard to ignore the buildings around you in this place."

"I was just thinking about thinking. It's a lovely idea but I can't see us getting time. I'm off on Thursday. I'm assuming you don't have any extra trips planned this time?" She narrowed her eyes as she asked.

"I might see what Will's doing," Tania said, with a big smile.

"You win. I deserved that." Another laugh, but this time quiet enough not to disturb the neighbours.

"Talk of the devil!" Tania was looking at the door. Claudia turned round, Andy and Will were just coming in.

They stood up; they had finished eating. "Good morning, boys." Claudia air-kissed Andy and nodded and smiled to Will. "We're seeing you at ten, I think."

"Yes," said Andy. "We'll meet in my suite. Will wanted to use a meeting room in the business centre but I said it's best he prints his presentation and we keep things quiet. With all the talk from Martha and Ozawa, I think we'd rather be in a leper colony than a business centre, there'd be less health risk."

"Nicely put, Andy," said Claudia, wearing her 'we are not amused' face. "Your number?"

"Eleven zero six."

"See you later."

***

"Well, Will," said Andy, more than an hour into their discussion, papers scattered on the floor and sofas, empty coffee cups and water bottles on the table. "I'll admit I was sceptical when Peter said his Japan expert hadn't been to Japan but you have an amazing grasp of Molloy and I know you ain't been there. So, I'm going to assume you understand this place." He paused. "But I'm obviously not suggesting Japan's as simple as Molloy."

"Oh, I've desperately wanted to come here but James, he's my boss, said I should wait until there was something in the pipeline."

"Frustrating?" asked Claudia.

"Yes, but I worked on both the China projects, so I've had a full plate and plenty travel, but I'm thrilled to be here at last. I'm going to stay on for a few days and look around. Are any of you staying?"

"I'd love to," Tania said, jumping in quickly, "but I have this tyrannical boss. I think she's worse than your James, so I have to get back to New York."

"I expect Will is more responsible when he travels." Claudia tried to look frosty to Tania and Andy, but they all ended up smiling slyly. Will, again, looked a little perplexed and embarrassed. "I thought you did a fantastic job there too, Will, thank you. I thought I understood Molloy, but I'd never focused on those financial perspectives, I suppose."

"Yeah," said Andy, "I was going to bring my CFO, but Peter didn't want me to involve anyone else yet. I was nervous, but you've given me a good feeling that you understand us." Now Will just returned to looking bashful.

"Can we go through how you're valuing Nakamura again?" asked Tania. "Yamamoto is going to be big on that this afternoon. I think he's good, but we should make sure we have different angles to see if the different methodologies give similar results." Claudia raised her eyebrows at her. "When Giddings bought Longshore four years ago, Dad wanted me to work on the acquisition team." *Yes, I guess you will be the CEO one day, girl.*

Will went through his options in more detail this time. Claudia glanced at Andy after a while; he smiled back, all the technical questions were coming from Tania.

The two were still talking intently when the ring at the door told them that lunch was being delivered. "I just ordered sushi, guys, that seemed to be the done thing." Andy directed the waiter to lay the table and raised his finger to his lips to the group to tell them to stop talking. Claudia began gathering all the papers.

Will and Tania seemed to understand quickly and began tidying everything near them. "Will, can I make you responsible for this? It's very good work." He paused. "Or do you guys want your copies with you this afternoon?" Claudia and Tania looked at each other.

"It might be better if you channel your points and questions through me," said Will, now seeming a little more authoritative having led most of the morning's debate. "There's a danger otherwise of discussions going off track as everyone sorts though different piles of paper. I think I've got a good grasp of your key concerns." The women looked to Andy, who seemed to reflect for a moment and then nodded.

18

Yamamoto met them in the lobby of the bank building. He shook hands with them all then spoke quietly with the receptionist. "Dickinson san and Ozawa sensei are already here," he said, as he guided them towards the lift. He pressed twenty when they were all in, and then twenty-one. Claudia noted that he had positioned himself next to her. He addressed her quietly. "Claudia san, would you please continue to level twenty-one? You will be met, Weddle san would like to greet you personally." Claudia nodded. Andy was talking to Will, but Tania noticed and raised her eyebrows. At twenty Yamamoto ushered them out and said, "See you shortly," to Claudia.

A slightly shorter dark-haired woman was waiting for her when the lift stopped again. "Claudia, I'm Martha, I'm sorry to steal you like this, please come through." They walked past a reception desk, where a PA, Claudia assumed, nodded to them. Martha led on through an open door into a large office; its outer glass wall gave a magnificent view of the city over the Imperial Palace. The two low leather sofas were side-on to the window. "Please have a seat," she said, closing the door. "I promise I won't keep you. Peter spoke to me this morning and I am so glad he did." She paused, allowing them to take stock of each other. Claudia would have to admit that she'd taken particular care, returning to her room to change before meeting the others for the taxi journey. Martha looked posh business, the black suit well-cut for a figure that, Claudia judged, found it hard to look elegant. The grey silk shirt looked classy and the face was softer than Claudia expected and actually quite pretty, although Martha would probably not have expected that description. "I know this is bizarre, but I do feel I know you. You are as lovely as he used to tell me," she said, with a warmth that surprised her.

"I know what you mean. It might surprise you to know how much he spoke about you."

"Well, he always said that he was very open with you. I got the impression that was at your insistence." She smiled. "That wouldn't normally be the male way, would it?"

Claudia felt awkward about how to respond, the woman was clearly being friendly. "No, I think he struggled, well, I know he did. Martha, I really do appreciate this little chat and I really would like to talk a lot longer, but I'm sensitive that the others are waiting."

"I know that, my dear, but I think we both know that this was far more important than any half billion-dollar acquisition." The smiles became laughs for both of them. "I won't keep you any longer now but I would like us to get together later. Is that OK with you?"

"That's very much OK with me, I was hoping you'd agree."

"Well, I would have wanted to anyway, but Peter mentioned something about some trouble Jack may be confronting in DC?"

"I'm hoping that's something and nothing. I'd just like to get together for a chat anyway."

"Attagirl, shall we go join them? We'll get together after dinner." It was more of an instruction than an invitation, but Claudia felt very comfortable about that.

The meeting room was quite large, but people had huddled to one end, leaving Yamamoto isolated by his computer in the end chair on the far side. Will and Andy were in the two chairs at the end of the table, with Peter next to Andy and Ozawa and then Tania to his right. They all had the wonderful view of the Palace. But once Martha had sat next to Yamamoto, Claudia felt the room would be unbalanced if she sat next to Tania and she wanted to be near Will anyway in case she had questions. In truth, she expected much of the discussion to be above her head — and so it was for the first half an hour as she struggled to understand Yamamoto's valuation systems. He, like Will earlier, had a great deal of data on Molloy and the two of them had plainly been collaborating closely and seemed to respect each other. When they compared some business performance metrics, she began to recognise data from her early work on Molloy and saw that it compared unfavourably with Nakamura.

When he began to look closer at Nakamura, he began with a 'Will and I see this similarly' and Will had nodded. "We see that in more recent years there has been less ambition to expand. The only real push has been into the US, and you could argue that that's an opportunistic response to the pull from US distributors." Andy breathed in heavily and nodded. "We just don't see great ambition to establish a base in China. Will?"

"Companies this size can easily be seduced by that opportunity, and while we'd recommend that you mount a serious effort, either as Molloy alone, or preferably in tandem, we're going to reduce our projected valuation to something conservative. China's a massive market, of course, but very difficult to succeed in. We'll still see that Nakamura looks a very good purchase even with an attractive premium on the stock price."

"And we're still saying that's fifty per cent?" asked Peter.

"In terms of the existing stock holders that would get you a very good uptake, we think. You would probably succeed with less, but you really only get one shot, so you need to be careful. I don't think you could go below forty. But if you get the family and directors on board, even that might do it for the bulk of the stock."

There was an awkward silence in the room for a moment.

"What the guys are saying," said Martha, "and we none of us are experts because these deals are rare, but there tend to be hidden costs in Japanese transactions." She looked hard at Ozawa. "Considerable hidden costs." His eyes were closed but he had pursed his lips and was nodding. "How high these are is something we should discuss later in a smaller group."

"I agree with that, Martha," said Peter, "but in the interests of educating the coming generations, I'm happy for you to explain why you want to limit that discussion. Normally the children are only asked to leave the room when naughty things are being discussed."

"Please let us not be so hasty," interjected Ozawa. "There will be delicate issues in the negotiations, and we should absolutely limit any open discussion of these arrangements. The significant protagonists will expect considerable confidentiality. Surely what we should be doing now is focusing on what Nakamura is worth to Molloy."

"I take your point, Ozawa sensei," said Peter, "but the boys and girls should just know that one or two people might try to squeeze more out of this for themselves. Nothing more sinister than that. In some countries it's still called business."

"In other countries it has some very different names," said Martha, quite mildly but she was looking sternly at Ozawa, who had returned to his eyes closed pose. "But one point that the negotiators should bear in mind, and I'm assuming that will be principally Ozawa sensei and Andy?" Peter nodded. "They should bear in mind that the dearth of export growth and a certain amount of stagnation in the home market, means that our offer will give us very little scope for any upside, to anyone."

"Well, we should move on and try to agree what that valuation is, please," said Peter, brightly, and that seemed to lessen the tension that had risen in the room.

Claudia could ask more about the background over dinner. It sounded like some key players and middlemen would be trying to take their own enhanced cuts on the deal and that, she assumed, presented legal and ethical conundrums.

Yamamoto and Will described their summaries of different valuation systems, but Claudia had to admit that topics like free cash flow and EBITDA were way beyond her comprehension, but all their systems seemed to yield a number in the seven to eight hundred-million-dollar area.

"And that includes the cash?" asked Peter.

"Of course," said Yamamoto.

Peter put on his patient look. "I have a small lump of anxiety, Yamamoto san, but before we get into that may I just say, to both you and Will, that your analysis and the clarity of your explanations has been superb, really excellent." Both the young men looked slightly overwhelmed. "But I'll come back to a worry Andy and I have. Is that cash solid where it is? Or could it somehow be siphoned off in some strange process while the deal is underway and we end up in three months, say, owning a company with an empty cash larder?"

"Oh, no, the cash is there, it appears consistently in the published accounts every quarter and the sum has been rising consistently." Yamamoto, having recovered from the compliment, seemed now to be defending Japan's honour. "It could not be touched without it being transparent to their bank, and therefore to us, once an offer process is underway. That would be part of due diligence."

"Steady Yoshi, Peter wasn't trying to impugn the honour of Japan or its banking system," said Martha. "Now, I'm not in the 'greed is good' camp but it behoves us to be aware that greed is certainly global, and we need to be very alert to what might happen. Could you comment on that, Ozawa sensei?"

"I think Dickinson san is wise to be cautious, these are areas where we must move forward carefully."

"Would that be the small steps through your fog of ambiguities, Ozawa sensei?" asked Andy.

This was plainly a private joke. Ozawa smiled broadly. "I am pleased you are such an attentive student of ancient Japanese wisdom, Molloy san." Andy laughed, Peter looked bemused but indulgent. Martha looked emotionless but Claudia judged she was concealing some animosity.

"Perhaps if I might add a small thought on this issue?" Even Martha now looked prepared to pay

Ozawa close attention and all nodded respectfully. "This two hundred million dollars is obviously very important to the economics of this transaction." He paused, allowing all to nod again, even Martha. "Our dilemma in all our discussions and negotiations is to give the impression that we have not even noticed this trifling amount." Peter smiled broadly, but Martha was not amused. "But to take rigorous steps at every juncture to ensure there is no inexplicable leakage because, forgive me, Yamamoto san, but on rare occasions some accidents can happen, even in Japan."

Now even Martha was nodding appreciatively. "I think you've put that very well, Ozawa sensei, if you don't mind me saying so. I'm sure Andy will have an excellent guide, well, a sensei, I suppose," she said, with a smile, plainly pleased with her almost-witticism, "to hold his hand through this process and to deal with these issues with the necessary tact and the equally necessary firmness."

"I think we have reached a point, ladies and gentlemen, where we must firm up our positions," Peter intoned, somewhat magisterially. Somehow the tone was necessary, and no one Claudia had ever met could carry it off quite like Peter. "I should like to go round the room and ask for your views on whether we attempt to proceed. I will tell you before you comment that my own mind is very far from being made up. Ultimately the decision is Andy's, but all of our opinions are important in helping him decide if he wishes to go ahead with this. Do you wish to add anything to that, Andy?"

Andy smiled at Peter. "No, mister chairman, those are important words of guidance to help me make my decision." Then, putting irony behind him, Andy said, "Seriously guys, I listen to my master's voice mainly because he will have to put lots of his money into this too, but I do need your honest input."

"So, Tania," said Peter, cutting across him, "your views first, please."

Claudia was a little stunned by the turn the process had taken and was worried about Tania being exposed to this. She was also concerned about what she might contribute when her time came. She didn't want it to be completely lame. Tania, as usual, surprised her. "The only acquisition I have worked on was far simpler. Our company, Giddings, it's logistics and mainly US based, had a regional weakness in the north east that was reasonably well covered by a local company, Longshore, who wanted to be bought out — the owner was old and his son was not a businessman — so he approached my dad. My dad is the chairman of Giddings. I think my dad could probably have bought it for less, but he always stressed that he wanted them, and that meant all of the Longshore company, to want to join us. So, he made sure we sold the Giddings idea to them and the merger, that's what we always called it, went very smoothly. It helped us offer a truly national package to our important customers and accelerated our growth rates as a few bigger accounts came on board and it even made Longshore a busier and happier place. But," she said, pausing for emphasis, "he did fire half of their directors in the first year for being not up to the job, but the funny thing there was, the morale at Longshore went even higher afterwards. So, Nakamura looks like a good deal to me, if it's available at that price." She looked intently at Andy and said, "But you have to be absolutely sure you can get these organisations to work with each other after the marriage."

Claudia could see Martha nodding appreciatively as, indeed, was Ozawa.

"Will?"

"I may have had enough airtime," he said, self-deprecatingly. "The numbers say it could be a good deal, but I do think Tania has made some important points." He turned to Andy, "It only works if you can get people to work together and I'm afraid I've no experience of that."

"He's being a little modest there," said Peter. "The two Chinese companies we bought into benefitted from our money, it's true, but they also benefitted from opportunities Will identified in the West and some contacts he helped them make."

"Thank you, Peter, but we didn't have to struggle with an arranged marriage like this would be."

"Fair point, and a good one. Yamamoto san?" It may be Andy's decision, but Peter was still orchestrating the proceedings, thought Claudia, still worrying about what her contribution might be.

"My numbers tell me this is a very good deal at the price we're considering but it would be a very rare deal, so I am unsure what to expect. There are complexities you have raised that I am unsure how to consider but if it can be bought at this price, retaining the full amount of cash, it looks a good deal, but I do respect the point that Tania san has made." He nodded to Tania, smiling. She smiled demurely back. *Does that little witch have two suitors?*

"Claudia, any observations?"

"I'm afraid the question's a little premature for me. I get the point entirely that the organisations must be able to work together, we've probably all seen examples of dysfunctional miscommunication — *wow, did I really just say that?* — in other pairs of organisations even sharing, nominally, the same language and culture — neither obviously applies here — but we also need to absorb a company that can fit to the Dickinson Group, and not just to Molloy. So, I can see the numbers look good, but I'm feeling a lot of pressure to study their business operations closely tomorrow and maybe then give you some views on how I see the possibilities." She tried to finish on a rising note, to leave the question in the room.

Peter, at least, was receptive. "Wise restraint, my dear. I did ask Claudia to be a check on our wilder instincts. That's a useful reminder that we're not pushing for a final decision today, so maybe I phrased the question incorrectly, but we're asking if you all think we should push ahead. Martha?"

"I'm going to say no." There was an audible intake of breath around the room. She paused — *OK, dramatic effect, woman, but I admire you for doing it* — "We're going to be talking later about what you want the bank to do. We've done a little already, but due diligence would consume much more resource. But you're also going to need us to facilitate around a half a billion dollars and I'm not yet feeling a compelling argument for us to do that. So, sorry guys, but at this point I'm saying 'convince me' and my sisters have just told you where the weakness lies. You mustn't underestimate how hard it is to work across these cultures."

Peter smiled. "I thank you, as always, for your lucidity and forcefulness." She could have become frosty at that — *I would have done* — but she smiled back at him, apparently with warmth. This must be a well-practised routine. "So, Ozawa sensei, are you going to stay on our side of the gender divide?"

Ozawa was nodding and waiting, somewhat theatrically, to begin. "I think some very good points are being made and, it seems to me, we do have some old heads on these young shoulders. We should clearly not attempt to bring incompatible organisations together since that would have destructive consequences. But we should also bear in mind that this is an important concern expressed in the limited discussions I have had with the other party. They will not wish for this merger, and I was very impressed by the way Tania san made that point." He turned to her, and smiled, Tania responded graciously — *but he's a lizard too* — "Unless both parties approach it with this thought as their main concern: how can these two organisations work together? So," *my God, this man speaks slowly*, "we should keep that thought uppermost in our minds in all of these discussions; what will be the health of the combined entity? And, who knows, if these discussions are convivial and productive, we might even be able to persuade Weddle san to view the transaction a little more favourably. For my part, from the preliminary conversations I have had, I believe this to be an attractive proposition."

Claudia sensed Martha struggling against an urge to respond but, she thought, why should she do that now? She's made her point, and they need to convince her, or it isn't going to happen.

"Thank you so much, Ozawa sensei," said Peter, with his usual charm. "I suppose it's my turn now. A key point that was made by both Will and Yoshi." He looked to Yamamoto. "Do you mind if I call you Yoshi?" Yamamoto almost blushed, but nodded. "Good, I am Peter, obviously. The point they stressed is that globally we expect this market to grow significantly. There are, therefore, it seems to me, big attractions in an enterprise with global scale and good geographic spread — but, as some of you have so wisely stressed, it would need to be an enterprise that can work harmoniously and coherently. So, I would be in favour, but only if we can satisfy ourselves on these points. Andy?"

"I've been warned since day one that the pursuit of an acquisition can bring out all of a man's worst instincts, so when I tell you I'm hot to make this happen, I am attempting to see both sides of the picture and stay quite restrained. But I think we can do so much more with double the resources focusing on agreed markets and we can widen our product range as well as our geography in ways that we've wanted to at Molloy but have held back because we were resource constrained. But I thank you for all the points you've made, they will be uppermost in my mind in all the discussions we have with Nakamura. So, long story short, I want to push on but know I can't do that without convincing you." He was looking hard at Martha, who didn't return his gaze but was nodding.

"Well," said Peter. "Let me thank you all again for your contributions today. I believe you're meeting some Nakamura people tomorrow, Ozawa sensei, Andy?" He looked to them, they both nodded. "You know what you have to keep uppermost in your minds and I hope you are right, Ozawa sensei, that they are moved by the noble purpose of creating a harmonious entity, but we shan't lose sight of our awareness that, among the dreamers, more venal motives can sometimes hold sway." Martha was nodding again. "Now, I'm told to expect that some of us will be invited to meet them tomorrow evening if tomorrow's discussions go well. Have I understood that correctly?" Ozawa nodded. "I think that will only involve Dickinson people, myself excluded." He looked hard at Ozawa, who seemed to nod reluctantly. "I'm sorry, Ozawa sensei, but they must focus on Molloy san as the man who will make the decision. If we deviate from that we open ourselves to being manipulated. Anyway, it means the rest of you can stand down for that, but I would like to provisionally book some time on Wednesday to summarise where we've got to and plan next steps. Are you around, Martha?"

"Tokyo all week but tied up until four on Wednesday."

"That would work, I hope. I know some of us are leaving Thursday. Can you make this room available?" She nodded. "Excellent, we'll meet again then, thank you all. I just need Martha, Andy and Claudia, please."

Claudia was surprised, almost shocked.

"We'll use upstairs," said Martha.

Claudia just caught Tania. "Breakfast at eight again?"

"Sure, of course." But she was clearly being set up for dinner with the two young men.

"This is absolutely spectacular," said Andy, standing in Martha's office window, looking out over the Palace and the gardens.

"You could soon be buying this view for half a billion," said Martha. Andy looked puzzled. "Nakamura has a small head office suite in the neighbouring building, it's more vanity than anything else. They'll tell you they need it for business connections but that's not really valid, certainly not these days. That's a little cost-cutting you could look at."

"But, for you, on the other hand, this majestic outlook is absolutely necessary." Peter was opening his arms expansively at the view, clearly teasing her.

She smiled. "Because my clients, Peter dear, are very, very important people whose colossal vanity inevitably and unfortunately demands excessively opulent surroundings, stunning views included. Shall we sit?" They moved to the sofas.

"This needn't take long," said Peter. "I just need to understand where you're coming from if we want to push ahead. We wouldn't attempt to do it without you. Well, we couldn't do it without you anyway, but that's actually less important to me than understanding if you think there's a way forward. I think you made your points clearly enough downstairs. But what would we need to do to get you feeling more comfortable?"

"I think my concerns are clear. One minor one is watching out for who tries to squeeze the extras out of these deals. No one's immune. The reason I said I wanted sensei to hold your hand, Andy, is that it will then be harder for him to put his hand in your pocket. Poor joke, I know, but you need to watch him. Just as we'll have to watch out for what they come up with, and whether it's excessive or illegal." She smiled at Peter, mildly flirtatiously Claudia thought. "It's what you rather broad-minded people call business." He feigned shock. "And you're one of the good guys." She took a sip of water. "But my biggest concern is whether you could knit these two companies together. There are few precedents and very many fewer that make happy reading, and I just don't know how you answer that one, it is a big risk, period! And I'll just make one final point." She looked hard at Andy. "You made a spirited case for a global business, conquering all markets with bigger product ranges. But was that vision there before Nakamura started eating your lunch in the US?" Andy hesitated. "Not trying to trap you into bullshitting me, Andy, I'm just pretty sure it wasn't. So, I liked your pose as the global visionary, applause, applause, but at the end of the day you're just a businessman trying to eliminate all competition so that you can make an easier buck." Andy looked a little crestfallen. "But," she added, "and here I must exclude you, Claudia, because I don't really know you, but I'm pretty certain I've just described the rest of us." They all laughed. "But we can all still do deals, for fuck's sake. My central question remains, however, could you make one business out of two very different halves?"

Peter was smiling, looking relaxed, not like a man whose half billion-dollar deal was imploding. "You're maybe slowly getting the picture, Claudia, of why I wanted you here so much." *Claudia isn't really getting it at all, Peter, if I'm being honest.* "This whole thing hinges on whether we can meld two different companies together successfully." He turned to Martha, sat beside him. "I don't know anybody better than Claudia at reading an organisation's DNA; she understands how they work, what makes them tick and how they can be developed." He turned back to Claudia and said, "So, no pressure, my dear, but you have one day tomorrow to try to get inside the mind of the Nakamura business. Is it something we could work with and develop? How do they think and act? And all that with the help of only one dodgy interpreter. I wanted you, Martha and I to be the three wise monkeys, but I'm on the borderline of jumping down to the jungle floor and joining the chase. So, what you two think, is very important but it's best if we just let you get on with it. Andy?"

"That covers it." He looked at Martha. "I will just underline what Peter said about Claudia. The Molloy turn around started when she came to us for a day. I wouldn't trust anyone more than her on an assignment like this." Claudia felt prickles of embarrassment but tried to look cool. Martha was looking at her through narrowed eyes.

"OK, guys, let's see where we get to by Wednesday. I hope, now we've covered all that ground, we can relax at dinner tonight. I'm afraid it's the same place, Andy, I've been promising Peter for a while. It's perfect Japanese, Claudia, I hope you'll enjoy it."

"I'm sure you will," said Andy to her. "I thought it was amazing and I'm normally steak and fries."

"Good, I will swing by and pick you up, it's on my way. Okura reception, seven o'clock."

Yes, thought Claudia in the taxi on the way back, a very impressive lady and, however strange the circumstances, she was looking forward to their conversation later. Peter was still actively in work mode. "Andy, I'm going to make a phone call or two. I would like you to have your own interpreter with you tomorrow. I'm guessing it was theirs last time?"

"Yes, Kitagawa san. I assumed he was good, his English was very good anyway, but," Andy said, his head nodding slowly, "I have no idea whether he translated everything exactly accurately and I think what you're telling me now is that Ozawa might translate words to fit his own thoughts."

"I wouldn't want to say that he's not our man but it's best to assume he's not entirely disinterested. And he's your fog of ambiguities man, I take it?"

Andy laughed. "I thought that was quite funny. But couldn't we have asked Martha? The bank must use people." Peter, turning from the front seat to face them, raised his eyebrows. "Duh! Sorry, you're saying you don't want the bank to know everything, of course."

"I wouldn't, ultimately, keep any secrets from Martha, but it's possible we may need to give her some distance and deniability. I will admit I'm struggling a little because my best conduit to Japan is through

Henderson." He looked to Claudia. "And these days I've begun to have doubts about him. If I can find someone, we'll have breakfast with you in my room so we can brief him together. Don't mention the topic this evening. And when Ozawa complains in the morning, just tell him I insisted. You can bullshit him about needing him focused, and translation being beneath him et cetera, but he will understand — and so will the Nakamura people if we find the right guy — and that won't be a bad thing, they'll see you as naïve, otherwise. Well, Mr Henderson is about to get a very early phone call. Let's make him earn his money."

***

Arriving at the restaurant had been a shock for Claudia: the little lane the big car couldn't enter; the long, dingy alleyway to the restaurant entrance; but, once inside, it had been charming, she found all of it entrancing, including the dishes she utterly failed to identify. With Andy there, she was not the least accomplished with chopsticks. They'd stayed off the topic of Nakamura, in spite of Martha's assurances of privacy, but with Peter in the party the conversation meandered over very diverse topics, usually with a humorous, but seldom cynical, slant. Martha had a few more trenchant observations about humanity but there was mostly laughter in their small room. Martha called for the bill.

"I'll get that," said Peter. "You'll just add fifteen per cent."

"I'll get it," said Andy. "You just do the same." They laughed loudly; the men had got well into the spirit of playing host with the sake.

"We'll drop you off, guys. Claudia's coming back with me to the Imperial. I'm going to wish you good luck tomorrow, Andy, watch yourself — and watch Ozawa!"

They waved to the men as they dropped them off at the Okura and stretched themselves out on the back seat of the Mercedes. "I love him," said Martha. "It's a shame he's unique. How long have you known him?"

"Peter? About four years. Someone introduced us and he got interested in what I was doing at Collins." She paused. "You must know quite a bit about Collins, one way and another."

Martha laughed, but warmly. "Well, they have, as you know, quite extensive operations in my region but, for a bank, they're very low maintenance. Peter is, fortunately, much more demanding — and therefore more profitable — but exciting too. The two Chinese deals were a lot of fun and they seem to be working out well."

"Oh, yes, definitely, I met the guys a few weeks ago at one of Peter's Gatherings and they seemed very switched on. There's no need for me, yet, but that might be an interesting project someday."

"I love China, it's so dynamic. I'm having to think seriously about relocating our headquarters. It's very quiet here by comparison, really, this deal is the most exciting thing to have happened in years for us. But I have to play the cautious banker, there's a lot could go wrong. Anyway, more of that on Wednesday. We were talking about Collins, but maybe we should settle down and get comfortable before we get back to that topic. I have a suite here. I'm going to have them bring us a bottle of champagne, this is going to be a conversation I couldn't ever have imagined happening."

"Well, amen to that." Claudia still felt some trepidation but had grown more relaxed about the prospect of being open with Martha through the afternoon and evening.

Claudia settled on the sofa, Martha in the armchair. She picked up the phone and ordered Taittinger — *Where did she pick up that habit? Jack, of course* — "Do you always stay here?"

"The group is a client, so it's preferential rates and bad form if I don't. I like it, but it is busier than your place. Can I get straight to my difficult question? Or would you like to start with yours?"

"No, you go."

"What happened?" she asked, emphatically. "He seemed so committed to making it work between you and then he leaves, and I find it's all over. My reaction, when I heard that, was that the bastard had been using you as a cover so that I wouldn't get too keen on building a relationship with him."

"He'd always told me that your relationship was very, well," she paused, "focused, can I say that? Confined to a limited area."

"You can say I loved him spanking and caning me. We probably won't get very far tonight if we mince our words and start using your beloved British euphemisms." They both laughed.

"I agree, and I'm afraid I made him tell me about it. I thought I was doing better by getting him to be open."

"Did it work?"

"Well, obviously not, and I really thought it would."

"So, back to my question, why didn't it?"

"I found out he'd not been telling me things and it seemed he was going way beyond a level that he'd already taken me to. I mean, he did spank me and cane me and did many other things, and I enjoyed it, I admit that. Much of it was new to a naïve wee girl from Scotland but I got excited by it. He even organised a gang bang for me with two guys in the States while he watched and then joined in. I'm a bit concerned about how far it went, looking back on it, but, at the time, I thought it was amazing." She couldn't discern any reaction in Martha beyond curiosity.

"So, what goes way beyond that?"

"Well, he'd said you and he weren't seeing each other for a while."

"That's partly true, but did he say why?"

"He sort of implied it was a mutual decision."

"Ha, it was, but it was mutual because I was falling for him and he seemed committed to you, so we both knew we had to take a break. I tried once or twice to make him break his self-imposed vow of abstinence, but he wouldn't do it with me, but he did agree to come to a club with me. It meant I could get the treatment I wanted, and I had a chaperone. I'm not going to deny that he enjoyed those evenings too, but I didn't see him doing anything more than he and I had done together — and a little less than you've done yourself, it sounds like. So, what's this about?"

There was a ring at the door. "Ah, champagne, excellent, they're quick here on the suites floor. Sorry to hold you up, this is really getting interesting." She let the waiter in, signed the tab, sat back and relaxed, and waited while he popped the cork and poured for them. "Cheers!"

Claudia clinked and drank with her, then waited until the door closed behind him. "Peter and I were about to sign our deal, then a contact of Peter's rang him with information on Jack, and I just lost it, I'm afraid. I felt like I'd always had to push him to be open and he'd pretended to be just that, but now there was stuff that went beyond that, that could have had him blackmailed, apparently, and it was all too much for me."

"Woah, I think I need some more background here. I'm not just being nosey, but I'm not aware of anything he was doing that was so dangerous, but maybe I didn't know either. Jesus, he'd have been a hell of a busy man. He worked very hard anyway and was always traveling. Can you tell me more about the story? And who's this guy of Peter's?"

"I'm a bit confused and worried now, and this network of Peter's is supposed to be ultra-confidential."

"Ha, I'm immediately suspicious. Whoever is doing that has a pretty good opportunity to organise things to their own advantage. *Cui bono*?"

"Martha, I think I may have been utterly fucking stupid." Claudia felt a large hole open up inside her.

"Hey." Martha moved beside her on the sofa. "Let us drink to the poor fucker who's never been that, wherever she may be — because I've never met her. What's the deal?"

Claudia told her about Henderson's network. Martha hadn't known about it but could understand why such an organisation might be helpful. Then she talked about Jack's call and his story about being set up in order to influence the situation at Collins.

"Wow, we'll have to talk more about that later, not tonight. I mean, we didn't agree formally on this, it's a girlie night, for God's sake, so everything's completely confidential, agreed?"

"Oh, completely, but, of course, if there's anything to it, I can understand why your bank would want to be in the know."

Martha hugged her. "Come on, drink, that's for tomorrow. Well, Wednesday actually, would you mind agreeing to talk to me after our four o'clock session so we can agree what I'm allowed to know?"

"No, that's fine, of course."

"Good, now can we get back to the important stuff. What's he supposed to have done?"

"Put simply, he was visiting kinky night clubs run by gangsters who could have blackmailed him."

"Bollocks!" Martha exclaimed vehemently. "What, in Singapore? Or somewhere else? Sorry, I shouldn't have jumped to that conclusion."

"I'd assumed Singapore, I didn't hear about anywhere else."

"Oh, honey, if it's Singapore I can imagine how that might be misrepresented," she said, pausing before continuing, "and I am saying maliciously misrepresented. There's a very smart club, it's actually called Smarts. That's a pretty lame pun for the spanking players, but it's all a bit of high-end fetish stuff. It's very expensive but Jack and I used to use it. Not often, but when I had the need and, like I said, I'm not going to paint him white, he enjoyed himself while we were there."

"But gangsters running it, blackmail and things like that?"

"Well, I can imagine someone making a story like that out of it but." Here, she went a little thoughtful. "Drink up! Let me pour us some more." She busied herself refilling glasses. "Could you respect why I have to limit what I'm going to say on this topic?" Claudia was puzzled but nodded. "I have a very good insight into the club owner's business operations and I'm almost certain that blackmail and gangsters would not be allowed to come into it."

"I think I'm getting the picture."

"The Smarts network tends to operate with a certain amount of understanding in the legal and political spheres so, as far as I am aware, there is a great deal of well-protected, and expensively acquired, confidentiality. So, what's Jack actually said?"

Claudia was relaxing, she felt stupid but maybe there was a way through this. "I'll have to say more about Collins. That's off the record until we agree it isn't, right?"

Martha nodded, drank, and then giggled, that led to a mini champagne explosion from her mouth, and they both laughed loudly. "Do you sometimes get those moments, they happen to me in quite big meetings when I'm supposed to be important, when you're suddenly very aware of the child inside you who thinks this is all a massive joke and you're just playing a very big game of make believe?"

"I know exactly what you mean, not on your scale of course, but I do get the point. I sometimes hear myself when I'm saying supposedly serious things and think: 'pompous cow'!" They laughed together.

"Well, let's be kids tonight, we'll do the serious stuff on Wednesday. What's he said?"

"He says that Oscar Maguire, the chairman and CEO at Collins—" She looked to Martha to confirm she understood. Martha nodded. "Well, he was getting concerned about how the network got its information, you know, if someone found there was hacking involved, it could quickly go pear-shaped in the PR area. And he may also have been getting worried about the potential for misuse. Peter uses Henderson and he says he's saved him lots of money. But Oscar's number two got wind of Oscar preferring Jack to run the place in the future, so he worked with Henderson, who by now was feeling threatened. First of all, they tried to block Jack's move to the States. That didn't work — Oscar ignored the accusations. Maybe that's what I should have done. Anyway, it probably turned Oscar even more against Henderson. But now, when Oscar is thinking about the CEO appointment, they're looking for ways to attack both of them, especially Oscar, maybe for financial misdemeanours."

"Ha, well, that wouldn't be difficult with most wealthy CEOs, but that's off the record too. We, obviously offer no help with that whatsoever." Claudia sensed that was meant ironically.

"It's feeling to me like Jack may have a point. But how bad is this club?"

A mischievous glint had come into Martha's eye. "I'm going to show you."

"What?"

"There's a Smarts in Tokyo, I've been wanting to try it, we can dress up on Wednesday night and I'll take you. It's best with a male but two girls can look after each other."

"Peter might chaperone us."

"What?"

Claudia immediately had regrets. She wasn't sure she wanted to go at all, she didn't think, and now she'd dropped Peter's name into the mix and that would need a lot of explanation. "I shouldn't have said that."

"But you did!" And now the mischievous glint was a big, evil smile.

"Can you pour some more champagne?"

"This is looking like the best bottle's investment I've ever made." It took a while to tell the Peter story, but Claudia had never had a more rapt audience.

19

The perspective was a little different, twelfth floor only and a little to the right of yesterday's building; the windows also were not full height, the building was older, but it was still a majestic view. Andy had a frisson of 'this would be mine' and that struck him as very strange; only on the official opening of the Molloy factory had he ever had a similar sensation. But that was in open country outside of Boston. This was the centre of Tokyo, one of the world's great cities and Andy Molloy would have an office overlooking the Imperial Palace! He slapped himself mentally. Peter would never think like that — but did he really understand Peter?

How had he managed to get Watanabe organised? He was already there when Andy got to Peter's suite for breakfast that morning. Andy had seldom seen a less imposing man. He was in his thirties, very short, small even for a Japanese, jug-eared and bespectacled, a poorly cut little mop of hair, and slightly shabbily dressed, as if he were still expecting to grow into his suit. He'd clearly been there a little while, the remains of their tea had looked cold in their cups on the table. Andy's impression had changed when the man spoke. "I'm Riku Watanabe, Mr Molloy," he said, in an incongruous West Coast accent. "I used to get called Riki in college, but I think we should stick to formalities in the meetings, OK?" Andy was quite taken aback by the man's almost assertive disposition, but he nodded. "OK, so I'll stay Watanabe san outside of this room."

"Your accent? Excuse me for being curious."

"Mostly San Francisco, college and work for a few years."

Then Peter had explained some background. This was no mere interpreter. Watanabe worked in the Henderson network on a variety of projects. "My business card says interpreter. It's a useful way of being in the room for some very interesting meetings and it sounds like today could be just like that."

It struck Andy even more forcibly, when introductions were being made with the Nakamura people, what a clever front this was. He could almost feel the disdain for this unprepossessing little fellow, yet it had been clear to Andy, when he'd outlined the business positions of the two companies, what a sharp grasp the man had. Ozawa had plainly been a little disturbed when they'd met at reception at the Okura. "Is this necessary, Molloy san?" — not out of Watanabe's earshot.

"Peter thought it important so that you especially can concentrate fully on what's going on — and we would look unprofessional if we expected them to do all the translating." Ozawa's eyes had narrowed, and he had nodded slowly before a slight smile appeared on his lips. At least Andy's team understood how the game was being played. Watanabe had done an excellent job of appearing appropriately abject and humble to Ozawa but, once Ozawa had established, by a few judicious questions in the taxi — which he posed in Japanese, but Watanabe responded to in English — *nice one Riki, you're my man* — that Watanabe was no ordinary interpreter, he seemed to relax and made one final comment in English.

"You are, I think, a very intelligent young man, Watanabe san, too intelligent to remain an interpreter. And clever enough, I hope, to avoid Nakamura becoming suspicious of that."

"*Hai, hai,*" said Riki, smiling and nodding but checking that Andy had understood his response.

"*Hai,*" said Andy. "That's my first word. And I know it doesn't always mean yes."

"Then you'll do fine," said Watanabe — almost as a friend offering reassurance, not, for now, merely the humble servant.

But humble servant was the role he seemed to be playing to perfection in the meeting room. There had been a little irritation when an extra person had to be accommodated. Ozawa explained who Watanabe was to the Nakamura party and Watanabe whispered a translation simultaneously to Andy. The bonhomie was not interrupted for long. Nakamura took the armchair at one end of the table with Andy opposite with his back to the window. Ozawa was just to his left, with Endo on one low sofa opposite Inui and Abego. An upright chair had been found for Watanabe and placed a little behind and to the left of Andy. Kitagawa had a similar chair immediately to the left of Nakamura, who seemed to have recovered his effusiveness after appearing disturbed by Watanabe's introduction. He was cheery enough when he addressed Andy: "Nakamura san asks if you like Japan, Molloy san, now you are here so often?" was Kitagawa's translation.

"I very much like Japan," said Andy, smiling, "and I hope to be here a lot more often." There was good-natured laughter when they heard the translation.

"And maybe this time you will see a *basho*?"

"I should very much like to see that." Andy was nodding and smiling, and Nakamura hadn't needed to wait for the translation.

"Yes, yes," said Kitagawa, "Inui san has tickets for you." Inui was nodding vigorously and smiling. "You will go on Thursday, I believe." He spoke to Inui, who nodded again.

Andy was genuinely pleased. He would enjoy it very much, but the gesture said something about the expectations of the parties. Still, the invitation could always be withdrawn or, more likely in this culture, quietly neglected, just as dinner might be this evening if the day did not go well.

Andy was asked to talk about how he saw the future of the joint enterprise. After one false start — he was expecting Kitagawa to translate too much — he got into a pattern of keeping his thoughts very succinct. (Watanabe had whispered 'sentences, not paragraphs' after his first mini-speech.) He talked about global markets, in particular the China opportunity, he talked about expanding product ranges, and about learning from the strengths of Nakamura in quality performance and he stressed, too, how much he would continue to value an R&D presence in Tokyo, deliberately concealing his reservations about how much — or how little — he would expose the Molloy innovations to the questionable security of an Asian environment. He was well aware already of how many patents of his own had been surreptitiously copied or circumvented, not least by Nakamura.

He found a little irony in some of the comments and responses. China was difficult because they blocked you at every turn and, much worse, they were always trying to steal your secrets. Andy had responded with a nod and a deliberate non-smile.

The vision, however, seemed to elicit mostly positive responses and they moved on to the guarantees for the workforce after the merger (Watanabe would reassure Andy later that the consistent use of that word was appropriate — no one would doubt who owned the place, but all egos would be tenderly handled by this terminology). But this was the difficult question that Andy had prepared for.

"You and I, Nakamura san, have grown very successful businesses over many years," — pause for translation, nods and smiles all round — "we occupy market leading positions in our different hemispheres," — pause, nods and smiles — "we have never had to reduce our workforces because we have always been expecting to grow." — pause — "When growth is weak, at Molloy we still keep employing our people, because we value them as people and we value their skills," — nods and smiles — "but I always say to my people: I cannot guarantee your future. I believe that future is very bright, because we are good people, with good products in a good market, but I cannot guarantee your future, only you can guarantee your future." He'd felt quite pleased with his Churchillian oratory and it provoked a lot of discussion among the Japanese themselves, only Abego stayed calm and was eyeing him carefully and nodding slightly, as if he appreciated the bullshit, but wasn't fooled by it. Andy turned to Watanabe, who was following the Japanese discussion intently, which calmed when Nakamura raised his hands to quieten Endo and Inui.

As he spoke, Watanabe whispered, "The others are worried about security. He likes the picture you're describing."

"We are very impressed by your vision, Molloy san," began Kitagawa, "but we are concerned about the livelihoods of our faithful employees. They must, of course, be committed to the future of our joint enterprise and enthusiastic about its prospects if they are to continue to give their best efforts."

While Kitagawa spoke, Andy and Nakamura eyed each other like two sumo wrestlers; it was not yet time to move, they were just throwing salt in the air. Nakamura spoke again, eyes fixed on Andy — *What's this about, they don't make eye contact? But he is the first guy I've seen do it* — "I personally believe very strongly in your vision, and I will be willing it to succeed, but I will be an old retired gentleman with no financial concerns, as will be my colleagues in this room also." Now Andy realised why he'd directed sideways glances to Endo and Inui while he'd been speaking. "The commitment of Nakamura employees to fulfilling this vision would be greatly enhanced by firm guarantees about their future."

Andy had learned enough from Peter to remain quiet at this point. He had his stalling response ready if Nakamura didn't follow up after this pause. Andy felt emboldened by Watanabe's whispers to sit tight a little longer.

But Nakamura was good, he sat and waited. Andy smiled, now it was time for him to strut and throw salt. "I stand committed to my vision. I hope I may say to our vision, because that is something we must all share." He looked carefully at Endo and Inui, whose blank expressions indicated either true incomprehension or excellent poker skills. Nakamura, meanwhile, was smiling and nodding — *gotcha Jiro, you understand more than you pretend* — "But I can understand why your employees, your family, I think I have heard you call them, would be worried about these strange *gaijin* with their terrible reputation for ruthless behaviour." Jiro had nodded and smiled almost brazenly at Andy, while Endo and Inui paid excruciating attention to Kitagawa's translation. When he finished, all eyes were turned to Andy, who was ready for his Nichonage, take the opponent off balance with a throw across your leg. "I will work very closely with you, if we agree this merger is desirable for all parties, to provide satisfactory guarantees to all of your, or maybe then I should say to our valued employees about their futures and about the future of our joint company." *What's a satisfactory guarantee and what's a valued employee will all be in the small print, my friend, but this is how we move forward.*

Nakamura looked pleased before Kitagawa began. Endo and Inui hung on Kitagawa's every word. Abego looked carefully at Andy with a grudging admiration. Watanabe whispered, "Nice work, boss." And this strange little interjection, from a funny little man that he had just met, would stay with Andy for years as one of the most rewarding commentaries on anything he'd achieved.

But, for now, there was still business to be done, no resting on laurels, and the sumo analogy, like all analogies, proved itself inappropriate. Nakamura was still there, smiling. "So you will agree, Molloy san, to write guarantees of future employment into the contracts of all of our workforce?"

But Andy was ready. "We will obviously draw up the details of this commitment as part of our deal, Nakamura san. It will be a contractual guarantee to every one of the workforce who has a good appraisal record."

Nakamura and Abego were instantly smiling. Endo and Inui, when Kitagawa had completed his translation, looked very concerned and there was another outbreak of heated debate among the Japanese. "We are concerned about appraisal records, Molloy san. We do not view our employees this way. We work with everyone to ensure their performance is satisfactory."

"And that will continue to be the responsibility of our managers in each country. As I said, I wish to work with you on the details of the guarantees to make sure that the workforce feels secure and can continue to perform at a high level."

Watanabe whispered, "Kitagawa's translation isn't perfect. I assume you're just kicking this into the long grass." Andy's nod was imperceptible to all but Watanabe.

Nakamura was looking to Endo and Inui, who finally seemed satisfied with the statement. "We are particularly reassured to hear you talk of the local managers continuing to be responsible for the performance of the Nakamura business. Perhaps we should move on to the level of your offer?"

Andy felt comfortable he'd left enough wiggle room for when the contract details would have to be signed. It would be good to move on. "I have been advised by my bank that, in situations like this, which are admittedly rare, a premium of thirty-five to forty per cent above the current share price is necessary to secure a high level of uptake from the investors."

Nakamura was plainly ready for that. "Our bank is suggesting that, since your ambition is to gain enough shares to enable you to remove Nakamura from the stock exchange, you will need to offer more than fifty per cent."

"That will obviously affect the economics of the deal. It is less attractive at fifty per cent than it is at forty. When we have agreed the premium, we should also discuss how you could help us sell this deal to your principal shareholders." Nakamura was again nodding before Kitagawa finished. This was the formulation Ozawa had suggested to Andy to open the door for Nakamura to negotiate a side deal for himself as a sweetener and to encourage him to be less greedy about the premium. Andy had agreed it with Peter, just as they had agreed that it would not be discussed in front of Martha. It would be down to the lawyers to find a method to make these special payments of dubious legality.

Andy looked at Endo as he listened to the translation, but Endo had the best poker face in the room. If he came back with no questions, however, then he had spotted the opportunity being opened up for him and his sister.

"Those will be important discussions, Molloy san. I am pleased you have recognised that our best efforts will be required for you to gain the level of control you require." Now even Endo was nodding. "I thank you for the answers you have provided to us this morning. We must now discuss the situation amongst ourselves. I hope we shall have the opportunity to entertain you this evening."

"I very much hope so too, Nakamura san." It was surprisingly abrupt end to the discussion. Andy looked to Ozawa, who didn't turn to look at him but nodded slightly, nevertheless. They stood up and there were cheery pleasantries. Inui was deputed to take Andy on a tour of the office suite, Watanabe went with them to translate. The meeting room and its three executive offices faced the park, all with the wonderful view. On the other side of a long corridor, after a reception area, there was a large, open plan office with twenty or so admin personnel. Down a flight of stairs at the far end of the corridor, he was shown a larger meeting room with twenty chairs round the central table and extra seats around the wall, but Inui was more keen to talk about Thursday evening's *basho*. Molloy san was very fortunate to be in Tokyo this week, he would see two of the current *yokozunas*, the third was currently injured. Watanabe looked slyly impressed as he translated Andy's comments and expectations.

"Inui san says you are very knowledgeable about sumo. You know more than most Japanese." Andy was nodding and smiling, as much for what that said about the state of the relationship than any vanity about his knowledge.

"You really do know your shit though, boss," Watanabe muttered, as they climbed back up the stairs.

The four senior Japanese were still in the meeting room when they returned. Kitagawa had plainly been sent on an errand so the grown-ups could confer, but there were smiles when Andy re-entered.

"It is not much, you see, just a humble office suite." Nakamura was plainly expecting Watanabe to translate. "But it is very important to meet our major customers. So, we shall see you this evening at Mama san's?"

"I shall very much look forward to that, and to hearing your splendid tenor voice again."

"Oh, Elvis, you are too kind." There were smiles and laughter, but Andy felt oddly out of synch with it while he waited for Watanabe's translation. "You will be inviting Tania san to join us? Abego san is keen to know." Andy, having picked up the names, had guessed what the topic would be, and why there was more laughter.

"I will also, if I may, bring Claudia san. She is a colleague of mine who is visiting your factory today," — *let's risk it* — "and Abego san will be pleased to hear that she is even more beautiful than Tania san." Even Endo smiled when that got translated. Andy couldn't truly say that their attitude jarred with him, his own business had too few women in its senior ranks for him to feel superior, but the responses here seemed so much more outdatedly sexist that it was noteworthy, even if he wasn't going to actually disapprove. But he realised that he had probably just committed Claudia's thigh to an evening of close manual attention.

"Then she will be very welcome to join us."

***

"So, sensei, what's the verdict?" Andy asked as the taxi pulled away.

"We should perhaps sit down over sushi in my room and talk this through."

"OK, Watanabe san, will you join us please?" This was probably what Ozawa was trying to avoid, but Andy didn't want to give him the opportunity. He liked his new little friend.

"Sure," called Riki from the front seat, and Andy could tell from Ozawa's expression that he disapproved. *Ah, fuck him!*

Andy was beginning to enjoy these lunches, they were light and make talking easy, although he was looking forward to steak at the weekend, but this was the continuation of a business meeting and the food would not prove to be a diversion.

"You will have gathered from the last conversation that dinner is confirmed," said Ozawa

"Yeah, got that. So, they're still positive, but how did you two read the critical points of the meeting? How much wiggle room have I negotiated on guarantees? I mean, I am pretty confident about business prospects, but I don't want to feel I have to pay all of them for ever. I think I got some flexibility there, didn't I?"

"Watanabe san, how did you see it?" asked Ozawa with an air that he would explain it properly later when he was having the last word.

"Nakamura himself really doesn't care that much. It's the other two, Endo and Inui, who are keen to fix the guarantees. Two things will help you: your words left you enough flexibility for the later discussions, you did that well, appearing to commit but not actually doing so and it helped that Kitagawa's translation was a little imprecise; the second point, and I believe that came from you, sensei," — *well done Riki, it doesn't hurt to flatter the old boy* — "is the offer of private deals, even Endo san seemed to relax a little at that point. Didn't you say he's effectively looking after his sister's money?"

"That is quite correct, Watanabe san, that will give us some flexibility and will soften Endo san's response. I do believe Inui san is very committed to the security of the workforce, so you will have to underwrite some guarantees, but we can make sure the wording will not be too onerous. As Watanabe san said, your words have left you enough flexibility. My own feeling is that Inui has been placed there tactically to keep pressure on you, so to speak. You will find that when the deal as a whole appeals to Nakamura san, that Inui san's principled objections may diminish.

"Our larger problem, and this has become clear in my conversations with Abego sensei, is that Nakamura feels that the cash on the balance sheet is his."

That left a silence in the room.

"That's the two hundred million you were talking about?" asked Watanabe.

"Yes," said Andy. "He thinks that's all his?"

"I don't think he is as unrealistic as all that, but he certainly feels that a large part of it is his due."

"Where is Endo in this?"

"I talk to Abego sensei. He deals with Nakamura. I must ask you Molloy san, and I mean no disrespect to you Watanabe san, but are you sure you do not wish to confine these discussions to the two of us."

"Oh, forgive me sensei, I had not meant to intrude, may I make one small point before I leave you?"

"Of course you can, Riki," said Andy, and took out his room key in its folder and handed it to him. "But afterwards, could you hang on a little while in my room until Ozawa sensei and I are finished?"

"Sure, thank you," he said, taking the key. "The point I wanted to make is that the two hundred million is in the accounts, it is part of the value that the stock market sees in the share price, so anything Nakamura or, for that matter, Endo takes on the side, so to speak, has got to be taken off the overall valuation. But I expect that's a point that had already occurred to you." Ozawa was nodding but Andy was glad to have had it expressed so clearly. "You will then have to struggle with how you can make those payments legally and confidentially, because it will probably suit you to keep Nakamura's deal secret from Endo, they didn't look to me like best of friends." He then stood up and addressed some remarks in Japanese to Ozawa, bowing low as he did so. Ozawa's expression changed slowly from pained irritation to calm appreciation.

"So, are you saying that Abego is trying to stitch up a deal for Nakamura that cuts the sister out?"

"Watanabe san has respectfully asked to be excluded from this next stage of discussion, Molloy san. He realises how these belong to the conversation of the principal actors."

Watanabe was edging towards the door. "I'll see you when I see you."

"Yeah, order yourself some lunch and thanks a million."

Watanabe left them.

"He is a bright young man, but we do need security and we must be very careful who we trust."

"But he comes to us from the Henderson network. You know them, I think."

"That is true but, I repeat, we should be careful whom we trust. There is a case in point here. There will be no trust between Nakamura and Endo. We must rely on Abego san to manage that relationship. I shall work closely with him."

Then food arrived and they moved on to observations about the individuals. Andy left feeling that a deal was quite likely, but he had awkward feelings about what might be required to achieve it. When he got back to his suite, Watanabe was just finishing his lunch.

"Thanks for hanging on, Riki. I don't know that I had anything specific, I just wanted to get a different perspective on the proceedings."

Riki smiled cheekily. "Because you don't trust your lawyer?"

Andy could only smile back. "Are you saying I shouldn't trust my lawyer?"

"I might be saying that no one should ever trust their lawyer. I'm sure he'll get you a very good deal, he seems very smart, but so does Abego sensei and you have to be prepared for them to be finding something in it for themselves. It's funny, these cash hoards are common in Japanese companies, but they're seen as something different from normal company assets by the executives of the business, and by their lawyers. But the institutions who will have to sell their shares will know the money's there. That won't stop Nakamura trying to grab as much as he can, but you may need to make the point about the amount of cash being well known to keep his greedier instincts in check."

"Riki, you've been a huge help. I want to keep in touch with you on this as the situation develops. Is that OK?"

"Of course it's OK. Peter had asked me to do that anyway."

"Is this your normal line of business?"

"We don't really do anything normal."

Andy smiled. "And I think you're telling me not to ask any more."

Riki smiled back. "Nobody said you were stupid, boss." Andy laughed. "Yes, please call me whenever you need to. It looks like a deal that could go through if you want it. I just want to make sure you pay only a fair price. Just don't expect to feel clean at the end of the process."

20

Claudia sat back in the car and tried to focus. Tania had commented at breakfast on how distracted she seemed but had the sensitivity not to enquire further. She had two strange evenings ahead of her and, sometime, she had to work out what to do about Jack. That could wait until the weekend, she knew, but it kept pushing its way to the front of her mind. Yet today was what she was here for, why she'd flown six thousand miles — then she had a moment just like she and Martha had discussed the previous evening, here was wee Claudia Brodie, being ferried through Tokyo in the back of a large black Mercedes, preparing to formulate her critical thoughts on a half-billion dollar acquisition!

"I know I've got a lot on my mind, I'm sorry, but I need to get very focused on today now. Can you help by going through what I should expect to see and what I should look for? I'm probably going to be in New York in two weeks. Sandy Nicholls thinks he's got two or three people we should see, and we can catch up on all your stuff if you can make your diary fit."

"Only if you promise we can have a girlie night out and I can learn more about your mysterious love life."

"Ha, if only." Claudia looked distractedly out of the car into the windows of offices that seemed to be almost touched by the barriers of the high-level expressway running past them. "We'll get an evening out together but I think you have more to report on in the love life area. How were the boys yesterday evening?"

"They were boys."

"Too young? Now I'm not going to have to warn you about forty-year-old men, am I? You told me you were utterly opposed."

"I am, I am and this is an important day, I know, so…" and Tania gave as detailed a description as she could of the Nakamura facility and how it compared to Molloy. She tried to explain the *nemawashi* process, where managers were expected to consult widely before making changes and how that had similarities with how the programme functioned in the businesses they worked with in the West. "But it's more institutionalised here, it's very healthy, really, I think. I wrote a paper on it in my student year here. I even gave a copy to my dad when I was nagging him to make changes at Giddings before you came along."

Claudia made a mental note to pursue that in some detail if she could, then pulled a notepad out of her bag — *should have done this before* — and began to list the aspects she would want to pay close attention to. By the time the car drove through the factory gates she had a full page of prompts and the one-hour journey had passed very quickly. The driver pulled up by the main entrance, Tania had a brief conversation with him. "He'll just wait. I've said I didn't know how long we'd be. I thought two o'clock might be a good guess."

"Four hours, well, who knows."

"Oh, and I'm Edwards san, that was our story before, and they know I speak a very small amount of Japanese but think I can't hold a conversation. I just hope we have a guide who speaks better English."

Claudia was glad to have been warned, the woman on reception rushed round to greet them, bowing low and smiling. "*Konichi wah*, Edwards san, *issho ni kite kudasai. Shibara kuomachi kudasai.*" They were led to a room and sat down, Tania appeared quite at home. "I think I'm allowed to understand 'please follow me' and 'please wait a moment', but I'll stop at that."

They had two guides, one plainly knew Tania from the previous visit and another whose English was very good. He was wearing a suit and tie, not the grey factory uniform, and he explained that he was not an employee, but he'd been brought in to provide support, even though Haraguchi san's English was almost perfect. Claudia hadn't known whether the irony was intended but Haraguchi san, the official guide, appeared not even to understand how the interpreter had just described his capabilities. At least Haraguchi san soon lapsed into speaking only Japanese. His attempts to speak English had left Claudia feeling thoroughly confused and, after having to repeat each question initially, Haraguchi had discreetly deferred to his assistant, as the interpreter had tactfully styled himself.

Claudia was fascinated by the place: so many similarities to Molloy in Boston; yet so many differences. Her questions, which were always couched in flattering terms — 'how do you achieve such consistently high quality levels?' — prompted increasingly detailed and enthusiastic responses from Haraguchi. When she asked how the *nemawashi* process worked, she felt she was almost being given a seminar, with the interpreter apparently adding his own take on how that functioned in Japanese industry in general. She was more cautious in her questions in the laboratories, not wishing to imply any sense that she suspected patent theft or illicit copying, but she at least gained the impression that there was a serious, independent development effort to keep the products ahead of competition. There was also a moderately reluctant acknowledgement that Molloy products were acquired, dissected, analysed — and admired — "How do you assess competitors' products, Haraguchi san?" she had asked. "Every business has to do that to stay ahead, doesn't it?"

She got them to explain every stage of the development, supply, manufacturing and logistics processes and tried to understand how the employees contributed at each stage and how they worked across departments. All the while, she was observing a pleasant hum of activity everywhere; when couples or small groups were talking, it always seemed to be around a screen or sheets of data, nothing looked like idle gossip — unlike many of the Western businesses she knew. She would have liked a conversation with HR to understand how groups worked and what incentive and motivation plans existed. Haraguchi's responses did not seem particularly well informed, but any exposure to more employees, and certainly to managers, would have risked blowing their cover. She was an advisor to a potential American distributor and Haraguchi had shown no apparent curiosity about that. Although, after three hours, he was beginning to flag and would probably have been very grateful to have passed them on to someone else — Tania had also put questions quite frequently, which had added to the strain he was beginning to show.

She asked at length whether they could have some lunch. Haraguchi had not planned for that, he said, or he would have ordered bento boxes to be delivered to the management suite. She was at pains to tell him that it was important to her to see the whole company, so the works cafeteria would be perfect. His embarrassment seemed to be moderated, but not eliminated. There were a few stares as they queued to make their choices but most of the diners seemed to be trying to remain politely indifferent, but two *gaijin* ladies must be a rare sight on the premises, or even in the community this far from the centre of the city. Claudia had tried to dress down a little to be appropriate to the day, after all, she wasn't meeting Martha, but she was still aware of standing out.

Finding four seats at the end of a long bench, she was able to ask more general questions that Haraguchi was happy to hand on to the interpreter. He was a lecturer in a local college and was able to talk a little more widely about business in Japan. Claudia felt relieved that, out of either politeness or a lack of curiosity, he was not asking any questions about them or their purpose in being there. In his view Nakamura was a very good company, they had a very good reputation locally, and his college saw many of the employees on day-release courses that Nakamura encouraged and supported financially. *Well, I guess you aren't exactly independent then, but it's a very encouraging point.*

Somehow, Claudia had targeted a two p.m. departure after Tania's communication to the driver and they were quite close to that as they were finishing lunch. She still had many questions but was sure she had extracted all she could out of poor Haraguchi, whose impressive impassivity was distorted by a limp smile when she explained that their visit was almost at an end. "Perhaps if we could have a brief tour of the management suite, Haraguchi san, and then we can get out of your hair."

Now even the interpreter looked troubled. "Excuse me, what is 'get out of your hair'?"

The women laughed politely. "Oh, I'm terribly sorry, we've been doing so well at avoiding those silly phrases. Or rather, you've been doing such a brilliant job at translating everything we've thrown at you. It means to get out of your way; to leave you in peace; we have taken a lot of your time and we are very grateful to both of you." The men were smiling, the torture was about to end. "You have both been extremely helpful, I really can't thank you enough." Now they were nodding as well as smiling.

The tour upstairs was brief and cursory: a few offices, with a chance to look into the empty ones; a large meeting room; a smaller boardroom; but nothing lavish anywhere, all quite modest, similar in its way to Molloy's high-tech minimalism and a world away from the Giddings' VPs' luxurious suites. They were soon outside in the car, waving goodbye to the deeply bowing pair, who had been joined by the lady from reception, completing the farewell party.

"I think we got as much as we could out of that. I think they were dead on their feet by the end."

"I saw three times as much today as I did with Andy, but where do you get the stamina? Where's your jetlag?"

"Oh, it's very much there. If I snore on the return journey, don't you dare wake me. I have a text from Andy asking us to meet him at four. We should be in good time for that. We'll just tell it as we see it. I don't feel any need to co-ordinate our thoughts on this morning, a snooze is much more important."

"I'm cool with that."

And Claudia drifted off, remembering Jack's stories about being driven places so that he could catch up on sleep during the day — *Jack, I've done well to ignore you for a whole morning.*

They were pulling up in front of the Okura when Claudia woke up, just dozy enough to wonder where on earth she was.

Tania was already there when she got to Andy's suite on time. "I just wanted to touch base briefly to make sure nothing was going wrong before we all meet for the evening. We'll have a chance to go over it in more detail with Peter and Ozawa tomorrow morning. Ozawa should have more from his mysterious conversations by then. I've also asked my funny little interpreter to join us. That will get Ozawa pissed."

"Why?"

"Well, Peter got hold of him from the Henderson network. He's a very smart guy, kind of posing as an interpreter." Claudia felt some disquiet about the network's involvement yet again, it was feeling like a spider's web. "I just got the feeling that he was more on my side. I don't always know what game Ozawa is playing. Well, it should be mine but sometimes I think it's his own."

"Well, you can relax, we had a good day, I think." She turned to Tania, who nodded. "I'll want some time to put my thoughts together properly, but I think, given the massive difficulties of language and culture, you're probably going to find that the underlying philosophy and approach is quite similar. I'm feeling uncomfortable because I have experience of only one Japanese business, but I was pleasantly surprised by the similarities. Tania?"

"I agree. I saw a bit more when I had my year here but it's as close to Molloy as anything I've seen. That doesn't mean it's that close, though. My God, it would still be daunting, but what a challenge!"

"OK, thank you. We had a good meeting today, I think. At least, we're still on for dinner tonight, ladies. I think it's the place we went to before. I'm afraid I've offered your leg to replace Tania's — you have to sit next to the lawyer."

"Who do I get? Please not Endo san, at least Abego had some life."

"'Fraid he's a big admirer."

"Thanks," said Tania, with her mock teenage resentment.

"Will Peter have to be there? I know he doesn't want to be."

"No, he's catching up on other stuff anyway, but, as you heard, he's very firm that they should focus on me. We don't want to confuse them about who's making the decision. That isn't just me, of course, but that's the impression he wants us to give them. In fact, he says, we should virtually deny his existence."

"Can I just ask what the purpose of this evening is?"

"I think Tania understands that as well as anyone. Tania?"

"Well, it's meant to feel like a friendly get together — too friendly, if you're sat next to Abego — but you'll get a few sly questions when they think you've had enough sake. They want to cross check that we're all telling the same story — that's a good point Andy's just made, if they've got wind of Peter's role, they'll try to find out more about him — but mostly it's about checking that the spirit is right, that we could all kind of get on with each other. It sounds silly, I know, but throwing yourself into karaoke is quite important. Can you do Tina Turner?"

"Oh, I'm a mean Tina."

"Brilliant, we have all bases covered. But try not to fall for Abego san. I don't think you will: he's too short."

"He's probably too old, as well."

"Not for you, though," replied Tania, and the good-natured laughter seemed to bring the chat to a close.

"Reception, six-thirty, see you both then. And thanks very much guys, great work today."

***

Peter opened the door with a phone in his other hand. He gestured to the sofa while continuing his conversation, which he quickly brought to a close.

"I didn't know you spoke French," said Claudia.

"Only moderately, my German is better. When I started out, I had a rule that I wouldn't get involved in businesses where I didn't speak the language, but I've rather abandoned that in China already and here I'd be doing the same. You see before you a man of flexible principles. Now, what was so important?" He sounded concerned, rather than annoyed. "Did you have some worries about today?"

"No, it wasn't that, the visit went well, I think. I was quite impressed. I want a chance to put my thoughts together before tomorrow morning's meeting, but I think I'm going to be positive. No, there are a couple of different points." She hesitated.

"Go on."

"Andy said you got someone from the Henderson network involved."

"Yes, Watanabe, funny little chap, very bright, Andy liked him, I think." He waited, smiling slightly when she didn't speak. "You're concerned?"

"I thought you were beginning to have doubts about that organisation."

He nodded slowly. "That's true, but I have no others to fall back on here. It's also true that Ozawa is a Henderson contact, so I may be compounding my error." He seemed relaxed, nonetheless. "We just have to ask the right questions and then evaluate the responses. People seldom tell you a direct lie, but equally they almost never tell you the whole truth, and my sense in this place is that the scope for interpretation is even greater than elsewhere. Anyway, I'm pretty sure that Watanabe and Ozawa aren't in cahoots. Andy says there was quite a bit of friction. So, we get an additional perspective on Nakamura from that, but I think it will be Watanabe's perspective and not Rod Henderson's." He paused, looking at her. "I'm not solving your problem, am I?"

"Well, I didn't think you would, I appreciate you can't, not so simply, but I'm grateful for the background…"

"But?"

"But there is a way in which you might help, and you'd be doing Martha a big favour."

His smile broadened. "Tell me more. I'm always happy to oblige Martha."

***

Claudia had been extensively briefed for the evening by Tania, but she found the experience extraordinary nonetheless: the dark, quiet streets of the nondescript quarter, such a contrast to all the garish neon they had driven past; the apparent step back in time to where ladies wearing beautiful kimonos attended a man's every whim; the unexpectedly loud bonhomie of a small gathering of men, almost more boisterous than a group in the West; the strange incongruity of ladies singing, dancing and playing primitive medieval instruments. And then the simple obviousness of a man's hand on her leg. She simply placed her hand on his, lifted it and returned it to his own lap. She'd toyed with giving him a hard stare but guessed, from all she'd read, that he would never return eye contact anyway.

When he tried again, five courses and not a little sake later, she added a quiet but firm 'no!' to the removal of his hand.

The girl to her left, who'd been assiduously refilling her sake cup, spoke a little English but she was seldom needed as Abego was reasonably fluent. The head translator, sat between Andy and Nakamura at the head of the table, seemed to spend all his time helping Andy discuss sumo wrestling with Inui, further to her left. Nakamura himself, a raffish but slightly seedy-looking old rake, spent the evening focusing on Tania, sat between him and Endo. Even Endo seemed a little caught up in the increasingly noisy flirtatiousness of that corner, but more of his time was spent talking to Ozawa across the head of the little girl plying them with sake and bringing them food.

Abego spent the first four or five courses talking principally with typical male vanity about himself and his travels in Europe and America but as the evening turned mellow and the sake's effects became noticeable — and his hand had been returned for the second time to his lap — he began to turn the questions on her and asked her about her role in the merger and about the mysterious Peter Dickinson: what was his business? Was he here? She was glad to have worked out her dumb platitudes in advance and she slowly hid behind a mask of simpering femininity when his interrogation began to feel like a barrister's cross-examination. His third attempt with the hand as the karaoke equipment was being wheeled out — *weird* — almost felt like a 'no further questions gesture'. She felt relieved, but didn't allow his hand to linger any longer, and relaxed enough to respond to the offer of the microphone when asked to sing. That she was following Abego's stomach churning 'To All the Girls I've loved Before', delivered principally with his eyes very obviously on her, only increased her determination to give them her very best Tina. 'River Deep, Mountain High' and 'What's Love Got to Do with It?' got such rousing applause that she was forced to offer a third song. So she sang 'Simply the Best' with her eyes fixed on Nakamura and the old roué at least had the good grace to appear to lap it up. And she got 'Pretty Woman' from him when he was next up on the microphone — and he sang it astonishingly well. Andy and Tania got through their slots with lots of applause, Claudia looked round the men when Tania was singing, all attentive. Abego, especially, had clearly decided his attentions were better directed there. When the party broke up a little later, he moved swiftly to Tania's side and began an earnest-looking conversation. Claudia caught none of it as she found herself cornered by a smiling Nakamura and his translator. There was a little flirtatious flattery, but the old rogue moved smoothly on to questions about her role in Tokyo and how the Dickinson organisation worked. By now she felt confident enough to offer a sly smile with her bland responses and quite soon he was smiling and nodding, obviously recognising that little Claudia Brodie wasn't so easily tripped up — *little? You're as tall as he is, good idea to wear no heels.*

The farewell party, soon convening outside, seemed to be waving very cheerily as their car pulled away. "Nice work, guys. What did you think, sensei?"

"That was a very successful evening. You made a very big impression on my colleague Abego, Claudia san."

"Well, he was trying to make a very big impression on me, but I quickly took his hand away."

Ozawa chortled. "But the Nakamura people are getting slowly more comfortable with you all. We must see what tomorrow brings."

She texted Jack when she got to bed.

I think there may be something in your worries about Henderson. C

But she was glad in the morning that she'd pressed Delete and not Send. After all, what was the real message there? She needed more proof. Shit, had she really been just reaching out?

21

They had planned to meet at eleven, Ozawa wanted time to have some conversations, he said.

That suited Claudia, she wanted to make notes on yesterday's visit and spend a little time with Tania reviewing their US activities. There were five clients already and some prospects on the West Coast. She'd debated with Sandy about whether they should travel to San Francisco for the recruitment, but he felt the search could be managed from his New York office and he'd assured her he had one very promising candidate who wanted to move back west anyway. It would have felt churlish to point out that Sandy had only a New York office, which he shared with another Dickinson business, and Tania when she needed a desk, and he might be arranging things for his own best convenience.

When they reviewed what they had and how their pipeline looked, Claudia realised she'd be looking for two new people anyway. Tania was working immensely hard but having to admit that she wasn't covering everything satisfactorily. All the clients were very positive about her, Claudia got that feedback consistently, but they all wanted more of her time — and when they went through the projects and planned activities, the Brodie bottleneck became even more obvious. "We need to build you a team, woman."

"Uh, oh, this is getting serious." Tania looked mischievous.

"What do you mean?"

"I'm normally just 'girl' when you talk to me like this." Claudia chuckled, that was true, and she could feel her attitude changing and her respect growing. And Tania's timeline might be only two or three years. Building a team was looking urgent. It put more pressure on the New York trip. Would she see Jack? — *Why the fuck, are you thinking about that?*

They went to Peter's suite at eleven. It was bigger than Andy's and seven people didn't feel uncomfortable. And, for all that Molloy was Andy's business and, for Nakamura, the acquisition would be his decision, this was Peter's meeting. He sat them around the dining table, putting Will and Watanabe on either side of him — *Yes, he is a funny-looking little man.*

"I'm going to begin by apologising to Tania." She looked as surprised as Claudia felt. "We had a meeting at the bank yesterday from which you were excluded. I hope you understand that we needed to let Martha feel comfortable — she was a little surprised even that Claudia was there but that will prove to be very important when we meet them at four this afternoon. And the ladies seem to have struck up a very close relationship, I'm glad to say." He smiled at Claudia who felt herself almost blushing, trying not to think about the evening ahead. "The point is, Tania, that we're going to be discussing the very delicate issues relating to the possible deal. Ozawa sensei will come on to those later." He looked to Ozawa, who nodded slowly. "You will see that these are extremely confidential but I'm very happy to have you in this discussion. We think you're already making a big contribution and we trust you completely to express your honest views — and if I understand Claudia correctly, it's impossible to stop you." It was said warmly and everyone smiled. "But you're big enough to realise that these conversations are for this room only. I have to make the point to you too, Claudia, no indiscretions with your new bestie, Martha." Maybe there was a little wickedness in his smile, or was she merely imagining that? *This is serious business, girl, focus.*

"The first area I'd like to discuss is Claudia's impressions of the business you reviewed yesterday. I know you're uncomfortable about how little time you've had — and we get a chance to go into much more detail in due diligence if we pull the trigger. But we, the seven people in this room, have to decide today if we want to make an offer — and then sell the proposition to a reluctant bank this afternoon. Is that clear?"

With Peter the switch from charming urbanity to ruthless decisiveness was a smooth one — but a very clear one. It meant that the questioning she received as she went through her views and impressions was intense and detailed. She was never cajoled or bullied but points were summarised and concluded sometimes with a 'that's important, but we'll just accept that the view is an impression, not a hard fact, but it's the best knowledge we're going to get'.

When she wrapped up, he said, "I'm amazed you got so much out of a four-hour visit but then, with you, I often am, thank you so much. Whatever we decide, I promise you your trip has been worthwhile." With that, charming urbanity was back for just a moment with a wonderfully warm smile.

But now the focus was on Andy, who was pushed very hard to say why he thought he could make the relationships work. "I'm hearing you Andy, but unfortunately we're talking about people who won't be there when the deal is done." Andy began to object. "Wait! The fact is, they will retire, and if they don't want to, you will almost certainly want them to, and then you'll have to force them to, so we'll have to try and tie that down with the deal itself." He looked to Ozawa, who nodded again. "You'll need to get someone here to run it for you. You may find it useful to keep your new sumo buddy on, but it's not going to be him who'll run it, is it?" Andy shook his head. Claudia felt a little sorry for him. "You can't find out much more yourself, we'll get Ozawa sensei's views in a moment on the quality of the next level of management, but Watanabe san here has done a little digging for me and it's a relatively reassuring picture." Watanabe nodded,

Andy looked relieved, but may have been thinking 'asshole'. "So, with that in mind, and before we come to sensei, are you still enthusiastic?"

"Yes, I'm still very enthusiastic, but I am interested in your 'reassuring picture' and in anything Ozawa sensei has been able to pick up on management quality. If they're not that good, I wouldn't be quite so keen to buy them but, in that case, I'd worry less about them competing aggressively in the US in the future."

"Very good point. Now sensei, is there a deal to be had?"

Ozawa went, in his habitually long-winded way, through the attitude of all the Nakamura protagonists, including Abego, which struck Claudia as slightly strange, why would that matter? But it seemed there was enthusiasm for a deal at the right price and with satisfactory guarantees about future employment. Peter's ears pricked up. "How firm are these guarantees going to be? We can't get locked in to paying people for ever."

"Oh, please do not concern yourself, Dickinson san. Molloy san was very careful with his words in our meeting and we lawyers will be able to give you enough flexibility — so far as the laws of Japan permit."

Peter looked moderately appeased. "OK, now before we come on to the grubby business about money, could you tell us what you've been able to find out about the next level of managers?"

Ozawa seemed to confirm Watanabe's findings, in sales and in operations they had two slightly younger managers who were very well regarded. Neither Endo nor Inui had been pushing their own number twos, apparently, but even to Claudia, that looked like it could be a play for future employment by the two of them.

"OK, thank you very much, but now we get to the hard bit. Do you mind if I summarise where I think you've got to?" Nobody minded, of course. "You said thirty-five to forty per cent premium," he said, looking at Andy. "They want north of fifty to motivate enough people to sell." Andy nodded. "OK, you were planning fifty, anyway?" Andy nodded again. Peter smiled now. "But there's this crazy attitude in some quarters that the cash hoard somehow doesn't belong to the company and should be made available to the family. Is that right?"

"Ah, well, I think you are putting that a little boldly, Dickinson san," Ozawa said, responding much more quickly than usual. His interjection made, he could now slow to his usual pace. "That is an attitude, perhaps, but it is not an expectation."

Peter smiled slightly, Claudia thought she read a 'gotcha' in that. "Well, I have to say that we do have an expectation: the money is on the balance sheet; it belongs to the business; and it is a factor in the stock price. But we also have an attitude: we may show some flexibility about how we pay for the company, but you and they will have to help us on that."

"That will be a very helpful attitude, I think, thank you." Ozawa said, smiling smugly.

"So, what sort of number would align their expectations with our attitude?" Ozawa, normally so phlegmatic, looked uncomfortably around the room. "I assure you, sensei, I have complete trust in everybody in this room." It occurred to Claudia that he probably did not include Ozawa in that.

"It is very difficult to predict that with any precision. This will require delicate negotiations." Ozawa failing to come to the point again, thought Claudia.

"Perhaps I may simplify things a little." Peter was sounding patient and polite. "I think we have concluded that an absolute upper limit on this deal, given all the uncertainties and difficulties of making a success of it, is six hundred million dollars. Andy?"

"That's the number but, of course, that's this team's maximum number. It would be very disappointing if our negotiating skills did not enable us to acquire everything, cash included, for less than that."

"That might be a very onerous objective, Molloy san."

"It's not as onerous as trying to make a deal work when we've paid too much money. But let me ask you, what's the key feature in getting the big shareholders, the institutions, to accept a particular price? Getting a forty per cent uplift in the current environment would be seen as an attractive return, wouldn't it?"

"It would not be seen as quite as attractive as fifty per cent."

"But how would they decide if forty per cent was attractive enough?" Peter had taken over again, probably judging that Andy's patience was not up to the task. "Would that depend on their own financial analysis, or would it depend more on the attitude and recommendation of the head of the business?"

"Well, it would depend on both, of course."

"But the attitude of Nakamura san would play an important part in them accepting the deal?"

"Yes, a very important part, but one must not ignore the attitude of Endo san also. He will be critical in determining the response of Nakamura Keiko."

Peter looked very hard at Ozawa. "Is that it, sensei, are they the critical people in this? Or is there anyone else who must be considered?"

If there was any hesitation or embarrassment in Ozawa's next response, Claudia failed to detect it. "It is customary, in cases as delicate as these where a great deal of persuasive work needs to be done, to recognise the efforts of the lawyers."

"And that would, I assume, apply to the lawyers on both sides of the deal?"

"But of course, Dickinson san, there is a great deal of work that goes into preparing the case for persuasion."

"I do accept that, sensei, but I suspect you would feel more comfortable discussing the details of that, both the nature of the persuasion and the level of compensation, with me alone, am I right?"

"Of course, that would feel more appropriate."

"Then you and I will sit together after this meeting. But the bigger question is how do we encourage the family to support our bid? Between forty per cent premium and fifty per cent premium, there is a gap of forty million dollars. The current fifteen per cent of the Nakamura family is worth sixty million dollars at today's share price. Is it evenly split?" Ozawa nodded. "So currently worth thirty million each. They gain twelve million dollars from the forty per cent uplift. If we add half as much again, do you think that would enable them to recommend the deal?"

"I suspect that Nakamura Jiro might feel that his role would be much more important than his sister's or Endo san's, and the sum you mention would not be enough to change his attitude."

Peter nodded quietly. "Ladies, this is what we will definitely not be discussing at the bank later today. I am going to call this 'business', we are merely encouraging some key players to help sell the deal to important shareholders and will recognise their efforts. Martha Weddle will have a different term for this and will call me some very bad names when she finds out how we have made this work. She will find out eventually, but if we are careful, it will be too late by then."

"I am also not sure that a bare forty per cent will be enough." Ozawa had a quietly forceful way of expressing his doubts.

Peter looked thoughtful. "I think the principles are clear, though, yes?" Ozawa nodded. "And our financial limits are also clear, yes?" again a nod. "Then I think you have some delicate conversations ahead of you in the next couple of days. You and I will also give some thought in a moment to how these payments are made. For the rest of you, and only for the rest of you, my first thought is that we will repatriate some of the cash hoard into the Group and channel it to the family through different vehicles offshore. Will?" Will nodded. "I emphasise that will all be absolutely legal in the jurisdictions we choose, but it is also likely to remain discreet and tax efficient. If the recipients experience any difficulties in repatriating the money should they wish to, that will be an issue for them. Sensei?"

"That would be both imaginative and very welcome, Dickinson san, in spite of the potential difficulties, as you say, of repatriation."

Peter smiled. "I suspect you would also prefer us to manage most of the legal fees in a similar manner."

"Very thoughtful, and also very welcome."

"OK, unless anyone has any objections, that's the case we're taking to the bank. I'll handle the outline, Claudia and Andy, you should expect a grilling from Martha, and I will need her on board to help with the financing. So, do your best." They both nodded.

"Sensei, I have the impression that it may be politic for you not to attend. There is a risk that there could be delicate questions that are no business of the bank's and we should not put you in an embarrassing position."

"I think you make a very wise point," Ozawa's features never moved much but Claudia was fairly sure she could detect smugness.

"OK, guys, sensei and I have some things to discuss, so I'll see you all at the bank at four."

***

If Peter's questions had been probing, Martha's were also relentless, so the bank meeting was an intense affair. Any thought that a new 'bestie' might give her an easy ride were almost instantly dispelled, there was no opportunity to conclude even the prepared remarks before the questions began. And they were very good questions but Claudia didn't make the mistake, she didn't think, of offering too firm or positive an assessment where she didn't have genuine conviction or relevant information, but they had been talking intensely for nearly an hour before Martha said, "I guess you're never going to make me feel comfortable, but I do appreciate the honesty with which you've presented your views. I know there's a whole host of things where we just won't be able to know." She turned to Peter, smiling. "If anything stinks, we'll find it in due diligence, but if we get that far, that's a huge commitment for us — and a huge cost for you, of course. I just wish I felt a bit better about this right now."

"Forgive me, but is it ungentlemanly to point out that similar things were said about the China deals?"

"Yes and no," she said, narrowing her eyes at him, "and gentlemanly, as you know, you charming bastard, is utterly irrelevant. Different reasons were given but the level of discomfort, I grant you, was similar — and in those cases you were keeping the business heads; here you're kicking them out, or you should be. Now, let's get on to your sweeteners. I assume Ozawa sensei is not here because he is conducting delicate negotiations?" Her scepticism was as palpable as her sarcasm.

"Absolutely right, we're in a hurry to get an agreement in principle while we're all here this week."

"And it has nothing to do with your reluctance to expose him to the bank's scrutiny this afternoon."

"Absolutely not!" said Peter. Claudia wondered if both parties know an outrageous lie is being told, is that so bad? This looked like a dance of scorpions.

But Martha was not glossing over it quite so simply, "So what sort of side deals is he empowered to discuss?"

"Well, there will be bonuses for important players when the businesses are successfully integrated, and we may retain Nakamura as a figurehead chairman of the business in Japan to help continuity with the customer base and that would need to be recognised financially. We'll see what Ozawa sensei comes back with."

This was dissembling, and Claudia wondered how much of it Martha saw through. Quite a lot, she guessed, but that wouldn't be a topic they could discuss later.

"Well, summing up, Yoshi, any thoughts?"

"I share your reservations, Weddle san. The financials look good, the difficulties look huge."

"Thank you, that's a very good summary, it also describes my position but, because we have due diligence if you get your offer accepted, we'll agree in principle to support you through the next phase. Yoshi and Will can work out a schedule of funding, OK guys?" They both nodded.

"Well, thank you everyone, I guess we've gone as far as we can." There was a large collective exhaling of relief.

"And thank you Martha, and Yoshi san," said Peter, "I know these meetings are tough, but they are necessary to get our thinking straight. Well done, everybody."

People stood up and began mingling. Claudia had a mother hen concern for Tania at the back of her mind, but her preoccupation now was with her Martha meeting and the evening ahead.

"I'm meeting with Martha now, Peter," she said, when the three of them were close together.

He smiled, and looked straight at Martha. "Then I shall just say see you later." Martha smiled and her eyes lit up. "Good luck with your meeting," he said, and he left them.

Claudia leant back on the sofa in Martha's office, finally beginning to relax.

"I thought you did very well. Was I too hard on you?"

"No, they were tough questions that needed answering. I just hope I made clear when I thought I couldn't give accurate answers, or any answers in some cases," Claudia said, and she chuckled to herself.

"Oh, you did that so well. I wish everyone were like you. It makes it so much easier to accept an opinion when you know you haven't been bullshitted." Now she chuckled. "Or you think you know you haven't been. Maybe you're just more brilliant at that than the others." They smiled at each other. "No, I really don't think it's that. Anyway, enough of Nakamura. You've got Peter coming, well done you! I'm quite excited about this now. How did he take it?"

"Well, that was a little strange, because when we talked it through, he'd heard of Smarts, and he thought it unlikely they would be the source of the problem, but he was going to find out more about them. The key question for him is whether Henderson is making up a story or Jack has been naughty elsewhere. So, there wasn't a real need, in his mind, to visit Smarts to prove a point but by then he was keen on the idea anyway."

"Well, I'm intrigued, and quite excited. Are you still up for it? You looked a little dubious."

Now that she was relaxing, it was easier for Claudia to say, "Fuck it. I haven't had fun in a long time."

"Wonderful. We'll need costumes to get in. There's a sex shop in Roppongi, and the upper floor is full of fetish gear, I'm told it's quite classy. Shall we go there when we're finished here?"

"Well, that'll be fun. I've always bought all my toys and things online. It'll be a first for me go inside an actual sex shop."

"Good, that's our next stop. But what about Collins?"

"What have I told you, officially?"

"Officially? Nothing."

"Can we stay unofficial for a while? There's a little more I'd like to say."

"It's all a bonus for me. You don't have to say any more at all."

"I feel I'd like to. It helps me to talk. Is that all right?"

"Of course. We just have to be clear with each other about this boundary. It makes friendship a little awkward, but you and I are worth it. Come on, give me a hug!"

And it didn't feel quite so strange as she thought it would, two women standing in a full height window of a bank headquarters, having a hug. It actually felt good. They sat down again. "I mean, you've probably heard things today in your preparatory meeting on Nakamura that I would be more interested in. I obviously take everything with a major pinch of salt, just to reassure you. There are games that Peter and I have to play with each other, and I am absolutely not expecting to see an expression on your face that I will in any way react to."

Claudia was relieved but she felt she'd managed to remain completely impassive.

"So, Collins, what do you want to say off the record?"

"Peter will be talking to Henderson, I think, and he'll let me know where he gets to. I'd rather just leave it with him. If there is a problem, it's a problem potentially for Peter, too, as well as for Collins. Can we leave it there?"

"Of course we can. We have a night out to prepare for!"

22

"Come in, I won't keep you a moment. Are you cold?"

"Peter, you are an imaginative man. This coat is staying on until we're inside the club."

He guffawed. "Well, if you'll forgive the observation, I'm sure it will be worth the wait. And Martha?"

"I'm pretty sure she'll be wearing a coat, too, but I didn't think this was a wardrobe check."

"No, please sit down. I wanted to put your mind at rest about something. Well, it may not put your mind at rest at all. It may make things more turbulent."

"Are we talking Jack? Are we talking Henderson?"

"Certainly the latter. I will leave the former up to you."

"What have you got?"

"When we were discussing lawyers' fees this afternoon, you may remember I told Ozawa I would want to talk to him on his own. He has work to do on the deal and I don't know how he and his kind stay out of jail, but that's by the by. I also told him I want more on the Henderson operation and that would affect his fee."

"Yes, I wondered what you were pushing for."

"He came to me via Henderson. I told him I needed to know how clean my operations were in Asia. I didn't ask for any specific cases, but I did say I had to know if there were any practices that would embarrass me if they came to light and that I would react by issuing stronger guidelines for any work done on my behalf. Well, he was quite brazen. In telling you what I am about to tell you, I can't swear you to secrecy exactly, because that might stop you acting in a situation that's very important to you, but I am trusting your discretion and your judgement. OK?" She nodded. "The practice of hacking is obviously very modern, and that, apparently, forms a part of Henderson's business practices. I suppose I'd guessed that but it's useful to have it confirmed. But here in Japan, nobody seems to bat an eyelid. There's a long tradition of opening mail, it goes back to shogun times, it's seen as a necessary element of control, and that moved smoothly on to the corruption of the postal service, which still goes on to this day — that surprised me, but there we are. I didn't press him on his research on the current deal, or I might find myself becoming squeamish. As I said, I am a man of flexible principles. But the reason that Ozawa and the other lawyer think they can moderate the family demands is that they hold information that should be completely confidential. But the family is aware that they would be prepared to use it in quite damaging ways. Anyway, if that is the norm here, I am not going to be the principled martyr, I just want deniability. But

I will set more stringent limits on Henderson, and I will tell him I'm on his case as far as Collins is concerned."

"But what if Martha's wrong?"

"About Jack, or about Smarts?"

"Either?"

"Well, she won't know about Jack because she won't know where else he's been, but I will probably find that out from Henderson, and I suspect you will know from Jack himself when you discuss it with him. As far as Smarts is concerned, as I told you, I've never been but I had heard about it. I do know more about it than I did yesterday, and I'm assured it's clean."

"So, we really don't need to go, is that what you're saying?"

"We don't need to go for the reasons that concerned you but, having been given the offer of escorting two of my favourite ladies to an establishment like that, I'm afraid there's no way I'm going to turn down the chance." The smile, this time, was definitely wicked.

Peter organised the transport. It would have been ungallant, he said, to expect that from Martha, and her usual driver might have drawn conclusions. The club was on the tenth floor of a building that wasn't too far from their hotel, but they'd made a round trip to pick up Martha, who giggled conspiratorially when she slid into the back seat next to Claudia.

A figure clad entirely in black, full head mask included, allowed them through the shiny black door with the small grille at eye level. Smarts was on a discreet plaque on the wall, only visible if you were searching.

"I'm delighted you've gone to all that trouble, you both look spectacular," Peter said when they removed their coats and handed them to the ninja gatekeeper.

"So how did you avoid the dress code?"

"It helps that I'm bringing you two beautiful, exotic creatures, but, if you didn't catch my sleight of hand just then, a hundred thousand yen and a business card is what swings it."

Claudia was shocked. "Aren't you worried someone will use it to contact you?"

"Not really, it was one of Henderson's." Martha guffawed. Claudia felt, once again, that Peter was confirming his doubts about him, and hers had solidified but, looking around, it seemed a silly time to concern herself with that. They now had to confront the party, and, ridiculous as she felt with the suspenders and, effectively, a bare arse beneath a small, black lace tutu, she realised, even from the first few bodies sauntering across the hallway, that she was quite demurely dressed.

The reception hall led to a large inner hall with four well-spaced large square red leather pouffes, three of which were occupied by groups of three or four people, mostly Japanese, as far as she could tell. Half were wearing masks, she slipped hers on and Martha followed. Little was happening beyond conversations but through the open double doors leading off she could see a number of wild activities and, from the uncoordinated cacophony, different music was playing in each of the three rooms.

"Well, you've brought me here ladies, very much against my better judgement, for nefarious purposes of your own. You are very well aware that no good deed goes unpunished, so we should deal with that first. Claudia, on the back wall, next to the large doorway, there is a rack of paddles and canes. I will not be too severe with either of you, I shall think of it as an *amuse-bouche* in order to stimulate your appetites for whatever enjoyments you have foreseen for yourselves later. But you will bring me a heavy leather paddle." Claudia felt a little perplexed, Martha had a knowing smile. "No point in smiling, Martha, I will simply be warming up on Claudia. Then, after your punishment, I am minded to look for a particularly muscular dom and pair you up with him later for my own enjoyment — and, only peripherally, for yours. I assume a male dom is to your tastes?" Martha now nodded and looked mildly enraptured. *This is Peter reading people?* Claudia walked to the rack. *Do I want this? I'm here, I'm free, I'm not vanilla any more.* She picked a long, stiff paddle from the rack and slapped her hand with it. *That will sting nicely — especially for Martha after all those questions!* She walked demurely back to Peter and handed it to him.

"Martha, you will stand with your back to that wall and observe closely!" He sat on the edge of the pouffe. "Claudia, you have been naughty enough times before.

You know what you must do. Place yourself across my knee and place your hands on the floor." *This is crazy, I actually want to do this, I've missed it.*

But she yelped loudly when the first blow cracked square across the middle of her bottom — *Christ, have I really missed it? Yes, I have. I spend all my time organising everything for everybody. Give me just a few minutes of being Peter's naughty girl. Let him take control of me! Just for a while!* After ten she realised how much she had missed it, as that familiar warm glow flooded though her, together with the sense of being under someone's power. Peter leaned down towards her and whispered, "As I suspected, your beautiful arse is gathering its admirers." She tensed and felt herself blushing, he leaned down to her again. "Give yourself to it my dear, bottom a little higher or I will remove your thong and spank you harder. Now count, the next is eleven." She relaxed and then wiggled to show herself off a little more. The next ten were harder anyway. Turning her head to look under her outstretched arm, she could see a gathering of legs of couples behind her. "Eighteen, ow." Peter was slowing down — *Christ, this is a voluptuous feeling*—. "Nineteen, ow, ow, ow." Then there was a long pause and the gentle caress of his hand on her cheeks — *he's never done that before*—. "Twenty — Christ!"

"Well, done, my dear, splendid, now be careful what you invite me to next time." She rose gingerly and there were appreciative noises from the couples, most of whom then mooched off to a side room. "Go and stand next to Martha." She obeyed. "Martha, come here!" Martha walked forward, head bowed. "Martha, you will undoubtedly be caned this evening." She remained motionless. "Do you understand?" She nodded. "Either you place yourself across my knee now and accept the paddle or you go to the wall and bring me a cane. In the former case, after your first punishment, I shall select, as I said, both the cane and your dom — and I shall choose someone whom I observe to be dealing severely with particularly naughty people. You have ten seconds to make your choice." He seemed to Claudia to allow her much longer than that, perhaps it was just the drama of the situation that was slowing time, like looking at a watch and being astonished at how slowly that first second ticks by, but Martha was undoubtedly hovering indecisively. Finally, Peter grabbed her arm quite roughly and pulled her across his lap.

Claudia had been surprised when Martha had taken off her coat, the full-body figure hugger with multiple zips had not been what she'd bought, she must have had it with her anyway — *well, maybe what she bought was a little too much like mine, that wouldn't have looked good — or maybe she just wanted to encourage me to buy* — Peter deftly unzipped the seam that ran up her left thigh, across her lower back, and down the right, rapidly exposing her well-rounded buttocks — *yes, a little bit large, did Jack like that?*

"You will count for me, Martha, up to twenty-five."

"But she only…" He slashed sharply at her, almost unseemly for him, but then she quietly laughed at herself for thinking such an absurd thought; he would have chosen the force very deliberately. Martha cried loudly, her bottom was colouring quickly.

"Twenty-five!"

"Yes, sir," she muttered meekly — *did she used to call Jack 'sir'?* —The couple who'd stayed, he, large with a muscled bare torso and a full head mask, she, petite in a white shirt, a very short tartan skirt and white, knee-length socks, turned to each other and nodded. Claudia's gaze moved between them, holding hands in rapt attention, and Martha's arse, reddening deeply as the strokes fell. She was counting but only emitting an occasional 'ow' to blows that seemed to Claudia to be very heavy.

After twenty-five, Peter caressed her gently and slowly zipped her. "You may stand, Martha, you are very red but otherwise unmarked, perfectly primed for the man I shall later select for you." He helped her to her feet. She had stayed very stoical, but it had plainly made moving difficult. She walked gingerly towards Claudia who opened her arms to greet her.

She watched Peter begin to rise but the spectator couple stood in front of him. The man addressed him. "Sir, this is one bad young lady." Claudia could barely make out what he was saying with the music coming from the different rooms, but she picked up an

American accent, which explained the large body and the paler skin. "I wonder if you would oblige me by applying some discipline."

Peter, for the first time in Claudia's experience, looked slightly nonplussed but quickly recovered his composure. "Of course, my good man. Tell me, has she been very naughty?"

The guy looked at his evidently Japanese girlfriend, her face was masked but her limbs had an Asian set and her skin was pleasantly olive-coloured. "Yes sir, she's been very, very naughty."

Peter looked directly at her, as if he were trying to look into the eyes behind the mask. "Have you been a very bad girl?" he spoke slowly. It was intensely arousing, thought Claudia, but also very easy for her to understand if her English were poor. The girl nodded vigorously. "Then I must be very severe with you, mustn't I?" Again, the vigorous nod. "I will ask my assistant to bring me a cane."

Her head spun to look up at her partner, Claudia assumed she was alarmed, perhaps expecting only the paddle. He merely nodded to her. She looked to Peter again and nodded. He looked up at the tall American. "There are four canes on the rack. Bring me the thickest!" Claudia heard the sharp intake of breath from the girl. "You have been a bad girl. This will not be easy." And there was both menace and solace in his voice, and Claudia, even with her arse still on fire, became aware of the growing heat between her legs.

The man returned with a thick, black-handled cane. Peter took the cane almost ceremoniously, nodded and then looked to the girl. "You must, of course, be bare-bottomed. Lie across my knee, then I shall ask my assistant to remove your panties." She turned to him briefly but then quickly settled down on Peter's lap. It made a sharp contrast to Martha's more bulky profile. "Assistant," he spoke quite loudly. Three couples had gathered around. "Remove these panties!" Claudia saw the girl squirm before her partner had even hooked his fingers into her pants. Claudia knew those twitches of anticipation. He pulled them off quickly and Claudia was quite surprised by the pert roundness of the perfect cheeks, she had expected a more shapeless, saddle-bagged flatness. She found herself moving to her left to have a view more from behind. She checked herself momentarily but found herself nudged further by Martha. She could move no further without her view being obstructed by the male.

"You must take thirty strokes," intoned Peter, casting a subtle glance to the American who nodded slightly. There was a simpering noise from the girl, but Peter's first blow landed with a startling crack. The girl shrieked, Peter looked up to the man, who nodded and smiled grimly. Peter waited, Claudia saw the livid line change colour and she began to worry for the girl, but Peter continued with long pauses between the strokes but no change in their intensity. The girl's mewling howls stayed equally constant. The only changes being the intense and increasing discolouration of her buttocks and the increase in the number of spectators the spectacle was attracting.

After twenty Claudia began to relax and her fears for the girl subsided. She turned to Martha who was transfixed in concentration. When Peter called "Thirty" it was as if a spell was somehow broken for her. She turned to Claudia. "Wow, I'm sorry, my God, I did enjoy that. Are you getting wet?"

Claudia was slightly startled by the question but had the honesty to nod slightly.

The man helped his girlfriend up. She hugged him and seemed to be weeping. Peter sat impassively with the cane across his lap. After a few moments the girl detached herself, turned to Peter, bowed, and seemed to say, 'thank you'. Peter, still sitting, gave a small bow in acknowledgement. The girl returned to the embrace of her partner.

"Young man," said Peter imperiously, "you should return this," and handed him the cane. He stood up and stepped towards his ladies. He waved the large, black disc that had been draped around his neck by the ninja on arrival. "This is free champagne, my dears. I, at least, have earned it." He put his arms around their shoulders. "I believe it's this way."

They walked through the door on the right of the main area. It was a long room. Claudia dubbed it instantly the fucking room — that seemed to be the principal activity of the non-spectators — and the music was quieter, she assumed because there were no screams to muffle, although one woman was howling in a loud orgasm at the far end that almost drowned the music. They turned right towards the bar area. There were a few small tables, most occupied, with black stools around them. Peter gestured to them to sit at one. They giggled at each other as they had to sit down gingerly, looking towards the longer half of the room. There were three large sofas, occupied but only with active twos and threesomes. In one far corner where the noise had come from there was a large curved metal pole with ropes dangling from it. The orgasm woman remained suspended by her limbs and was made fully available to anyone who wanted to penetrate her or lick her. It had been the latter that had led to her screaming, but she was now being serviced by a young man with well-rounded bouncing buttocks. In the other far corner was a table on which a rather tubby young woman had been strapped, leaving her arse and pussy available to all who cared, but few did, she attracted the odd desultory spectator who would then move on to stand behind a sofa on which a lithe young woman was being vigorously spit-roasted by two young men with a small queue of others standing by to replace them. "Is that for you later?" asked Martha cheekily, when she saw Claudia studying them. Claudia smiled but shook her head vigorously.

Peter returned with a bottle and three glasses — *Moet, thank fuck it's not Taittinger* — "And this is where you've never taken me in Singapore, Martha, that will be ten extra from your dom later!"

"I never knew you were a player, Peter."

"I'm afraid I'd guessed you might be." She looked a little startled although, with the mask over her eyes, it was hard to tell. "Is this similar?"

"Very, one room for fucking, one for gays, that must have been the one on the left earlier on, and one for discipline. Isn't that the one we'll be heading for later?"

"We certainly shall," said Peter, and Claudia surprised herself by nodding.

"But this must be a home from home for you, if I understand Claudia correctly?"

"Well, Peter's place is vastly more stylish and opulent."

"But the activities themselves, as we can plainly see, are universal, and I just believe in people being free to enjoy themselves. I've had couples make connections, that's always lovely, and some people just find out more about themselves, but no one should take it too seriously. Have you ever done parties like that? What was your voyage of self-discovery?"

"I'd had two bad marriages, my fault, not theirs. Simple version, although life is always more complex than clichés, isn't it?" There were attentive nods. "They were charming men, but weak. I'd never been attracted to macho, alpha types. Ha, you can probably understand that." They both sniggered. "But I was once with a guy, it wasn't a date. I was still married but away from my husband. It was a meeting, late, in my office in Singapore and we weren't getting anywhere with a topic and I think, to be honest, I was being a little shitty, and he suddenly said 'there's only one way we're going to resolve this!' and he pulled me across his lap and just pounded my ass. I didn't scream, I was outraged but I didn't think it was dangerous and I didn't want it to come out in public. I struggled at first but then I found my skirt up and my panties were no protection and after a dozen hard slaps I just lay there, stunned. Then he asked, 'Enough yet?' and by then I knew enough to say 'no' and he gave me more — he still didn't get his deal, but I was a convert. I needed to build it into my life. Is that weird?" She looked at Peter.

"It's surprisingly common, but usually people have had feelings of disquiet, or curiosity, or both for some time before, but it's not unique to have suppressed those feelings, as it sounds like you did, and maybe even to overcompensate in some way. You became your own alpha male. Does that make sense?"

"Kind of."

"And I would guess that you never have any dominant instincts during sex, you always want to be the submissive?"

"Absolutely, that's weird. You're right, of course."

"I don't want to be platitudinous but that may be why your marriages to charming men never had a chance." She looked thoughtful and nodded. "Well, one day I really must meet Jack Stephens, the only man on the planet who arouses feelings of envy in me. I really hope Rod Henderson screws him." He smiled, but Martha looked as anxious as Claudia felt. "Oh ladies, your reactions, I'm sorry. I mean absolutely no jest about my jealousy. He enjoys the affections, the devotion, I suspect, of two of my three favourite ladies in the world, but I'll admit to some concern about what's happening to him. And you and I, Claudia, will talk about that some more when I've spoken with you-know-who, but first I must find an adequately sadistic dom for Martha. I shall survey and return." He refilled their glasses and left them.

They got engrossed with themselves and Martha was pouring the last of the champagne when Peter returned with the tall American. "Martha, this is Jeff, and I've been very impressed with his work."

"Oh, I'm in the presence of a master, sir, those were beautiful stripes you put on Kimiko earlier. Well, I was impressed, so was she."

"And where is she?"

"Oh, she's watching somewhere, sir. I think she's even more into this than I am."

"Nevertheless, Jeff, we need your services. Martha, here, has been extremely naughty and needs to be dealt with on the X-frame. We shall use the little assistant there also."

"The little assistant?" Martha sounded concerned.

"You will do as you're told Martha. Come with us."

Claudia guessed, roughly, what the X-frame would be. It stood in the centre of the room, but she was distracted by the surrounding benches on which men and women were tied. A few of the punishments looked severe, one girl had a particularly vivid pattern of bright red welts but her dom was still applying a thin whippy cane, but at most stations it was hand spanking or the leather multi-thonged floggers that she and Jack had tried — but they almost tickled, rather than hurt, so there was a general air of gaiety, albeit serious gaiety, about the room. The only disquiet she felt was at one station where a woman was secured with wrists and neck in stocks, albeit comfortably padded stocks. Two men and a woman were clustered behind her. A row of very large dildos and plugs was arrayed on the top of the stocks, but one of the trio seemed to be pushing a whole hand into her. Claudia didn't study it long enough to see which orifice was being abused but, since the victim seemed to be vigorously fellating the first of a small queue of men waiting in front of her, she could only guess that the woman was happy.

The X-frame was empty. Martha, clearly understanding the process, lay herself on to it; it was padded and tilted away from her slightly. She raised her arms and Jeff buckled them into place. Claudia barely noticed the dwarf in the ninja costume who lurked behind the frame. Martha looked alarmed when she saw him but by then he had already strapped her ankles. She gasped when he appeared to unzip the front of her costume, just below the crossover of the X. Then he strapped her waist. Claudia couldn't hear the buzz because of all the music but when she moved to one side, she could see him applying a large vibrator to Martha's now open clit and that was plainly calming her, and then almost exciting her. Then the dwarf took the vibrator away and nodded to Jeff. Jeff, quite elaborately and ceremoniously, unzipped Martha as Peter had done. Peter handed him a paddle, Claudia could just make out 'ten first with this'. Martha's cheeks were still red from earlier, but the colour deepened quickly. Martha was gasping a little but didn't seem seriously discomforted. A few spectators had gathered round, this was clearly the focus of the room. Jeff handed the paddle back to Peter and took the cane from him, the same black-handled thick one that Peter had applied to Kimiko earlier. Jeff smoothed his hand over Martha's cheeks, slightly lasciviously, Claudia thought, but Martha wiggled eagerly in response and the dwarf applied his vibrator to her briefly again. But the first swipe, when it came, looked savage and Martha yelled loudly. That brought more spectators. Jeff looked to Peter, who merely nodded, but the line on Martha's ass looked livid, even on the crimson background. Jeff proceeded slowly, Martha howling each time, but whenever she seemed too distressed the dwarf would apply the vibrator again and Jeff would take a longer pause. After twenty there were a lot of people gathered round and Claudia found herself transfixed, but not in the slightest envious. She turned to Peter, who also appeared transfixed, but she was shaken when she saw Kimiko, kneeling in front of him, having unzipped him, fellating him very deeply. She looked away quickly, suddenly attacked by the most confusing emotions. She looked back to Martha, where Jeff had restarted. Claudia left and went back to the bar, where the barman recognised her and brought another bottle to their table. He popped the cork and poured her a glass. It was some time before Peter and Martha returned, she was holding on to his arm and walking unsteadily. "There you are, more champagne, a splendid idea," he said, and he poured two more glasses. "You will not be sitting, my dear, I assume."

Martha chuckled. "I'm going to find the taxi ride hard, but it was so worth it. Wow, cheers!" They drank together. She looked at Claudia. "Are you going to be trying anything?"

"I was quite happy with the paddling and the entertainment," replied Claudia. Peter looked at her in a way that told her she hadn't fooled him.

"Well, guys, I wouldn't want to rush anyone, but I will leave as soon as you want to. I'm afraid I need some attention on my ass to help me function tomorrow."

The taxi was easy, although Martha struggled to find a comfortable posture on one hip, much to her own amusement. When they pulled up outside the Imperial she said, "I've had a wonderful evening guys, thank you for indulging me, but I hope that's shown you it's probably not run by blackmailing gangsters. But I'll let you two worry about that one."

They were quiet during the short trip to the Okura. He offered his hand as she got out of the cab. "We go our different ways tomorrow and you've a whole day of flying and sleeping. Please come up for a few minutes now. We have some loose ends."

She nodded but said nothing.

They got to his suite. It had been an intense and memorable four days and she still had to decide what she would do about Jack, but that wasn't why she was feeling so awkward. What was that?

"Please sit down, you're not rushing off. Would you like some of my irresistible green tea?" She smiled weakly but shook her head. He sat down beside her. "Have I disappointed you?"

"Oh, no, Peter, it's something very different from that."

"Should, I guess? Was it something to do with Kimiko?"

"Of course it was, you fool. Oh, Peter, I so wanted that to be me!" And she fell on to his chest, sobbing.

He held her to him, but it was a long time before he spoke. "Oh, my dearest, dearest Claudia, that is such a lovely thought, my wonderful girl, but you mustn't think like that. You can't, please."

She sat up to look into his eyes, puzzled. "Why not? Can you tell me?"

"Because I'm far too close to loving you already."

23

I could talk this evening if you would like to. It will be quiet after 10. C

Five on Friday should suit him, if it really was that important.

It was lovely to be back, the trip had given her so many vivid memories, which she'd begun to try to digest on the long flight home. The most astonishing, perhaps, was her last conversation with Peter but now, with a little time and distance — and with an important and apparently successful meeting with a new client behind her today (Alan, bless him, had been superb) — she hoped she was getting a calmer perspective on that and not reacting to the febrile emotions of an extraordinary evening — or an extraordinary week. And, even had he been truly serious, she couldn't make herself responsible for the emotions of a three-times married man of his age, whatever she felt for him — and it was, she knew, something a little like love.

Thank you. I'll call you then. J

And when the phone rang exactly at ten, that confirmed it was important. She couldn't imagine him turning a new leaf on telephone punctuality.

"What were you doing in Tokyo?"

"It was business. I think you'd rather get on to the important bit, wouldn't you?"

"I suppose I'd better say yes."

"Let's just get the main thing out of the way. If you want to talk afterwards, well, I'm not doing anything, but I'll warn you I'm tired."

"I'm not surprised. I used to find coming back from the Far East easy, but I always wanted to sleep when I got back."

"OK, small talk over. It appears you might be on to something."

"Go on."

"Just might be, OK? I'm going to ask you some questions and you have to be absolutely honest or there's no point."

"You're doing this for me, I'm not going to fuck you about on that."

"I'm actually doing it for someone else, Jack, but you were good enough to point out that other people I might care about were in trouble, potentially, just as you thought that you and Oscar were, so I owe you something."

"Accepted. So, what's the question?"

"There may be more than one."

"I'm ready."

"You said there was a time when you weren't seeing Martha. How long was that?"

"Is this to do with Henderson?"

"Do you want me to help?" *Is this really so difficult for him?*

"You know that Martha and I had a particular sort of relationship."

"I don't actually know anything, Jack." She didn't know whether she was enjoying his discomfort or not. Peter had enough information to follow through with Henderson and that would, presumably, prevent any problems arising there in the future. OK, so Jack had given her that knowledge, but she wanted questions answered, old hurts salved.

"Are you going to help me with Henderson?"

"Are you going to answer my questions?"

There was a long silence. "Actually, Claudie, no. I'll take my chances. I've just realised how pleasant it's been to be free of the neurotic fucking interrogations of someone who couldn't even be honest about herself and her own affairs. Good luck!"

And the phone went dead.

She felt like she was falling and had no idea how or where she would land. And she didn't, in that moment, care.

24

He was still on the sofa looking out at the darkening sky when Lavinia came in half an hour later. He'd left the front door unlatched for her, as in their previous life, and she stood in the doorway to the living room clutching a bag of groceries.

"Oh, I didn't realise it was going to be the old sort of a Friday evening."

That startled him, he leapt up. "Oh, I'm sorry, my love, here, let me take that." He quickly took the bag and placed it on the dining table, then wrapped his arms around her and kissed her. It took her a moment to relax into that.

"I'll take my coat off and enjoy the next one even more, OK?" But she was looking questioningly at him as she leaned back in his embrace.

"I'm sorry, let's put these away and pour some drinks and I'll tell you about it." He kissed her again, lightly this time.

"And I'm going to tactfully assume that the 'my love' I got a moment ago was a lazy English colloquialism that shouldn't be taken too seriously."

He smiled sheepishly. "Not too seriously, no. Come on then." He saw the tell-tale overnight bag by the front door as they crossed the hall. He put the groceries on the kitchen worktop for her to do with as she wished while he went to the wine fridge. "I hope the bag in the hall means you're staying."

"I am if you have no objections, my love." But her warm smile was a big tease.

"You know," he said, as he pulled out a bottle and was preparing to open it, "one of the nicest things about our change of status, if I can call it that, is seeing what a lovely smile you have."

She put down the pack of fish, stepped towards him, held him and kissed him again, then, smiling, said, "Thank you. I actually prefer that to last weekend's effort."

"Last weekend's effort?"

"Yes, one of the nicest new things then, apparently, was finding out that my pussy was waxed." She smiled again but he laughed and felt embarrassed.

He showed her the bottle. "It's Pouilly-Fumé, I'm hoping to redeem my reputation for romance."

"Oh, Mr S, I'm afraid you're a lost cause. Come on, pour two and let's go and sit down. Can we leave the bottle here? I don't want you drowsy after dinner."

"We can leave the bottle, but we're not waiting until after dinner." He poured two large glasses and put the bottle in the fridge.

"I think you want to get this other thing off your chest first though, don't you? Come on."

She leaned back against his chest as they almost lay on the sofa. "You know I rang Claudia last weekend."

"Yes, it wasn't very helpful, you said." There was no tension, no attitude in her comment, just a very welcome matter-of-factness.

"Well, I must have planted a seed because she rang back just now."

"This isn't hard. It wasn't very helpful, was it?"

"Well, maybe it was, she's obviously followed up with someone, that would be Peter, I assume, and it must have triggered something, but instead of telling me, she started one of those old interrogation routines about me and…"

"And? Am I about to learn about more dark, old secrets?"

He felt tense for a moment but then relaxed, what secrets could he have from Lavinia? "I just don't want this to get boring but there was a relationship in Singapore and it's in some way related to this blackmailing story but instead of getting into how she came by that, and its obviously questionable authenticity, she wanted to start by dissecting that old relationship. I just lost it. Not a proud moment, I'm afraid."

"So, not a relationship I'll be asking questions about any time soon."

He laughed. "You can ask all you want, I'll tell you anyway, but you must know about it already. Miss X, the regional head of a global bank, had certain specific tastes."

"Would those be the tastes that I am not unfamiliar with?"

"Exactly, and it was Martha Weddle."

"I know, you were right, that was in the file of course."

"And her tastes?"

"Also of course. That's how I felt confident when I approached you that you might be responsive to my proposal."

He kissed the top of her head. He couldn't see but he felt she was probably smiling. "I'm feeling a little manipulated and outmanoeuvred here."

"Well, if you will try and mix it with the superior gender, what chance do you stand? But I should just point out to you that it ended up being your cane and my bottom, not the other way around. Furthermore, master, I never heard a word of complaint from you until just now."

"Well, you used to be so obedient then. And you have a fabulous bottom."

"Well, if something's changed you can always apply some of your old magic."

"I will. I think we'll set next Friday as an appointment. I think I'm still going to want the old ritual from time to time."

"Yes please," she said, and turned and lifted her face to kiss him. "But now we still have to work on the

Oscar/Jack problem, and you seem to have cut off a major source of information."

"I felt really stupid when I put the phone down. That's not really like me at all, but I had a flash of thinking how much I had not missed being questioned about everything."

"But I can understand why she would do that." She sat up and took his hands in hers. "When you stood in front of me in the hotel room, holding out your hands out to me, I forgot for a moment about all this Rod Henderson crap. I was just telling myself: 'don't do it, you'll fall in love with him', and then I thought I would want to know every detail about what you were up to, who you were seeing, what you were doing with them, everything, period." She relaxed and smiled. "Phew, thank God I didn't make that stupid mistake!" she said, and fell on him and kissed him again. "Do you think you need the information she's got?"

"I don't know. Probably I do. I don't really have enough to take to Oscar, not enough to give him a case against Rod."

"Well, I've got stuff that could do that."

"No," he said, very firmly. She looked startled. "I'm sorry, just no! You've done more than enough already. Look, the best outcome is that Rod gets a warning shot, cleans up his business, rehabilitates himself with Oscar and goes back to doing good work, with you coordinating his operations. That may sound naïve but it's the most desired outcome."

"Yes."

"Yes, what?"

She took his hands again. "It does sound naïve, my love, but thank you for trying to protect me." She kissed him lightly. "And don't worry about the 'my love', I was just paying you back."

"That's fine, I'll just add ten next Friday," he said with a smile. "There's still a good chance this will get resolved from the other end. Peter whatsisface must be a significant client."

"It's Dickinson, my love, not whatsisface, and he is one of the biggest, certainly in terms of the complexity of operations. There are more than thirty businesses spread over three areas."

"My love?"

"Yes, I'm going to want another ten on top next Friday. God, I'm so hot for you my wonderful man, I don't know if a simple fuck is going to do it for me this evening."

"Let's find out."

"I think I'm getting addicted to that." She was fiddling with the lube tube. "Isn't that what you said would happen?"

"I think I said it might happen."

"Well, it has, so how are you going to keep them both happy?"

"Interesting question. I'm hoping the new toy will arrive tomorrow."

"The new toy?"

"Yes, it's big and it's buzzy. We're going to DP you."

"Am I going to enjoy that?"

"Who cares? I will." And she laughed and slapped him. He pulled her to him and kissed her passionately.

***

He poured the last of the wine. "That was wonderful, thank you, do you cook a lot?"

"Because I'm on my own, do you mean?"

He looked at her and decided she wasn't trying to make a point. "Do you enjoy it, is what I should have asked."

"For appreciative diners, yes, and I think you just about qualify. 'Wonderful' is kind of a minimum. I'd prefer to be in the amazing to fabulous range on the spectrum."

"Like the sex, you mean?"

"If you say so, master. But you're providing dessert, remember?" He looked puzzled. "I'll give you a clue; I'll be sitting on your face while I'm eating it." They smiled and clinked glasses. "But don't worry, you've plenty time to prepare it. We have to come back to our topic. What happens next?"

He was thoughtful. "I really don't feel like ringing her again."

"Do you have anything to hide?"

"I don't think I do, but I didn't really hide things, anyway. I suspect she kept more from me in the end than I did from her, but she's convinced herself I'm not a credible witness and I just don't want to go through all that crap again."

"Could you write? Tell her everything relevant and see how she responds?"

"If she responds. But it's a good thought. I have actually nothing to hide — and anything from her might be useful. Will you help me write it, or at least check the draft?" She looked puzzled. "You know the background, you can tell me if you think you'd respond. Plus, we're kind of in this together. I want to be completely open about it."

"Now stop that, Jack, please. I have no idea where you and I are going, if anywhere, and I'm very happy with the spank and fuck routine. But whatever it's going to be, it's not going to be on a 'we tell each other everything' basis. I know I might want that, but I think you've demonstrated that it doesn't work, and I've never been in a position to expect it, even in the early years of my marriage."

"Agree, but could we make that a spank, cook and fuck routine? The fish was amazing!"

"Don't push it, buddy, or I'll be ordering a strap-on!" They laughed. "Other options?"

"To strap-ons? Or to the letter?"

"I could always use the cane on you."

"Nah, you're a sub, you couldn't."

"Nah, you're a wuss, I couldn't. But you're probably right about me being a sub. Anyway, apart from the letter?"

"I could ring Martha and find out if she knows anything about this."

"Mm, that's an option. What about Peter Dickinson?"

"I don't know him at all. That would seem just too desperate. So maybe I just tell Oscar what I've got. Other people in the Far East think the story's made up, he might try approaching Rod with that."

"My hacking evidence is more convincing, and our file details about the Singapore business."

"Both of those put you in the firing line. There's a better option here."

"You're setting up a fight between hope and hardheadedness. Only one winner there, Jack."

"Oh, dear, sexy and wise, killer combination."

"Come on, let's see if a letter gets us something. She's going to be feeling very emotional right now, and maybe a little guilty herself."

Dear Claudie,

I am very sorry I lost it. I had asked for help and you were trying to give it, and you got an unfair and probably very hurtful reaction. I am truly sorry.

I thought I might write down all the facts of the events as I saw them from two years ago. If they're corroborated by whatever else you have learned, then that may provide additional evidence for any other potential victims of what appear, to me, to be some serious transgressions and distortions. I'm assuming that there may be some tie-in with Peter Dickinson, and he might be exposed by Henderson's practices moving outside the ethical zone, but I don't need to know that.

The only club or similar establishment I ever visited in the Far East was a place called Smarts in Singapore. I went there a few times with Martha. It was a large, luxurious, exclusive and very expensive apartment designed for kinky sex games.

When I told you I'd stopped seeing her, that wasn't true. I had stopped her coming to me because her feelings were changing, she'd admitted to wanting more than our dom/sub arrangement, but she was aware of my feelings for you. So, we agreed that she and I would curtail our joint activities, but that I would escort her to Smarts occasionally for her to enjoy a little 'fun'. To complete the picture here, I will admit that I enjoyed those visits myself.

She and I never considered that Smarts might be in the hands of gangsters and blackmailers, so I was shocked when Henderson rang me. Rather than cast doubt on his allegations, it was easier to accept them and commit to desist. I didn't tell the story to anyone. Quitting Smarts was more of a problem for Martha than it was for me, I simply told her I no longer wished to go there. But I did agree to see her again on the old basis, as long as that arrangement would not lead to romantic complications. With my subsequent job change there was only one final visit to my apartment in Singapore. That's the visit you and I have discussed.

We now have other concerns in Collins about Henderson going rogue and endangering the organisation by framing Oscar with similarly fictional embellishments. If there were any other evidence of practices that go outside guidelines, it would be very helpful to learn of them.

I know, from the limited feedback you gave me, that you have found my information helpful. If the foregoing adds weight to any actions your friends feel they need to take, then I am glad to have been of some help. You have given me enough for me to feel vindicated about Singapore. I'm just sorry it had such unfortunate consequences.

All my best,
Jack

"Do you think 'unfortunate' is the right word?" He looked at her. "Are you sure you're not being a little too sensitive to my feelings? Wasn't it 'tragic'?"

He looked into her eyes, and thought for what seemed like a long time. "No, yes, and no." She looked quizzical. "No, unfortunate is not the right word. Yes, I was thinking about your feelings. And no, it wasn't tragic. We're all still alive and at least one of us is happy, thank you."

She smiled. "Happy, but worried. I like the rest of the letter. Please change that word. I don't need to know what you put there."

"Deeply regrettable."

"You didn't have to tell me that."

"I know. But there's a difference between being straight up open and having to admit things under duress."

She nodded slowly. "OK, change it and press 'Send'. It's time for my dessert."

25

Claudia could see her drive from the kitchen window. The big Range Rover swept in five minutes early. She wiped her hands and rushed to the front door, just checking in the mirror as she passed.

"You found us! Well, of course you found us, you found this in the first place. Small kiss, please, the kids might be watching, the gravel drive alerts them."

So, small kiss, but a big embrace — and then the flowers, grand, but not obviously romantic, and a small gift box. "What's this?"

"It's a moving in present, of course. OK, maybe it's four months late but you've only just invited me." He smiled.

"That is just such an outrageous lie."

"But it's more ungentlemanly to point out that you prefer to meet at Coworth. Let's go in, I'm dressed for out here, you're not."

She held the box, he held the flowers and his arm was around her shoulder as they moved back in.

"Guys, come and say hello!" she called up the stairs. "If I'm lucky they won't have headphones on. Come on through, you know where everything is. Although, that's silly, you must see hundreds of properties." She walked through to the kitchen, and he followed.

"That's true, but I have a surprisingly good memory of most — and this one was rather special." She was taking the flowers, but they spent a moment looking into each other's eyes. Abbi came in.

"Alphonse, this is Abbi, my eldest. Alphonse found this house for us."

"Ah, cool."

"Did it pull you away from your mates?"

"A bit, but they like coming here to hang out, especially when the tyrant's away," she said with a smile. "Gran's much more understanding. Is she coming to lunch, did you say?"

"Yes, she wanted to meet Alphonse too; she wants to thank him for her office. Can you send your brother down? I don't care if he is just saving the world from whatever forces of darkness. We're not eating until one or so, by the way, but come down whenever you want to."

"Cool," she said, and skipped off.

"My God, she's as beautiful as you are!"

"Thank you. And thank you for not telling her."

"Oh, enough people will, but it would just feel creepy coming from an old man like me."

She stopped as she was putting water into the large vase. "Gosh, I never think of you that way, but I suppose she probably would. Look, I hope you don't mind Pat coming."

"No, absolutely not. I've been wanting to meet her — and I've had many occasions to be grate…"

"This is Jo, the younger, Alphonse."

"Hi Jo." They shook hands, Jo a little diffidently. "Saving the world?"

"Nah, Fifa football."

"Who's your team?"

"Chelsea."

"Mine, too."

"Really?" Claudia was surprised.

"Of course, it's my local team, but I was a fan anyway before I moved there."

"Do you go to any matches?"

"The big ones, yes. Who's you favourite player?"

"Hazard. Who do you like?"

"I've always liked Willian, I don't think they use him properly. He's so committed, he plays everywhere and never gives up. Do you ever see any games?"

"Nah, just telly."

"Would you like me to try to organise something?"

Claudia couldn't remember a look like that on Jo's face since the small child Christmases. "Are you sure?" — *please don't let him down on this* — "How would you do that?"

"It's simple. I'll just pick a Saturday afternoon game and come and pick him up."

"Wow! That would be fabulous. Ha, my mates will be soooo jealous. Thank you."

"You'll be very welcome."

"Wow." Jo then rushed off upstairs again to attack his video game with renewed purpose.

Claudia looked a little doubtful. "Are you sure about that?"

"Yes, I can get tickets, property connections, my dear."

"But an afternoon out with a fourteen-year-old boy."

He looked patiently at her. "Claudie, for a reason that should be very obvious to you, I get no opportunities to play 'dad' ever. It will be a serious treat for me."

"OK." She snuggled in to him for a long kiss.

"That's lovely, my love, but aren't you supposed to be showing me around?"

"I thought I might let Pat do that, she's at least as proud of the place as I am. Then you can get to know each other while I'm getting lunch. To be honest, I wanted some time with you, and it suits me all round. She won't be here for an hour. George will be with her, but Jo will make him play video games."

"OK, I thought there were hints of trouble at the corner of your dazzling smile. How was Tokyo?"

"God, where do I start? Coffee?" He nodded.

They were in the sitting room and she was trying to give as condensed a version as she could, but she kept spilling out into descriptions of meals and places and people. He put his hand on hers. "I think, unless you've bored the family with this already, you can tell me all about that over lunch. Well, maybe not the bit about your leg's limpet lawyer, but the rest of it will be news to Pat and George as well as me. The little I know of kids tells me that they never think their parents are interesting anyway," he said with a smile. "But there's something really troubling you and you'd better get that out. I have a free day, by the way, so it doesn't matter if we come back to it later but I'd rather you told me what the big thing is now."

She fell on to him and let him put his arms around her and let herself weep a little. After a while she sat up and dabbed her eyes. "The problem goes back two years. You remember when you met me at Coworth and told me about Jack?"

"Of course. That was a tough day."

"Well, Jack thinks he was set up by Rod Henderson. He says that the threats were gross exaggerations. He doesn't deny going to kinky places, but he says he knows the dangers were inventions"

"Why would Henderson do that? Peter's used him for years."

"Jack says he's plotting at Collins because he's worried about being ousted from there and there would be follow-on damage to his network elsewhere. But I also have some independent evidence that all was not what it seemed two years ago."

"Does Peter know?"

"Of course. I talked to him about it last week. He seemed to take the point seriously and was going to follow up with Rod."

"And the red eyes? They tell me you've been talking to Jack."

"Oh, Alphonse, please stay this evening." She fell into his embrace again.

"I have no commitments."

"Thank you, the guest room's kept ready." She sat up and looked at him. "You can pretend to sleep there." She smiled, and said, "I'm going to promise to be quiet."

"You know I'd stay anyway."

"Yes." She smiled. "But who better to christen the house properly with?" She kissed him. "Thank you. Now we've got time, you can help me in the kitchen."

But Pat soon turned up to drag him away. Claudia avoided commenting on the new Sunday-best look, it was so close to being too smart and certainly risked attracting comments from the guys. Even George had been forced into a suit. What had she told them about Alphonse? Then it struck her, Pat had probably made two and two come to five; Alphonse was the new man. Perhaps it wasn't a good idea that he stayed. Oh well, it was done now. And she did want to talk to him about Jack's letter. And about Peter? No, not about Peter. Definitely not about Peter.

She was dishing up when her phone rang: Peter. Shit! "Hi, I'm just getting lunch. Can I call you back?"

"OK, try not to leave it too long, please, it's already nine in China."

"By ten, I promise, thank you."

"Talk soon, bye."

"Peter," she said to Pat, for no good reason. They took the meat plates through. George would normally have been told to carve the lamb, but the males had occupied one end of the dining table and were engrossed in football talk. At least that had freed up Abbi for vegetable duties. Claudia had carved, not her favourite job.

"That was Peter just now," she said to Alphonse as she put the plate in front of him. "He's in China. I said I'd call back in an hour." He nodded almost imperceptibly, not letting his concentration waver from George's denunciation of the treatment of Mourinho by Abramovich. When she sat down and began serving herself, she couldn't resist smiling when it became clear that George's disapproval of Abramovich wasn't strong enough to let him turn down the opportunity of going to a game with Jo and Alphonse. Somehow, Alphonse moved the conversation around to Japan and she found herself talking about karaoke and kimonos — and raw fish — "Raw fish?" she got in stereo from the kids. "Yes, and you eat it with chopsticks!"

"What's the most disgusting thing you've ever eaten, Alphonse?" A sixteen-year-old girl was bound to try to engage the attention of probably the most dashing man she'd ever met, even if he was 'ancient' — as she later described him when she finally accepted he was 'mum's'.

"Well, I struggled with Bosintang, that's a Korean soup and it tastes good, but it's based on dog meat."

"Yeugh," came from both grossed out children.

"But actually eating? I guess I had the most problems with Casa Marzu. It's a Sardinian cheese and you can only eat it when the maggots in it are still alive."

"Oh, gross!"

"But your mum is no great fan of birds' claws, I gather." He smiled at her.

"Where did you eat them?"

"Where didn't I eat them is the right question." The talk then moved around the table on favourite foods and places with even George feeling relaxed enough to join in sometimes. She'd barely got dessert on the table and it was nearly two.

"Can I leave you guys to it? I must make this call."

***

"Peter, I'm sorry I couldn't talk earlier. It's a family Sunday lunch and Alphonse is here."

"Alphonse?"

"Yes, I've been trying to get him to come for ages to say thank you for finding the place. You'll be next. It was your money."

He laughed. "It's your money, my dear. My money was an investment, nothing more. But I'd be delighted to come to lunch, of course." — *and, of course, we both know you can't possibly be serious, thank goodness.*

"How did the week finish for Andy?"

"I think they're very close. We'll let Ozawa work his little tricks next week and Andy would need to go back after that if the deal is going to come off. But I'm ringing about our more urgent issue, of course."

"Of course." She leaned back on the bed. It struck her that the office might have been a more sensible place, but she wanted to be in a space that felt safe and personal.

"I had a long talk to Rod this morning. He's not admitting anything, of course, that isn't the way he operates. But when I asked if his old Singapore case was built solely on Smarts, he hesitated, then said he couldn't remember and there had probably been more to it than that. He was alert enough, even at seven a.m. on a Sunday morning, not to fall into the trap of trying to tell me that Smarts was gangster-run. So I told him that your man might be challenging him to provide more evidence about that case. Are you in touch with Jack?"

"Oh, Peter, can I just say we're communicating?"

"That's good enough for me. Look, I haven't threatened Rod yet, he still could be valuable to me but I've insisted he check that my guidelines are being observed in all Dickinson businesses but, as he points out, even he can't check where some of his information comes from and some of the stuff those two criminals are using in Tokyo…"

"Criminals?"

"The lawyers, my dear. Ozawa would almost be blackmailing the family with what he's found out and we none of us know how he's come by what he knows. I'm in my squeamish zone but, if the deal goes through, I'll just have to assume everyone is happy. But I'm not happy about Singapore, and if that case doesn't stack up, he knows I'll be getting back to him. And when Rod says, 'leave it with me', I expect it to get sorted."

"What should I do?"

"One of the many things I admire about you is that I know you will answer that question for yourself. Now, you get back to your guests. I'm back in your time zone on Wednesday. I'll be available then, OK?"

"Peter?"

"Yes?"

"You're wonderful, thank you."

"Oh, my dear, I would do anything for you anyway but in this case I'm partly responsible for your problem. You make up your mind about what you want to do but I'll be disappointed not to get a progress report by Friday."

"Yes, sir. Love you, bye."

"Bye."

Probably not what she should have said, but it's what she felt.

They were still at the table when she came back down. "Come on," said Pat, "let's clear up and give your mum some time with her guest."

Alphonse got up and started moving plates to the kitchen. "I'll be right back," said Claudia, "I'm just going to print out an email." She was back before they'd finished clearing. "Do you feel like a walk into the village when you've read that?"

"Sure."

They turned left out of the gate, it was the quieter walk. "That email gives me half a picture, are you going to tell me what Peter said?"

"He'd spoken to Rod this morning. Rod was cagey and claimed not to remember the details. Fair enough, I suppose. So, Peter suggested that I get in touch with Jack and ask him to challenge Rod on what evidence he had in the Singapore case."

"And you're pretty sure this Smarts place isn't run by gangsters?"

"I probably should give you more background, but I couldn't do it in the house." Early November, walking on a carpet of sodden, dead leaves along a narrow lane of denuded poplars poking accusingly at a dull grey sky, and she was talking about a byzantine apartment in the centre of Tokyo where colourful, weird creatures indulged their strangest, most imaginative and most decadent customs. She spoke freely; he knew Peter well enough and he wouldn't meet Martha. She held his hand. "And you know I have a little bit of a taste for some of that stuff."

He stopped and put his arms around her, smiling. "I enjoy some of your adventures very much." He kissed her. They walked on.

"You're not really into that dom/sub scene, are you?"

He laughed. "Well, it amuses me a little but it's not a major turn on. I'm quite vanilla, really."

Now she laughed too. "We've done some non-vanilla things together."

"True, but we can talk about them later. Seems to me now that there's evidence to support Jack. I suppose I want to ask you what your feelings are, but it seems to me it's simpler than that, isn't it?"

"I should just let him know what Peter said, you mean?"

"I think so, it will weigh on your conscience if you don't."

"I won't have a conscience about Jack." The row of poplars had ended, and they were looking down over open fields to the huddled roofs of the village, wisps of smoke rising from a few chimneys.

"We both know that's not true, and maybe I don't need to ask about your feelings."

"They're not simple."

"Of course they're not. But I think the next step is simple, you know that. And you can always take the easy way out and write to him — although the written word's an overrated medium in my view. It's a haven for cowards and dissemblers."

"You think I should call him?" She sounded shocked.

"Not first off. But we both know you'll have to someday, if you want to find out how it should have ended, or whether it should have ended."

"Well, it's ended now. He's probably got somebody else anyway."

"Ha, now we've got to the bottom of it. That's your main worry, isn't it?"

"No, it isn't," but she didn't convince either of them.

Dear Jack,

Thank you for writing. It did make it easier to deal with.

And thank you for finally being honest about your relationship with Martha, which makes more sense now.

Peter Dickinson has a great deal of respect for Rod Henderson and a long history of a successful commercial relationship. He has, nevertheless, probed further on the Singapore case because he was the source of my information and he was aware of how much distress it caused me. Henderson's recollection of those distant events was not clear. Peter's suggestion is that you take it up directly with him and ask him to provide the evidence for the position he took at the time.

Peter's own view, after some background research, is that Smarts is unlikely to be the source of any real problems and it may be that Henderson was being over-

cautious but that is something that you might be able to establish more directly if you are sure there were no other incidents that could have led to these allegations.
Best wishes,
Claudia

"I don't think you need that 'finally'."

"I did wonder about that. Anything else?"

"To me, it still feels like you're overdoing the injured innocence thing. On balance, without knowing either Henderson or Jack, my money would be on Jack to be telling the truth in this instance. Then all you have against Jack is that he wasn't completely open about how he was managing Martha and it seems to me that reflects quite well on what his feelings were for you. He was stopping her getting too close because of you — and you've even had her corroborating that. Are you sure you're not just putting up walls to defend yourself? If you two ever do sit down and talk, you'll have to tell him about you and how close you got to Martha, and then who would have the right to complain about a lack of openness?"

They were side by side on the sofa in the sitting room. She kept her face fixed resolutely on the screen of her laptop. His arm went round her shoulder. "That will do the job for you, although I would remove 'finally'," he chuckled. "But I would never forgive you if you wrote me an email as snotty as this one."

"Shut up."

But he just laughed again. "Look, this solves his problem if he's been telling the truth. It gives him the chance to set Collins straight, rise to the fabulous riches of the CEO position and settle down with his new ladylove in a splendid colonial town house in Alexandria and keep a seventy-two-foot Sunseeker on the Chesapeake."

She slapped the screen down. "I never thought I'd hate you." But they both laughed, and she snuggled in to him. "I'll finish it later. I'd better get some tea for the guys. It will only be cheese on toast, are you good with that?"

"That will be seriously wonderful." *He was taking the piss, wasn't he?* "I brought a 1995 Gran Reserva to have with the lamb but didn't get a chance to open it. It will be perfect for cheese on toast."

She slapped him. "And you knew we'd be having lamb?"

His eyes met hers, smiling. "Can't say you're in love with someone unless you can read their mind."

26

Dear Jack,

Thank you for writing. It did make it easier to deal with.

And thank you for being honest about your relationship with Martha, which makes more sense now.

Peter Dickinson has a lot of respect for Rod Henderson and a long history of a successful commercial relationship, but that doesn't mean he doesn't have concerns and suspicions. He has probed further into the Singapore case because he was the source of my information and he was aware of how upset I was.

Henderson's recollection of those events was not clear — whose would be at seven a.m. on a Sunday? Peter's suggestion is that you take it up directly with him and ask him to provide the evidence for the position he took at the time.

Peter's view is that Smarts is unlikely to be the source of any real problems and it may be that Henderson was just being over-cautious, but that is something that you should be able to establish in a conversation with him.

Best wishes,
Claudia

"Does that give us enough?"

"Probably not, but it's enough to take to Oscar before I talk to Henderson."

"I wish you'd let me help."

He sat up. "You really do have the loveliest smile."

"Thank you, but it's the other lips that have been getting the most attention," she said, and pulled the duvet up, "but I am absolutely not complaining about that. I'm only complaining about not being allowed to help." He put his phone back on the bedside table, lay down again and pulled her to him. "You can't distract me with sex for ever, Jack Stephens, but I love it that you're trying. I don't know what meal it will be when we get up, but I am getting hungry."

"I think we're down on supplies."

"I only planned for Friday night and you run a bachelor fridge."

"I'm glad you stayed."

"Glad?" she said, with mock horror. "You've come, on a conservative reckoning, at least seven times in the various orifices of my body this weekend and you're only 'glad' I stayed? What would it take to make you delirious, for heaven's sake? Or even just happy?"

"Well, I'll settle for eight, but shall I get some pizza in?"

"Pizza's fine. And number eight will be fine too but I'm going to close off one of your options. You've made me particularly sore in one place."

"Oops, sorry!"

"Don't apologise, you've made me an addict, but twice a day there seems to be a little more than enough."

"You need more practice."

"I've been getting it with that new toy of yours. I enjoyed that too, by the way."

"I did notice."

She slapped him. "Order pizzas, I'm going for a shower."

***

"I'm not ruling out involving you completely. I'm just saying give me a chance with what we've got. I'd still like to bring everything back into line. I can see some value in what Henderson does. But if Oscar is still seriously threatened then I will ask you to help."

She looked uncertain but had just taken a mouthful of pizza, so could only shake her head. "That may be too late," she got out eventually, still chewing. "I don't see the stuff his finance hackers get before he does, and he may use it straight away. And if Saunders gets hold of it, Oscar still has a problem even if he does deal with Rod."

"I'd rather protect you."

"Honey, if Rod pulls this stunt off, I'm not staying there anyway."

"Please let me talk to Oscar first."

"OK," she said, slowly, "but I'm ready to step in if that doesn't go as it should. Right, that's one thing we disagree on. Let's establish some other incompatibilities before we go back for number eight. Old movies, what's your choice for this afternoon?"

"*Casablanca.*"

"No! Really?"

"Of course. As long as you don't mind seeing a man weep when Rick gets to the piano."

"And he says, 'I thought I told you never to play that again'."

"And their eyes meet; 'Hello Rick'."

"Hello Ilsa," she laughed. "We seem to have got our roles reversed. Anyway, you're too tall for Bogart. Shall we see if it's available?"

"I have the DVD anyway, of course. Shall I organise that while you get some champagne?"

"You're drinking tea, Master Jack, you've promised me number eight and I'm not having you fall asleep on me before we get there."

"Deal."

***

It didn't seem worth worrying about Ken Saunders, Oscar would know what the topic was. If Saunders tried to muscle in, Oscar would deal with that. Jack realised there was little downside in asking for a conversation.

"We have a meeting starting at nine, you know that. Will this take long?" But Jack knew from Oscar's look that he realised the topic was important.

"You might want to come back to it later but, for now, it's only a few minutes."

They'd barely sat down when Saunders came in. His corner had been empty when Jack had approached Oscar. "Do you guys need me?"

Oscar smiled, and appeared friendly. "We're good thanks, Ken. It's just a small personal thing of Jack's." And Oscar's smile was a little wicked, as if he was enjoying keeping Ken tense. Maybe it had struck him as strange that Ken should appear so quickly — just as it had struck Jack. Or maybe it was the confirmation Jack was looking for! But that was fanciful, Oscar didn't yet know about yesterday's communications. But Jack felt it was safe to assume that Henderson and Saunders had talked yesterday.

"I'm getting it confirmed that my disgrace of two years ago was a set-up."

"So, you hadn't actually been to any naughty places?"

Jack knew he would have to break through this thick crust of scepticism. "I plan to ask Henderson for his evidence about Singapore."

"I doubt whether it was strong. He didn't push me very hard when I told him I planned to ignore it."

"But he'd told me that, if I agreed to desist, as he put it, then he wouldn't even tell you."

Oscar gave him a very patronising look. "And you think I pay him lots of money to keep secrets from me?

Are you going to grow up soon, boy? He can keep his secrets for when I need deniability."

"Oscar, I've got somebody richer than you calling Henderson at seven on a Sunday morning because he's sufficiently concerned about Henderson's operations."

"I'm going to assume that I'm not wrong, and that you are a pretty savvy individual. I know you're charismatic and imaginative, and yet you're still pretty grounded about delivering business results. So, you must have something you're not telling me, because you can't possibly expect me to act on this nebulous crap."

"I do, but I'm not telling you." Could this work?

"Not buying that, Jack. If you can't trust me with your secret sources, then why the fuck should I trust you with anything? We've been round this loop before."

"OK, can we talk this afternoon? I'll tell you all I've got and why I want my source protected."

Oscar seemed to relax. "OK, Jack, it's a deal. And, well, I'll give it to you," he said, as he smiled slyly, "you do seem to stick your little friend in some very attractive places." Jack knew he was blushing — and struggling forlornly for a response. "And you get one piece of good free advice this morning: don't ever play poker! I'd guessed your source was Lavinia the last time we spoke. That's why I listened. But I didn't know until you just confirmed it." Jack exhaled, smiled, and relaxed. "And I actually didn't know absolutely for sure then, but you really have confirmed it now."

Jack was shocked and felt stupid.

"Jack, your only excuse is that you trust me — and I'm disappointed that I've allowed you to feel that way. But here we are, we know you're pretty naïve — and, even though you're absolutely right to trust me, you shouldn't have let me find out about Lavinia so easily, that poor woman deserves better than Rod and you. But your credulous stupidity has at least made me believe you might have a point. Can we say four, this afternoon?"

Jack nodded glumly.

"Don't look so miserable, Jack, you're not the worst poker player in the world. Ken Saunders, as you saw earlier, is a lot worse than you are." And there was that wicked smile again.

***

"OK, Mr Paranoia, what have you got?" was Oscar's opening gambit when they sat down again. Saunders had been hovering, but he didn't ask to join them — *probably gone to ring Henderson.*

"Lavinia has evidence that Rod's IT team use hacking quite extensively to get their information, and these are people with military or banking experience, so the capability's there. She's also got evidence that there's a focus on you."

"Why might that be?"

"She thinks it's because you're trying to push Henderson out; you're worried about his methods becoming a major PR embarrassment. But, if you push him out, some other high-profile clients might follow and he can't sustain his operations, it's become a pretty extensive network and that's a major selling point, but it now has very high running costs and a bunch of people who just know too much. So, he's tied himself to Saunders to get guarantees of keeping Collins, but that only works if Saunders gets CEO and they push you out or up to a very neutered chairman role soon. So, they were looking at me again because they got wind of me being the CEO option and they wanted to kill that off."

"Well, that wasn't hard to get wind of. When I meet the board, I have to talk about senior executives and succession. Henderson knew about that option three months ago. So?"

"Full disclosure. I've been seeing Lavinia occasionally for a year or so now and she was disturbed when this latest move started up, both for me personally, and because she thought they were doing good work at Networks but staying clean. I've told her that I would like this resolved without bloodshed, i.e. we get Henderson to clean up his act and guarantee continuity here and she can keep her place at Networks. She's pushing to offer more hard evidence but I'm saying no because that would make it obvious where the source was."

"A regular fucking Sir Galahad, aren't you Jack?" said Oscar, with warmth rather than malice. "But that does sound like a preferred option. Then you've always got the back channel in the future," he chuckled, "as long as your little friend there keeps her happy. But what's this other connection of yours? Who's the guy that rang Rod on a Sunday morning? How are you in touch with him?"

"He owns the Dickinson Group." Oscar shook his head. "I'm not surprised you haven't heard of them. It's an odd kind of global conglomerate, a network of loosely linked businesses. He uses Rod for surveillance on his operations."

"And your connection with them?"

"Brodie Associates is now part of his network. I'm still in touch with Claudia Brodie."

Oscar rolled his eyes. "Is that the woman that used to work for us?" Jack nodded. "And we now pay ten times as much to?"

"Five is probably a fairer number, but you're right. Dickinson has set her up."

"Smart man. But you have no direct connection with him?"

"No, but I'm told he also has concerns about Networks."

"Concern enough to call Henderson on a Sunday morning?"

"Well, that was done more as a favour."

"For you? Why?"

"Not for me, no, for Claudia Brodie."

"Jesus, Jack, is your pecker going to keep taking us into these places?" He sighed heavily. "No, I don't want an answer. What I want is a contact with Dickinson. It sounds like we both have an interest in not being outmanoeuvred by Mr Henderson. Can you set that up for me?"

"Of course." *I have no fucking idea actually, Oscar, I just hope my poker skills are better this afternoon.*

"You'd better get on to it quickly. If there is a problem, we need to get ahead of the game."

Can we talk? J
We did better when we wrote. C
I'm trying to get two other people talking. J
What's that about? C
Talk would be better. J
Call in ten, then. C

***

"Why do we have to talk?"

"If you think about what we're worrying about, we don't want to put anything in texts and emails that triggers a search."

"That's all a bit cloak and dagger isn't it?"

"Peter may have got on the case just as a favour to you, or he may have done it because he has some worries, and they might be worries about cloak and dagger operations, as you put it. I can tell you that Oscar has worries, I've just been talking to him, and when I gave him some background, he said he'd like to talk to Peter. Does that make sense?"

"Not really, but it's not for me to judge the risks of that. I'll get a message to Peter, but I can't talk to him until Wednesday and it sounds like I shouldn't be sending any details in the message, far-fetched as that seems to me."

***

It was Wednesday afternoon when Oscar called him into the meeting room. He seemed to have abandoned all concerns about Saunders. Jack thought he'd detected a change in atmosphere in any meetings they attended together: a coolness from Oscar towards Ken, and a nervousness in Ken that he had never seen before.

"I've just had a long conversation with a charming man." Oscar was smiling and seemed to drift into a reverie. "Have you ever asked yourself how many phone calls men make that last more than fifteen minutes?"

Jack nodded. "Well, I know it applies to me. And if I've had you on the phone it's never more than five minutes."

"And that's only because you talk too much," he said with a mock gruffness, but smiling. "But here's what's going to happen. I'm calling Rod in here for a meeting on Friday afternoon at four. You need to be in the office, but I won't call you in unless I'm happy we have an agreement. It won't be a long meeting. It'll be nine in the UK, which is where Peter will be if we need him, or if Rod wants to cross-check with him. But I'm telling Rod that we're staying with Networks, but only with guarantees about their practices as far as they affect our businesses, that's Collins and Dickinson. He's going to tell us there's a twilight zone that's essential for his operations — and we neither of us can rule that out. Dickinson's got something going on in Japan where he thinks some dirty tricks have already happened — but we're both going to insist that we know of any incidents affecting our businesses that breach our guidelines. If he agrees, I'm going to call you in. You'll need to tell him that you'll keep him on when you take over."

"Take over?" Jack was stunned.

Oscar looked irritated. "Come on, Jack, that's fucking obvious. It can't possibly be Ken Saunders now. In fact, you and I have to decide if we want to keep the bastard on as head of operations."

"Will he stay? We don't really have a number two."

"It's a good question," Oscar said, thoughtfully, "and now I'm thinking it might be better to just let him go anyway. There are other ways of managing that job, there are people in the regions we can bring in to cover different bits of it. I'm quite attracted by that but we're getting off the point. Are you happy to keep Henderson?"

"If we're not endangered by his activities."

"Good man. Let's be pragmatic about this. What did my new friend say? Yes, 'a man of flexible principles' is how he described himself, but I think he's genuinely worried about some of this stuff and why, ultimately, we can't be too hard on Henderson. You know, that's the first real conversation I've ever had with a man in a similar position. To my other US-based chairmen, talking Networks operations would be like discussing a fart. That's what Henderson can play on, and why we can't afford not to watch him. OK?"

"Sure, let's see what Friday brings."

"Jack, not a word to Lavinia, or the other one."

"Not even a thank-you note?"

"I worry about you sometimes. Stop trying to line up future appointments for your pecker. It has accidentally helped in this situation, but it usually won't."

***

Lavinia rang that evening. "Rod's changed his travel plans for Friday. He was due to be taking Eleanor on holiday. It must be serious."

"Serious enough for me to have to postpone our Friday appointment."

"Oh." The disappointment contrasted sharply with her initial breathless excitement.

"We'll find a different way of weaving some role play into the evening."

"Ah, so we're still on for the evening then?"

"Oh, definitely, please. I don't know what time I'll get there, it shouldn't be too late. What if I leave a spare key with the concierge? You can let yourself in, OK?" There was a long silence. "What's up?"

"I don't know how to put this. I just want to reassure you I'm not reading too much into anything."

"I don't know what you're reading into what, but we can talk about that at the weekend. Or do you have some plans?"

"I told my mother I'd see her. She's in Annapolis. I've already pushed it back from Saturday to Sunday. I thought Friday night might have consequences."

"It very well might, but I'll tell you more on Friday. Right now, I'd just like to cuddle you, but I expect the dom will turn up some time on Friday."

"I shall look forward to meeting him again, not the wuss I had to put up with last weekend. See you Friday, my love," she said, laughing.

***

Oscar called him over to his desk. He'd been with Henderson about half an hour. "I've left him in there to talk to Peter. It seems he thinks I might be bluffing."

"Have you made progress?"

"I don't know. He might not actually be ringing Peter, but he had to do something after he challenged me on it."

"Did he ask where your information came from?"

"Sure, and I told him." Jack looked horrified. Oscar laughed and shook his head. "I told him Martha Weddle."

Now Jack was stunned. "Martha Weddle? She knew nothing. I deliberately didn't tell her."

"Just accept that story and nod quietly if it comes up, we're playing poker, for fuck's sake. I'll explain later."

Henderson emerged from the meeting room and nodded to them. He looked quite calm, a good poker face. They joined him and went in.

"It seems I should congratulate you, Jack."

"Thanks Rod, but I'm not sure for what."

"Well, for fucking my PA, for a start."

Poker face, Jack. Shrug impassively! "Not guilty."

"Meeting at the Ritz?"

"Like I said, not guilty."

"I know you were at the Ritz."

Oscar was keeping quiet, watching them.

"I pleaded not guilty to fucking your PA, Rod." *Now shut up, Jack.* He thought he caught a slight nod from Oscar. "That was your 'for a start', was there something else?"

"CEO at Collins, I gather."

"Perhaps, but that's going to need board approval. You'll get a chance to vote that down."

Finally, there was a small smile on Henderson's face. "I shan't be doing that, Jack. I shall value good relations with the new CEO. Congratulations."

Jack waited unsmiling, and then nodded slowly.

"I'll have to apologise, of course, for acting over-zealously on some information I was given two years ago. I'm sorry if there was any fall-out." He was staring hard at Jack; he may not have caught Oscar shaking his head very slightly. Well, there was no mileage in talking about Claudia and their disrupted lives.

"I'm here now. You obviously didn't push it too hard with Oscar at the time. Although you'd committed to me that you would say nothing to him." *The bastard's trying to unnerve me, does he really expect us to have a good relationship after this?*

"A little lesson, if I may, Jack. I actually told you there was no need to let him know, that's not the same as committing to not telling him. I always phrase those conversations very carefully — and most people, even pretty sophisticated people, like yourself, hear only what they want to hear. But, looking forward, if we're going to work together," he said, turning to Oscar, "can I talk about what we've agreed?"

"You'd better. I'd like to hear what you've understood in your own words anyway." Oscar wasn't looking friendly.

"If we work together, I'll try to give you background on what I think you should know. I will make sure that you aren't given any information that you can't deny, should it be necessary for you to do so. In the future," he said, looking to Oscar, "and this is the new bit, none of this information for Collins, or for Dickinson, will come from unethical sources, i.e. nothing hacked, nothing stolen. But this is the bit I insist on, because we can't always avoid straying into grey areas: if we unveil stuff like that, and it's material to you, I will flag it, but not communicate it. You will have to decide what you want to know." He looked again to Oscar, who nodded. "That's what I've also agreed with Peter Dickinson just now."

"Good," said Oscar, tersely.

"Does that wrap it up?"

"Yeah, leave Saunders to me."

"Of course."

"Not just 'of course', Rod. This is an instruction to you to have no communications whatever with Ken Saunders at all, unless you get clearance from Jack or me. Tell me you've understood."

He grimaced. "I had understood. No communications."

Oscar seemed to relax. "OK, Rod, thank you for seeing it from our point of view. I'm pretty sure we'll recover our relationship, but I am still feeling pissed at you today."

"I understand, and thank you for taking the bigger view. This stuff isn't easy."

"I know that, man." He smiled and stood up. "Now, we've already delayed Eleanor's holiday enough. Please apologise for me."

"I will, thank you." And he shook hands with each of them and walked swiftly out, both of them checking that he didn't stop at Saunders' desk. They returned to their chairs. "He'd have been pretty stupid to do that. I'd better get Saunders in now, although it's past my closing time already."

"Martha?"

"Yeah. She was in Tokyo last week, working with Peter on that deal of his, so he had a chance to talk to her. That convinced him that Rod had bigged up the story. Shame for you though, seems your Claudia didn't take so relaxed a view as I did — and I'll admit the incident did add to some seeds of doubt about the Networks operation that were already in my head then. That's one of the reasons why I started thinking about moving away from them. Well, he's earned one more chance, but he knows you and I will be watching, as will Peter. OK, I have to stay late and see Saunders, you can go off and fuck Rod's PA."

"I…"

Oscar laughed. "Ha, gotcha! But you did well with Rod on that one, he really tried hard to provoke you. I thought there was a chance we might make a poker player of you yet, but now I know I couldn't let you play snap with my grandson. Have a good weekend, Jack, and keep your pecker up!" Even Jack laughed at that, but Oscar exploded.

Some big questions had jumped into Jack's head but now wasn't the time to pursue them. What hadn't Claudia told him? Had she spoken with Martha? What were those connections? But they probably didn't matter. A big threat had been dealt with and, hey, he'd be CEO next year. Time to go fuck Henderson's PA.

She was waiting, although it was only five thirty. She walked up to him anxiously as he came through the door.

"Hey, everything's fine sweetheart, lots to tell you, most of it good."

"Shall we sit down? What's the bad bit first?"

They got to the sofa, he'd thrown his jacket on a dining chair. "He thinks I'm fucking you." She looked shocked. "I didn't respond, but he mentioned the Ritz. Is he following me, or you?"

"It must be me. There was nothing unusual about you being there. He's had someone follow me!" Her face was white. "I know we do that sort of stuff, especially in DC, but it's horrible when it happens."

"Steady, steady! I wouldn't jump straight to paranoia. If you have a lot happening in DC, do you stake out the Ritz?"

"Sometimes, not often. That would have been very unlucky. I'm a bit shaken."

"I can see that. Anyway, I denied it, but you were already worrying when the room service guy came in. If they were checking on me, wouldn't they ask the staff who my visitors were?" She thought for a while, then nodded slowly. "But Oscar obviously knows about us now, and he's happy enough. There's lots to tell you. You're still looking pensive?"

"Yes," she said, hesitating. "I'm just wondering whether it's worse being caught spying for you or fucking you," she said, her smile returning, "there's a lot of damage to my reputation either way."

"I can just spank you for being naughty, you don't have to choose between those two felonies."

"I think you're going to tell me about the rest of your day while we have a drink and then you can think of how to build the spanking into our lovemaking later."

"I've been thinking about that anyway."

"You look like you're going to tell me something."

"Yes, look, we've been good at role play." She looked as if she was about to interrupt. "Wait, we've been absolutely amazing at role play."

"That's better," she said in a mock harrumph.

"And we're not denying that we both enjoyed the events themselves, the assignments I should say, very much."

"True, where is this going?"

"But it probably couldn't have stayed like that, there were feelings growing." She snuggled in to him. "But now everything's changed, we've found ourselves making love sensually and passionately and, well, normally."

"There was nothing normal about how my ass felt last weekend, but I did think it was wonderful. So, what's your plan?"

"Well, you said it earlier, spanking in lovemaking, we need to make it work for us. Here's what's going to happen. There's a bottle of Taittinger waiting, that comes through into here. That will be our egg-timer on the conversation about today. Then the dom will arrive and you will do exactly as you are told while your body is abused and played with and, above all, enjoyed and the spell will be broken not when you come, because that may happen two or three times, but when the last drop of my cum has passed your lips."

She was turning her face to kiss him, her hand sliding on to his cock.

"No, my love, you have to wait for the egg-timer."

"Sorry master, but you have kind of made me impatient. I love your plan."

"It's your plan, really."

"Fuck it, I'm thrilled to call it our plan."

"So," he said, as he shared the last of the champagne between their glasses, "he's committed to clean up operations as far as we're concerned, and I'm including Dickinson in that, but his teams will still be covering some pretty dirty areas. That wasn't what you signed up for, was it? What will you do?"

She was pensive. "I don't like it, but I guess I knew, deep down, that we'd already crossed some red lines. I think I've been turning a blind eye. Is 'flexible principles' the phrase of the day? I don't know if that's a way I can work."

"You could talk to Rod about what you're prepared to cover, he might welcome some internal controls, or at least reference points."

"You don't know Rod, and if I bring up the topic that will confirm we've been talking."

"How long do you want to keep that a secret?"

"I was thinking of you."

He smiled. "Ah, love, let us be true to one another! For we are here as on a darkling plain, where ignorant armies clash by night. I'd rather put the secrets behind us but Rod may get very uncomfortable, so it's your decision. I'm for being open."

She nodded her head slowly. "I think I am, but I can take the weekend, can't I?"

"Of course you can."

Now her smile went a little wicked. "After all, I've yet to see how you're going to integrate spanking in love-making. Has anyone brought that fabulous beast to life?"

"Not so far as I know." *—But I thought I was so close once.*

"Well, while you're trying to work that out, can you promise me an extra slap for every line you just missed from the last stanza of Dover Beach?"

"That would be six, I think, but you don't know how that's going to work yet."

"Fortunately, that's your job, I'm merely the sub. Jack, we have the weekend for this, haven't we. I'm getting impatient."

He smiled. "Yes, we have the weekend. Am I meeting Mom on Sunday, to get the stories about the early boyfriends?"

"I like the thought, but let's kick that one down the road, please. I'd be subjected to ceaseless interrogation every phone call. It'll help me, too, to walk by the water and think what I'm going to do."

"Will you come by on Sunday evening to talk it through?"

"I'd like to, Jack. Will that be OK?"

"Of course it's OK. You're in this mess because of me. That's the least I can do."

"I'm in this mess because the business I work in is a bit corrupt. That's what I have to deal with." She picked up her glass. "But that's Sunday thinking. I'm more interested now in how you can integrate discipline into love-making. Cheers, let's drink up."

He smiled and raised his glass to her. "This is one of the most fascinating challenges of my life. Cheers! Can I rise to it, I wonder?" They put the empty glasses down. "You will dim the lights and then stand by the drapes."

She walked to the doorway, taking the empty glasses and bottle and placing them on the dining table. She lowered the lights.

"No, that's too much, I wish to enjoy the view of your naked body." She turned them up slightly, he nodded, she walked to the large window. "Pull the drapes open wider." She hesitated and said, "You have correctly deduced that I am about to tell you to remove all of your clothes. I will be happy if anyone can see you, you have a beautiful body, but it is unlikely that anyone is training binoculars on us at the moment, unless it's one of Rod's goons spying on you from those distant apartments on the far side of the Potomac. Once you have undressed, most of our activities will not be visible because of the balcony but, for now, you must stay where you are, remove all your clothes, and throw them on to the chair — and remember, you are doing this to please your lover, nice and slow, please."

A sultry look spread across her face. She began, very slowly, to unzip her dress. She draped it carefully over the chair to her side. He smiled, the suspenders and stockings, the tiny lace thong and the low platform bra had plainly been chosen for a traditional Friday evening.

"Turn around for me, slowly." She was slightly more statuesque than he would have chosen, but it was a beautiful, womanly body. "I was going to have you stand fully naked in the window but, like that, just as you are, you please me. Turn around once more, even more slowly. I want to admire that beautiful ass."

She stopped when she had rotated fully, their eyes firmly fixed on each other's.

"I will tell you what's going to happen. Soon, I will tell you to remove the rest of your clothes, you will do so and remain standing in the window while I make further preparations. When I return, I shall have a number of toys, none of them small, and, of course, a large tube of lube. I shall sit here, as I am now, but naked of course." Her gaze was unwavering. "You will drape yourself across my lap. I want to feel your skin against mine." Now she nodded slowly. "I will feast upon your body with my eyes and my fingers, I will slowly excite you by only manual means, touch alone will give you your first orgasm. That will be the first of four phases. The later ones will be explained as you are recovering breathlessly from the first climax. Do you understand?" She nodded, a serious look had replaced the smile. "Good, now remove your bra." It came off tantalisingly. She held the cups after the straps were loose, then let her sumptuous breasts sink slowly and voluptuously. He stood up, walked towards her, embraced her and cupped each breast in turn, squeezing the nipples enough to make her wince. He left her and resumed his seat. He allowed himself to smile as she stared, once again, into his eyes. "That wasn't in my plan, but they looked so beautiful, I couldn't resist." Now she smiled a little. "I want the stockings off. You will walk towards me, turn around, and use the armchair seat as a rest when you undo them and take them off. I wish to stare at your ass and your pussy while you are doing this." She moved slowly and turned. She bent over as she rolled the left stocking down towards her toe and bent even further to present him with an even more intimate view.

"Stop! Before you remove the other stocking, you will take off your panties. Your ass and pussy are a beautiful sight, I wish now to enjoy them naked." She smiled at him and nodded, then slid the panties down. Leaning forward he could have touched the beautiful bare pussy, but he stayed leaning back. She turned, bowing even deeper as the right stocking came off. He exhaled heavily. She was smiling when she stood up and turned to face him. Now you must return and face the window. She stood tall there, her early inhibitions had dissipated. "Discard the garter belt." She did so and draped it nonchalantly on the chair. "You are to stay exactly where you are. I shall return soon."

He tried to move slowly but his excitement was rising. No coolly draping his clothes on the bed, he cast them off quickly and retrieved the toys from the bedside drawer and pulled the cock ring down on to his stiffening cock. He put a bathrobe on and then managed to walk slowly back into the main room. She hadn't moved. He stood in front of the sofa. "You may turn and face me." She watched him place the items on the coffee table in front of the sofa: the tube of lube; the new vibrator, yes, not small; a bright red butt plug, she looked concerned, in truth he had been a little surprised by its size when it arrived — but all the more fun to help her relax — and, in spite of her complaints about soreness, she had been relatively easy to penetrate, unlike poor Joanna; and the paddle, it was leather, but very stiff, he wanted to keep her on his lap, he wanted her warm, soft skin against him, he wanted to feel her responding at all times, he did not want the separation that the cane would impose. He desired her very deeply, this would be exciting, but it should also be very intimate. He would want constant contact with her skin, with her body. He cast his robe aside, she smiled at the cock ring on his half-stiff penis.

"Come to me here," he said, as he patted the seat. "Then lay yourself across my lap." She moved slowly, elegantly, and knelt beside him. He ran his hand down her back, across her ass, and down her thigh. He looked up into her eyes, she smiled and brushed her breast across his face, and then stretched across him, snuggling in to let her hip squeeze his hardening cock. "This is beautiful," he breathed, and ran his hands all over her back, bottom and thighs. He could feel her moving in anticipation, he slapped her hard, once, on the right cheek. She twitched, that had been unexpected. When his hands went between her thighs, he eased them apart, there was no resistance. One hand and forearm moved on to her back to restrain her, his fingers moved to her pussy, she was drenched already, but he would still want the lube. He reached across, squashing her bottom with his chest, it felt gorgeous. He squirted a large amount between her cheeks. "Now it's playtime," he said, "don't worry if you have to come quickly, there is plenty time, there are plenty toys." He slowly eased his fingers inside her, one behind, two in her vagina and the pinkie began to play with her clit. She sighed deeply. He let his left hand move now to caress her bottom, it was beautiful, round and firm, and now adorned with a vivid red handprint. Quite soon she was breathing quickly. He took his pinkie off her clit. "You said I could come quickly!" He took his hand away completely and slapped her again on the other cheek. She had expected that, but it provoked a quiet 'ouch'.

"I know, but I love just touching you like this." Now both hands were caressing her back and ass and she relaxed on to him again. He squirted more lube. "More lube?" he slapped her, not so fiercely this time and somehow that felt more warmly sensual.

"More fingers." And his left hand spread her cheeks and he slid two fingers into her. He could feel her hips gyrating gently, she felt pleasantly tight around him, but three would feel wonderful, he pushed further, she was breathing heavily, she moved her legs to push her clit down on to his thigh. "Oh, a little more, a little more." He pushed all three in as far as he could. Her clit was rubbing him fiercely, it would be wrong to stop now. He was a dom, not a sadist. She was becoming noisier; he loved the feeling of exploring deep inside her. She was relaxing easily around him, pushing back harder and almost screaming as she came. He eased out slowly as her breathing subsided. "Oh, wow, just from that, wow, I'd never have thought."

He slapped her gently. "It wasn't just that, you were pressing your pussy on me, cheating. You're lucky I'm not a cruel man."

"And the coffee table?"

"Are instruments of pleasure for you."

"I'll be the judge of that."

He slapped her, much harder this time. "No, my love, I will be. You can tell me later." But his hands were moving across her, over all parts of her body, he loved the smoothness of her skin, the firmness of her bottom and thighs. "I find it immensely exciting to bring you up like that, but this is almost more gorgeous. I think my friend is telling you that."

"And you think you can make him wait?"

"Well, everyone has a plan, as they say, until the battle starts, but I would like to try to stick to it."

"You were going to explain it to me after phase one, you said."

"And I shall. Of course, you have cheated at step one, but that gives me confidence that step three will work."

"But step two first, yes?" Her head was turned towards him so he could see her smiling.

"Yes, so let's not get ahead of ourselves. But sit up and kiss me first."

"Is that a command?" She smiled again — he laughed.

"No, and it wasn't in the plan, but we're trying to integrate our special needs into love-making and I want to kiss you."

She sat up, he felt her full breasts squash on to his chest as their lips met tenderly, then passionately. "You're beautiful," he said, as she pulled away, "but we're worrying about him, aren't we?"

"Yes," she said, but knelt down, held his cock in one hand, and slowly enveloped its head in her mouth — but only briefly, then she stretched out languidly across his lap again. "What's next, master?"

"This is where two toys will stretch you and stimulate you."

"Am I allowed to say that your new red thing scares me?"

"As my lover, you can tell me. As your lover, I will be caring and sensitive, recognising, as I do, that it's rather larger than I expected." She nestled in more comfortably across him. "As your dom, however, I'm determined that you take everything, whatever the discomfort. The plug will be inserted first, then the vibrator, and we will try to sustain you on a plateau so you can enjoy the voluptuous sensations of being more full than ever. Then, when I judge the moment is right, my fingers will gently touch your clit and I will make the rhythm of my touching and pressing match yours as you rise to your second climax."

"Let's see what you can do with the red thing."

"I may touch you first."

"You're the dom, but it's no longer a secret that I love that, wow."

He squirted more lube and loved the ease with which his fingers could now enjoy exploring her. Her soft moaning was a delight as he moved deeper. She was relaxed, now was the time to try. He leaned across and picked up the plug, squirted lube on its tip and said, "Stick your bum a little higher."

"It's my bottom." He slapped her hard. "OK, sir, my bum is coming higher."

The first part was easy, but she began to squirm when the thickest part was still some way away, he eased back but she pushed her ass up again. "Don't you dare stop now, you wuss!"

He pushed again, further this time. She was panting and saying 'oh, oh,' loudly. He eased back again. "Did I say yellow?"

She hadn't said yellow. He squirted more lube around the thing, pushed a little harder when, suddenly, she pushed back quickly and, with one loud scream, it was all in. She collapsed on to him, breathing very heavily. "Oh, give me a moment, please, but that just feel amazing. Let me lie here and enjoy it, wow."

"Oh, sweetheart, take your time, I'm enjoying you," he said, and his hands and his eyes enjoyed her body.

Slowly he began to feel her hips moving on him. He reached for the vibrator. "Oh, I really don't know about him as well." He slapped her hard. "Ow, sorry, master. I am yours." When it was only half way in she was moving violently. "Touch me, touch me." He'd meant to wait but they were learning, making love would be touching her now, concentrating on her pleasure, and she began screaming as soon as his fingers touched her clit. He even found himself saying 'shhh' to her and, oddly, she seemed to respond but her movements felt violent for what seemed like minutes until she slowly ebbed into an easy rhythm. He tossed the vibrator onto to the table. "Oh," she said, still moving, "you'd better pull that big thing out too while I'm still relaxed."

He pulled on the plug carefully, but she still gave a loud squeal as it came out.

"I think it's cuddle time again," he said. She sat up and swivelled to sit on his lap. They kissed.

"Are you open to a little negotiation?" He eyed her suspiciously. "Oh, don't worry, I'm not trying to escape the paddle. I'd never fantasised about that before, all my discipline thoughts were caning, but now, with bare skin across your lap and my clit on your thigh while you spank me, I'm getting so excited about it. But I'm worried about him. I'd be thrilled if you ordered me to kneel down and suck you dry now." She looked momentarily horror-struck, her hands flew to her face to cover her mouth. "I can't believe I've actually just said that!" They both laughed. He pulled her closer to him.

"I'm not an unreasonable man. We'll try it your way in a moment. Hold me for a while first, though."

She snuggled in, he wanted to feel all of her on his skin. It was not a small body, there was not a fragile delicacy about it, it was a body that could be embraced, pushed and pulled, slapped and spanked without inhibitions. He was feeling free to utterly enjoy himself with her. He cuddled her tenderly, even his friend began to relax slightly.

She wiggled her hips. "I like it that he's relaxing. It means I don't have to rush now, and I'll have the joy of feeling him grow in my mouth later."

"I love that thought but I've no idea how it will affect my spanking motivation later."

She pulled away slightly to look in his eyes. "Jack, my love," she said, and smiled, almost laughed. "I have no idea what to expect but I'm not finding it so hard to switch from dom/sub to lovey dovey. I think, in spite of just now, I still want to discover how it feels to be spanked, with all this bare skin, in something like a loving relationship. This has been wonderful so far. I am worried about your poor little fellow, I think he deserves a treat, and I so want to taste you coming. Don't worry about later, but whatever you do, she will need more attention." She kissed him again. "Now please lean back and let me enjoy you. I will try to make you come slowly but do not, please, hold back. Let me have everything." And she slid off him and knelt between his knees.

He slid down the sofa to give her full freedom to play with him as she wished but although it felt like electricity as she held his shaft in one hand and carefully stroked the underside of his balls with the other, it was her eyes that completely captivated him. It was wonderfully erotic to watch the top of a head bouncing on his cock but to be held like this and to stare into those beautiful warm dark-hazel eyes was heavenly, and when the head of his ugly little monster disappeared between those gorgeous full lips and the other sensations began, it was still the eyes that held him captive. So, when she closed them, and leaned further forward to take more of him, the thrilling sensations coursing through him somehow failed to compensate for not seeing her eyes. But the sense of loss was fleeting, the habitual urges began to reassert themselves. He was feeling enormously stiff, her tongue and lips seemed to be touching every nerve, but her fingers, gently caressing his balls, were almost pulling the trigger on him.

"Woah, please, just a moment, could you ease back and look at me again for a moment."

She pulled back, lifted her lips from his cock and looked up at him with the most delightfully wicked smile he had ever seen. "As my master commands."

"I know silly things get said in moments like these, but you have the most beautiful eyes I have ever seen."

"I believe you, master, but I still think you would like me to suck your cock some more." But she had to wait a while until he had stopped laughing, and then, just before her mouth enveloped him again, she said, "This will be it. Please lean back and give yourself to this. Our little friend has been waiting while I have had two wonderful orgasms. He must have some splendid gifts for me. Just relax, focus on him and my mouth — and give me everything."

It was time to abandon plans and agendas, it was too easy to overthink, too hard to try to keep control, now was the moment to give himself. He felt her enveloping him, not just his stupid, stiff and utterly excited cock, but all of him and he knew that, as the unstoppable flood began, that he was giving all of himself to her. He stayed in a state of bliss for an unimaginable time, almost unaware of physical feelings. Then only slowly did he feel her arms resting on his thighs, her breasts brushing his legs, her dark brown hair still bobbing gently as she sought the last few reluctant dribbles, but then they moved to embrace each other, lying along the sofa to feel all their skin touching while their lips melded into the tenderest of kisses.

They lay in silence for a long time. Finally, he said, "That was so wonderful but I've a great fear that I'm going to disappoint you." He could feel her chuckling. "OK, so you know what I'm going to say."

"Always, master," she said, and she laughed lightly. "But I so wanted that and I'm certain he did, but you're going to tell me now that you can't play dom with the paddle." She snuggled in a little tighter. "But for a first attempt at integration, I thought that showed great promise. I adored it, but maybe we start with the paddle tomorrow?"

"That's a wonderful idea. I just want to play lovebirds for the rest of this evening."

"You make me very happy, my beautiful man."

27

"Ozawa sensei, what news on this fine, well, it's what…"

"Eight a.m. in Tokyo, Molloy san."

"I'm very grateful you're prepared to do this on a Saturday morning." He thought a moment. "Or should I be worried?"

"No, no, I believe I have good news, but I wanted to reach you before you begin to enjoy your Friday evening too much. It is six p.m. for you, I believe, and I thought I might catch you before your dinner, I hope I am right."

"You are exactly right, Ozawa sensei," said Andy, but he was doing his own calculations. "Am I right in assuming that your own Friday night could not be interrupted, and you couldn't therefore ring this morning?"

"I was engaged in discussions with Abego sensei yesterday evening and while the important points of our agreement are now very clear, I did not feel at eleven p.m. yesterday evening that I could aspire to my habitually lofty heights of lucidity. Abego sensei had some quite erroneous views on which is the best Junmai Daiginjo and I felt compelled to educate him. It is strange that a man of his education should be, in this respect, so ignorant. I suspect he has rather risen above his family, certainly I had never heard of them. But he is, nevertheless, a man of considerable insight and persuasive skills. I think you will be quite pleased with what he and I have provisionally agreed but I was not, how can I put this, not in a position to give an exact description of the details earlier in your business day, indeed I am still awaiting his written version of our understanding. I will transmit mine to him simultaneously with his transmission to me, but I do not expect that for another two or three hours and I felt I should give you the outline before you begin to enjoy too much sake yourself this evening."

"What I drink will have bubbles — and I would rather it was Bollinger than Bud. So, what's the deal?"

"Our proposal is that an offer of sixteen hundred yen per share should be made to ensure we can reach ninety per cent take-up of the shares."

"I'm speaking to you on the phone that I rely on as a calculator at the moment, so I can't do the math, but since that's a round number, I know that's forty-four per cent or so uplift. I suppose that's what I expected. That's the easy bit. What else?"

"Endo san feels that his sister would be content with a facilitation bonus of five hundred."

Andy knew this might be tricky, but he didn't want to lose momentum. "Just one second, please, sensei." He covered his phone and called out, "Jen!"

A slightly grumpy face emerged from the kitchen. He hissed, pointing at his phone. "It's Tokyo, can I borrow yours, I need to make some calculations." She shrugged, looked exasperated, but pulled her phone from her back pocket and dialled into the calculator screen. "Thank you, my darling." She shook her head and turned back into the kitchen. Maybe the frostiness would end when the deal was done — but he doubted it.

"That's a little over four million, sensei, that's not too bad."

"Thank you, but Endo san himself would require a similar sum for his role in facilitation."

"But he's already getting a forty-four per cent uplift on the value of his shares."

"But you should see this as a completion bonus on his retirement."

"And when does he retire?"

"Publicly not for one year, that way you can demonstrate continuity to your major customers."

"So, his payment is not due for one year?"

"That would not be so persuasive for him, Molloy san. He might lack the motivation to speak appropriately to his sister."

"And how much flexibility do I have on this number?"

"I have spent many hours in discussions, Molloy san, and I am afraid I have expended a great deal of your money on expensive sake to reduce the requirement to this level. We must regard that as the minimum we are able to achieve."

"Well, let's park that. I'd like the full picture. Nakamura himself must be the big one."

"You are right of course. He is the chairman and is prepared to remain in that position for two years, if you wish, while undertaking to do no more than liaise with key customers."

"For which he would require an expense account?"

"Of course, but it would not exceed his current level of expenditure."

"I think I might let the new chief executive take a look at that, or is it something I need to commit to now?"

"It would be better to commit, but there may be scope to reduce this element slightly. I mean, the entertainment budget must remain the same, but Nakamura san may take less than full access to it."

"OK, that's a wash, the money's going out anyway but it's part of future business expenses. Like I said, I'm going to see that as a local challenge."

"A wise attitude, if I may say so."

"Thank you," — *he can probably detect already that I'm impatient and pissed* — "but we need to get to the bigger number now. What does he want for a completion bonus?"

"Twenty."

"You've stopped talking yen, haven't you?"

"Yes, Molloy san, that's twenty million dollars."

"Paid if the business sustains profitability for two years after the merger?"

"Oh, it will undoubtedly do that."

"I am slowly learning to decipher your perfect English, Ozawa sensei, you are about to explain to me which of my assumptions is incorrect."

"I have come to appreciate the incisiveness of your insights over these past few months."

"So why am I smelling something here?"

"Well, the terminology of completion bonus will naturally make the sum more palatable to the bank and other key players, but Nakamura san will, of course, expect the payment to be made on the completion of the merger transaction. After all, his key contribution will be to ensure that the institutional shareholders are attracted by the deal. In this, of course, Endo san will also have a role to play."

"I think I know the answers to my next questions. Does Endo know what Nakamura will get? Will Endo's sister know what he's getting?"

"I think you already do know the answers to those questions. Abego sensei and I have gone to great pains to ensure a high level of confidentiality in all these discussions. Endo san knows what his sister will receive, he would not have agreed to receive less, but otherwise all information is secret between the parties."

"OK, I'm calculating now that you've spent six hundred and five million, that's above our upper limit."

"You are very quick, Molloy san, but I believe you are using an older exchange rate. My calculation yesterday evening showed the sum we have discussed so far to be a little under six hundred million dollars. Closer to five nine nine, to be exact."

"Well, I would say congratulations, but when you use the term 'discussed so far', there's obviously something you're still going to tell me."

"We do need to add the legal fees, Molloy san."

"Are we discussing your thirty some odd dollars per minute? That will not be part of the acquisition fee, surely, I will expense that against my business." Andy knew this was an argument he would lose, but sometimes you just have to give in to these urges to demonstrate resentment. *Let's just tell myself I have to keep the pressure on.*

"We are not discussing those fees, of course, Molloy san. Perhaps I may refresh your memory of the conversation we had with Dickinson san when we discussed our targets. I quite clearly pointed out that there is usually a completion fee paid to legal counsel upon a successful transaction."

You have to hand it to the old boy, thought Andy, this was a level of shamelessness that he'd never encountered elsewhere. "You're quite right, sensei, I do remember the discussion, but I had assumed a successful transaction was one where we stayed within our financial parameters and, even with your best exchange rate assumption, we are already there. That, for me, would be just about successful, but you are proposing to add how much to the transaction cost?"

"Well, the appropriate completion fee would be two and a half million dollars."

Andy knew he means each. *I'm not going to dick around with that one.* "I assume you mean to each party."

"Of course."

That probably wasn't said in as patronisingly smug way as Andy felt it was — *it's only two fucking words, for Christ's sake* — but he could tell he was getting prickly. "That puts us four million above our limit." There was just a silence — *a silence at thirty dollars plus a minute* — Andy got himself calm again. "When we look at these components, sensei, where do we have the most flexibility to adjust the numbers?"

"My own view is that the upper limit you have set is best viewed as a guideline. You will be paying, after you consider the cash, approximately four hundred million for a business that will be worth eight hundred to you, according to your financial analysis. The attractiveness of that can scarcely be upset by four million dollars."

"You can try to call it a guideline, sensei, but Peter Dickinson and I were very clear that it was a limit, so something else needs to be adjusted. This is where I may be about to show my habitual weakness, my impatience. I presume the family numbers have already been discussed." —*Slow yourself down, Andy!*

"And agreed, that is correct, they could no longer be adjusted if the deal is to proceed."

"So, the offer comes down to fifteen seventy yen per share. That's still around a forty-two per cent uplift."

"I think the round number, sixteen hundred, was seen as important to Nakamura san if he were to be able to sell this deal to the important shareholders."

"Well, the round number of six hundred million is seen as extremely important by Dickinson san and myself, or the deal does not go ahead."

"And that is the current view of you both? I am acting in this for Dickinson san also, do you not think we should obtain his views?"

Now Andy Molloy was managing to overcome his impatience. "I will, of course be discussing this with him over the weekend, but it would be remiss of me if I allowed us to conclude this call with an impression in your mind that he might take a different view from me."

—*My God, Andy, are you beginning to sound like this cunt?*

"I do understand, and I thank you for your frankness, but it would be equally remiss of me if I failed to point out that the numbers I have given you, are anything less than firm."

"I will talk with Peter, but I must request that you have a further conversation with Nakamura san, and we should talk again on Monday. I can make six a.m., is eight OK with you?"

"That will be fine for me, I will have all Monday for further discussions."

"I will get a message to you after I've spoken with Peter, but I'm pretty certain you'll be starting Monday with a four-million-dollar target and I'm guessing fifteen seventy yen per share is your best way of getting there."

"I look forward to hearing from you on Monday, and I do retain high hopes that we will see you here at the end of next week to sign an agreement."

"I retain hopes, sensei, but I'm not calling them high. Anyway, I don't want to seem churlish, you have got us very close. Please just see if you can push them over the line."

"I will, of course, do my utmost. Please enjoy your weekend."

"You too, sensei, bye."

"Do I get my phone back now?" Jen asked, acidly.

Andy smiled and handed it to her. "Wanna come to Tokyo with me next week?"

She took the phone and squinted at him. "All that way for jetlag and raw fish? Don't think so."

He knew it was wrong but, as Jen turned and went back into the kitchen, Tania came into his mind.

Dear Sensei, I have had discussions with Peter Dickinson and we have agreed that six hundred million, including all associated costs, is our limit and not a guideline. I hope this helps. Good luck with your discussions tomorrow. Best regards, Andy Molloy.

The discussion with Peter had been a strange one. He'd never known Peter quite like it, he was unusually uncomfortable, and Andy had insisted on knowing why.

"I think we'll get the deal we want, Andy, at least in terms of money, because I've learned a little more about how these guys operate. You know something of the work that Henderson's organisation does for me?"

"Yeah, a little, twilight zone stuff."

"I think we're in a pretty dark twilight. I had to talk to him yesterday after I'd spoken to someone else who has similar misgivings, and we decided we'd apply much clearer and tighter guidelines to the work he does for us. Well, we're tidying that up but, in the meantime, I discover they have been digging up stuff on your Mr Nakamura and, effectively, blackmailing him with it. So, he's pretty likely to be the way that Ozawa bridges the gap — and, I'd guess, since there are more of us addicted to the drug of greed than to the elixir of success, that he'll choose the option of sticking to the twenty million for himself and lowering the offer price. It's unlikely that the institutions are going to turn down forty-two per cent. Well, if they do, they'd have wanted fifty and that's way uneconomic with all these other costs."

"You wanna pull the plug?"

"What, and revert to your lingering death scenario?"

"Easy now, having got to know them, I think the finance guys were right. The US was just an opportunity for them, it wasn't a strategic commitment. I don't detect a real drive for expansion in that business, not nowadays, and I think the competitive threat will wither, especially with the progress we're making here."

"I hear all that, and if you work harder you might persuade me, but there's an opportunity to build a real global enterprise for you. It's a well-run company, everything we've seen tells me that. My problems are with the lawyers and with the owners and, above all, with how this is being done. But that's happened, *amor fati*, let's accept that it's fate, embrace it and move on. I won't do business this way again, Henderson knows that, but he thought he was acting in my best interests. Well, don't let me sound too naïve here, he was also very much acting in his own best interests and that's got him into serious trouble with my new friend Oscar. It's also what caused Claudia's relationship to crumble — but that's another story. On the matter in hand, I'd stick with your position and I'm confident they'll find a way of making Nakamura bend." Then, suddenly, he sounded cheerier. "Another point for you, my boy, Will and Yamamoto are keeping a very close eye on the accounts and the latest cash number is going to come out at two hundred and ten million. It doesn't sound like Ozawa sensei is quite up to date. I'd stick with your limit nevertheless, after all, you wanted to come in under that. It looks like you might beat it by ten million. That would be a job well done. Maybe you will have to fly there to sign. What's the plan?"

"Signing on Friday, so I'd leave here on Tuesday."

"Are you taking Jen? You've been away a lot."

"I've offered, she was pretty unenthusiastic."

"I know what you mean, I've tried to get Yvonne out to China but that hasn't worked."

"Are we heading for bachelorhood?"

"Who knows, but I have checked the wording on the pre-nup," Peter said, and gave a hollow laugh. "Anyway, good luck with the deal — and with Jen. I think of myself as Cupid, I'd hate to see you two fail, try and get her to go. And you can't take Tania this time, I don't know what Claudia would do to me if you tried."

Andy never normally set an alarm, he always woke before six, but to be safe this morning he'd set it for five forty-five but forgotten to switch it off. He came out of the bathroom with it buzzing and Jen groping to stop it. He took it from her.

"What the fuck, Andy? What's that about?"

"I have a call with Tokyo, sorry, it's important."

"It's always fucking important." She pulled her duvet around. Morning was never her best time. He pulled on a tee-shirt and some jogging pants — *get the call out the way first and then dress properly*. He was just leaving the room when she called out, "Is this what it's going to be like? Away half the time and six o'clock calls when you're not?" She was sat up again now, and scowling.

"Maybe this call will tell me that the deal's off and we'll have nothing to worry about anyway."

She shook her head. "We still have plenty to worry about, Andy," she said, and pulled the duvet over herself again.

Normally, he could avoid starting the day like this. He would leave tea by her bedside and, mostly, be gone before she even woke. The tetchy exchanges, always skirting the real issues, happened usually at dinner and led to them retreating to their separate workrooms to spend the evenings not speaking.

"Ozawa sensei, what news do you have for me?"

"I believe I have some very good news for you, Molloy san." Andy felt a stab of excitement, he had primed himself for a rejection. "Nakamura san thinks that, at fifteen eighty, you will receive a satisfactory uptake if he puts all his efforts into persuading the institutions. In this he will also be supported by the best efforts of Endo san."

"I don't wish to seem ungrateful, sensei, but looking at my notes from yesterday, we needed fifteen seventy to meet the target. Has he agreed to reduce his bonus?"

"Oh no, that would not be appropriate."

"So, we are short of our target. How do we bridge the gap?" Andy snorted, "I don't think you're going to tell me that the lawyers have reduced their fees." Andy could somehow picture him smiling smugly in some office in Tokyo.

"Of course not, Molloy san, but I was speaking to Yamamoto san earlier today. You know who I mean?"

"Yes, I know who you mean. Yoshi at the bank." *You cunning old goat!*

"Well, it appears there has been a revision in the cash estimate and that our offer, as now agreed with all parties, is eight million dollars below the limit you gave us."

Andy was shaking his head in grudging admiration, and smiling. "Well, I must say an enormous thank you, sensei, and congratulations."

"Oh, no the congratulations are entirely due to you. You have given very clear guidance and shown, ahem, if I may say so, impressive patience. Now we must plan for Friday. Nakamura san will convene a meeting of all the directors on Friday. He would like to introduce you to them for you to talk about your vision."

Andy was cagey. "Will this be before we sign our agreement?"

"Yes, but that is a formality."

"But they all have to agree, don't they? Couldn't the deal blow up if one of them objects?"

"Oh, that will not happen. They will follow the guidance of Nakamura san."

"But what about all this I hear and read about consultation and bosses listening and gathering the views of their subordinates?"

"That is a much-misunderstood idea about how Japan works, and it is important that you appreciate the reality if you are to guide this business successfully. The leader consults, but the clever worker always understands the leader's wishes and offers appropriate opinions. So, you should take the opportunity on Friday to present your vision of the future of the global enterprise and they, those who you wish to retain, will be enthusiastic to pursue those goals. There are some very good people, Molloy san. And do not worry, the signing will take place at four p.m."

"To be followed by an evening at Mama san's?"

"It is a place where we can guarantee security. The deal must remain secret until completion of due diligence. We must allow three weeks for that, I am told."

"And we can maintain secrecy for that long?"

"That will not be a problem, the directors will commit to Nakamura san's guidance and he will be very clear about the need for absolute confidentiality."

"Sensei, I will appreciate a little help on a rather difficult topic that relates to secrecy and confidentiality." Ozawa must have known what was coming, but he certainly wouldn't break the silence. "I understand you have found ways of influencing the family to accept this decision."

"Abego sensei and I have been able to persuade them to accept our numbers. The principle of the deal itself was accepted early on. It is in the family's interests almost as much as in yours."

"I'm not going to get squeamish about this, I promise you that. I'm assuming you've got me protected so I can't be sued for anything?"

"Of course."

"But I do want to understand how this process of persuasion has worked. Dickinson san and I both have concerns about how these processes are managed."

"We will talk when you are here, but it would be unwise in global operations to expect similar values and principles to apply universally. We have worked within our Asian norms."

"Let's talk on Thursday, OK? I'll work out my travel schedule and email you later."

"Very good. I look forward to seeing you Thursday."

Well, it was going ahead, and Andy found it easy to quell his concerns and become overawed and excited about what he would be doing. Peter was in Europe — he sent a text to get him to call. Who could he speak to, to share this with, to be excited with him? Obviously not Jen, but he would try another attempt at persuasion later, add a few days, make it a holiday. He found himself surprisingly unenthusiastic, unwilling to put the effort into the necessary cajoling. Claudia, yes, he must ring her. He hesitated, then dialled Tania.

"Andy?" The voice was sleepy.

"The deal's going ahead!"

"Yeeeeee, that's amazing. Oh, absolutely brilliant. I am so completely thrilled for you. Wow, well done, my man. Wait, what the fuck time is it?" But then Andy heard an alarm in the background. "Oh, six thirty, I'm getting up anyway. Wow, have you just heard?"

And he talked about all that had gone on and gave her some hints about the darker processes — the woman would run her own business one day, and didn't they have a Henderson connection?

"When are you up here again?"

"Next week, I think, I'll have to check. Why?"

"Can you stay over? Have dinner with me and we'll celebrate?"

"I'd love to, thank you."

"We should also spend a little time on Henderson. Doesn't Giddings have something to do with him?"

"Yes, he and Dad are old Yaleys. He scares me."

"Well, we'll talk about that too. But right now, I have to plan for Japan this Friday."

"I am so excited for you. I think it's a stunning opportunity. Wow. Does Claudia know?"

"Not yet, I was going to call her later."

"Please do. She's here at the end of this week and I don't want to tell her. She's a mother hen about me, won't let me spend time with dangerous men." She paused, and said, "Especially you, for obvious reasons."

He laughed. "See you next week, angel." Angel? Oops, that was new.

"See you, Andy."

28

Tania had picked Hakubai. It was an easy walk from the office. "We can celebrate for Andy, although I suppose we still shouldn't be overheard talking about it." Claudia nodded. "But I thought we're very unlikely to go to Tokyo again soon, so Japanese food just seemed the right way to round it off."

It was New York City but, once they were in the restaurant, it had a pretty authentic feel, and she knew the food would be easier than confronting a steak — and leaving half of it because of its size.

It had been a good day. They had seen three good people and had already agreed that the West Coast man and the woman who could re-locate to DC, were probables. Claudia would go through everything on the phone with Sandy in the morning. He was busy on another recruitment now, which was good — it let them enjoy their promised girlie evening, although Claudia was still on UK time She'd only flown in the day before, so this wouldn't be a late one — and they had an early start in the morning to get to DC. She'd left Collins too long, it was time to check in, although Tania had kept the account buzzing, Davis was always enthusiastic about her when she called him. So, did she really need to go? Davis had been fairly insistent.

She'd texted Jack, hoping he'd take the hint and be working elsewhere. Was that what she really wanted? Hadn't she been looking for texts with a dinner invitation, hoping she'd have a reason to postpone the flight back?

But she'd be seeing Peter on Saturday, for dinner. He hadn't said why — 'just catching up, my dear, we'd bemoaned the loss of our careless hours, why not grant ourselves a few'. It hadn't felt right to enquire about Yvonne when he said it would be just the two of them. Flying back in on Saturday morning, which is what she would have to do if Jack sprung a dinner invitation, wouldn't be the best way to get ready for Saturday evening. What were the unresolved feelings from Tokyo? For him? And, when she thought about it, for her? Would these hours be so careless?

Tania was still bouncing about Andy's news when they sat down. "But I must shut up about it now. He'll tell me about it next week. He's asked me to stay over so he can take me to dinner to celebrate." Claudia scowled at her. "And don't give me that look! I completely behaved when I was in Tokyo last time. You were the one having suspicious evenings. What's the deal with that old guy?"

Claudia snorted. "I'm not going to respond if you call Peter old." But she realised from the triumphant smile that she'd fallen in to Tania's trap.

"Ha, see, there is something. But he's married, isn't he?"

"Oh, there's a lot more baggage than that."

"Are you going to tell me more?"

"Not until you grow up. Anyway, you've got Andy to worry about. You don't normally stop over, do you?"

"No, I fly there and back, or I fly on somewhere else. But he said he wanted to talk to me about Henderson." Claudia felt shocked, but realised quickly that she shouldn't be, the tentacles of that arrangement were spreading everywhere. "You don't like him either, do you? Don't you have some more background?" Claudia was silent a long time. "You're going to have to tell me something. This has obviously triggered a train of thought in you." Tania was looking serious.

"Well, I guess it fits in with Andy's deal. I don't know where to begin. I mean, I ought first to say that Henderson gave me a big break at Collins, well, gave me a lot of support anyway, and set me up to meet your dad, even though I wouldn't shag him." Tania choked on her sparkling water, laughing as she tried to drink. "Pretty noble, don't you think?"

"Nobility isn't the first word that pops into my head when I think of Henderson," she said, smiling broadly, "but he hasn't even tried to shag me. What's wrong with me?"

"You'll be fine. My job is just to make sure you stay busy, your father's instructions, keeping you chaste for David." She thought a moment. "Wilkins, wasn't that his name?"

Tania's eyes went heavenward. "Yes, I still get calls occasionally, but I try to ignore them. What did you think about him?"

"We talked about that on that first evening. I thought he had no personality, and you would dominate him, but, hey, who am I to give relationship advice? Maybe you settle down with him and have a row of Andys for fun."

"What do you do, though?" She looked serious for a moment. "Apart from your gorgeous sugar daddy."

Claudia closed her eyes. "For a moment there I was almost trapped into taking you seriously."

"I would like to know, though. When I first met you, I thought you had something going with someone. Was it the job that stopped that, getting your business set up?"

"No, not really. Maybe I should say more about Henderson but, at the end of the day, I should have handled things differently."

"There's a lot I'd like to understand. I don't want to pry but, if you'd like to talk, I'd be a very grateful listener."

So, Claudia talked, as tactfully as she could — the table beside them had filled — about the concerns about Henderson's methods and how Collins and Dickinson were reining him in — and she went on to talk about the

Singapore plot and the fallout from that and its impact on her relationship.

"Isn't that something where you can just say sorry? I apologise for being goofy, but, duh!"

"It's never seemed that simple. We tried to make a long-distance relationship work, tried to be open about everything and, ultimately, now, I find out that he had been open, more or less. More than me, probably, well," she said, then paused, "certainly more open than me. But, looking back, trying to be open about everything doesn't feel like it was the right thing to do, everyone should have their little bit of private space. So, I think we've ended up not liking each other very much. He got very resentful of the 'fucking interrogations', as he called them." She drifted off into thought again. "Well, maybe we find out tomorrow."

"Tomorrow?" Tania looked puzzled.

"Yes, he's still at Collins, it's where we met. Well, we worked together in the UK of course, but we seem to have become global citizens. But he's DC-based now. I've warned him I'll be there. I'm hoping he'll be somewhere else."

"Do you really mean that?"

"I actually think I do. I'm happy now, I have a lovely friend who I see occasionally, and I think that's enough, although I do have a mysterious dinner invitation from my sugar daddy for Saturday. And I don't think I want the pain and worry of all that other stuff. And I actually think that's not such a bad plan for you, by the way, the one with David."

Tania looked thoughtful. "Does that mean I can shag Andy next week?"

"No, certainly not!" But they were both laughing.

29

I have to be in the office this afternoon, I'm afraid, I have a meeting with Oscar at 3. Hope you can work around that. J

Yes, she could work around that. She was booked on the 18.25, she could just leave a little early. But there was a late flight if he wanted to talk. Why was she even thinking that?

They got to the office by ten and Davis was ready for them. He'd appointed someone new to run the Collins programme and wanted to introduce her and get an update on the current status from Claudia and Tania. Claudia's mild irritation at the change was softened by its cause: Arnold's promotion. He would join them to make it a handover meeting. She and Tania both liked him, and he had done very well over the two years — and head of HR for the US unit, a big step up, meant that leading the programme was gaining higher recognition and the candidates for the new head were being chosen from a bigger talent pool this time around.

Arnold's wish to take them out and celebrate hadn't fitted Claudia's schedule, but there was time for big smiles and hugs when he came into the goldfish bowl meeting room.

Claudia remembered Céline, his successor. She'd been working in France when Claudia had been running the programme and had been a very capable and enthusiastic supporter, so there were more smiles and hugs when she came in and it meant Claudia could introduce her to Tania.

Davis was sat there getting increasingly edgy as the good wishes and the happy memories were being effusively traded. "I hate to break up the wonderfully warm reunion, guys, but we have quite a lot to get through. I'm hoping you're going to give us a status update, we only have you today. Arnold's got a little more time to take Céline around." Claudia smiled at Tania, Davis had an ambivalent attitude to the programme; it was the one responsibility area for which his department got plaudits, but he was, personally, always assumed to be distant from it. He was strangely uncomfortable with employee engagement and his lip service was widely recognised for what it was. And Claudia guessed that the latest issues around the leadership changes, as far as she could deduce from Jack's messages, would have placed him outside a magic circle that he would have felt he should have belonged to. So, a man a little at odds with his situation, but maybe that was how Oscar liked to manage, keep your senior people uneasy.

That thought was reinforced when, as she was

concluding her introduction, she saw Davis, with a flicker of irritation, look over her shoulder to the doorway. "Davis, I'm going to steal this young lady for a little while." She looked round, astonished to see Oscar Maguire standing there. She stood up; he was smiling broadly at her. "Can these people manage without you for a little while Claudia? We have some things to discuss."

"Er, yes, Mr Maguire."

"Oscar," he said, quite sharply, almost as if he were admonishing her for not using his first name.

"I'm sure Tania can cope." Then, her presence of mind kicked in. "Oscar, can I introduce Tania Gunter? She works with me, she's the main Collins contact now."

Tania stood up, he offered his hand and narrowed his eyes, as if dredging his memory. "Hello Tania, I'm Oscar. Gunter? Aren't you Giddings?" Tania beamed at him. "My God, you're Arthur's girl!" She nodded. "Well, I'll be damned, you had braces when I last saw you. My goodness, well, you help these good people please while I take Claudia, but do come over when you're finished and tell me how your parents are."

"I will, of course, sir."

"Hah, sir, indeed, you call me that to make me feel old. Your father always said you were the cheekiest. My God, it's lovely to see you. Anyway, apologies guys, but I'm sure I'm leaving you in capable hands. Claudia, come this way please."

Claudia shrugged at Davis and followed Oscar out. He led her to the meeting room near his desk, it had always seemed to be a holy of holies when she'd visited in the past, entered only by very senior executives, directors and a few visiting VIPs.

"Please, take a seat. Can I get you a coffee?"

"No, I'm fine, thank you, Oscar, really."

"I'm sure you can guess why I've grabbed this opportunity."

"Jack used to say that you started every conversation with an open question or a neutral statement when people's defences were down, and you found out more that way than by any incisive interrogation after they were ready for you."

He laughed very loud. "Well, young lady, I really wasn't trying to trap you into anything, but I'd rather play poker against him than you any day." Now was the time to smile and see what he said. He studied her carefully and smiled back at her. "One big thing I wanted to do was say thank you. I don't know how much Jack or Peter have said to you, but we were quite close to a big mess here. We're lucky you had the connections you did." He waited to see if she would speak. "And we're lucky you managed to get over your problems with Jack, but I'm guessing that helping Peter was a big motivation." He waited again, and then smiled when it was obvious she was saying nothing. "I count myself fortunate to have made that connection, by the way, he's an impressive man. I don't suppose our paths will cross but it would be good to get together some day. At least I feel he's someone I could call any time now, one of the very few I would trust. Now, we'll get back to that in a minute, but what's the story with Tania?"

Clever, she thought, this would get her talking. "I did some work at Giddings. It was while I was still here, but Rod Henderson wanted me to help Arthur Gunter. When I went down there, I met Tania. She really impressed me and wanted to run the programme there, which she did very well. Then Arthur asked me if she could work with me for three years to broaden her experience. I agreed immediately, she's been brilliant but, longer term, I think he hopes she'll run the place."

"Will she do that?"

"It's always difficult when people are young, isn't it?" He nodded. "But she's one of the most talented managers I've ever met, so, yes, there's a good chance if she wants to."

"You make a good point. People keep evolving. I've been seeing that even in my senior people and one or two haven't been happy with the way they see their careers going." He stopped, thought for a moment, and chuckled. "Well, with the way I see their careers going, really. But I'd concluded that Jack was the best fit to succeed me and that'll happen in a year or so, but it almost got derailed, that's why I wanted to say thank you to you, especially, but also to Peter. Do you see him soon?"

"Yes, Saturday."

His eyes narrowed and he waited. "Well, please do say thank you from me. Will you be seeing Jack today?"

"It doesn't look like I shall. I know he's in later, but I'll probably have gone by then."

He waited a while, eyeing her carefully. "Could you tell me a little about how you see Henderson? I wanted to say hello and thank you while you were here, but this is the other reason for calling you over."

She relaxed and smiled. "I think you've made your Faustian bargain, haven't you?" He breathed in deeply and nodded. She shrugged. "I can't paint a simple picture for you. At one level, I'm grateful, he saw the potential of the programme and pushed both it and me." She eyed him levelly. "I think he might have wanted a different relationship with me." He grimaced and nodded. "But his support never wavered when that didn't happen. He's always seemed seriously interested in lifting corporate performance. But then he does things that, well, I don't know, you see more deeply into that dark side than I do. I think Peter's had to make his peace with that, or Japan wouldn't happen for him. I thought you two had a meeting of minds."

Oscar looked pensive. "I think we did, but we also both have uncomfortable feelings because the basis of trust has been, well, let's not get too dramatic, it's been disturbed. Now, may I take you back a moment to a point you made in passing? You said he wanted a different relationship with you. I don't want to be indelicate here Claudia, but what you said next is very important…"

"That his support never wavered?"

"Yes. That tells me something, I think…" He waited.

"He never made me doubt that making the business better was the prime thing for him. Exporting it to Giddings was his idea — and although it gave him a chance to approach me on my own," she said, then stopped. "I'm sorry, it's not easy to talk about."

He smiled. "Hey, I know that, I don't want to underestimate the seriousness of harassment and it's important background to what you're saying. So, I very much appreciate you being frank about it. I know this is clumsy of me but the key point for me here, and I think for Peter, is understanding Rod's prime motivation."

"Well, his advances were clear, but not really offensive. He even told me once that he knew I didn't fancy him that way," she said, smiling at the memory, "but you guys shouldn't underestimate just how threatening even those casual advances can be."

"I do appreciate that, and we try to deal with it."

"I know that, when I worked here, we stamped on it pretty hard. So, sorry, I didn't mean to derail this conversation."

"No, no, that's fine, as long as you don't mind treating it as background for these purposes."

"That's OK, the important point is that he really was dedicated to doing the best for the business. I was with him and Arthur Gunter at Giddings, closing out the visit, and he was very blunt with Arthur, his old Yale buddy — and they do seem like the best of friends — he told him straight that even he would be under threat as chairman if the business didn't improve. I was shocked, I have to admit, but he managed it very well. He asked him if he wanted a job, or a business — I thought that was quite clever."

"Oops," he said, smiling. "I shall have to be careful what he says to me, then. But, seriously now, thank you very much for that, I know it's not easy to talk about. But I feel a little more comfortable now. I'm going to worry still about his dirty tricks and keeping us insulated from them, but at least I can worry a little less about his motivation." Now he sat up a little straighter. "And I'm going to resist the temptation to apologise on behalf of all men. I'm afraid I'd spend too much of my life doing that if I went down that route," he chuckled evilly. "That's a good job to keep Davis busy. But the stupid thing I often observe is the vanity of men. I mean Rod's a smart enough guy, quite presentable, I suppose, really, but he makes advances to a beautiful woman who already enjoys the devotion of two of the world's most charming men. It's crazy! Well, I know we never really met before, but I was always very aware of what you were doing and, as you know better than anyone, it has had a profound effect on us and, although I tease the guys about letting you go, I'm happy you're exporting the stuff so successfully. Peter's a very smart and lucky man. Jack, of course, is a little bit stupid, so maybe you've outgrown him, but," he said, breathing in deeply, "I guess he's still smart enough to run this place." He laughed lightly. "Now, is there anything you need from me?" She shook her head. "Then I'm going to let you get off, I've already got Davis pissed at me again." He was obviously untroubled by the thought. "And I'm just going to say thank you one more time and please give my very best regards to Peter." He stood up and offered his hand.

"And thank you very much for your time." She had the sense, as Jack had always told her, that, even in the little asides, every word had had a value.

The discussion, when she re-joined the meeting, was very animated but seemed positively focused on taking the programme forward, only Davis looked like a passenger. She looked at him for a while, apparently trying to contribute to a discussion sweeping rapidly past him, the HR head of a big corporation, but clearly seen by the boss as a poodle. All that aspiration, all that apparent achievement — and to end up like this. But she had no complaints, he'd given her the space to flourish — and then she was pulled into the debate.

They wrapped up by twelve with Claudia feeling good about Céline. She sent Tania to see Oscar and hung on to the room. It gave her a chance to call Sandy. They agreed on the woman and on West Coast man. Wow, a base in San Francisco, two of Peter's businesses were there, both of which had asked her to look at them.

That would take a lot of her time. She was feeling more and more pressure and would need to talk to him. Maybe the hours on Saturday wouldn't be so careless.

She looked around. The office, which seldom seemed busy outside staff weeks, had almost emptied as people went for lunch. In the far corner she could see Tania and Oscar chatting animatedly and some of Oscar's words came back to her. What was he really saying about Jack? About Peter? What had he really taken out of a one-hour conversation that must have focused on some serious business issues? What was Saturday really about?

Then Jack was there! She'd been daydreaming, but here he was, sat opposite her.

"Hi Claudie. Sorry, it felt too cowardly to skulk around outside. Tell me to go of you want to."

"No," she said, and hesitated. "No, of course not. How are you?"

Oscar suddenly leaned into the room. "I'm just taking Tania out for a snack. Oh, Tania, you'd better meet Jack Stephens. Jack, this young lady is our prime Brodie contact and I've seen her in dungarees swinging from my apple trees."

Jack stood and shook hands; even Tania looked uncomfortable and glanced quickly at Claudia.

"Well, you guys won't want to join us, we'll see you later." Oscar would have known how awkward it was but bludgeoning his way through it was the only way, she thought. Tania looked over her shoulder as she left.

Jack smiled, slightly nervously, she thought. "Did you know that?"

"No, it was surprise to all of us this morning. I met her at Giddings and her dad wanted her to work with me for a few years."

There was an uneasy silence.

"You might remember, Henderson took me down there."

"I remember it well, he was after you."

"That's partly what Oscar wanted to talk about." Jack looked puzzled. "He's trying to assess whether Henderson is worth the risk. I suppose that's something you'll have to worry about, isn't it?"

He shrugged. "We'll see. Best laid plans, and all that. We've both had some very big surprises, haven't we?" He left a pause. "So, what did you conclude?"

"I told him about the support I got, and I told him a story about Giddings. I feel uncomfortable about Rod, but I have to admit that some good things get done. I guess the question for you and Oscar, as well as for Peter, is can you manage the risks. How did you get wind of all this anyway? It came from you originally, didn't it?"

He seemed to think for a long while, then looked straight at her. "Not from me really, Claudie, it came from Lavinia. You remember her?"

And Claudia knew, in that instant, that she was being told much more — *try and stay composed* — "I never met her. But I got a lot of help from her. She's Rod's PA?"

He nodded, but the silence was awful. Suddenly, Sarah burst into the room. "You devil, why didn't you say you were coming?" She hugged Claudia, who'd barely had time to stand. Sarah turned to Jack. "Sorry Jack, but this bad beast is too important for little me these days."

"It's only…"

"I know, I know, it's only a flying visit but I warn you, if I don't get ten minutes and a cup of coffee before you leave," she said, drawing a deep breath, "your programme's gonna have some serious budgetary issues." She laughed and hugged Claudia again.

"I'll drop by, I promise." She sat down again. It felt like a squall had passed. She looked at Jack. "Lavinia and you?" He nodded. She exhaled, then smiled. "Thank you. No interrogations, don't worry. I'm sorry about Singapore. I should have trusted you more. My new bestie tells me that."

"Martha?"

"Yes," she said, and they smiled. "I can't tell you how weird those conversations felt but it turns out you were being quite noble."

He shook his head slowly. "It never felt like it. I always felt like I was somehow in the wrong."

"That's 'cos you fucking well were!" But she was laughing before the alarm spread too far across his face. It took a while for the next sentence to come. "I guess we've arrived at different places, haven't we?"

He seemed to nod reluctantly. "It looks like it, my love, it looks like it."

She stood up slowly. "Guess I'd better go see Sarah or Tania will have no budget."

30

She'd wept in the taxi. She'd wept in the plane. First class — *upgrade, fuck it, I need space to myself.* But somehow, on the M3 in the slowly lifting gloom of a damp November morning, she began to look ahead. George would have already driven the guys to school and Pat would be waiting with tea and updates. She'd already scanned the emails on her phone in the car but the real news, the colour, the music and the gossip, was waiting with breakfast. And she had a lot to tell Pat.

"You've been upset, love," said Pat, sliding a mug across the table, "you've got that brave face on."

"I saw Jack yesterday, Pat. He came into head office." Pat nodded slowly and waited. "He's got somebody else." Suddenly, she was sobbing on to Pat's shoulder, great heaving shudders that almost unbalanced them as they stood and hugged.

"Just let it out, dear," Pat mumbled, hanging on to her tightly. It seemed to take minutes to pass, but slowly the shakes subsided, and they separated and sat down. Then suddenly, taking a big tissue from the box on the table, she was able to laugh through the tears and snot, and blowing her nose made her laugh again.

"Oh, that was good." Another laugh. "I think I've been waiting two years for that. Thank God it's out now."

Pat still looked concerned.

"Oh, I'm not kidding myself it's all gone. I'm sure there'll be plenty more of those horrible empty nights."

"But you've got Alphonse, haven't you?"

Another laugh. "Oh, Pat, I do adore you, but Alphonse is a special sort of friend."

Pat nodded as if a realisation was dawning. "Ah, I thought he looked a little…"

"Too good to be true?"

"I wasn't going to say that, Claudie, you're a beautiful woman but…"

"Just a little more stylish than most men?"

Pat smiled. "Well, they usually are, aren't they? But he seems like a very good friend."

"He is, a very good friend, but…"

"No, I won't be telling George."

"I'll wait until after the football before I tell Jo."

"But what's tomorrow night then? You don't normally see Peter at a weekend. Well, you don't normally see Peter, full stop. I get his travel schedule from Penelope, just so I can always tell you where he is. I don't know how anyone does it. I mean, yours would kill me."

Claudia smiled. "Sometimes I think it's doing that to me. I'm planning a quiet weekend. At least we've got the American recruitment nailed down, that was worrying me. But it does mean I'll have to be a couple of weeks in San Francisco in the new year.

Pat looked at her with sympathy and shook her head. "And we used to think it was glamorous. Anyway, are you out tomorrow night?"

"Oh, I think so. Oh, Christ, I hope he doesn't think he's coming here. No, he can't do. 'Can we do dinner' is what he said. I'd better check."

"Penelope will know, she'll have made the arrangements. I'll call her."

Claudia went to unpack while Pat went to the office. In spite of the misery, she'd managed a few hours' sleep on the plane. She unpacked and showered and pulled on sweatshirt and jogging pants; just a good, slobby day of catching up. She crossed to the office, Pat was on the phone. Claudia smiled to herself. Pat looked smart, she had to admit — no slobby days for Pat.

She came in to Claudia's office soon after. "He's picking you up at six, apparently, and you're booked at the Latymer, it's in a hotel near Bagshot. I hadn't heard of it, but she says it's supposed to be very nice."

"Yeah, OK, good." She was distracted by a text: *SIGNED!!!* and a row of emojis from Andy. "Oh, brilliant, sorry, Pat, that was Andy in Tokyo — the thing I can't tell you anything about — he's going to buy the Japanese company — but it's still schtum!"

"That won't involve you anymore though, will it?" Pat eyed her suspiciously, she was getting ever more zealous about diary management. It was wonderful to have their client roster, but she knew recruitment wasn't keeping pace with projects.

"No, definitely not — but I never know what Peter's going to spring on me next. I hope he doesn't turn up with some new idea tomorrow."

"He'd better not!" Pat was trying her fierce look, but she knew it only made Claudia laugh. "At least Alan Jeavons has got someone for you to see next week. You need more help."

"I know, I know, as long as he doesn't try to recruit from our clients again."

"I told, him, I told him." And she mooched off back to work.

It was a good catch-up day. Pat came in frequently with cups of tea — obviously on a Jack-watch to make sure Claudia wasn't getting too down. They were well-judged interventions, but Claudia wasn't looking forward to the evening. She hoped Abbi would find something stupid for them to watch together after the Chinese. The guys had only met Jack once, but it had left a surprisingly long legacy — not that he was ever spoken about. Abbi was too sensitive for that, but it had left a void, even for the kids. They'd known of his existence long before they met him — and then they met him — and then he wasn't there anymore. But now the two years of not quite admitting that were at an end.

He'd still looked good. A little older, a little more careworn. But good. Fuck! The tissues came out — and another cup of tea came in.

Mid-afternoon a call came through. "It's Peter," said Pat.

"Hi Peter, brilliant news about Andy."

"Wonderful," he said. "Now our troubles really begin. But that's not why I'm ringing,"

"Don't tell me, you have this new business prospect in Australia and there's only one person who can truly evaluate it for you." There was a long silence. "Peter," she said slowly, "please tell me it's not something like that."

"Well, no and yes, my dearest love. You've completely unnerved me. I am looking at something there but that wasn't going to impact you at all, not in the short term anyway. No, I was ringing about tomorrow." She prepared for a disappointment. "What plans do you have?"

"Well, I thought the world's most charming man was taking me to dinner and I was getting quite excited."

"But earlier in the day, do you have any plans?"

"Not really, my two will tell me where they want chauffeuring but that's it. Why?"

"Could we meet for lunch?"

"Instead of dinner?"

"No, I'd like you to keep the day free, could you?"

This was very strange. "Yes, of course, are you trying to catch up on careless hours?"

"That's exactly it. May I pick you up at twelve?"

"Of course. I'll get things sorted here. Where are we going? What do I wear?"

"Bring a change, we'll still do dinner as planned, but wrap up warm for a walk by the sea."

"Fine, I'll look forward to that, I think. And you promise no Australia."

He laughed. "Short term, definitely not, see you at twelve tomorrow, my love."

"See you." She put the phone down slowly. Pat was in the doorway. "So, I'm not the only one looking after you then?"

Claudia shrugged a little helplessly. "Well, we'll find out tomorrow."

And it kept her sufficiently intrigued that the evening wasn't quite as painful as she'd feared.

***

She was quite relieved when he arrived in an S class, she'd feared something more ostentatious. The guys were out, so she was spared introduction duties and got straight into the car, throwing her bag on the back seat. After his mansion in Barnes and his vast yacht she wasn't going to show him round what would seem like a modest cottage. And he was plainly preoccupied anyway.

But he seemed cheery enough. "We're doing fish and chips by the sea and then it's a bracing walk."

"I'm delighted, man of mystery, but what's this really about?"

"Its purpose is morphing. I had a call from my new friend yesterday."

"Before you called me? I assume you mean Oscar."

He smiled. "I knew you'd know. Yes. He was worried about you — and he knew I would be."

"You'll realise, being the perceptive man you are, that I find that very strange."

"Yes, but you'd met Jack. He told me. He didn't think that was easy for you."

"No shit, Sherlock!" She had a laugh that was a half-sob and she reached for tissues. "No, it wasn't easy, but I was glad I faced up to it. I'd been trying to avoid it."

"I know. I still feel very guilty about it."

"Oh, Peter, bless you. We had ages to rebuild if we'd really wanted to. I don't know if pride was the enemy, or mistrust, or whatever it was, but I know that only two people were responsible." She was weeping gently. "I mean, I know Henderson's a bastard but that was the funny thing about the Oscar conversation. Deep down, Henderson seems to be trying to do the right thing. Do you think it's the intelligence background that makes him so amoral? I suppose that's silly, those values and attitudes form much earlier, don't they?"

And she talked about Oscar, and Collins, and Andy, and Tania, and Sandy and recruitment and the muddy hills rolled by, the A3 now missing all the little villages it must once have terrorised until they crested a hill and saw the channel, the Solent and the Isle of Wight beneath them.

"I used to bring the kids down here. Are we going into Pompey?"

"Yes, the Still and West, fish and chips overlooking the harbour."

"I've been dribbling on for an hour, I'm sorry, but it's actually been good therapy for me. What about you though? Where's Yvonne?"

"Antigua. We have a small place there. She likes it in November. It is the dreariest month here, isn't it?"

"So when do you escape next?"

"On Tuesday, New York for the hedge funds and then California for some property deals Alphonse wants to look at."

"Do you ever want to slow down?"

"Today is slowing down." They were in Old Portsmouth and he found a parking spot facing the old sea wall. "We'll walk along the top later if the rain stops. At least there are spaces in the bad weather." It wasn't far through the little lane to the old pub. His arm was round her shoulder and she snuggled in to him.

He seemed too big for the space somehow, but the little table, squeezed behind a doorway, had a clear view of the harbour, for her out to sea, watching the odd little boat trying to beat its way in against the fast ebbing tide, for him up into the harbour and on to the chalk-scarred hill beyond. "I'd promised myself fish and chips, are you going to join me?" He smiled at her.

"Of course, nothing else would be right."

"We're having fish and chips," he said to the girl hovering with the menus. "May I just have a very quick look at the wine list?" He instantly picked out a Chablis and handed the list back.

"Water?" the girl asked.

"Yes, please, just tap is fine." He looked to Claudia. "You disapprove?"

"No, I'm just pleasantly surprised. My lord can mix with the common folk."

"But I am common folk, my darling."

"Never in a million." She paused. "Look, Peter, my darling, this is wonderful and it's precious, but why are we here?"

"I love the sea, I love boats bouncing on it, and so do you, I thought."

"But why have you brought me here. Just to help me get over Jack? We can celebrate Andy later, that must be worth a bottle of Krug…" She looked at him helplessly.

"I was hoping you might have an idea."

Now she shook her head. "I don't, none I can make sense of — and I've learnt from your new friend this week, seen it in operation, just ask open questions and wait. You're doing it to me and I'm going to turn it round on you. What is this about?"

He waited, apparently in some turmoil, but she knew he was going to speak. "Let me put it in business terms first. It is all getting too much. It's principally the Group. Property and hedge funds are easier, they have very good people running them, but the Group is already too large. I need help."

"I can understand that. You want to put someone in? I'd miss the contact, hah, the little I get, but I can understand you'd want someone to pull things together. It would give you more time to look at new stuff, unless you're finally going to be sensible and slow down."

"I'd like to do both."

"Now you get radio silence again. Explain yourself, sir!"

He looked, momentarily, curiously child-like. "Would you do it?"

The wine came. Fortunate. A moment to draw breath.

"Just pour, please, I'm sure it's fine." He was looking hard at her, ignoring the waitress who was waiting for him to taste, even though she'd poured two glasses. Claudia moved her eyes to make him look up. He took a quick sip. "That's fine."

"Do what, Peter, please say? I'd rather appear thick than stupid, if that makes any sense at all," she said, and they both laughed suddenly. "I don't suppose it does really. I just don't believe what I think you're asking."

"I want you to be group CEO."

There was a very long silence. she looked over to Haslar and the small boats in the marina beyond; a large ferry came by, almost, it seemed in touching distance, like the Tokyo offices right beside the high-level expressways; a pilot boat pottered out, swiftly pushed by the tide to whatever bigger ship was waiting. She turned back to look at him, puzzled.

"I've talked to a few of the guys. They're all independent, of course, but everyone thinks that the sort of light-handed guidance would be much better managed by you than by me, they say I'm inaccessible."

"Obviously, I'm stunned. What about Brodie Associates? We're just getting going. No, don't even go there. This is nonsense."

He looked perturbed, but then he slowly smiled. "I'm glad I've given myself the whole day to do this." That made her relax and laugh. "Shall I do the easier bit first?"

"Oh, please." But then the fish arrived, monstrous battered slabs that had them laughing again. "Pompey tempura," she said. "I love it, but I'll do without the chips, I think. So, easy bit?"

"Brodie Gunter Jeavons. Tania and Alan are both doing well, and you can pull back from client contact. Obviously, you need more people but Sandy says the recruitment's gone well."

"You've spoken to him?"

"Of course, and about the big idea, he's very much in favour. He's been pushing me to do something with the organisation and he thinks you're the best person."

"I'm stunned."

"Of course, but let's talk through how it's going to work."

'Going to work', not 'might work', that was his way, a leap of imagination, think of a different future, and, by the time the coffee came, it seemed ridiculously plausible. Then she blinked as a sudden shaft of sunlight hit the table.

"Right on cue," he said. She looked puzzled again. "I wanted to save the difficult conversation until last. We can talk while we're walking."

"The difficult bit? For fuck's sake," she whispered.

"You see, that's why I love you," he said, smiling. "Well, partly."

The rain had stopped but the wind was whistling through the lane now. They walked up the tower, past the smells of urine and disinfectant, on to the sea wall, to be buffeted by the wild gusts. He put his arm around her again. Mad gulls hung on the breeze and then dived raucously to the sea. Occasional sunlight caught the bright wind-whipped waves.

"So, what's difficult?"

"It's only difficult if you don't like the idea."

"I'm afraid this is where you get the Oscar silence."

"Ha, my new friend isn't good for you."

"I think he is good for me, though."

"Well, I do believe in the plans I've outlined. I want to push ahead with that if you'll agree, both the Brodie Associates plan, and the Group CEO, even if you reject the third idea."

"I haven't accepted ideas one and two yet. It doesn't sound like I'm going to like three any more. What is it?"

"It's about us."

"Us?" she almost shrieked, glad that the wind was noisy.

He almost seemed emboldened by her response. He stopped and turned her to face him and smiled. "The principal driving force behind all this is me wanting to spend time with you. I have no idea what sort of a relationship that could be. I know it would be a working relationship. I would have that anyway if you agree to the first two steps and you're the person I trust most to work with. But I'd like it to be more."

"Yvonne?"

"Yvonne's not coming back."

They started walking again. "Are you sad about that?"

"A little, not very."

"Divorce?"

"Oh, yes, but we'll still be friends."

She laughed. "I don't know if I've been propositioned or not."

"You have been, dearest love, but take your time."